AYESHA AT LAST

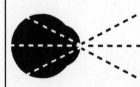

AYESHA AT LAST

UZMA JALALUDDIN

THORNDIKE PRESS
A part of Gale, a Cengage Company

GALE
A Cengage Company

Farmington Hills, Mich • San Francisco • New York • Waterville, Maine
Meriden, Conn • Mason, Ohio • Chicago

LIBRARY OF CONGRESS CIP DATA ON FILE.
CATALOGUING IN PUBLICATION FOR THIS BOOK
IS AVAILABLE FROM THE LIBRARY OF CONGRESS

ISBN-13: 978-1-4328-7081-2 (hardcover alk. paper)

Published in 2019 by arrangement with Berkley, an imprint of Penguin Publishing Group, a division of Penguin Random House, LLC

Printed in Mexico
1 2 3 4 5 6 7 23 22 21 20 19

For Imtiaz,
who said "when," not "if"

CHAPTER ONE

He wondered if he would see her today.

Khalid Mirza sat at the breakfast bar of his light-filled kitchen, long legs almost reaching the floor. It was seven in the morning, and his eyes were trained on the window, the one with the best view of the townhouse complex across the street.

His patience was rewarded.

A young woman wearing a purple hijab, blue button-down shirt, blazer, and black pants ran down the steps of the middle townhouse, balancing a red ceramic travel mug and canvas satchel. She stumbled but caught herself, skidding to a stop in front of an aging sedan. She put the mug on the hood of the car and unlocked the door.

Khalid had seen her several times since he had moved into the neighborhood two months ago, always with her red ceramic mug, always in a hurry. She was a petite woman with a round face and dreamy smile, skin a golden burnished copper that glowed in the sullen March morning.

It is not appropriate to stare at women, no matter how interesting their purple hijabs, Khalid reminded himself.

Yet his eyes returned for a second, wistful look. She was so beautiful.

The sound of Bollywood music blaring from a car speaker made the young woman freeze. She peered around her Toyota Corolla to see a red Mercedes SLK convertible zoom into her driveway. Khalid watched as the young woman dropped to a crouch behind her car. Who was she hiding from? He leaned forward for a better look.

"What are you looking at, Khalid?" asked his mother, Farzana.

"Nothing, Ammi," Khalid said, and took a bite of the clammy scrambled eggs Farzana had prepared for breakfast. When he looked up again, the young woman and her canvas satchel were inside the Toyota.

Her red travel mug was not.

It flew off the roof of her car as she sped away, smashing into a hundred pieces and narrowly missing the red Mercedes.

Khalid laughed out loud. When he looked up, he caught his mother's stern gaze.

"It's such a lovely day outside," Farzana said, giving her son a hard look. "I can see why your eyes are drawn to the view."

Khalid flushed at her words. Ammi had been dropping hints lately. She thought it was time for him to marry. He had a steady job, and twenty-six was a good age to settle down. Their family was wealthy and could easily pay for the large wedding his mother wanted.

"I was going to tell you after I'd made a few choices, but it appears you are ready to hear the news. I have begun the search for your wife," Farzana announced, and her tone brooked no opposition. "Love comes after marriage, not before. These Western ideas of romantic love are utter nonsense. Just look at the American divorce rate."

Khalid paused midbite, but his mother didn't notice. Her announcement was surprising, but the news was not unexpected or even unwelcome. He resumed eating.

"I will find you the perfect wife — modest, not too educated. If we can't find someone local, we will search for a girl back home."

"Back home" for Farzana was Hyderabad, India, though she had lived in Canada for more than thirty years. Khalid had been born in a suburb west of Toronto and lived there for most of his life until his father's death six months ago, before Farzana and

Khalid had moved to the east end of the city. Farzana had insisted on the move, and though Khalid had been sorry to leave his friends and the mosque he had frequented with his father, deep down he thought it might do them both some good.

Their new neighborhood had felt instantly comfortable. From the moment they'd arrived, Khalid felt as if he had finally come home. There were more cars parked three or four deep on extended driveways, more untamed backyards in need of the maintenance that only time, money, and access to professional services could provide. Yet the people were kind, friendly even, and Khalid was at ease among the brown and black faces that reflected his own.

Farzana neatly flipped another paratha flatbread onto her son's plate, though he had not asked for more. "The wedding will be in July. Everyone will want an invitation, but I will limit the guest list to six hundred people. Any more is showing off."

Humming to herself, she placed a small pot on the stove, adding water, milk, cinnamon, cloves, cardamom, and tea leaves for chai. Khalid's eyes lingered on the chipped forest-green mug on the counter. His father's mug. Ammi had used that mug for his Abba's chai for years. This was the first

10

time he had seen it out of the cupboard since the move. Maybe his mother was finally beginning to make her way through the cloud of grief that had paralyzed her after Abba's death.

There was so much of the past they did not talk about. Khalid was relieved she was thinking about the future. Or rather, his future.

The idea of an arranged marriage had never bothered Khalid. A partner carefully chosen for him, just as his parents had been chosen for each other and their parents before them, seemed like a tidy practice. He liked the idea of being part of an unbroken chain that honored tradition and ensured family peace and stability. He knew that some people, even his own sister, thought the practice of arranged marriage was restrictive, but he found it comforting. Romantic relationships and their accompanying perks were for marriage only.

At the thought of romantic perks, Khalid's attention drifted to the window once more — but he stopped himself. The girl with the (broken) red mug would never be more than a fantasy. Because while it is a truth universally acknowledged that a single Muslim man must be in want of a wife, there's an even greater truth: To his Indian

11

mother, his own inclinations are of second-ary importance.

CHAPTER TWO

The Toyota lurched down the street, wheezing and anemic. Ayesha reached for her travel mug, but her hand closed on empty air. In the rearview mirror she spotted the red shards on the asphalt. *Blast.*

She had been in such a hurry to get away from Hafsa. Now she would have to face her first day as a substitute high school teacher without the comforting armor of chai.

No matter, it was worth it. The moment she had spotted the red Mercedes convertible pulling onto the street, Ayesha had known why her cousin was visiting so early in the morning, and she didn't want to hear it.

Besides, there was one rule repeatedly drilled into her at teachers' college: A teacher can never, under any circumstances, be late.

Ayesha had graduated from teachers' college last June. It had taken nearly seven months of papering local schools with her résumé to secure a substitute teaching position. Now her stomach flipped over as she parked in the staff lot of Brookridge High School, a squat, two-story brown brick building constructed in the 1970s, ugly and functional.

The building was similar in layout and atmosphere to her old high school. It had the same well-tended shabbiness of a public building, the same blue-tinted fluorescent lighting, and waxed and speckled linoleum floors. The same mostly white staff dressed in business-formal slacks and skirts; the same mostly brown and black students slouching in jeans, track pants, and too-short dresses. Ayesha tugged self-consciously at her carefully chosen teacher clothes: blue button-down shirt and serviceable black pants. Her hands nervously smoothed the top of her purple hijab.

Part of both worlds, yet part of neither, she thought.

Such existential thoughts were really not helping to settle the butterflies in her stomach.

She entered the large, open foyer, its concrete walls painted a dull green and smelling faintly of industrial cleaning solvent. The familiar scent calmed her, and she smiled slightly at a female student in black leggings and a blue hoodie carrying an overloaded backpack. The girl gave her a dubious look before shifting her bag and walking purposely down the hall, reminding Ayesha to hurry. A teacher must never be late.

The secretary, Mary, was waiting for her in the main office with forms to sign. The principal, Mr. Evorem, was absent today, Mary explained. "He'll want to meet you tomorrow to welcome you properly."

A white man in his early thirties with a short black beard walked into the office just as she was finishing the paperwork, and Mary asked him to take Ayesha to her class. He peered over her shoulder at her schedule.

"Grade-ten science?" His eyes were wide. "You're covering for Rudy?"

"Who's Rudy?" Ayesha asked as they walked toward the stairs.

"He's the last teacher those little shits scared off. I think he chose early retirement over that class."

Ayesha looked at him, waiting for the punchline. There wasn't one. "Nobody told me that."

"I hope you're light on your feet. The

bastards like to throw things."

Forty minutes later, Ayesha crouched on the toilet in the staff bathroom, bookended by feelings of self-pity and guilt. Instead of teaching, she was hiding from her class. Even worse, she was writing a poem in her purple spiral notebook.

I can't do this.
This thing that I should do.
I can do this.
This thing I don't want to do.
I want to be away, weaving words of
    truth.
Not here, trapped between desk and
    freedom and family.

She should be teaching, not writing. She had vowed to leave this part of her behind when she'd left for work that morning. Instead, she hadn't been able to resist placing the purple spiral notebook in her bag, like a child's security blanket. She gripped her pen tightly and tried not to stare at her cell phone.

"Come on, Clara," she said out loud. Then she held her breath, hoping no one had heard. But of course they hadn't. This was the staff bathroom, and it was the

16

middle of the school day. The other teachers were teaching, not hiding and writing poetry.

She squinted at the page, rereading her words. Correction: writing *bad* poetry.

Her phone beeped: a text message from her best friend, Clara.

> What do you mean you can't do this? You just got there.

Ayesha texted back.

> My class hates me. They were throwing things at each other, and they didn't listen to a word I said. Can you call the school and tell them there's an emergency at home?

Her phone rang.

"You picked the wrong profession." Clara's voice was low.

"I'll come back to teach tomorrow, when I'm ready," Ayesha said.

"Babe, you are never going to be ready to teach. You know what you're ready for? Writing poems. Exploring the world. Falling in love. Remember?" Ayesha pictured Clara in front of her — blue eyes wide with concern, fingers fiddling with strawberry blond hair. "I bet you're writing a poem about this right now. Aren't you?" Her friend's voice was accusing and impatient. They had had variations of this same conversation so many times, Ayesha couldn't blame Clara for being sick of it. She was sick of it herself.

Her eyes flicked to the notebook, and she shut it firmly. No more. "Poetry is for paupers. I'm not Hafsa. I don't have a rich father to pay my bills, and I promised Sulaiman Mamu I would pay him back for tuition."

She remained silent about the other two items — exploring the world, falling in love — the first as impossible as the second. She had no money, and falling in love would be difficult when she had never even held someone's hand before. "Hafsa is getting married this summer," Ayesha said instead. "She came over this morning to tell me, but I already knew. Nani and Samira Aunty have been talking about her *rishtas* for weeks."

Clara, an only child, loved hearing about Ayesha's large extended family. She was particularly intrigued by the traditional rishta proposal process, which Ayesha had explained in hilarious detail. Prospective partners were introduced to each other after being carefully vetted by parents and fam-

18

ily. Ayesha had received a few rishta proposals herself, years ago, though they had never led to a wedding. She hadn't really connected with any of the potential suitors, and they must have felt likewise because she'd never heard from them after the initial meetings.

"Hafsa can't get married! She's a baby!" Clara exclaimed.

Ayesha started laughing. "She's got the entire wedding planned already. All she needs is the groom."

"Your cousin is crazy. You're the one who should be getting married. Or me. Rob still flinches whenever I mention weddings, after ten years together."

Ayesha was starting to regret this topic of conversation. "If Hafsa wants to get married, I'm happy for her," she said. She imagined twenty-year-old Hafsa reclining on an ornate chaise as she surveyed a parade of handsome, wealthy men. She pictured her cousin languidly pointing to one man at random, and just like that, the marriage would be arranged.

So easy, so simple, to find the one person who would cherish and protect your heart forever. Everything came easy for Hafsa.

Clara pressed her point. "When do you get to be happy? When was the last time you went on a date, or finished and performed a poem?" Clara thought Ayesha was afraid of love because of what had happened to her father and afraid to dream because of her family's expectations.

Ayesha disagreed. "My family is counting on me to set a good example for Hafsa. I'm the eldest kid in the family. I want to set the bar high for everyone else. I can't let Mom, Sulaiman Mamu, or Nana down, not after everything they've done for me. All that other stuff can wait."

Clara sighed. "Why don't you come to Bella's tonight?"

A long time ago, a different Ayesha had performed poetry at Bella's lounge. Another reminder of the road not taken. She smothered a laugh that sounded like a sob.

"Ash, you got this," Clara said, her voice softening. "Do all that teacher stuff. Send the troublemakers to the office. Make a seating chart. Stop hiding in the bathroom."

There was a discreet knock on the stall door, and Ayesha ended the call with Clara.

"Miss Shamsi?" Mary said, sounding awkward. "Your class said you might be in here."

They're not my class, Ayesha thought. *They need a circus trainer, not a teacher.* She flushed, wiped sweaty palms on her pants, and tucked the purple notebook back inside her bag. Mary stood outside, a look of pity on her face.

"There was an emergency, but I'm better now," Ayesha said with dignity. "When does the class end?"

"You still have another forty minutes, honey." Mary patted her on the shoulder. "I'll send an assistant to help with your first class. She'll keep an eye on them when your back is turned. Oh, and I forgot to give this to you earlier."

Mary handed Ayesha an ID badge with STAFF written in bold letters at the top.

Ayesha stared at the official-looking badge. This was why she had attended teachers' college, why she had worked so hard at her in-school placements. Her mother and grandparents had left behind so much when they immigrated to Canada. She wanted their sacrifice to mean something.

There was no turning back, not now.

Her thoughts drifted to the purple notebook in her bag. Maybe if she worked on the poem tonight, she could perform it at Bella's sometime . . .

But no. All of that lay behind her. It was time to focus on the road in front.

"Everyone starts out right here. You'll get the hang of it," Mary said.

Mary meant to be kind, but Ayesha knew that not everyone started from the same place. Some people were always a little ahead. Or in her case, constantly playing catch-up.

The rest of the day was not as dramatic as the morning, yet Ayesha felt deflated when she drove home after school. Teaching was not what she'd expected and nothing like her training, where she'd had the comforting guidance of a mentor teacher. The entire experience had been nerve-racking, and she had felt perpetually caught in the bored tractor-beam stares of twenty-eight teenagers.

All she wanted now was to go home, drink a cup of very strong chai, and reconsider her life choices.

She turned onto her street and spied a red Mercedes parked in the driveway.

Hafsa was back, and this time there was no escape.

CHAPTER THREE

Khalid kept his head down as he walked through the narrow back hallway of Livetech Solutions, his employer for the past five years. He was dressed in his usual work attire — full-sleeved white robe that skimmed his ankles, black dress pants, white skullcap jammed over dark brown hair that curled over his ears. His beard was long and luxuriously thick, contrasting sharply with his pale olive complexion.

He was a large man, tall and broad, and the corridor was narrow. He looked up to see his coworker Clara standing in the middle of the hallway, whispering into her cell phone. Khalid did not wish to disturb what appeared to be an intense conversation; he also did not wish to brush past her in the hallway. He had been raised to believe that non-related men and women should never get too close — socially, emotionally, and especially physically.

"When an unmarried man and woman are alone together, a third person is present: Satan," Ammi often told him. Khalid found this reminder helpful, especially when paired with cold showers. There wasn't much more that a twenty-six-year-old virgin-by-choice could do, really.

He didn't mean to eavesdrop, but Clara had raised her voice. "When do you get to be happy?" she said sharply into her phone.

Khalid blinked at the question, which so neatly mirrored his own thoughts.

His cell phone dinged with a new e-mail, and he opened it, grateful for the distraction. His heart sank when he read the subject line and recognized the sender: his sister, Zareena. He hadn't told her about their move. He hadn't been sure how she would react to the sale of their childhood home. It looked like some other busybody had thoughtfully informed her instead. He began to read.

Re: the last to know?

Khalid,
I can't believe I had to hear the news from my father-in-law. You sold the house and moved? I loved that house. It was so easy to sneak out of my bedroom.

But I guess it was too hard after Abba died.

Guess what? I got bored and started volunteering my time for a Cause. You would be so proud of me. I'm teaching English to a class of little girls at the local school. My students are super sweet. Their parents can barely afford to send them to class. Half the time they show up with no lunches, but their clothes are so tidy, their hair in neat braids, and they want to learn so badly. Not like when I was in school! They always bring me a flower or a fruit they stole from someone's garden. I sneak them rice and dal sometimes.

— Zareena

P. S. Maple donuts and Tim Hortons hot chocolate.

P. P. S. Thanks for the gift. Can you use Western Union next time plz? It's closer and you know how I hate to walk.

Zareena's e-mails and texts arrived every few days and reported on her daily life. Sometimes she complained about the dullness of her days, or which of her dozens of in-laws were irritating her. Sometimes she asked him about work, or if he had talked to a girl yet . . . or even made eye contact with one.

The one thing she never asked about was their mother. The second thing she never discussed was her husband.

The postscript was always something Zareena missed about Canada. Her words brought the taste of maple dip donuts and too-sweet hot chocolate to his lips. Their father, Faheem, used to treat them on the way back from Sunday morning Islamic school when they were kids. Before Zareena went away.

After she left, whenever Khalid mentioned her name, his father would freeze and Ammi would become upset. Soon her name became an unspoken word in their home.

Clara's call had ended, and he noticed her examining him as he read his e-mail. They knew each other, but had never spoken. He wondered if she was uncomfortable with the way he dressed. Some people found his robes and skullcap difficult to reconcile with an office environment. But Khalid had long ago decided to be honest about who he was: an observant Muslim man who walked with faith both outwardly and inwardly, just as some of his Muslim sisters did by wearing the hijab.

Still, sometimes it made people nervous. Though Clara did not seem wary. She appeared almost . . . appraising.

Which made him nervous.

Khalid motioned in front of him. "After you," he said politely.

Clara didn't move. "My friend is having a crisis. Her first day at a new job."

"That can be difficult," Khalid said, looking directly at her.

Now she looked curious. About him? Women were never curious about him.

"It's sort of my first day too," Clara said, leaning close. "I was promoted to regional manager of Human Resources."

"Congratulations." Khalid inclined his head in acknowledgment. "I know you will fulfill your duties with integrity."

"My boyfriend, Rob, is happy about the pay raise," Clara said with a smile. "I'm reporting to Sheila Watts. Do you know her?"

Khalid shook his head. Sheila had replaced his old director a few weeks ago, but he had yet to meet his first female boss.

The door behind Clara opened and a petite woman with black hair and blue eyes stepped out. She was shorter than Clara, dressed in a sleeveless top and tight black pencil skirt. Above her right breast was pinned a large crystal brooch in the shape of a spider, its winking red eyes matching her lipstick.

Clara stepped forward with a friendly smile.

"Sheila, I wanted to introduce myself — I'm Clara Taylor. John promoted me just before he left the company."

Sheila looked at the outstretched hand and beaming face before her. A faint expression of distaste lurked at her lips and she briefly shook Clara's hand, using only the very tips of her fingers.

Khalid knew what was coming next, and he felt powerless to stop it. Usually when he was introduced to female clients and co-workers, he had time to prepare beforehand with a carefully worded e-mail about his no-touch rule.

As the women talked, he subtly edged away from their conversation, taking tiny steps down the hall. But it was no use; Clara's friendliness foiled his escape.

"Sheila, this is our e-commerce project manager, Khalid Mirza," she said, and both women turned to him.

A hard glance from Sheila took in Khalid's white robe and skullcap. Her eyes lingered on his long beard.

Her gaze was the opposite of appraising,

28

Khalid thought. She looked annoyed.

Then everything went from bad to worse. Sheila leaned forward and stuck out her hand for him to shake.

They stared at each other.

"I'm sorry, I don't shake hands with women. It's against my religion," he blurted.

Sheila left her hand outstretched for another moment, cold eyes locked on his face. Then she slowly pulled back and raised an eyebrow. "I should have assumed as much from your clothing. Tell me, Khalid: Where are you from?"

"Toronto," Khalid answered. His face flamed beneath his thick beard; he didn't know where to look.

"No," Sheila laughed lightly. "I mean where are you from *originally*?"

"Toronto," Khalid responded again, and this time his voice was resigned.

Clara shifted, looking tense and uncomfortable. "I'm originally from Newfoundland," she said brightly.

"I lived in the Middle East for a while," Sheila said to Khalid, her voice low and pleasant. "Saudi Arabia. I found it so interesting that the women wore black while the men wore white. There's something symbolic about that, isn't there? Half the population in shadow while the rest live in light. You must be so grateful to live in a country that welcomes everybody." Sheila's laughter sounded high and artificial. "Of course, when I was in Saudi Arabia, I wasn't afforded the same courtesy."

Khalid's eyes were lowered to the ground, his head bowed. "I apologize, Ms. Watts. I meant no disrespect," he said finally. "Please forgive me." He turned around and walked back the way he had come, hands trembling.

He took the long way around the floor and caught the service elevator down to his small office in the basement. It was sparsely furnished with two gray metal desks squeezed together, a black bookcase wedged behind the door and a sagging blue couch against the back wall. Rumor had it this office used to be a maintenance closet, but he was grateful for the privacy, especially when he prayed in the afternoon.

It was nine thirty in the morning, earlier than usual for Amir to already be at his desk. Though judging by the rumpled suit, his coworker had spent last night at the office. Again.

"Assalamu Alaikum, Amir. I thought we talked about this." Khalid hid his shaking hands by folding his arms.

"My date wasn't exactly interested in a sleepover, if you know what I mean. Bitches, am I right?" Amir reached for a water bottle on his desk, opened it, and began chugging rapidly.

Khalid winced at his description. "I can't keep covering for you."

Amir had been hired the previous year as part of Livetech's "Welcome Wagon" program for immigrants. Technically, Khalid was his manager. Most days he felt like a babysitter.

"Last time, I swear. This would never happen if you came out with me and stopped me from committing my many sins. I promise I'll introduce you to some pretty girls."

Khalid was tempted to confess Ammi's plans to find him a wife, but instead he stuck to his usual line. "Out of respect for my future wife, I don't believe in sleeping around before marriage."

Amir only laughed. "Classic Khalid. I tell my friends about you all the time. They don't believe half my stories. All the other Muslim guys I know scrub up for Friday prayers just like you, but they know how to have fun."

Khalid ignored him and settled down to check e-mails; the most recent was from Sheila, sent only moments ago.

Khalid, I'm glad we met today. I'd like

to begin our working relationship with a performance review. I look forward to a frank discussion of your strengths and many areas of improvement. The meeting is scheduled for Monday at 3 p.m. I trust this appointment will not interfere with any religious obligations.

Amir, noticing Khalid's concerned expression, got up to read over his shoulder. He whistled. "What did you do?"

Khalid shrugged. "I declined to shake her hand."

"K-Man, you need to edit. Figure out what works for you, throw out what doesn't. It's not like we're still riding around on camels, right?"

"I'm not sure what you mean."

Amir punched Khalid lightly on his arm. "You're too old to be this naive. Watch your back, brother."

Khalid kept silent. He knew how Amir saw him — as an anachronistic throwback, a walking target for ridicule.

Sometimes he wished he were different. But even if Khalid "edited" everything about himself — his clothes, his beard, his words — it wouldn't erase the loneliness he felt every day. The loneliness he had felt ever since his sister left home almost twelve years ago.

His white robes and beard were a comfortable security blanket, his way of communicating without saying a word. Even though he knew there were other, easier ways to be, Khalid had chosen the one that felt the most authentic to him, and he had no plans to waver.

Besides, the robes provided great air circulation.

And everything happened by the will of Allah.

CHAPTER FOUR

Sheila had an entire wall of windows in her office, Clara noted. Her new boss sat at a large black desk so shiny it reflected her perfectly poised image. She was typing an e-mail, and she looked angry, her red nails stabbing the keyboard. Clara was seated on a lethal-looking chair; the curlicued metal embellishments on the back felt like they had been filed to a knife's edge.

Sheila sent her e-mail and then stared at Clara for a moment before leaning forward with a confidential air. "Five years ago, I was in customer support, and now look at me." She spread out her arms to encompass the large, airy office. "Hard work, that's the key. And it doesn't hurt to look good doing it." Her tight smile revealed tiny white teeth.

Clara shifted uneasily. The scene outside with Khalid was still fresh in her mind. As the new regional manager of Human Resources, she felt responsible.

Sheila straightened in her chair. "People are intimidated by a woman in power, Clara. They think it goes against the natural order of things. But the world is changing, and it's important that we embrace the transformation. You grew up in Newfoundland."

Clara blinked, head spinning at Sheila's abrupt topic change. So her new boss hadn't been simply ignoring her outside in the hallway.

There had been rumors about Sheila Watts. When Clara was first promoted, her coworkers had warned her about the new boss.

"They call Sheila 'the Shark' because she always circles her prey before she attacks," one remarked. Clara didn't take gossip seriously, but now she was worried.

If only Khalid had shaken Sheila's hand, things would have been so much easier. Her friend Ayesha had no problem shaking people's hands, and she was Muslim. But this was HR 101: Everyone was entitled to their own interpretation of faith, even if it did make her job especially challenging. Also, her new boss's repetition of that question — *Where are you from?* — hadn't sat well with her. If Khalid had been awkward, Sheila's reaction had been no less so, though Clara doubted her new boss would see things that way.

Ayesha thought she had it bad standing in front of bored teenagers. Finding a way through the tricky waters that made up people's backgrounds and beliefs was even worse. She reined in her thoughts and focused on Sheila's words.

"We're fortunate at Livetech to employ people from all over the world. Diversity is essential in today's global marketplace, but it can also present unique challenges," Sheila said.

"I grew up in a diverse neighborhood, so I'm used to living and working with people of different ethnicities and cultures," Clara said.

Sheila waved her words aside. "I'm going to let you in on a secret, Clara. Livetech Solutions is ready to join the global technology stage with our new product launch, but there are bad apples polluting the orchard. That's where you come in."

Clara's laptop was open now, and she was taking notes. *Polluting the orchard. Bad apples.* Her fingers hesitated over the keyboard. "Are you asking me to *fire* someone?" she said, not quite masking the squeak of terror in her voice. "So far my HR work at Livetech has focused on mediation, conflict resolution, and mental health initiatives."

"Termination is a last resort, and proper protocols must be followed. We wouldn't want Livetech to be involved in any legal unpleasantness." Sheila gave Clara an arch look. "Let's start with Khalid Mirza. I want you to prepare a file on his work habits, how often he misses deadlines, and his inappropriate behavior toward women."

Clara was typing furiously but slowed down at Sheila's words. "Is this about what happened in the hallway earlier?"

Sheila lowered her voice. "You saw what he did," she said. "He's clearly one of those extremist *Moslems.*"

Clara leaned back, fighting to appear calm. The chair pinched her shoulder and she winced. "I'm not sure what you mean."

Sheila's tinkling laugh rang out. "You are so innocent. I love working with a blank slate."

Clara's sense of unease grew.

"I was headhunted by a big conglomerate in Riyadh, the capital city of Saudi Arabia, a few years ago. I lasted six months." Sheila's teeth gleamed. "Khalid would fit in with my former employers perfectly, right down to the bedsheets and dirty beard."

Clara's stomach clenched. "You can't get rid of someone because of their religious beliefs," she said carefully. "And his beard looks presentable to me. He told me he dry cleans his robes every week."

Sheila's eyes narrowed. "Livetech is a growing global player. Our senior team must maintain a certain professionalism, and that includes a uniformity of dress." She leaned across the desk. "Sweetheart, you'll find this type of behavior the higher you climb. Men afraid of a woman with power, men who can't handle a woman's ambition. There are limits to religious accommodation — and it's your job to find those limits. I've set up a meeting with Khalid for next week, which is more than enough time for you to compile your report. I do hope your promotion was the right decision for Livetech."

When Clara left the office, she felt uneasy. She thought about Ayesha and her family, who had embraced her when her own parents had moved back to Newfoundland during freshman year. They prayed five times a day and wore "funny" clothing too.

Khalid might have chosen to follow his faith in a way that appeared conservative, but that didn't mean he deserved to be fired. By all accounts he was respectful and hard working, if a little quiet. How could Clara, in good conscience, allow this to hap-

38

pen? She'd gone into human resources to advocate for people, not to promote inequity.

Yet Sheila had made it very clear that her job was on the line. Clara had been so proud of her promotion, so excited to begin climbing the corporate ladder. But already her new role was turning out to be more difficult than she had imagined.

There had to be a way out of this.

An idea popped into her head. Perhaps there was a way she could help Khalid, and Ayesha too. Her friend needed to have some fun, and her coworker needed to loosen up and learn how to talk to women. Besides, Sheila had asked her to investigate Khalid, not fire him. As the new regional manager of Human Resources, she had the responsibility of seeing both sides of any workplace issue.

Clara took the elevator to the basement. Standing on the threshold of Khalid's shared office, she tried to see him the way Sheila did, as a dangerous, sexist outsider. But he looked like the other Muslim men in the neighborhood where she'd grown up, like Ayesha's grandfather dressed for Friday prayers. She knocked on the door and entered the office.

"It was so nice bumping into you in the

hall today, Khalid," she said.

He looked up from the screen, surprised. "How was your meeting with Sheila?"

The less said about that, the better. "Do you enjoy listening to poetry?" Clara asked instead.

Khalid considered this, puzzled. "I read the Quran. It is a very poetic book."

Amir snickered. Khalid's obnoxious office mate stared at her, eyes on her breasts. She ignored him.

"Have you heard of Bella's? They're having an open mic poetry night on the weekend. I'd love it if you joined me and my friend."

Khalid looked uncomfortable. "I do not think that would be appropriate —" he began, but Clara cut him off.

"I'm launching an initiative at Livetech that I hope will be of interest to you. I want to organize a workshop on diversity and religious accommodation. I could really use your input."

Still Khalid hesitated.

"Come on, K-Man," Amir said. "It will be fun. I'll bring my boys."

"Is Bella's a bar?" Khalid asked. "Will there be alcohol?"

Clara shook her head, fingers crossed behind her back. "It's a lounge, not a bar. I really appreciate this. In return, maybe I can offer you a few suggestions for your meeting with Sheila next week."

She left before Khalid could ask how she knew about his meeting, or the difference between a bar and a lounge. Or who her friend was.

Clara smiled to herself. *Khalid Mirza, have I got a girl for you.*

Chapter Five

Ayesha parked her car in the driveway and slowly removed her key from the ignition. It was six o'clock, and she had survived her first week as a substitute high school teacher. Barely.

In the bag beside her were two books on classroom management strategies, along with the tenth-grade science curriculum. All of which would eat up her entire weekend.

But not tonight. Tonight she was going to party like she was still an undergrad. Which meant takeout pizza and old Bollywood movies.

What time should I come over? Ayesha texted Hafsa.

Whatever. It's not like you have time for me anymore, career-lady.

Ayesha sighed. Hafsa was upset because

she hadn't responded to her texts or phone calls all week. *Because I have a job, because I can't skip work to go for a facial,* she thought, and then she felt guilty. Hafsa was like a baby sister, and sometimes baby sisters threw tantrums. The best way to deal with a temper tantrum was to ignore it. She quickly texted Hafsa again:

I always have time for Bollywood Night! Come on, we are going to have FUN! :) We need to celebrate your husband search! I'll be there in an hour.

Ayesha knew she shouldn't dawdle in the car. The "Bored Aunty Brigade," as she had nicknamed her gossipy *desi* neighbors, were likely peering through their windows right now.

Ayesha Shamsi took her sweet time going inside, she imagined them saying. *Up to no good. No husband yet. Who will marry her now?* Cluck, cluck, cluck.

She flung open the car door, fake smile plastered to her face. Let them stare. She was too old to care what the Aunty Brigade thought of her!

" 'Oh, she doth teach the torches to burn bright,' " a soft voice called from the front lawn. " 'Beauty too rich for use, for earth

43

too dear. So shows a snowy dove trooping with crows. As yonder lady o'er her fellows shows.' "

"Nana, are you smoking again?" Ayesha's frozen smile thawed into a more natural one as she surveyed her grandfather on his favorite green plastic lawn chair, hiding behind their lone scraggly maple tree. Ayesha's grandfather was a retired English professor from Osmania University in Hyderabad, India. He had a soft spot for the Bard, and quoted him often.

"No," he said, blowing cigarette smoke thoughtfully into the emaciated branches, which were just starting to turn green. Spring in the city arrived slowly, a lazy cat stretching after a long winter nap. "This is just an illusion, as is most of reality. This is not a cigarette. I am not hiding from Nani and waiting for you. And you are not working too hard. We are all just cosmic players in the eternal dance of life."

"Nana, you talk too much *bakwas.*" Ayesha carefully removed the cigarette from her grandfather's unresisting fingers and kissed him gently on the cheek. "You're not even wearing a jacket. It's cold."

"I am a Canadian. I feel no cold." But he got up gingerly from the lawn chair and followed her into the house.

"Smoking is bad for you. It causes lung cancer and emphysema. It is also very unfashionable. You said you quit during Ramadan," Ayesha scolded as they entered the house and stood in the tiny entranceway to remove their shoes.

"I always quit during Ramadan. I restart after Eid. And I do not care if it is unfashionable. I am a nonconformist."

Ayesha hid her smile and held her hand out. After a slight hesitation, he placed a half-empty pack of cigarettes in her palm.

"Who's your supplier?" Ayesha asked as she pocketed the package.

"I'll never talk." He smiled rakishly at her. "If it truly disturbs you, I promise to stop. Just as soon as you promise to quit your job. Nice girls from good families shouldn't work outside the home." He twinkled at her.

"Nana, you're so sexist," Ayesha said. "Who said I'm a nice girl?"

"Beti, you are the *nicest."*

When Ayesha, her mother, Saleha, her brother, Idris, and her grandparents had first immigrated to Canada seventeen years ago, they had felt unmoored in their adopted home and by her father's sudden, violent death in India. Saleha was in mourning, Idris was an infant. Her grandparents had stepped in, caring for Ayesha and Idris while

45

their mother grieved. Ayesha grew especially close to Nana, who had read to her every night. She joked that she had learned to speak "Shakespearean" English before "Canadian" English.

Ayesha and Nana walked into the kitchen of the three-story townhouse. Ayesha's mother had use of the third-floor loft, while the two bedrooms on the second floor were occupied by Ayesha and her seventeen-year-old brother. The small kitchen and family room were shared, and her grandparents had the basement suite.

Their home was located in the east end of the city, in a suburb named Scarborough. The neighborhood consisted of mixed housing, their aging townhouse-condominium complex set among single homes with large backyards and double-car garages, as well as smaller semi-detached units. Driveways modified to accommodate three or four vehicles were common, with luxury brands like Mercedes and BMW sprinkled among older, more affordable types. Minivans dotted most driveways, and many garages were furnished with sofas and TV screens and used as additional gathering spaces for family and friends. Homes had side entrances used by extended family, or for rental basement suites.

Ayesha's townhouse complex was old but well maintained, part of a larger neighborhood made up of a high concentration of immigrants from Asia, the Caribbean, and the West Indies. Their community also boasted the best kebabs, chicken tikka, dosa, sushi, pho, and roti in the city, most of which were made in the kitchens of residents.

Nani was at the stove, stirring a fragrant curry and sprinkling minced coriander on top, when Ayesha and Nana walked into the kitchen. Her grandmother screwed up her nose at the smell of tobacco but otherwise kept silent.

"Challo, ghar agay, rani?" Nani said in Urdu. *You're home, princess?* She added curry leaves to the pot before warming oil for mustard seed and black cumin in a separate frying pan, the final touch in every dal. She placed another pot on the stove and deftly filled it with milk, dropping in whole black peppercorns, cardamom pods, cinnamon sticks, cloves, and three heaping teaspoons of loose-leaf black tea.

"Where's Idris and Mom?" Ayesha asked her grandmother.

"Idris is in his room pretending to complete math homework. Saleha is on a double shift at the hospital until midnight," Nani

47

answered. Her grandmother spoke to her family in Urdu, though Ayesha knew she understood English perfectly.

Ayesha made her way upstairs, picking up socks, scattered mail, and a jacket as she went. She opened her brother's door without knocking. Idris was at his desk, hunched over the keyboard. The lights were off, and he whirled around when she flicked them on.

"Jesus! Can you knock?"

Idris was tall and had the lankiness of a teenager unused to his growing body. He was wiry and stubbly, but when Ayesha looked at him, she saw the little boy who used to beg her to play. His thick black hair was standing on end from frequent finger-raking, and his glasses were smudged, obscuring his light brown eyes.

"I hear you're hard at work. I had to see for myself," she said.

Idris turned back to the screen. "Nani was nagging me again. I had to get her off my back."

"You're not watching porn, are you?"

Idris didn't respond, and Ayesha peered over his shoulder.

"I e-mailed your math teacher. She said you didn't do that great on your last test. Don't forget your English essay on *Hamlet*

48

is due next week. Nana said he'd help you annotate the play and think of a thesis."

Idris hunched lower and typed faster.

"Did you hear me?"

"Yes! I heard you! Can you leave me alone?"

Ayesha sighed and placed her hand on her brother's shoulder. "Are you writing code again?"

"Somebody's gotta make it big in this family. It's certainly not going to be you, Little Miss Poet."

Ayesha was stung, but she squeezed her brother's shoulder lightly. "Don't forget me when you're rich and famous."

When she returned downstairs, her grandparents were drinking chai in silence. A large mug of milky tea was waiting for her, and she sipped the fragrant brew gratefully. Chai was so much more than a caffeine kick for her. She knew how every member of her family liked to drink their tea, how much sugar or honey to put in each cup. Chai was love, distilled and warming. She drank and relished the silence.

"Are you going to Hafsa's house?" Nani asked after a few moments.

"It's Bollywood Night."

" 'Self-love is not so vile a sin as self-neglecting,' " Nana remarked into his mug.

Ayesha ignored his unsubtle jab at Hafsa and gulped the rest of her tea. "I'll be back soon."

When they'd first emigrated from India to Canada, Ayesha and her family had moved into the three-bedroom townhouse with Hafsa's family. It was a tight fit for everyone, but her uncle Sulaiman insisted on hosting them. He had immigrated as a young man almost two decades before, and he was happy to have his family join him in Canada, despite the devastating circumstances.

After two years of living together, Sulaiman, who owned several halal butchers and Indian restaurants in the city, gave the townhouse to Ayesha's mother, mortgage-free. He constructed a new home on a parcel of land he had bought five blocks away, which he shared with his wife and four daughters.

"This is what family does," he said. As eldest brother, it was his duty to take care of his widowed sister and their parents. The townhouse was a generous gift, one that Ayesha didn't know how her family would ever repay. In return, she had looked out for her younger cousins, especially Hafsa.

It was a brisk fifteen-minute walk to her

cousin's house — which Ayesha secretly called the Taj Mahal. Sulaiman Mamu's new home was large and ostentatious. It had never really appealed to her. He had built it envisioning a villa similar to the ones he had grown up admiring in the wealthy neighborhoods of Hyderabad, so completely out of reach for the son of an English literature professor. The house was Spanish colonial, set well back from the road. With its adobe roof, sandstone walls, and ten-foot-high custom-made door embellished with metal flowers and vines, the construction had initially drawn the ire and envy of neighbors. The building featured a large courtyard, circular driveway with stone fountain, four-car garage, six bedrooms, and eight bathrooms. There was even a small guest cottage, kept ready for Nana and Nani whenever they wanted to spend the night. So far, they preferred their cozy basement suite in the townhouse.

The main house was decorated in bright colors, with dark maroon accent walls and warm syrupy-toned paint everywhere else. The floors were covered with red, blue, and green wool rugs that had been imported from India. The wall decorations were Islamic prayers filigreed on metal, embroidered on tapestries, and painted on canvas, and the large central family room had pictures of famous places of worship, including an oversize one of the Kaaba in Mecca. The furniture was traditional and ornate: overstuffed brocade couches, Queen Anne armchairs, and heavy drapes. The light fixtures were all brass, polished weekly by a cleaning lady.

Hafsa's mother, Samira, answered the door. She was a petite dumpling of a woman, round-faced and excitable, who had married young and birthed four daughters before she was thirty. She spent most of her days taking an avid interest in the goings-on of her neighbors.

"Ayesha *jaanu*!" she said, using the Urdu term of endearment. "You're finally here! Hafsa was afraid you were too busy for her now that you are working." She enveloped her niece in a massive hug. "Let me fill you in on all the news. The Nalini girl ran away with her boyfriend, and the Patels are about to file for bankruptcy because their daughter is being far too demanding about jewelry and clothes for her wedding. She had her dress made by that fashionable Pakistani designer. So sad when people spend money they don't have, no? Also, Yusuf *bhai* down the road is divorcing his second wife! Imagine!"

Ayesha's eyes twinkled. "Samira Aunty, you're better than CNN. Do you have a newsfeed I can subscribe to?"

Hafsa's three younger sisters — Maliha, sixteen; Nisa, fourteen; and baby Hira, eleven — all rushed toward Ayesha.

"How do you like being a substitute teacher?" Maliha asked. "Dad said teaching is a good job for a woman. He refuses to consider enrolling me in the engineering program in New York City because he said it's too far from home and he would miss me." Her cousin rolled her eyes. "Can you try to convince him? Please?"

"Are we going for bubble tea this weekend? You promised!" Hira piped up.

"Did Ammi tell you about the rishta proposals that came for Hafsa?" Nisa asked. "Five this week."

"Nisa, *chup*!" Samira Aunty reprimanded her daughter, and there was an awkward moment as all three girls looked at the floor, embarrassed.

"Only five?" Ayesha asked lightly. "I'm surprised Hafsa hasn't received fifty proposals this week alone."

The girls exchanged knowing looks and Ayesha's cheeks turned red. Samira shooed her daughters away before turning to her niece.

"Ayesha jaanu," she began carefully. "Since you brought it up . . . Well, I hope you aren't comparing your situation to our little Hafsa's many rishta proposals. Even if you *are* seven years older and only received a handful of offers. Only consider Sulaiman's status in the community and Hafsa's great beauty, her bubbly personality. Well, we are all blessed by Allah in different ways."

Ayesha knew her aunt was trying to be kind, in her way. "Don't worry about me. I'm too busy to go husband shopping."

Samira Aunty smiled, but a look of pity was still fixed on her face. "Just don't leave it too late. I was married at seventeen, and Hafsa will be married before the end of the summer. A girl's beauty blooms at twenty, twenty-one. After that, well . . . Finding the right person can be difficult. Perhaps I can send a few proposals your way. The ones that aren't suitable for Hafsa."

Ayesha's mouth twitched, but she kept a straight face. "Thank you. I promise I will think seriously about your offer."

In truth, the only thing Ayesha envied her cousin was her massive bedroom suite. Hafsa had a separate seating area, with a large bay window and cozy reading nook. Her walk-in closet was the size of Ayesha's bedroom, and best of all, one entire wall contained a built-in bookcase filled with books that her cousin, never a great reader, kept for decoration. The room was painted a screaming hot pink, Hafsa's favorite color.

Hafsa was in her room, sprawled on the reclining leather sofa in front of a sixty-five-inch flat screen TV so thin it resembled a painting. Two boxes of pizza and chicken wings and a bowl of halal gummy bears were in front of her.

"*Apa!*" Hafsa squealed. *Apa* meant "big sister" in Urdu, an honorary title. "What took you so long?"

"I was talking to your mom."

"They didn't tell you about my proposals, did they?" Hafsa's mouth pursed in a pout. "I wanted to tell you first. Here, check out the pictures. They're *hilarious.*"

Her cousin was wearing yoga pants and a furry pink hoodie that exposed her flat stomach when she reached for her cell phone. Samira Aunty was not idly boasting — her twenty-year-old daughter was lovely. With large eyes framed by dark lashes, the high cheekbones of a Hollywood starlet, and a sweet smile, Hafsa was easily the most beautiful girl in the neighborhood. She was always laughing and joking, the incandescent center of every social gathering. In contrast, Ayesha was the calm, steady, responsible cousin. *The boring one,* she thought wryly.

Hafsa passed Ayesha her cell phone, to examine the pictures of her suitors. "I missed you so much!"

"It's only been a week. I saw you on Monday when you told me your news. Haven't you been busy with school?"

"I'm not really sure interior design is the right fit for me," Hafsa said. "I told Abba that I'm super interested in event planning. I could start by planning my wedding and then launch my business."

Ayesha reached for a slice of pepperoni and pineapple pizza and a handful of honey-garlic chicken wings. "So you've already picked one of the five proposals?" she asked, scrolling through the pictures.

Traditional arranged marriages were a bit like horse trading, Ayesha had always thought. Photographs and marriage résumés detailing age, height, weight, skin color, job title, and salary were sent to the families of prospective brides and grooms before the first visit was even arranged, a sort of vetting process for both parties. Details about family were often sent through a trusted intermediary, usually a mutual friend and sometimes a semiprofessional matchmaking aunty.

Hafsa looked over Ayesha's shoulder, supplying details — this one was a doctor, that one lived in India and was obviously looking for a visa-bride. This one had a pushy mother.

"All rejects. I'm not going to pick a husband until I get a hundred proposals."

Ayesha laughed. "Why not hold out for a thousand?"

Hafsa squinted at her cousin. "I don't want to be unreasonable. If I'm going to be a kick-ass wedding planner, I need to start now, when I'm young."

"Yes, launching a business is a great reason to get married," Ayesha said.

"You know what would be even better?" Hafsa said, ignoring her cousin's sarcasm. "A storybook romance. Every business needs a good origin story. If I met someone who swept me off my feet, imagine how great that would play for my clients. I could call my company 'Happily Ever After Event Planning.' "

"Or you could just start a company without the wedding."

"Don't be silly, Ashi Apa," Hafsa said. "I don't want to turn into one of those women who never gets married. No offense."

None taken, Ayesha thought as she took another slice of pizza. She pressed Play on a nineties Bollywood classic, *Pardes,* and the girls settled in to watch the movie together.

It was after midnight when the movie finished, and Hafsa was fast asleep on the couch, curled up under a pink cashmere throw. Ayesha gathered the half-empty pizza box and empty wings container, turned off the TV, and closed the bedroom door.

The light was on in the dining room when she crept downstairs, her uncle Sulaiman at the large table with stacks of paper in front of him.

"Ayesha." He smiled, standing up to embrace her. "I didn't know you were here."

Her uncle resembled a kindly shopkeeper rather than the family savior. He was a portly man a few inches taller than his niece and dressed even at this late hour in a white-collared shirt and dress pants, though he had removed his jacket and tie.

"I wanted to talk to you about something." He motioned to the chair. "I am so proud of your hard work and choice of profession. We were a little concerned when you started performing those poems, but I told Saleha you would settle down. Teaching is a good job for a woman."

"Thank you, Mamu," she said. "I'm going to start paying you back for my tuition as soon as I get my first paycheck."

58

Sulaiman Mamu waved his hand magnanimously. "I am worried about Hafsa. She told me she wants to be an event planner now, but I am afraid this is another phase, like all the others."

"Hafsa has many interests," Ayesha said diplomatically. So far Hafsa had tried her hand at cosmetology, landscape design, and culinary school, and she had yet to complete any of the programs she'd started.

"I have a favor to ask of you. As you know, I am involved in the masjid," he said, referring to the mosque.

Ayesha smiled. Her uncle was more than just involved. He had spearheaded the mosque building committee and donated generously over the years. Everyone knew he was the reason the Toronto Muslim Assembly could afford to keep the lights on and salaries paid.

Sulaiman Mamu continued. "The masjid is planning a weekend conference in the summer. Since Hafsa is so intent on pursuing event planning, I suggested they make use of her services. I know you are very busy with your new job, but . . ." Sulaiman hesitated. "You have always been so sensible, jaanu. We want to see Hafsa settled, but she thinks these proposals are a game. I worry that these boys might be more interested in my money than in her. I want my girl to be happy. I don't want her head turned by some rascal, and I don't want her to waste another chance to graduate with a diploma. Could you go to the planning meeting with her, help her take this seriously? It is time for Hafsa to grow up."

Ayesha nodded. Her uncle needed her, and after everything he had done for her family, she could not possibly refuse this simple request.

"Leave it to me, Mamu. I'll keep an eye on her and make sure she sees reason."

CHAPTER SIX

Virgin Shirley Temple, 9 p.m. My treat. You deserve it after your first week of teaching. I'm so proud of you!

Clara's text arrived late on Sunday afternoon, and Ayesha frowned as she read it. The only thing she was looking forward to tonight was an early bedtime. But loyalty ran deep in the Shamsi clan, and Clara deserved a best friend who could stay up past eight.

Clara was the first friend Ayesha had made when she'd immigrated to Canada. They'd both joined their school midyear in grade five, both transfers from faraway places — Ayesha from India, Clara from Newfoundland. The girls had bonded over their newcomer status. When kids made fun of Ayesha's Indian accent or Clara's "Newfie" lilt, they had each other's backs.

One time in health class during a lesson

on menstruation, the triumvirate of Mean Girls kept giving Ayesha surreptitious looks. At recess Sara, Kimmie, and Suzie surrounded Ayesha.

"Does your mom wear a Paki dot?" Sara asked her.

Ayesha had no idea what a "Paki dot" was, or why her Indian mother would wear one. Didn't these girls know she was from another country entirely? She turned to walk away, but they followed.

"Ever wonder why Paki dots are red?" Kimmie asked Sara, handily blocking Ayesha's path.

"No, why are Paki dots red?" Sara said, speaking loudly. A small crowd of students had gathered around them.

"Leave me alone," Ayesha said quietly.

"Leeee-ve meee all-oowwwn," Kimmie mocked in an exaggerated Indian accent. "Paki dots are red because *Pakis* use their own period blood to put them on."

The three girls laughed out loud and the crowd gasped in shock. "Eeeew!" someone said. "Nasty."

A tear slipped down Ayesha's cheek, but she kept her head lowered. She would not give them the satisfaction.

Clara pushed through the crowd to stand beside Ayesha, fists balled at her sides. "You

Angishore jinkers," she snarled. Her New-foundland accent became particularly pronounced when she was incensed. "Everyone knows you use your period blood for lipstick!"

Clara later told her she'd known her words made no sense — or at least, no more sense than the Mean Girls' Paki dot comments. But Clara had used the girls' momentary surprise to drag Ayesha out of the circle.

When they were safe, Ayesha thanked her. "But can I ask — what's a Paki dot?"

The memory made Ayesha smile all these years later, and her hesitation vanished. I'll see you at 9, she texted back.

Clara responded almost immediately. They have open mic tonight. In case you're feeling poetic.

When Ayesha arrived at Bella's at eight forty-five, the place was buzzing, the dance floor covered by stage and sound equipment. Their usual spot had been taken over by a group of guys, so she claimed the table beside them. Settling in, she ordered a Shirley Temple for herself and a white wine for Clara. She took out her purple notebook and looked around for inspiration.

"Hey, beautiful." A tall man holding a bottle of Heineken smiled seductively. "I'm

Mo. I bet your parents don't know you're in a place like this, dressed like that."

A veil-chaser. Ayesha could spot one a mile away.

Veil-chasers thought women in hijab were an exotic challenge. Like the pimply white guy who had asked Ayesha to prom every year in high school, and even offered to wear an "Indian outfit and turban" if she acquiesced. Other veil-chasers had tried to pick her up at bus stops and malls, and on one memorable day, a veil-chaser had administered her driving exam. She'd passed and even given him her (fake) number.

Mostly, they were a pain. They always commented on her headscarf and usually said something ignorant. As if on cue, Mo gave her a smoldering look. "If you're getting hot in that thing, you can take it off. I won't tell."

"Mo, I'm not interested. Why don't you go smile at those girls?" She waved toward a small group of young women crowded around the stage.

He didn't look away or even blink. "You're so mysterious. Can I buy you a drink?"

"I don't drink," she said coldly. "And if your name is Mo-short-for-Mohamed, you know why. Now please go away."

"Not until you let me buy you a drink."

Ayesha looked around until she caught the eye of Andy the Bouncer. "I'll take a Hyderabadi Mud-Slam," she said. "Ask Andy, he knows what I mean."

When Ayesha had come to Bella's on a more regular basis for open mic nights, a few of the veil-chasers had been relentless. Any time she used the term "Hyderabad," Andy knew it was code for "Would you please have a friendly discussion with this gentleman about respecting a woman's right to say no?"

"Anything for you, my brown princess." Mo winked and loped off.

Mo's buddies, who were sitting at the next table, started laughing loudly and she glanced over. Two of the men were true to type — greasy hair, greasy smiles, tight pants, the tabletop in front of them full of shot glasses. The third man gave her pause. He looked bored and aloof, and the clothes he was wearing caught her attention. He was dressed in a long white robe and kufi skullcap, his beard well past acceptable hipster levels. Their eyes met briefly. A tiny spark of electricity passed between them.

Ayesha looked away, and then back again.

He was a good-looking man, she acknowledged. Large brown eyes in a pale face, sensual mouth pressed into a severe line.

His dark beard was thick and long, accentuating a square jaw and sharp cheekbones. The white robe, so stark against the sea of tight jeans and T-shirts, hinted at broad shoulders and a powerful chest. He kept his gaze on the table in front of him, finely sculpted brows furrowed.

He was not the sort of man Ayesha usually looked at. He looked a bit like a priest in a strip club, she thought with a smile. He looked up at her again, eyes dark as they observed her expression. She shivered, though the lounge was warm.

Clara came flying in at that moment. "Sorry I'm late. I've been feeling rotten about our conversation. I didn't mean to give you a hard time about school and your first day. I'm just worried you're giving up on your dreams . . ." Clara was babbling, her eyes roaming the bar, looking for someone.

Ayesha's eyes were still pinned on the strange man.

Clara followed her gaze. "Khalid," she said, relieved.

"You *know* that guy? Is he lost?"

"Said the woman in hijab," Clara shot back before walking to the neighboring table.

"You invited me!" Ayesha called. She

fished in her pocket for lip gloss, and her fingers closed around a small rectangular box. Nana's cigarettes. She pulled them out and peered inside the packet.

"Having fun, Khalid?" Clara asked.

"Not particularly," Khalid said. "I don't feel comfortable here. Clara, you know Amir from work. This is Ethan and Mohamed." A chastened-looking Mo nodded at Clara, and Ethan smiled brilliantly.

" 'Sup, pretty lady," Ethan said.

Clara ignored him. "You took my advice. It's so important to invest in our work relationships."

Amir tried to muscle into the conversation. "I agree, Clara. After all, we probably see our coworkers more often than we see our family . . . husband . . . boyfriend . . ."

Clara ignored him too. "We grow by exposing ourselves to new experiences."

Khalid sat stiffly at the table. "This is certainly a new experience for me. I had no idea lounges smelled so bad."

Clara leaned in close. "Maybe it's not the lounge," she whispered, nodding at the three other men. "If you're bored, why don't you join us?" she said, loud enough for her voice to carry. "I'm here with my best friend. She's Muslim too. Why don't you

67

meet her? I'm sure you have a lot in common."

Khalid glanced at the young woman at the next table, and his expression of disapproval deepened. Ayesha was now holding three cigarettes in her hand and had a colorful cocktail in front of her. The look on his face betrayed his doubts about the Shirley Temple's virginity. "I do not wish to be introduced to your friend. I stay away from the type of Muslim who frequents bars," he said.

At the neighboring table, Ayesha stiffened.

"To be honest, I regret coming here tonight," Khalid continued. "My companions are only interested in drinking alcohol and accosting women, and it will be impossible to have a serious conversation. I hope I haven't offended you, Clara. I try not to judge other people's choices."

Ayesha was gone before Clara returned to their table. Had her friend heard any of that exchange? It was loud at Bella's, so probably not. She hoped.

On her way to the ladies' room, Ayesha ran into Andy the Bouncer. "I talked to that guy for you," he said. "I hope he's behaving."

Ayesha nodded, her mind spinning. Who did that bearded fundy think he was? *I try not to judge people's choices . . . I stay away from the type of Muslim who frequents bars.* Of all the judgmental, sexist jerks she'd ever met, he was the worst!

"You going to perform tonight?" Andy asked. "It's been a while."

Ayesha blinked at the smiling bouncer. "Thanks, Andy. All of a sudden, I'm feeling really inspired."

The crackle of a microphone caught everyone's attention.

"Hey, everyone, it's time for our weekly Open Mic Poetry Slam!" Andy the Bouncer (and part-time poet) announced. "We are so excited to have a special guest. She's been busy teaching, but tonight she is going to school you all with a special performance. Please welcome award-winning poet Grand Master Rhyme-Slam Shamsi!"

The small crowd in front clapped, and Ayesha walked onto the stage, an expression of intense concentration on her face.

"Uh-oh," Khalid heard Clara mutter at the next table, and he looked up.

"Hello, everyone. I'm so honored to be here tonight. I'm going to perform a poem I wrote a long time ago. It's called 'What do you See?' " Ayesha took a deep, steadying breath and focused her mind. Then, in a different voice, one rich with melody, she began to recite:

> What do you see when you think of me,
> A figure cloaked in mystery
> With eyes downcast and hair covered,
> An oppressed woman yet to be
>   discovered?
> Do you see backward nations and
>   swirling sand,
> Humpbacked camels and the
>   domineering man?
> Whirling veils and terrorists
> Or maybe fanatic fundamentalists?
> Do you see scorn and hatred locked
> Within my eyes and soul,
> Or perhaps a profound ignorance of all
>   the world as a whole?

The crowd roared. Her body swayed slightly, eyes liquid and focused on a spot at the back of the room. She continued.

> Yet . . .
> You fail to see
> The dignified persona
> Of a woman wrapped in maturity. The
>   scarf on my head
> Does not cover my brain.
> I think, I speak, but still you refrain

70

From accepting my ideals, my type of
   dress,
You refuse to believe
That I am not oppressed.
So the question remains:
What do I see when I think of you?
I see another human being
Who doesn't have a clue.

Ayesha looked directly at Khalid as she
recited the last two lines.

Clara clapped along with the enthusiastic
crowd and Ayesha smiled slightly and
headed directly for the bar. Khalid's eyes
followed her.

"That girl gets around," Mo said. "She
wanted me to get her a Hyderabadi Mud-
Slam. You think that's a sex thing?"

Khalid shook his head. "Amir, I'm going."

"No way, K-Man. I have to introduce you
to some pretty girls," Amir said, sloppy-
drunk by now. He put an arm around Khalid's shoulder.

Khalid carefully disentangled himself from
Amir's embrace and placed some money on
the table. "Promise you'll take a cab home,"
he said.

He left Bella's without another look at his
drunk friend, or anyone else.

Sulaiman Mamu texted Ayesha as she pulled up to her house, close to midnight. Her uncle had only recently learned to text, and she smiled at his carefully worded message.

Assalamu Alaikum, Ayesha. This is your uncle, Sulaiman. I am writing this letter to remind you that the first conference planning meeting will take place tomorrow, 8 p.m., at the mosque. Hafsa will meet you there. Best regards, Sulaiman Mamu.

She unlocked the front door quietly. A light was on in the kitchen. Ayesha's mother was alone at the small breakfast table. Her shoulders were slumped, and she had a ceramic mug in front of her, filled with the nuclear-strength coffee she drank by the liter.

Ayesha greeted her as she walked toward the staircase. Saleha stopped her.

"You were out late," her mother said.

"I was with Clara."

Saleha smiled, the expression making her seem younger, the similarity between mother and daughter more apparent. "Remember when she used to sleep over every

Friday night after school? I haven't seen Clara in so long."

That's because you're never home, Ayesha thought. A few months after they'd first immigrated to Canada, her mother had enrolled in nursing school. She had put in years of study to achieve her current position and now worked days and nights at Scarborough General Hospital. For a long time, Saleha had been the only working member of the household, and she routinely took on double shifts, overtime, and holidays. The dark circles under her eyes were permanent; she didn't bother with concealer anymore.

"It was crazy at the hospital. Every time I sat down to eat or drink, I was interrupted."

Ayesha felt a pang of guilt. "I'm working now, Mom. I can pitch in."

"You have your own expenses, and you need to pay back bhai," Saleha said.

"I have some extra money. Maybe you can work fewer shifts," Ayesha said. *So we can see you more often.*

"I don't need your money. I've supported us for years without help. I want you to see that a woman doesn't need anyone to take care of her. This business with Hafsa . . ." Saleha trailed off, looking exhausted once more. She tried for a lighter note. "I hear your cousin has been collecting rishtas."

"She's aiming for a hundred," Ayesha said. "Someone told her there's a cash prize for frequent-rishta club members."

Saleha smiled faintly at her daughter. "Sulaiman has old-fashioned ideas about marriage. Marriage is not a bad thing, if you find the right person and your judgment isn't clouded by emotion. I hope you're not thinking about marriage too, just yet. You need to focus on your new job and career. A husband can be such a distraction."

"I'm fine, Mom," Ayesha assured her. "Rishtas and marriage are the furthest things from my mind."

Saleha took another sip of her coffee. "I don't want you to be disappointed in love. Men are selfish, Ayesha. They will not put you first. A woman should always have a backup plan, for when things fall apart. You must know how to support yourself when they leave."

Ayesha wasn't in the mood for this. She didn't want to hear her mother's unsubtle hints about her parents' marriage. She knew if she asked specific questions about her father, her mother would just shut down. She said good night and climbed the stairs to her tiny bedroom on the second floor.

While it wasn't as grand as Hafsa's,

Ayesha's bedroom was her favorite room in the house. With her twin bed pushed against the wall, she had plenty of space for books, every one of which she had read. Her desk was full of textbooks and resources from teachers' college, and there were posters of Shakespeare and Jane Austen on the wall. She smiled a greeting to both as she un-pinned her hijab and shook out her curly brown hair, which had been tied up in a bun all day.

There was a knock at the door, and Nana peeked in.

"I heard you talking to Saleha," he said, coming in to sit on her rolling desk chair. Nana had spent so much time sitting in that chair, talking and reading to her, that she couldn't look at it without thinking of him. Ayesha settled on the bed, folding her arms.

"She told me husbands are a distraction and that I should never rely on a man."

Nana sighed. "Aren't you too old to be angry at your mother?" he asked gently. "Saleha has not let go of her anger, and it has made her so unhappy. I don't want to see that happen to you as well."

"I don't think she'll ever forgive Dad, but she won't talk about it either. It's not his fault that he died."

Nana looked down at his hands. "It was

such a shock," he said quietly. "Such a time of darkness in our family. Your mother was not raised to expect . . . She was not ready to deal with the aftermath of such a tragedy. Your Nani and I — we wanted nothing but the very best for our children. I thought it would break her, but she survived. She wants you to be stronger, ready for any catastrophe."

Ayesha drew her knees up to her chin, curling her body against the headboard. "It's like she hates him. She doesn't have any pictures of him, and she never talks about Dad. I lost something too when he died."

" 'We know what we are, but know not what we may be,' " Nana quoted. It was not lost on Ayesha that he was quoting Ophelia. "Her anger is so strong because it once fueled a very great love."

Nana's loyalty to Saleha was instinctive. Ayesha only wished he was more forthcoming about her father. Her mother and her grandparents were silent on the circumstances surrounding his death, and she had tried in vain to tease out details in various ways over the years.

"Don't you miss Hyderabad?" she asked instead.

"My life is here, with you," Nana said, as

he always did. "Sometimes I miss my classes at the university, and my books. My library took over the entire first floor of our house. Nani was jealous of my collection. She said I loved it more than her. She was wrong, of course. I brought *her* when we moved, not my books." His tone was wistful, and Ayesha felt a well of sadness for all those orphaned volumes. "Your mother loved the Hardy Boys and Agatha Christie mysteries best of all."

And now I get to live one, Ayesha thought. Whenever Ayesha and Idris asked questions about their father's death, they were deflected or ignored. At first she thought it was because the subject was too painful. Lately she had started to wonder if her father had been involved in something illegal, a scandal that justified her mother's anger.

"What sort of man was my father?" she asked. "Was he a good man?"

Nana was silent once more. "Goodness is for Allah to judge. But I can tell you this, jaanu. I have never met a man of more honor than Syed Ahmad Shamsi." Nana stood up to leave and Ayesha rose too. She wanted him to continue talking about her father.

"Samira Aunty offered to send Hafsa's

excess rishtas my way," she said. "Did you arrange Mom and Dad's marriage?"

Nana hesitated. "No," he said. He reached for the doorknob.

"I thought all marriages were arranged in India."

Nana started laughing. "Young people. Do you think you invented love and romance?"

"What do you mean?"

" 'No sooner met but they looked, no sooner looked but they loved, no sooner loved but they sighed, no sooner sighed but they asked one another the reason, no sooner knew the reason but they sought the remedy; and in these degrees have they made a pair of stairs to marriage,' " Nana recited as he walked out into the hallway.

Ayesha followed him. "Can you please stop quoting Shakespeare for one minute. They fell in love and you let them marry?"

"They were so happy, jaanu," he said simply. "I could never be a barrier to such happiness. Saleha must remember that and find her peace."

His words held a note of finality as he wished her good night. Ayesha returned to her room, pensive, and set the alarm. It was already past midnight, and tomorrow would be another long day spent managing students, and then managing Hafsa at the conference meeting. She was too tired to be angry at her mother and her secrets, or at fundy Khalid and his comments.

Besides, it was not as if she would ever see him again.

CHAPTER SEVEN

A headache throbbed behind Khalid's eyes, making it hard for him to concentrate on the code he was troubleshooting for one of his developers. The script kept blurring on his monitor and the office felt stuffy and airless. Sleep had eluded him last night. Now, no matter how hard he tried, he could not stop thinking about Bella's.

They had been joined there by Amir's friends Mo and Ethan. The trio had high-fived and cracked jokes, Khalid's presence a source of great amusement.

"Yo, this a prayer meeting?" Mo asked when Amir had introduced Khalid. Ethan snickered.

"You got any shawarma hidden under that robe?" Ethan asked. "How about a Persian rug?"

Khalid knew they were trying to be funny, but their teasing, combined with the loud noises and unfamiliar smell of alcohol, made him feel irritable and ill at ease.

"You look like you belong in one of those videos Amir likes to watch, with the unveiled girls," Mo said, but Amir hushed him.

The trio began downing shots and Amir was soon drunk, Khalid bored. A thought drifted into his mind: *How would it feel to behave as Amir did, so loose-limbed and free of inhibitions? Would he be happier if he drank alcohol too, instead of just watching from the sidelines?* He looked at his friend. No, that was not for him.

Khalid was eyeing the exits when he noticed the woman in hijab. She looked comfortable sitting alone at her table, golden-brown skin shadowed in the dimly lit room, her face arresting and familiar. He made the connection after a few minutes: the girl with the red mug! His disappointment hollowed out his stomach and loosened his tongue.

He had only seen her in their neighborhood, bathed in early-morning sunshine and filled with purpose. Not sitting comfortably in this seedy lounge. A good Muslim would never frequent such an establishment.

He felt the weight of his white robe at that moment, the skullcap on his head bearing down. He knew he had no right to be upset, but he couldn't help it. She didn't belong here.

Or rather, the person he'd thought she was didn't belong here.

Then the girl with the red mug was on-stage. He had tried to keep his eyes modestly lowered, even when her voice moved over him like a silken caress. But when she flung her final lines at the audience — *What do I see when I look at you? I see another human being who doesn't have a clue* — Khalid was on his feet and walking toward the exit. He knew he would do something incredibly foolish if he stayed.

Like walk up to her and ask, "What is a good Muslim doing in a place like this?"

Or worse: "Do you want to leave with me?"

Now Khalid banished his ricocheting thoughts and knocked on Sheila's half-open office door. His boss motioned for him to take a seat and gave him a discreet once-over, her eyes lingering on his white robe and skullcap.

"Thank you for coming today, Khalid. I'm eager to discuss your performance and future at Livetech," she said, shuffling papers around until she found a file with his name on it.

The door to the office opened and Clara

walked in and smiled warmly at Khalid.

Their familiarity was not lost on Sheila, who fixed cold blue eyes on Khalid. "I met your office mate, Amir, on Friday," she said, pronouncing his friend's name *Ahhh-mare.* "We chatted for a while. I found it interesting that he had no problem shaking my hand. He seems like a good fit at Livetech."

There was an awkward pause.

Sheila continued. "Khalid, let me start off by saying that according to your employee records, your performance has been consistently acceptable. Clara has talked to many of your coworkers, and everyone said you are an asset to the team. I called this meeting because I wanted to discuss a few matters. I believe in a transparent work relationship between management and employees."

Clara took a deep breath and seemed to plunge in. "As the regional manager of HR, Khalid, I think it's important to hear Sheila's concerns. In particular, she has some thoughts about your emphasis on religion in the workplace."

"What do you mean?" Khalid asked, taken aback.

"Are you comfortable reporting to a female director?" Clara asked, her eyes conveying a subtle warning.

Khalid was confused. "I have no problem

working with women. I have no wish to cause discomfort through my actions or words."

Clara gave Khalid an encouraging smile before she continued. "Since we are on this topic, I also wanted to bring your attention to the Livetech employee dress code. Sheila is concerned that your . . . cultural clothing stands out in a work environment. We want to ensure that you feel comfortable with your colleagues."

"As a member of the Livetech executive team, you are required to look professional at all times," Sheila added, her eyes flicking to Khalid's white robe and beard. She smiled stiffly at him. "We have to present a united front to our clients."

Khalid looked down at his clothes, heart sinking. Not this again. "I don't understand the problem," he said, keeping his voice flat. "If you can wear a dress to work, why can't I?"

Both women, momentarily speechless, stared at him. He forced himself to stand, despite his shaking legs.

"Clara, Sheila, thank you for your concern, but I am very happy at Livetech. I must return to my office to attend to urgent matters." He nearly ran for the door, closing it firmly behind him.

84

The women exchanged glances: Clara was chagrined and embarrassed, Sheila furious.

"I'm very disappointed with your performance today," Sheila said. "His coworkers must be covering for him."

Clara gathered her files and tried to keep the note of impatience from her voice. "I talked to everyone he's ever worked with. People find him a little odd, but he's also reliable and hard working. If you get rid of him, he might sue for religious intolerance. My advice would be to leave him alone."

"What if he's one of those undercover Islamists? Just this morning I asked him about the empty water bottle he carries to the bathroom. He said that *Moslems* have to purify themselves with water every time they use the facilities. Who knows what they really keep in there!"

Clara flushed red at Sheila's words, irritation tipping over into anger. "I think you've been watching too much Fox News," she said evenly. "I also don't think you should refer to Khalid, or any other Muslim, as 'they' or 'them.' We have employees from all over the world and from all religious backgrounds at Livetech. Academic studies have consistently demonstrated that diversity among employees leads to greater creativity and higher profits."

Sheila's eyes were narrowed. "I thought we understood each other. Your job is to help me remove the rotten apples from the orchard, not to attempt rehabilitation. Clara, you don't know what these people are like. In Saudi Arabia, I wasn't even allowed to leave the compound by myself!"

"We're not in Saudi Arabia, Sheila."

"Someone should tell that to Khalid."

"Actually, I think his background is South Asian."

When Clara left the office shortly after, she was sure of two things. One, Khalid needed help, and as the new HR manager at Livetech, it was her job to make sure he wasn't unfairly dismissed. And two, the only rotten apple in this orchard was sitting in the director's office, googling "Islamist water bottles."

CHAPTER EIGHT

Khalid sat at his desk, mind spinning after the conversation with Sheila. It was clear that his boss didn't like him, but why? Was his job in jeopardy because of the way he dressed? He had worn white *thawbs* to work every day for the last five years, with no complaints. His old boss, John, had even complimented their elegance.

Amir noticed his distraction. "Why did Sheila ask to see you?"

"I don't know. She had a file folder with my name on it." Khalid couldn't keep the note of panic out of his voice. Nothing like this had ever happened to him before. "When she requested a meeting, I didn't think HR would be there. That's a bad sign, right?" Khalid's throat felt like it was closing and he forced himself to take deep breaths and calm his racing heart.

Amir shook his head. "I thought there was something going on. That hot chick, the new

HR girl, was asking about you. Maybe you should just shake Sheila's hand and she'll call off the witch hunt."

"But it's forbidden!"

"Forbidden is relative. How about losing the robe and prayer cap? I'll help you pick out some nice shirts."

"I like the way I dress."

"You won't last ten seconds if she's out to get you. You know her nickname is 'Sheila the Shark,' right?" Amir sounded exasperated. "This political shit is everywhere. The least you can do is stay under the radar. Adopt some camouflage. That's what I did when I moved here. I learned to blend in."

"I thought I did blend in. I speak English, I work hard, I do my job well. What is the problem?"

Amir shook his head. "You're being stubborn. It's not about what you do. It's how you look while you're doing it. Start small: Stop washing your feet in the bathroom sink before prayer."

"My religion is not something I'm willing to compromise."

"Brother, don't be an idiot."

Khalid hid in the office for the rest of the day, feeling hunted and vulnerable, and when five o'clock rolled around, he hurried toward the subway station. He was so upset he didn't even read his Quran on the train. Instead he looked around the subway car.

The passengers directly across from him — an old man, a young corporate type, a few students — were all staring into their phones or newspapers. He caught the eye of a man in a business suit across from him, who shifted uncomfortably and looked away.

Are they afraid of me? Khalid wondered. *When Sheila looks at me, what does she see?*

The assumptions he saw in strangers' eyes as they took in his beard and skullcap were painful to acknowledge. Khalid had considered shaving or changing his wardrobe many times over the years. It would be easier for the people around him, but it wouldn't feel right. *This is who I am,* he thought. This thought was quickly followed by another: *If it comes down to my clothes or my job, there's no contest. I'll quit.*

Except he couldn't quit. He needed the money. Not so much for himself — Khalid lived simply — but for his sister. He sent Zareena money every month, and he knew she counted on it.

Khalid didn't feel like going home right away. His mother would ask about his day, and then he would have to lie. If he told her about the conversation with Sheila, she would demand that he go to the Human Rights Commission, or that *he* be made director of Livetech.

Instead he headed to the only place he felt entirely comfortable: the mosque.

The Toronto Muslim Assembly was located at a busy intersection five minutes away from their new home. It had taken the working-class congregation twenty-five years of fund-raising to gather enough money for the land and construction of the building, which included a large prayer hall, a small gym where teenagers played basketball and floor hockey, and a dozen offices and classrooms. With its minaret, large copper dome, and white stucco exterior, the mosque was instantly recognizable among the surrounding fast food restaurants and industrial units.

As Khalid entered the building, his shoulders relaxed. His fists, which he hadn't realized were clenched, loosened and he took a deep breath. He made his way to the large prayer hall, an empty space banked by ten-foot-high windows. The floor where congregants lined up for the five daily prayers was covered in two-foot strips of alternating olive-green and beige carpet. Brass wall sconces cast a warm glow, and an enormous crystal chandelier hung above the oak pulpit where the imam delivered his weekly sermons. According to rumor, the chandelier had cost over $100,000, a gift from a wealthy business owner looking for a tax write-off.

The prayer hall could hold more than two thousand worshippers, and on occasions like the twice-yearly Eid celebrations, the building strained with people packed into hallways, gymnasium, and classrooms. But for the five daily prayers, the building sat almost empty.

The prayer hall was enveloped in the hushed quiet of an art gallery. An elderly man sat in the back corner, worrying *tasbih* prayer beads. A large man in a bright-blue robe sat beside the pulpit bent over a book, forehead furrowed in concentration. The man spotted Khalid's approach and broke into a broad smile, calling out "Assalamu Alaikum."

Khalid returned the greeting and shook Imam Abdul Bari's hand.

"I was just about to take my tea. Will you join me?" Abdul Bari asked. Without waiting for a reply, the burly imam walked on graceful feet out of the prayer hall.

Once inside the office, the imam removed his blue robe to reveal a bright floral Hawaiian T-shirt and khakis. Khalid, used to the imam's peculiar sense of dress, didn't say a word.

Abdul Bari busied himself with the kettle and tea bags. "I don't usually see you until the evening prayer. What brings you here so early today?"

Khalid lowered his head. "Just some trouble at work. My boss doesn't like the way I dress. My coworker Amir suggested I adopt some camouflage, but it feels dishonest."

The imam handed Khalid a cup of weak tea and settled down in his swivel chair. "Honesty is an admirable trait," he said carefully. "However, one of the cornerstones of a functional democracy is the willingness to accommodate. Does the thought of camouflage feel dishonest, or are you uncomfortable conforming to other people's expectations of you?"

They drank their tea in silence while Khalid considered the imam's words. Abdul Bari was better at giving advice than making tea, though he was generous with both.

"I don't know," Khalid said.

"It is always good to analyze your *niyyah* — your intention — before making decisions. The Prophet Muhammad, may Allah be pleased with him, said: 'Actions are judged by intentions, and everyone will have what they intended.' So be clear of your motivations, Khalid." The imam set down his cup and clapped his hands together. "Perhaps what you need is a distraction. I have great news: Our mosque has been chosen to host the 'Muslims in Action' conference this year. I hope I can count on you to help organize? Our first planning meeting is tonight at eight."

Khalid agreed to help, and their conversation moved on to other topics.

When he returned home, his mother was on her way out. She had a guilty look on her face, which she replaced with an imperious one.

"I am going to buy vegetables from Hakim bhai," she said.

Hakim Abdul, known by everyone as Hakim bhai, owned the nearby grocery shop that sold essential items: bread, onions, garlic-ginger paste, and halal meat. It was also the best place to hear neighborhood gossip.

"I'll go," Khalid offered.

"No!" Farzana said. "You've been working all day. Aliyah said she would meet me there also." Aliyah was Farzana's new friend, a woman with grown-up children and time on her hands.

As Farzana peered into the hallway mirror

and carefully pinned her bright-blue hijab, Khalid noticed a large gold bangle with red stones on her arm. The bangle had been a gift from his father years ago; she had not worn it since his death.

In their old neighborhood, his mother had loved to chat with the other aunties. Maybe Aliyah would introduce Farzana to new friends among the coriander and lemons. Her absence would also allow him some time to think.

And to engage in his secret hobby.

Khalid moved quickly as soon as his mother was out of the house. He assembled everything he needed: onion, turmeric, chili powder, garam masala, and chickpea flour. While canola oil warmed in a small frying pan, he chopped up onions using the special chef's knife he hid behind the mixing bowls his mother never used. Khalid listened to a recitation of the Quran on his iPhone as he worked, mixing together spices and onions, dropping tablespoons of batter into hot oil, watching the onion pakoras brown and grow crispy.

Khalid loved to cook and feed others. When he was younger, he would make desserts and simple pasta dishes for Zareena. He subscribed to *Gourmet* magazine and watched Food Television. Lately his focus had been on Indian dishes. He was experimenting with different techniques to grind the perfect garam masala spice mix.

Farzana hated it when Khalid cooked. She claimed he left behind a mess, so he only cooked when she was out of the house, and he made sure to air out the kitchen afterward.

The pakoras were delicious, and he made a note in his recipe book to add more whole coriander seeds next time. He read a new biography of Prophet Muhammad while he snacked. His phone pinged, another e-mail from Zareena:

Hey K, guess what I'm doing? Cooking. I made breakfast. Then I made lunch. Now I'm making dinner. The fun never stops here. I can guess what you're doing. You're at the mosque, volunteering, or maybe performing some extra prayers, am I right? My pious little brother, making up for the sins of the sister. Wish I was there to poke you and force you to do something fun!

I've been thinking about you a lot lately. I miss you. Also, can you do me a favor? Same as before, Western Union plz. You're the best!

P. S. Boiling-hot showers and that crazy snowstorm every April, just when you think winter is over.

Khalid sent Zareena money every month, but lately her requests had become more frequent. He didn't mind — he enjoyed taking care of her. It made her seem less far away. He missed having her in his life, even though it had been hard to keep her secrets.

The first time he had caught Zareena sneaking out, he was thirteen, his sister seventeen. It was nearly midnight, and he had been getting some orange juice from the fridge when he heard her light footfall on the stairs. She was just about to turn the door handle, shoes in hand, when Khalid spoke.

"Going somewhere, Zareena?" he had asked.

She froze, then turned around with a mischievous smile on her face. She was wearing eyeliner, which made her eyes look huge and smoky, and her lips were a shiny red. Khalid didn't know Zareena owned lipstick, let alone knew how to put it on. His mother hated makeup on women and forbade it in the house. She was wearing a gauzy black hijab that barely covered her hair and a pair of jeans so tight they made

96

her legs look like pipe cleaners.

The look on his face must have said everything, because she walked over to him, smiling as she swiped his orange juice.

"I'm meeting some friends," she said, taking a sip. "It's no big deal, but you know Mom freaks out every time I leave the house. I'm not asking you to lie for me. Just pretend you never saw me."

"Where are you going at this hour? Will there be boys?" he asked.

She rolled her eyes. "No, only girls. I'm going to a sleepover. I'll be back by Fajr. It's no big deal, honestly." Fajr, the dawn prayer. She would be out all night.

"Maybe I should come with you," he said.

"To a house full of girls? What will people think?" she said, smirking playfully. "Then again, why not. My friends think you're cute."

Zareena's friends were all popular and pretty, always smiling and joking. They made him nervous.

"No, that's okay," he said. "If you're just going to a girls' sleepover, there's no harm. I won't tell anyone. Just make sure you're back by Fajr."

"I'll be back *before* Fajr," Zareena said, grinning with happiness. On impulse, she gave Khalid a big hug. "Thanks, K," she said. "I won't forget this." She smelled like soap and flowers. Was she wearing perfume too? She grabbed her shoes and ran out the door.

Khalid followed just in time to see her open the passenger door of a waiting car. It was dark, and he couldn't make out who was driving. Thumping music spilled into the quiet street, abruptly cut off by the car door slamming shut. He returned to bed but stayed awake until just before dawn, when he could faintly make out the sound of a key in the door and soft footsteps climbing the stairs.

In the morning, Zareena beat him to breakfast, dressed in a shapeless black abaya with a black hijab and no makeup. She was chatting with their mother and didn't give Khalid more than a cursory smile.

Lying for his sister made him uneasy, and that night wasn't the only time. Later, after she was sent away forever, he felt awful about all those times he had kept silent.

His mother didn't know he sent money to Zareena. She didn't know they communicated. Khalid was certain Ammi and Zareena hadn't spoken in almost twelve years, not since Farzana had flown her only daughter to India and returned two weeks later without her.

Khalid hated thinking about this, hated thinking about his sister. He should have told his parents what was going on. Maybe then Zareena would still be here, instead of on another continent, miserable.

CHAPTER NINE

Khalid returned to the mosque after dinner for the conference meeting. He was early, and headed to the prayer hall. He sat cross-legged on the carpet and leaned against the beige-paneled wall. The mosque was quiet and warm, and he felt cocooned in the peaceful stillness. His breathing slowed as he enjoyed this momentary respite from the world.

When he opened his eyes, a soft golden glow engulfed the empty prayer hall. He checked his watch and stood up. It was time for the meeting to start.

A bundled shape on the other side of the room caught his eye. The bundle moved, and without thinking, he stepped closer. It was a young woman, fast asleep. Her face looked peaceful, and her even breathing matched his own.

The Toronto Muslim Assembly employed a casual segregation policy. Unlike most other mosques, where men and women prayed in separate rooms and sometimes even on separate floors, the mosque had no physical divider. Khalid cautiously moved toward the women's section.

The young woman was clutching a book in her hands, but he couldn't make out the title. He looked away to avoid staring, but his feeling of peace was broken. His eyes were drawn to her for a second look, and he recognized her now: the girl with the red mug; the girl from the bar.

He wondered if she was following him.

Today she was wearing a blue hijab, dark blue cardigan, and long black skirt. If she hadn't shifted position when Khalid glanced over, she would have resembled nothing more than a pile of prayer sheets. Prayer sheets that softly hugged the sharp curve of her hips, outlining elegant legs hidden by dark fabric.

Khalid felt strange. His heart was beating fast and his mouth had gone dry. He didn't intend to approach her, but his feet moved him even closer and he stood staring down at her. *Sleeping Beauty,* he thought.

She opened her eyes and they looked at each other wordlessly. Then she sat up. "Were you staring at me?" she asked, voice unfriendly.

"No," he said. The lie came automatically to his lips. Lying inside the mosque! He was going to hell.

His heart was beating even faster now. Her eyes were two large pools of inky brown, and he couldn't look away.

"I mean, I was about to leave and then I noticed you sleeping. I thought you were a pile of prayer sheets and was going to fold you and put you away. Then I realized it was you. A person, I mean. A woman. You." He looked stupidly at her.

She seemed amused, but then her expression hardened and she stood abruptly. "I have to go. I try to stay away from the type of Muslim who stares at sleeping women in prayer halls."

In her rush to exit, she left her book behind, a plain purple notebook, the type used by students. He picked it up to return it but sat down instead, his legs jelly.

Ayesha had grown up attending Sunday school and Friday prayers at the mosque, but she had not visited the Toronto Muslim Assembly in a long time. The prayer hall looked older and shabbier. The green-and-beige striped carpet was frayed at the edges, and there was a faint but distinct odor of socks. The walls had dents and black smudge marks made by running children. Still, the room retained some of the majesty she remembered, even if the crystal chandelier now looked like it belonged in a Trump casino.

Ayesha had been early for the meeting, and after she'd found a spot in the empty prayer hall, she took out her purple notebook. But it was no use. She was too tired after her late night at Bella's, and the confusing conversation afterward with her mother and Nana. Instead her eyes had felt heavy and she slipped into a deep, dreamless sleep.

When she awoke, she felt rested and at peace. Her eyes had slowly opened to see a man standing in front of her, staring intently. He looked surprised but hadn't looked away. *I know you,* Ayesha thought, half-asleep.

He had been wearing a rumpled white robe, the kind her Nana wore sometimes to Friday prayers. They locked eyes, and a hum of energy rose around them. With a jolt, she realized who the man was — Khalid, the bearded fundy from Bella's!

"Were you staring at me?" she asked, jumping up quickly and straightening her skirt.

"No!" he said, looking guilty.

A smile had twitched at the corner of her lips at his blatant lie. Then she remembered she was sleeping in an empty prayer hall, and Khalid was a judgmental jerk and possibly a Peeping Tom.

Now, as she hurried out of the prayer hall, she ran straight into a large man wearing a blue Hawaiian shirt. Flustered, she apologized. "Brother, do you know where the conference planning meeting will be held?" she asked.

"Assalamu Alaikum, Sister," the man said. "You must be Hafsa. You look so much like Brother Sulaiman. I am Imam Abdul Bari."

"No, I'm not . . ." Ayesha said, but the imam was gently steering her toward a conference room beside the main office.

"I am so thrilled to have an actual event planner help with our conference. It is so kind of you to donate your time."

"Imam, there's been a misunderstanding," Ayesha was saying firmly when Khalid entered the room. "Are you following me?" she said to him instead.

The imam, who seemed to have selective hearing, offered Ayesha a chipped mug filled with a cloudy-looking liquid. She accepted the tea and scowled at Khalid.

The imam handed Khalid a cup as well. "Have you met Sister Hafsa? She's the official event planner for our conference."

Khalid looked embarrassed and confused. He selected a seat far away from Ayesha and stared at his hands.

Ayesha put the cup on the conference table. "Imam, my name is not —"

A tall man in a tight black shirt entered the room, and Ayesha stopped speaking. He was the most beautiful man she had ever seen. His long face was accentuated by sharp cheekbones and he had the jawline of a Disney prince. His tawny eyes contrasted with terra cotta skin, and his generous lips curved in a wide-open smile as he surveyed the room.

"Sorry I'm late," the beautiful man said, his smile increasing the temperature in the conference room by several degrees. Even his voice was sexy, Ayesha thought, like drizzled honey. And he had big hands. She watched the beautiful stranger greet the imam and nod cheerfully at her with his perfect, manly chin. He even had a dimple. Seriously, who was this guy?

"Sister Hafsa, Brother Khalid, please allow me to introduce Tarek Khan, the president of the Muslims in Action organization," Imam Abdul Bari said. "Let us open with a recitation of Surah Fatiha."

Khalid recited the first chapter of the

Quran in Arabic, his voice clear and deep, and not remotely as sexy as Tarek's, Ayesha thought.

The imam continued. "Thank you all for attending our first planning meeting. Our mosque has a unique opportunity to host an important youth conference. I have asked all of you here today to form the central organizing committee."

The imam's words brought Ayesha crashing back to reality. She texted under the table.

Hafs, where are you? The mosque conference meeting started already, and the imam thinks that I'm YOU! Hurry!

Her phone buzzed almost immediately.

I can't make the meeting. Can you take notes for me? Don't tell them your real name, it will be like *Freaky Friday.* Sooo hilarious! You're the best! xxx

Ayesha sighed. Typical Hafsa. Why tell the truth when an entertaining lie would do? She opened her mouth to clarify her name when her eyes slid to Khalid. He was still looking down at his hands, a block of immovable, judgmental, unsexy concrete. A

106

sudden impulse washed over her.

Hafsa had pulled so many pranks over the years. Her cousin was always laughing and having fun while serious, responsible Ayesha was expected to do the right thing.

But her fun-loving cousin wasn't here today. Or was she?

Khalid paused in his contemplation of the desk to look briefly at Ayesha. The expression in his eyes was disapproving, and his words to Clara rang again in her ears: *I stay away from the type of Muslim who frequents bars. I have no wish to be introduced to your friend.*

Ayesha smiled grimly. *If he doesn't want to be introduced to me, that can easily be arranged.* A spark of exhilaration filled her with heady spontaneity.

The imam asked everyone to officially introduce themselves. When it was her turn, Ayesha didn't hesitate. "I'm Hafsa Shamsi," she said, trying to sound young and vacuous. "I'm an event planner, and this is, like, my first event ever! I'm so excited!"

The imam and Tarek smiled, but Khalid gave her a strange look. She ignored him and reached into her bag for her notebook, but it was gone.

The imam continued. "The youth conference will be held during the July long

107

weekend, which leaves us with only a few months to prepare. We will have to meet at least two or three times a week to ensure our success."

Tarek opened his MacBook and turned on the LCD projector. "I have a short presentation prepared," he said, smiling at the group, eyes lingering on Ayesha. He talked rapidly, moving through the slides. "Our yearly summer youth conference is aimed at ages eighteen to thirty, and we try to keep the sessions as small and intimate as possible, with lots of interactive activities. The big draw is the Singles Mixer on Saturday. Last year we had more than five hundred people attend, and this year we are anticipating twice that number. We have access to many well-known speakers, including Sheikh Rafeek."

"Brother Tarek, that sounds impressive," Khalid interrupted. "But I'm unclear as to the purpose of your organization, and why you have chosen our mosque."

Tarek looked at Khalid for a long moment without speaking, so long the silence became uncomfortable. "Muslims in Action is a grassroots organization that partners with local mosques to raise funds and encourage young people to participate in the community," he said eventually. "Imam Abdul

Bari tells me most of your congregation are middle-aged and senior citizens. It's time to attract the next generation."

When the slideshow concluded, Imam Abdul Bari leaned close to Tarek to confer quietly with him for several minutes. Khalid used the opportunity to discreetly slide the purple notebook to Ayesha.

"I apologize for my rudeness in the prayer hall," he said in a low voice. "I assure you, it is not my habit to watch women sleep inside the mosque. Though to be fair, there usually aren't any to watch." Khalid smiled slightly.

"Is that a joke?" Ayesha said, grabbing the notebook. "Someone who looks like you should avoid humor. You'll only confuse people."

"And someone who dresses as you do should not frequent a bar," Khalid said. "Hijab and alcohol don't mix."

"It's a lounge, not a bar, and I could say the same of you. What were you even doing at Bella's? Designated driver?"

"I was attempting to socialize with my work colleagues. However, the experience was not pleasant. I will not be returning."

"Bella's will be lost without you," Ayesha snapped.

"I suggest you do likewise. You don't want

to attract the wrong type of attention," Khalid said, thinking of Mo and his comments.

Ayesha was furious now. "Maybe that's the whole point, Khalid. Maybe I like to stick out. You should know all about that — you're the one walking around in bedsheets."

Khalid's head was lowered, but she could see his lips twitch. Was he laughing at her?

"You are free to do as you please," Khalid said after a beat. "I was simply trying to look out for a fellow Muslim, Hafsa."

Ayesha flushed with embarrassment. She'd been trying to have some harmless fun with her "Hafsa" impersonation but now she found herself arguing with Khalid. Why couldn't she just let him be? It was not as if she cared what he thought of her.

She gathered her bag and notebook and left the room. She had no plans to return to this stupid conference committee with its stupid, judgmental Peeping Tom. Sulaiman Mamu could find another babysitter for the Real Hafsa.

Khalid was about to leave when Tarek stopped him.

"Brother Khalid, right?" Tarek smiled and clapped him on the shoulder. "You look so familiar."

110

"I'm at the mosque a lot," Khalid said. He wanted to follow Hafsa and apologize again for staring at her in the prayer hall. Though he had limited experience with women, Khalid could tell when he had pissed one off. He didn't want her to be angry with him, since they would be working so closely on the conference.

Tarek shook his head. "I don't live in the area, but I feel as if I know you. This is going to bug me." He scrunched his face, thinking hard. "Wait. Do you have a sister?"

Khalid stopped fiddling with his bag. "What?"

"You're Zareena Mirza's brother," Tarek said, smiling broadly. "You look just like her. How is she doing?"

Khalid picked up his bag and Quran. "I'm sorry, I have to go. My mother is waiting for me." He rushed out of the room before Tarek could ask anything else.

CHAPTER TEN

The next day, Nana was on the couch watching a gardening show when Ayesha returned from work. He was holding a sketchbook and drawing carefully. She flopped down beside him.

"Strategizing already?" she asked her grandfather.

"I don't know how Mr. Chen sleeps at night. His win was clearly fraudulent," Nana said, not taking his eyes from the screen.

"His roses looked pretty big to me."

Nana stared at her, indignant. "Size has nothing to do with the quality of the flower. My chrysanthemums were smaller because they were bred that way. Their delicate colors were most attractive. Mr. Chen seduced the gardening board with his tacky pink roses."

Ayesha smothered a laugh. Mr. Chen, who lived two houses away, was Nana's frenemy. The men constantly compared the success of their children and grandchildren, and were bitter rivals in the neighborhood Garden and Beautification Competition. Nana had lost three years running and was determined to win this time.

"What's inside the Victory Garden this year?" she asked.

"My muse and I are still discussing. 'The rose looks fair, but fairer we it deem, for that sweet odor, which doth in it live.' "

"A Winter's Tale?"

" 'Sonnet 54.' I think you need a refresher course in Shakespeare, jaanu."

Her cell phone rang. "Ayesha, come quick! Hafsa said she will not meet him without you," Samira Aunty's panicked voice shouted down the line.

"Meet who?" Ayesha asked.

"Whom," Nana said absently, adding petals to his sketch.

"Please, Ayesha! They will be here any minute and Hafsa is still in her room!" Samira Aunty hung up. Ayesha looked blankly at her grandfather.

"Your Nani is already there. I do not approve of this outmoded mating ritual," said Nana. "Also, *Garden High Life* is on the television. If you wish to offer Hafsa moral support, I suggest you hurry."

Ayesha sighed. She was not sure what was

going on exactly, only that Hafsa was dragging her into this ridiculous rishta quest whether she liked it or not.

She walked slowly to the Taj Mahal, smiling at the grandmothers and little kids she met along the way. When she arrived at her cousin's home, the front door was unlocked and there was a flurry of activity inside. Hafsa's three sisters were wiping down counters and frying samosas in the kitchen, Samira Aunty pinning her hijab in the hallway. She motioned Ayesha upstairs.

Hafsa was sitting on her bed, staring off into space. She jumped up when she caught sight of her cousin and fell into her arms. "Oh Ayesha, you're so lucky you never had any rishta proposals. Waiting is the worst part! What if he's the one? I've only had twenty-two proposals so far. He'll think I'm giving it up too easily."

"You've had seventeen proposals since Friday?" Ayesha asked.

"This is the first one to show up at the door. Mom said they were really insistent. I guess word is starting to spread about my availability." Hafsa applied pink lip gloss and reached for a floral-printed hijab. It had bright-pink roses on it, Ayesha noted.

"From the way Samira Aunty was talking,

I thought there was an emergency," Ayesha said.

"I told her I wouldn't see the guy until you came. I need my Ashi Apa to hold my hand." Hafsa twirled. "How do I look?" She was wearing a white-and-pink shalwar kameez, a long tunic with pants. It was decorated with delicate gold embroidery along the hem and sleeves. Her face was flushed; she looked like a painted porcelain doll.

"Perfect," Ayesha said simply. "You're going to break his heart." Ayesha was still in her work clothes: black straight-cut trousers, a white dress shirt, and an unflattering black cardigan, ready to play the unwanted spinster relation.

When they emerged from Hafsa's bedroom, they heard voices downstairs in the living room. Ayesha and Hafsa tiptoed into the kitchen.

"What's going on?" Ayesha asked her younger cousins.

"Not sure. Mom told us to stay here and get the tray ready," said eleven-year-old Hira.

"Hafsa has to bring in the tea and snacks," Maliha said. "Don't drop it."

"That tray is too heavy for me," Hafsa said. "I'll get chai all over my new shalwar."

"I'll do it," Ayesha said. She picked up the

treat-laden tray, which held brightly patterned bone china cups, a teapot, milk,
sugar, a bowl of spicy Indian *chaat* mix, and
a plate overflowing with samosas.

Hafsa stepped daintily into the living
room. Ayesha followed close behind and
placed the tray on an ornately carved walnut
coffee table before taking a seat beside Nani.

Two women were perched on the gold
brocade couch across from them, both
wearing bright shalwar kameez and hijabs.
The prospective groom was nowhere in
sight. After a beat of silence, one of the
women leaned forward and looked at
Ayesha.

"Did you make the samosas yourself?" she
asked abruptly. The woman was younger
than her companion, in her midforties. The
shawl draped loosely around her neck
revealed a color difference between the
lighter foundation on her face and the rest
of her body. Her clothes were fashionable,
and she wore gold rings on every finger,
including her thumb.

Ayesha was confused. "No, we bought
them from the grocery store."

The other lady, older and severe looking
despite her bright-blue hijab and orange
shalwar kameez, frowned. A massive gold
bangle, two inches in diameter and inlaid

with red stones, dwarfed her small hand. "My son is so fond of homemade samosas. Tell me, what do you cook at home?"

Still confused, Ayesha answered, eyes on the winking, opulent bangle. "I'm not much of a cook. My nani is a gourmet. She spoils us rotten." She smiled at her grandmother. "I'm very busy with work right now."

Severe Aunty frowned even more, cementing the lines on her face. She looked dissatisfied as she gave Ayesha the once-over, taking in her entire outfit from top to bottom.

"Are you a receptionist of some kind?" she asked Ayesha.

"I teach high school."

"I suppose that is an acceptable job for a woman. After marriage, you will quit your job."

Her words dropped like a bomb in the room, and Ayesha couldn't help herself. She laughed. Severe Aunty and Foundation-Mismatch Aunty both stared at her, highly affronted.

Samira Aunty interjected. "I'm afraid you are mistaken, Farzana and Aliyah. This is my eldest daughter," she said, indicating Hafsa. "Ayesha is my niece. She is seven years older than Hafsa," she added.

Both women turned to look at Hafsa and

examined her with more interest. They began their interrogation without giving Ayesha another glance.

"Did you fry these samosas?" Aliyah, aka Foundation-Mismatch Aunty, asked.

"My sisters did. I made the cookies, though," Hafsa answered.

Farzana, aka Severe Aunty, picked up the biscuit — store-bought Chunky Chips Ahoy, Ayesha noted — and took a bite. "My son likes cookies," she said.

The questions came lightning-fast:

Do you pray five times a day?

What did you study in school?

What are your hobbies?

Do you know how to read the Quran? Can you recite Surah Yaseen by heart?

Hafsa answered as best she could, stammering and blushing prettily. Samira Aunty and Nani were shocked into silence by the interrogation, until finally Ayesha interrupted. She could stand their rudeness no more.

"Where is your mysterious son?" she asked.

Both aunties shifted uncomfortably. "He is very shy. We are here to arrange matters for him," Farzana said. "If things go well, I will show him a picture of Hafsa and let him decide."

"I think the girl in question might have some say in the matter," Ayesha said evenly. "Hafsa, do you have any questions you would like to ask? Maybe the boy's name?"

Hafsa blushed. She clearly did not appreciate Ayesha's question, or her lack of rishta game.

"How about his age, his job, his hobbies, whether he prays and if he can recite Surah Yaseen by heart?" Ayesha asked sweetly.

Samira Aunty cut in. "How long have you lived in the neighborhood, Farzana?" she asked.

"A few months only. Your husband does well, I see," Farzana said, looking at the ornate furnishings. "How much money does he make every year?"

Ayesha looked sidelong at her Nani, who was sitting ramrod-straight and observing the conversation impassively. Nani squeezed her hand, trying to compel Ayesha to hold her fire before it became a bloodbath.

"How much money does your mysterious son make?" Ayesha asked, undeterred.

Farzana looked at her dismissively. "It is so difficult to find a truly well-trained girl these days. So many modern ideas about education and careers. When I was growing up, a girl knew her role."

"So true, Farzana," Aliyah said. "A girl

should know how to cook at least three different types of rice, twelve or more meat dishes, and at least as many vegetable curries. When I was married, I had sixty-five recipes memorized," she added.

Farzana nodded. "Finally, she should show a deference and modesty of character. She must not speak when her elders are talking. She must be quiet and refined, never gossip or joke. I find a girl who laughs in public has been raised in a very inferior household. She must never talk back to her mother-in-law, and should spend her days sewing, cooking, and reading the Quran."

Ayesha smothered her laughter. "I never met such a woman," she said. "Such a young person does not exist outside Pakistani dramas. Besides, any man who would be happy with such a dud is probably not worth marrying."

The two aunties stood up. "Thank you for the visit," Aliyah said. They hugged Nani and Samira Aunty, smiled at Hafsa, and turned their backs on Ayesha.

Ayesha was clearing the dishes when Samira Aunty returned from walking Farzana and Aliyah to the door. "Jaanu, if it's all the same to you, next time you should probably just stay at home."

■ ■ ■ ■

Ayesha left without saying good-bye to her cousins, anger increasing her pace to a walking run. Nana was right; she wanted no part in this outmoded dating ritual! She was halfway to the townhouse when Hafsa caught up to her.

"You walk fast," her cousin said, panting.

Ayesha slowed down. "I don't know how you could just sit there. Those ladies were awful."

"I've read worse on the rishta forums."

"What are you talking about?"

"The subreddit, Ashi Apa. Compared to what some girls post, those aunties were baby dragons. Though it was a little weird they didn't bring their son. Maybe he's really hideous. Or maybe he's really famous!" Her eyes lit up. "What if he's a Bollywood movie star?"

"Is this how you want to get married?" Ayesha faced her cousin.

Hafsa shrugged. "It's actually kind of fun to meet the rishta and his parents. Think about it — all these guys drive to my house to take a look at me. I feel like a princess being courted by suitors. It's like I'm on *The Bachelorette.*"

"Well, I'm glad you see it like that."

Hafsa bit her bottom lip. "Listen, the reason I chased after you is because I need to ask a really huge favor. Imam Abdul Bari told Dad I came to the conference planning meeting yesterday. Dad was so happy he promised to give me money for my event planning business. Could you not mention the mix-up? I'll be at the next meeting, and I'll explain everything to the imam myself."

Ayesha gave her cousin a shrewd look. "Where were you?"

Hafsa waved her hand airily. "Getting my eyebrows threaded. You're the best!" She gave her a big hug.

Ayesha walked home in a more thoughtful mood. She wasn't sure where Hafsa had been last night, but she did know one thing: Her cousin's eyebrows hadn't been threaded in weeks.

Then again, if it meant skipping all future conference planning meetings guilt-free, she would keep her mouth shut.

Ayesha was too annoyed to go home. Instead she drove to the condo Clara shared with Rob. She smiled at Malik, the security guard sitting at the condo reception desk. She came over so often, he just waved her through.

Rob opened the door, dressed in running shorts. "Clara's on the can." He motioned her inside. Their home was still full of Ikea furniture from university days, though they were both working "real" jobs now. "Clara!" he yelled. "I'll be back in an hour." He winked at her. "She's in a mood. I'm heading down to the weight room."

Ayesha settled into the gray couch and put her feet on the frayed leather bench.

"What are you doing here?" Clara was wearing a bathrobe, her hair wet.

"I'm thinking of divorcing my family," Ayesha said. "What are you up to?"

Clara laughed. "What happened this time?"

"Hafsa got a rishta proposal. She needed me there to hold her hand."

"She probably wanted you there so she could show off."

"The aunties thought I was the bride until Samira Aunty pointed them in the right direction. You should have seen the way they jumped on Hafsa. They were practically drooling."

"You hate the bride-viewing thing," Clara said. "I remember when you had a few rishtas in university, you didn't even want to meet the guys."

Ayesha absently etched circles on the

couch with her finger. She wasn't upset at the aunties' cursory glances or their quick dismissal. Not entirely. "I know I said I don't want to get married. It's just . . . I don't know how this is going to happen for me. You met the guy you wanted to be with forever when you were eighteen. I'm twenty-seven and I've never even been on a date or held a guy's hand."

"Well, there was Kevin in high school. He asked you to prom three times." Clara started to laugh. "And don't forget Mo from Bella's. He's cute."

"I don't want to date the guys I meet at Bella's. It's too much work to explain all of this," Ayesha said, indicating her hijab. "They wouldn't get it, and even if they did, that's not what I want."

"What about Khalid?" Clara asked, her voice casual.

Ayesha stared at her friend. "The guy from Bella's? Forget it. He's the kind of guy who scares people in shopping malls and gets randomly searched at airports. Khalid is a fundamentalist — he'll stick out wherever he goes. I don't want any of that."

Clara looked at her blankly. "He's not a fundamentalist," she said. "You're being judgmental."

"I know his type," Ayesha said darkly,

124

thinking about the prayer hall. "The whole rishta proposal was so frustrating, and everyone just sat there like it was normal. Hafsa said she enjoyed the attention. What's wrong with her? Or is there something wrong with me?"

"What did Nana say?" Clara had a soft spot for Ayesha's grandfather. Her own grandparents lived in Florida and rarely visited.

"He called it an 'outmoded mating ritual' and stayed home to watch the gardening channel."

Clara laughed again and settled next to Ayesha. "Your family is better than any soap opera. I just don't get why you have to play the martyr."

"Shut up, Clara. Haven't gone furniture shopping yet, I see. I think that bench is going to split down the middle soon."

"Shut up, Ashi Apa."

"Rob said you were in a mood."

Clara sighed. "It's nothing. It's the same thing. I don't want to talk about it." Clara and Rob had lived together for the past three years. She had been dropping hints about a wedding, but so far he remained clueless, or was choosing to ignore her.

"You know, Prophet Muhammad's wife Khadijah proposed to him," Ayesha said.

"Among us atheists, it's still the man's job to drop to his knees."

Ayesha's hands were clasped in her lap. "Maybe he's happy with the way things are. Maybe he doesn't want to rock the boat because he's afraid that something new will ruin all the good momentum."

Clara leaned close to Ayesha. "Sometimes the only way to move forward is to rock the boat. Otherwise you risk losing everything. That's why you went to teachers' college, right?" Ayesha had worked for three years at an insurance company before returning to school.

"I guess," Ayesha said. "Teaching is a good, stable job. I'm sure I'll get used to it."

"You should write copy for the teachers' union," Clara said. " 'Be a teacher — it's a boring job, but you'll eventually learn to like it,' " she mocked.

Ayesha sighed. "You want me to be an artist and travel, my family wants me to be a teacher and settle down. Do you ever wonder what I want?"

"You don't know what you want. That's why you should listen to me." Clara picked her laptop up from the coffee table and pulled it close. "Okay, let's strategize. You need to stop this substitute teaching thing and get hired permanently."

"I didn't come here to talk about my job! What about my crazy family?"

Clara ignored her, opening a new document on her laptop and saving it with the file name "Save Ayesha from Herself." "I think you need to coach a sports team. Or maybe put together a fund-raiser. Also, kiss the principal's butt. Bake him some cookies. Trust me, benign bribery always helps. I'm the regional manager of HR for a very important company. I know these things."

Ayesha smiled. "So now you think I should be a teacher."

"I think you should always have a plan. While you're working, you can spend evenings and weekends writing poetry until you make it big. One of Rob's friends helps organize that arts festival in August. You should audition. You were really great at Bella's." Clara stopped typing. "I'm sorry about Khalid. He's a good guy, just a bit awkward around women."

"He's a freak."

"You sound like my new boss, Sheila. I know Khalid is a good person. If he trimmed his beard and got some new clothes, he might even be a hottie."

Ayesha laughed out loud at the thought of Khalid in tight jeans and a mesh tank, with his hair slicked back and a hipster beard. "He would look even more ridiculous than he does now. I don't think he cares what people think."

Clara's typing slowed and she looked sidelong at her friend. "That can be quite sexy in a man," she said.

"Khalid has no interest in me, and the feeling is mutual."

"You deserve to be happy, Ayesha."

"What I really want is to be happy and free. I don't think I'm going to be either of those things."

Nana was still in the living room when Ayesha returned a few hours later. He was watching TV with Idris and ignoring the clatter from the kitchen. Nani was upset about Hafsa's rishta visit, and she was taking it out on her pots and pans.

Ayesha approached her grandmother carefully. "Nani, I'm sorry I was rude, but they started it. And I meant what I said. You're the best cook in the whole neighborhood. So what if I can't boil water? I'm never moving out anyway."

"You made me look bad in front of those horrible women," Nani said in Urdu. "They're going to think we didn't do a good job raising you. I'm going to teach you how to cook, right now. Grab some onions and garlic-ginger paste."

Ayesha looked alarmed. From the living room came Nana's voice. "Beti, you promised to take me to Tim Hortons."

"But Nana, you just had tea," Idris said, his lips twitching. Unlike his older sister, he got a kick out of causing trouble.

"I wish to purchase an apple fritter," Nana said with dignity. "I shall be waiting in the automobile."

"You can teach me to cook when I come back. Or maybe tomorrow," Ayesha said. She kissed her grandmother on the cheek and hurried outside.

Nana didn't say a word until they got into the car and were driving toward the main street. "Your time will come," he said.

"What are you talking about?" Ayesha turned into the Tim Hortons' drive-thru.

Nana's expression was serious. "Sometimes I worry you have been scared off by Saleha and Syed."

Ayesha's grip on the steering wheel tightened. Nana never talked about her mother and father. But she was not in the mood to hear about failed relationships or might-have-beens.

"Welcome to Tim Hortons, can I take your order?"

Ayesha turned to the drive-thru window and spoke quickly. "Two steeped teas double-double, and one apple fritter please."

"Beti —" Nana started again.

"I'm fine. Really. My life is unfolding exactly as planned. I'm happy, I promise."

CHAPTER ELEVEN

Khalid was even more silent than usual at breakfast the next morning, but Farzana didn't notice. She placed two overcooked paratha flatbreads on his plate and busied herself with the dishes, talking the whole time.

"The mosque executive board is meeting this morning and I plan to be there. I will get rid of this silly youth conference idea once and for all. Imagine, Khalid — boys and girls mixing at the mosque. They should all stay home and listen to their parents. If they just stopped being so *besharam* and texting each other all the time, they wouldn't have all these mental health issues or wear leggings. It's disgraceful." His mother had recently joined the mosque's governing council. On the one hand, Khalid was happy that Farzana had something to occupy her time. On the other hand, he worried she would get caught up in petty political in-fighting.

Khalid silently mopped up his spicy tomato and egg curry with the second paratha and washed it all down with the watery chai his mother had made.

He hadn't slept well last night, and he'd almost missed getting up for Fajr prayer. His head was pounding, so he got up to go in search of pain medication.

"Khalid, where are you going?" Farzana asked him. "You haven't eaten the *kheer* I made."

His stomach flipped over at the thought of spooning down too-sweet gelatinous rice pudding. "I should leave now if I want to catch the bus."

"Imam Abdul Bari thinks the conference is a good idea, and the treasurer, Sister Jo, agrees. I have to get President Aziz on my side. That shouldn't be a problem. He's easy to persuade."

"Ammi, the imam knows what he's doing. The conference will be good for the community, and the mosque can use the money. Please don't try to take over everything."

Farzana narrowed her eyes and looked at her son with suspicion. "The mosque doesn't need money. Everybody knows the Shamsi family makes a big donation every year to cover all the expenses. Did you know there are four daughters? The eldest is Hafsa. She is very beautiful and modest."

Khalid froze. His mother must have heard about the conference meeting from one of her friends, maybe Aliyah. "I have to go," he said, and he made his way to the foyer.

Farzana followed him to the front door. "The family is quite prominent and wealthy too," she said. "They have almost as much money and property as we do. Make sure you say salam next time you see them."

"Yes, Ammi," Khalid said. He hated it when his mother talked about the family fortune; he was very aware that the money belonged to his mother, inherited when her own father had died and left a vast estate in India for his children. Khalid didn't really think about money very often, so long as he had enough to send to his sister and pay his few expenses.

Farzana beamed at her only son. "You're such a good boy. I've never had any problems with you."

When Khalid arrived at work, Sheila was waiting at his desk. "You're late," she snapped. "I asked you to be here at seven thirty for a very important meeting. Don't you check your e-mail? Or do you think you can ignore me?"

Khalid looked at her blankly. He had checked his work e-mail that morning after he'd prayed Fajr, at five thirty. He must have missed her message.

Sheila sighed loudly. "Well, thanks to your lack of response, we had to move the meeting to eight thirty. Don't be late again." She stalked out, her stiletto heels stabbing the tile floor.

Khalid scrolled through his inbox. "She never sent me an e-mail," he said out loud.

Amir rose like a costumed Egyptian mummy from the sofa, enveloped in a blue blanket. "K-Man, she's snapping you."

"What?"

"She's snapping pics of you to paint a picture. You know, like the politicians do. Take a photo of a guy shaking hands with the wrong person, and then run it in every attack campaign."

"What do I do?"

Amir shrugged. "Make powerful allies. Boast about your success. Buy some dress shirts. Throw someone else under the bus."

Khalid sat down at his desk. "They promoted me to manager. The last director said I was the most diligent and hardworking employee he had ever hired."

"None of that matters if the Shark is out for blood."

Khalid walked to the meeting in the conference room like a condemned man. The room was filled with middle-aged women in colorful pantsuits. They turned to face him when he entered.

"How nice of you to join us, Khalid," Sheila said in a nasty tone. "Better late than never."

Khalid checked his phone. It was 8:25 exactly.

"I'd like to introduce you to your new client, WomenFirst Design. You've read my e-mails and the report I attached, so you're familiar with their portfolio."

He looked around, bewildered. "Sheila, what e-mail? I manage e-commerce. I'm not the right person for client-facing meetings."

"Don't be so modest." Sheila smiled at him. "Your résumé clearly states that you are proficient in numerous programming languages, including Java, Python, and Urdu."

"That last one is actually not a coding lang—" he began, but Sheila interrupted.

"At Livetech, everyone must be comfortable wearing different hats and working in flexible roles. I'll leave you to it." She walked out of the room, smiling grimly.

The suited ladies turned to look at him.

"Oh, honey," a heavyset white woman

with blond hair and red glasses said. "Now you're in for it."

The ladies laughed, and Khalid considered running after Sheila. "I assure you, I have done nothing wrong."

That set them off again, into more gales of laughter. After they calmed down, the blonde introduced herself. "I'm Lorraine. This is Vanessa." She nodded at a black woman who was smiling at him. "You don't know who we are, do you?"

"Umm," Khalid stammered.

"I never liked that woman," Lorraine said to Vanessa. "Never trust a skinny woman in stilettos." She turned back to Khalid. "Honey, we're your clients, WomenFirst Design. We design and sell lingerie for plus-size women, and you've just been put in charge of setting up our entire online sales structure."

Clara reminded herself to breathe when she knocked on Sheila's office door at nine that morning. Her boss had called her upstairs for an update on the "Khalid situation." Clara rehearsed what she wanted to say in her head again.

Sheila, I think you would benefit from some sensitivity and diversity training. Have you considered visiting a mosque or maybe talk-

ing to other Muslims? Clara frowned. She doubted Sheila would take kindly to that suggestion, especially since she had lived in Saudi Arabia, a majority-Muslim country, for a few months. Though it sounded as if she had lived in some sort of sheltered compound full of expats.

Maybe she should tell Sheila that Khalid went to a bar last weekend. That might help. She knocked and opened the door, pasting a friendly smile on her face as she approached Sheila's massive shiny desk.

"Good morning!" she singsonged. Sheila looked up from her monitor, frowning.

Dial it back, Clara told herself. *Sheila needs to see you as an ally, not a scolding teacher.* Working in HR meant constantly navigating a tightrope of competing interests. Her clients were management as well as employees, which often led to uncomfortable conversations. Ultimately, she knew that her role was advisory at best; her boss didn't have to listen to her.

"That's a lovely pin," Clara said, indicating a bright-red jeweled scorpion pinned to Sheila's shoulder, matching her red-and-white dress.

Sheila gave her a thin-lipped smile. "I have a collection of them. Snakes, spiders, scorpions, sharks. I like to give people fair warning."

Clara laughed uneasily, but Sheila's face remained impassive.

"You wanted to see me?" Clara said.

"I wanted to give you an update on our little problem. Khalid showed up late for a meeting this morning. They're not terribly important clients, but he showed a lack of professionalism and was completely unprepared. Is that enough of a reason to fire him?"

Clara sighed and opened her laptop. "Who were the clients?" she asked, taking notes in the document she had created.

"WomenFirst Design. They make lingerie for . . . larger women." Sheila stopped and bit her bottom lip, smiling. "I guess everyone can dream, right?"

"I'm sorry?" Clara hoped she had misheard.

Sheila's smile was wide-mouthed, teeth tiny points of white behind red lipstick. "Can you imagine? Saggy flesh encased in lace." She shuddered delicately. "They wouldn't leave me alone. They want a new website and they kept calling and calling, even when I told my assistant to get rid of them. So I've set them up with Khalid. I'll be killing two birds with one stone."

Clara's typing slowed. "I'm sorry?" she said again.

Sheila looked up, eyes sharp. "This is business, Clara. There is no room for squeamishness. Livetech is ready to take the global stage. We need to be associated with young, edgy, popular clients. Not someone like the Large Ladies Lingerie company." Her laughter rang out, and all the color drained from Clara's face.

Sheila didn't need sensitivity training. She needed to be muzzled.

"That's not very . . . You shouldn't be speaking about women like . . . Khalid isn't . . ." Clara floundered for something to say.

Sheila's laughter cut off abruptly and she leaned forward. "I'm giving him a chance to prove himself," she said to Clara. "They're a small company, barely worth our time. If he can't handle them, he can't handle anything."

"But Khalid is the e-commerce manager. He doesn't design websites."

Sheila shrugged. "He can quit if he doesn't like it. He can go back to the Middle East where he belongs."

"He's Canadian, Sheila. He belongs here."

There was a knock at the door, and Dev Kanduwallah, the CEO of Livetech, walked into the office. Sheila immediately stood up and strode over to give her boss a friendly hug.

"Dev!" she cooed. "What are you doing here? I thought you were still in Seattle."

Clara joined them, curious to meet him. Dev was originally from Bangalore, the tech capital of India. He was a tall man in his late fifties, well groomed in an expensive gray suit and Italian loafers, his skin a warm russet. His intelligent brown eyes missed nothing, and he nodded politely at Clara. "I was in town and thought I would drop by and see how you were settling in. I hear you had an important client meeting scheduled for this morning."

Sheila looked puzzled. "All of our clients are important."

Dev laughed, his voice a rich tenor. "You always know what to say. But then, some are a bit more important than others," he said, tapping the side of his nose. "Women-First Design, for instance. I'm sure you are aware they cleared twelve million dollars last year in revenue. The plus-size lingerie market is ripe for the taking, and with their new online business, they'll probably make over twenty million this year. Congratulations on setting up the meeting."

Sheila had an excellent poker face, Clara

had to admit. Her body froze only for a moment before she laughed merrily alongside Dev. "You know me! Always on the lookout for emerging markets. Don't worry about a thing. I've got my very best resource on it."

Dev squeezed Sheila's shoulder, hand brushing the jeweled scorpion. "I expect nothing but the best from you. Keep me updated on this one. It might open up a whole new design platform for us." He smiled again at Clara and left.

Clara's hands gripped her laptop. "I should get back to my office," she said, edging toward the door.

Sheila's eyes narrowed. "Not a word of this to anyone," she hissed. "Unless you want your life to become very uncomfortable."

Clara nodded quickly and closed the door behind her with a gentle *click*.

Khalid had never blushed so much in his life. He felt grateful for his long beard — at least it covered up part of his face.

"I'm really not the right person for this," he kept saying to the ladies — clients — from WomenFirst Design. "I manage e-business contracts and take care of the server and virtual machines. I need to talk to Sheila. She's doing you a disservice by

141

assigning me to your project."

But the women insisted on showing him pictures of scantily clad plus-size models in teddies, bikinis, and edible thongs, as they continued to talk about "accessibility openings" and their large array of fasteners.

"Please," he said firmly. "I need to speak to Sheila."

Vanessa stopped him at the door with a question.

"Khalid, is there really any point?" Brown eyes blinked at him behind large electric-blue frames. "She's setting you up, honey. I don't know why, but she doesn't like you. Sometimes that's just the way it is. Maybe she doesn't like the way you look, or dress, or that fluff on your face. We know how that goes, don't we, girls?" The women around the table nodded in understanding. "Same thing happened to us when we worked at a lingerie company we'd rather not name." She winked at him and he stared back, confused. Khalid couldn't name a lingerie company if he tried. Whenever he went to the mall, he always averted his gaze from the flashing neon bosoms in the window display.

"They didn't like it when we told them you can't make lingerie for a larger woman by adding more fabric. You've got to design with her in mind," Lorraine said. "So when they showed us the door, Vanessa and I, we started from scratch. Livetech is the seventh company we've approached for our online business." She looked around the table. "What do you say, ladies? We're a democracy," she said to Khalid. "We all have to agree on the big business decisions."

There was a murmur of voices as eight women huddled at one end of the board table. A few of them glanced at him, scrutinizing his face, lingering on his white robe and beard.

Finally, the huddle broke and Vanessa said, "We like the look of you. I think we'll try you on."

Khalid was surprised. "You don't know anything about me. I haven't designed a website since high school, and I don't know anything about women's lingerie."

"We like that you're honest. It's endearing in a man," Vanessa said. "Livetech has a great reputation. We'll get the contract started with HR. And honey, men never notice lingerie. It usually doesn't stay on long enough."

Khalid blushed an even deeper red. "I'll have to take your word on that. I'm not married."

Lorraine and Vanessa started laughing.

"You are too much!" Lorraine said, wiping her eyes. "What does your girlfriend say about all this?"

Khalid shifted uncomfortably. "My mother will find a wife for me. In the meantime, I have many interests to keep me busy."

Vanessa smiled slyly. "Are you telling me that a good-looking man like you doesn't have someone in mind?"

Copper skin and sharp brown eyes flashed in Khalid's mind. "No," he said. "That's not the way this works for me."

"Oh, honey, nobody knows how this thing works. It just happens. Your heart and gut take over, and your mind has to go along with them, because it's going to happen no matter what. Sometimes you get a sign, and sometimes the sign gets you."

Khalid mulled this over while Lorraine and Vanessa discussed inventory and design.

Sheila strolled into the conference room. "Everything all right here, ladies?"

Vanessa's face grew cold. "Khalid is such a godsend, Ms. Watts," she said. "We'll be sure to tell Dev how happy we are with his willingness to help us out with our little company. There's really no reason for you to check up on us. We'll deal with Khalid exclusively from now on." The meeting quickly wrapped up and the ladies filed out with promises to be in touch.

Sheila glared at Khalid once the room had emptied. "They seemed happy."

Khalid gathered his laptop and notepad. "I think we understand each other."

"I hope so, Khalid," Sheila said. She circled around to the other side of the conference table. "WomenFirst Design cleared twelve million dollars in profit last year. In fact, they're so important I'm taking you off e-commerce to work exclusively with them. I hope that's not a problem?"

Khalid thought about the existing projects waiting for him, the server upgrade and virtual machine testing he had planned for this week. Sheila expected him to drop everything and design the website for a product he didn't even understand. His stomach clenched with disappointment and frustration, but he kept his face expressionless.

"No problem at all," he said. "I look forward to the challenge."

It was probably the extra-large helping of chicken curry so late at night, but Khalid had trouble sleeping again. His biryani burps kept him staring at the ceiling for hours. When he did drift off, he dreamed of his father. He got out of bed at five, showered, and drove to the mosque.

Khalid used to attend Fajr almost every day with his father, back in their old neighborhood. Ever since his dad had died, he hadn't been so diligent about attending the pre-dawn prayer at the mosque and usually prayed at home.

There were only a dozen people in the congregation that morning. He nodded and smiled at a few familiar faces before sitting down cross-legged at the front of the prayer hall, thinking more about his father, Faheem Mirza.

Faheem had been a gentle, quiet man. He'd worked for the government as an accountant, auditing large companies. He was one of the first openly religious Muslim men in his department in the early 1980s, and Khalid knew that his coworkers had not been kind about his teetotalling and diligence for afternoon prayer. Faheem had missed opportunities to advance while his coworkers ingratiated themselves with superiors over drinks after work.

After Zareena's scandal had been fully revealed, Faheem retreated from the family, staying later at work and allowing his wife to deal with the situation. When Zareena had left home nearly twelve years ago, Faheem had said nothing at the airport. Khalid thought it was because of the shame he felt, but in the weeks that followed, he had often caught his father weeping silently. He never talked about his daughter, and as the years passed, he spoke less and less to anyone else. Khalid remembered him at the outskirts of conversations, listening with a faint smile on his face. But his curtain of sadness never fully lifted.

A massive heart attack had killed Faheem instantly last fall. The janazah funeral prayer was attended by nearly five hundred people at their old mosque. For a quiet man, he had many friends.

Zareena had not been among the mourners. Khalid had broken the news to her himself, violating their e-mail-and-text-only arrangement to call long distance. He couldn't stand the thought of his only sister finding out about their father's death through some gossipy neighbor. She was quiet on the phone and hung up quickly.

Six months later, Khalid still missed his father deeply. His mother made him feel like a young child, but Faheem had never been like that. A man of few words, he'd listened to Khalid and only given advice when asked.

Though in this instance, Khalid wasn't sure what advice he wanted. *What do you do when you can't get a woman's face out of your mind?* He would be too embarrassed to ask his father such a personal question. And there was only one answer: You do nothing.

Khalid reached for his cell phone and quickly composed an e-mail to his sister.

Salams, Z,

It's early morning and I was thinking about Abba. Remember when he took us fishing, except he forgot to buy the bait, or ask for instructions? Thank God that nice family took pity on us and shared their worms.

By the way, I wired you the money, as requested. I'm glad to hear you are volunteering at a school.

As for me, I'm busy with the usual — work and mosque events. The imam wants to host a youth conference over the July long weekend, which doesn't leave us a lot of time. Another woman is working with me to get things organized. I think you'd like her. She's a poet and I made her angry when we spoke. I'm still not sure why.

I miss you.

K

He pressed Send and lined up as the prayer began.

When Khalid arrived home at six, his mother was still sleeping. He removed some sourdough bread from the fridge and beat three eggs with cream and cinnamon. One at a time, he dunked four slices of bread into the batter and fried the French toast, spreading each slice with a peanut butter and Nutella mixture. His phone pinged with an incoming e-mail just as he was sitting down with breakfast and a large mug of chai.

Salams!
Got the loot, thanks so much. I hate to do this, but I need a bit extra, if you can manage. I have some more gifts and stuff to distribute. I promise to pay you back. In fact, I'm going to start paying you back right now, with some advice: Go for it!

In all the long, tedious years you've been writing to me, you have NEVER, not ONCE, talked about a girl. I was starting to wonder what team you played for, not that I'm judging.

I mean, it's not as if you're the easiest guy to talk to, not if you still wear those white dresses and refuse to trim your

149

beard. (Seriously, it's like you WANT to be racially profiled.) Btw, she's probably mad at something stupid you said.

Take my advice. Keep talking, try to smile (you know how to do that, right?). You're not completely repulsive when you smile.

And keep me posted! This is better than a Pakistani drama!

— Z

P. S. Hollywood scandals and those sprinkle donuts from Tim Hortons.

Khalid nearly spit out his chai as he read, and then he looked around to make sure his mother was not there. He quickly typed a response.

Z,

I'll wire the money tonight.

There is nothing going on with me and the woman from the mosque. This is not the way things are arranged. Ammi will find me a suitable wife. Love blossoms after marriage.

— K

His sister's e-mail had one good effect — if she thought he should pursue Hafsa, then he needed to do the exact opposite.

CHAPTER TWELVE

Ashi Apa, something super important just came up and I can't go to the conference meeting. Can you pretend to be me for one more night? xox

Hafsa sent the text fifteen minutes before the meeting. Just enough time for Ayesha to either leave for the mosque or call her cousin demanding to know what was going on. Mindful of the promise she had made her uncle, Ayesha grabbed her car keys and vowed to get to the bottom of Hafsa's well-timed disappearance later.

When she entered the conference room, Tarek smiled lazily at her, looking gorgeous in a fitted blue shirt that showed off his broad chest. Khalid didn't raise his eyes from the table, and Imam Abdul Bari beamed as she settled into her usual spot by the door.

"Sister Hafsa, we need your expertise for

the conference program," the imam said, pointing at a board filled with agenda items.

Ayesha felt irritated and grumpy as she looked at the whiteboard, silently fuming at Hafsa for putting her in this situation again. She scowled at the lineup of events and speakers. "I thought this conference was supposed to engage young people. The agenda is full of boring lectures."

"Our attendees expect inspiring speeches and big-name speakers, like Sheikh Rafeek. We're giving them what they want," Tarek said.

Ayesha frowned. "You mean you're giving them what they're used to."

Khalid looked up from his examination of the table.

"I also see a big problem with the diversity of your speakers," she continued.

Tarek was confused. "This is a Muslim conference. The speakers will also be Muslim."

Ayesha shook her head. "They're all men. Where are the women? Why does fifty percent of your demographic have no representation in your speaker lineup?"

"It's a question of availability and quality. The more well-known speakers are men," Tarek explained with a smile. Ayesha looked askance. His Prince Charming good looks seemed less overwhelming today.

"You said this conference was meant to engage young people. This is the perfect opportunity to try something crazy, like maybe inviting the same number of male and female speakers. You should stand behind your name, Muslims in Action. That means you actually have to act."

"There simply aren't any women —" Tarek continued, the smile on his face slipping.

"Sister Hafsa is a poet," Khalid interrupted.

"I don't mean *me,*" Ayesha said.

"I've seen you perform." Khalid held Ayesha's gaze. "You would electrify any audience."

"An excellent idea!" Imam Abdul Bari said, smiling broadly. "Homegrown talent will be a wonderful addition to our conference. Sister Hafsa is right. We should make gender equity among speakers a priority."

Khalid went back to his contemplation of the table. Ayesha turned over his words in her mind. *Electrify?*

"Any other suggestions, Sister Hafsa?" the imam asked.

"You need more of an online presence. I tried googling our conference the other day, and I found no mention of it on your

153

website, not even the date."

A look of alarm crossed Tarek's face. "Our website is under construction," he said.

"You said this conference was being put together quickly. How can you get the word out if you don't post promo videos on YouTube and information about it on social media? If you want to target youth, you have to spread the message where they live. How did you attract people to your last conference?"

Tarek shrugged and smiled at her. "Word of mouth. News spreads so quickly in our community. Even faster than the internet."

Ayesha was not moved by his charm. "If you want to attract more than a thousand participants, you need a media campaign. It's already late to really get the word out in a big way. You need to announce details online immediately."

Imam Abdul Bari muttered, "Excellent, excellent," as he wrote down her suggestions on the whiteboard. He looked up. "Sister Hafsa, since you have a way with words, can you put together something for the bird and the book to say?"

Ayesha was confused.

"He means Twitter and Facebook," Khalid said with a sidelong glance.

"And Brother Khalid, you work with

computers. Can I ask you and Sister Hafsa to set up things on the worldly computer system?" Abdul Bari asked.

Khalid looked blank.

"I think he means a website," Ayesha said.

The imam beamed at them. "You are both so talented. May Allah reward you. Brother Tarek, I have some ideas for female speakers. Would you come with me to my office?" He stood up and motioned for Tarek to follow him outside.

"You don't look like someone who listens to poetry," Ayesha said to Khalid when the other men had left.

"I enjoy a well-written turn of phrase. There are many methods of self-expression, Hafsa," Khalid said carefully. "Or do you prefer to go by Grand Master Shamsi?"

Ayesha flushed. "Why does my name matter? You're so quick to put a label on my identity. Does an outspoken woman offend you that much?"

"Clearly you have never met my mother," Khalid said. "I can understand why you use a stage name. It is easier to say some things from behind a mask."

Ayesha frowned. Was Khalid trying to be funny again? His eyes were lowered so she couldn't tell. Regardless, he was hitting too close to home. He hadn't wanted to be introduced to her when he thought she was a boozy Bella's patron. It was none of his business if she wanted to pretend to be someone else at the mosque too.

Besides, a man who grew a beard that thick knew a thing or two about hiding.

"The last line of your poem was very powerful," Khalid said. " 'What do I see when I look at you? I see another human being who doesn't have a clue.' People are so quick to judge others based on appearance and first impressions."

That sealed it. Khalid did not deserve to know her real name. He just wanted to put her in a box he could label; she wasn't in the mood to be so easily defined.

"You mean the way *you* did, at the bar when you first saw me," Ayesha said. She smiled thinly at him. "And you can call me Hafsa."

"As *you* did in the mosque when you first recognized me, Hafsa," Khalid said. "And I believe Bella's is a lounge, not a bar."

Definitely trying to be funny. Ayesha's lips twitched despite her best effort. She wanted to continue feeling angry but found it difficult to maintain her irritation. Khalid was surprisingly easy to talk to.

"So you admit you misjudged me. Yet you think others misjudge you. That makes you

156

a hypocrite," Ayesha said.

Khalid shrugged. "My hypocrisy or lack thereof is for Allah to judge. Nobody is perfect. Everyone has a tendency to some particular evil that not even the most fervent prayers and education can overcome."

"Your defect is a tendency to judge everyone," Ayesha said.

"And yours," he said with a smile, "is to willfully misunderstand them."

Khalid's smile transformed his face, like a cold room warmed by a portable heater. She felt it warm her, and her heart began to beat faster. *Oh no,* she thought. *Not him. Anyone but him.*

Khalid continued. "While I don't think women should perform onstage, if you were dressed modestly in a long robe, it would be all right. Or you could stand behind a screen, as they do in blind music auditions."

Ayesha's momentary flare of attraction vanished. "Stand behind a screen? Wear a long robe? Are you serious?"

Khalid was mystified. "I'm simply suggesting a few ideas."

Ayesha sat back in her chair, contemplating the bearded man before her. She knew she should take him to task for his ridiculous ideas, but he looked so confused, she couldn't help but smile.

"What is so funny?" Khalid asked.

"You are, and you don't even know it."

Khalid patted his head and shoulders. He wiped his mouth. "Is there something on my face?" he asked, bewildered.

Ayesha laughed out loud, a throaty chuckle. He blushed a deep red and dropped his eyes to the ground.

"You have no idea what you look like, do you?" Ayesha asked. She was still smiling at him, and he shifted uncomfortably.

"There is a mirror in my bathroom I use on occasion," he said.

Ayesha laughed again, and Khalid's face changed.

"I'll be right back," he said abruptly, and he walked out of the room.

Which was just as well, Ayesha thought. They had no real business speaking to each other; after all, she wasn't supposed to be here. In fact, she wasn't really here at all — Hafsa was.

In the bathroom, Khalid splashed cold water on his face and quickly made *wudu,* a ritual purification that involved washing hands, face, arms up to elbows, ears, and feet. The familiar rhythm calmed Khalid's mind and cooled his cheeks.

Women didn't usually laugh at him. Amir

made fun of him, and Zareena used to tease him, but he had never experienced this before. Hafsa's laugh had slid over his ears like caramel.

Was he funny? Khalid looked in the mirror, smoothing down his hair, which fell below his ears. Maybe he was funny looking.

Hafsa's poem came back to him again. *What do you see when you look at me?* He saw her onstage again: eyes that missed nothing and looked at him with irritation and humor, full of life. When he looked at her, he was not sure what he saw.

But he was starting to feel something.

Oh no, he thought. *Not her. Not like this.*

When Khalid returned to the seminar room, it was empty.

He wandered around the mosque looking for Hafsa, but she had disappeared. He found the imam and Tarek inside the prayer hall, deep in conversation.

"The May long weekend is not possible," Imam Abdul Bari said. He looked distressed.

"If the Toronto Muslim Assembly wants to host the conference, you don't have a choice," Tarek said.

The imam's hands were clasped in front

of him, and the furrow in his brow deepened.

Khalid stepped forward. "Is there a problem, Imam? I thought the conference was scheduled for the July long weekend."

Tarek smiled brightly, showing off white teeth. "Unfortunately my team has a conflict. We just signed a contract with another, larger mosque in the west end of the city for the same weekend. If your mosque still wants to host a conference, you will have to move it up to the May long weekend. I'm so sorry," he said, looking anything but.

Khalid looked at Imam Abdul Bari. "Four weeks is not enough time. We will have to cancel the conference." A small voice in his head protested, but he ignored it. The meetings would come to an end, and then he would have no reason to speak to Hafsa again. Which was probably for the best.

The imam stared at the ground, arms wrapped tightly around his body. "We cannot cancel, Brother Khalid," he said quietly. "There is something you should know. Something I have kept from you and the congregation, may Allah forgive me. The mosque is in debt. Attendance is dropping, and despite generous contributions from community members, we are barely afloat." The imam lowered his voice. "The executive board is thinking of selling the property."

Khalid stared at him. Sell the mosque! The Toronto Muslim Assembly was the heart of the community, one of the oldest mosques in the city, and the first to be designed and built by Muslims. He looked from Tarek to Abdul Bari, waiting for one of them to burst out laughing and singsong "Just kidding!" They remained silent.

"The mandate of Muslims in Action is to help communities," Tarek said. "As I mentioned, we are a nonprofit organization. In exchange for hosting our summer conference, the mosque will be given all proceeds, less our administrative fee. We have a proven model for success and can raise a large sum of cash in one weekend. However, considering the situation, I'm not sure we can help you out of this financial mess."

"Ammi thought the conference was a bad idea," Khalid said. "Maybe she was right."

Tarek looked at Khalid. "Your mother, Farzana?" he asked, his voice sharp. "She didn't want the conference to happen?"

Khalid didn't hear Tarek, his attention focused on the imam's bleak expression.

"I prayed for a miracle, and Allah sent me Brother Tarek," Abdul Bari said.

"We can't sell the mosque," Khalid said.

161

"I would hate to see such a well-established mosque community suffer," Tarek said, his voice casual. "Maybe we can help you out after all."

The imam nodded, determined. "Then it is settled. We must ensure the conference is a success and move the date to May. I see no other option." He turned to Khalid. "Sister Hafsa had to leave early. Can I count on you to coordinate with her to spread the word on social media? I know you would be heartbroken to see our beloved mosque turned into a strip mall."

Khalid agreed reluctantly. He resolved to call Hafsa from work, where there would be less chance of their conversation being prolonged. He would be succinct and businesslike, with no unnecessary laughter. And definitely no more smiles.

CHAPTER THIRTEEN

Ayesha played the movie *Mean Girls* during first period. She had been substitute teaching for a few weeks now, and she knew the drill. When teachers called in sick, they usually left work for students to finish, or a group assignment. English teachers loved to throw grammar exercises at their classes, and science teachers usually left textbook work. But math and history teachers always left movies. As a substitute teacher, she had sat through Marvel superhero movies and Pixar adventures, but the most popular choice by far was *Mean Girls,* the classic portrait of high school life, starring Lindsay Lohan.

Fifteen minutes into the movie, just as Cady Heron was being inducted into the popular crowd, a shadow detached itself from the class. The door opened, letting in a shaft of light from the hall and illuminating a small figure.

Ayesha sighed. There was a runner in every class. She followed the student into the hallway.

"Where do you think you're going?" she called after the speed-walking teen.

"Washroom, miss," the girl said. She leaned her weight on one leg and looked Ayesha up and down. "Mrs. Gerard always leaves that movie. Someone needs to get her a Netflix account." Ayesha remembered the girl from attendance. Tanisha Mills, back row, far left.

"You're not supposed to leave the class without letting me know first," Ayesha said.

The girl huffed. "I had to pee. I know the way."

"I'm the teacher. You need to let me know before you walk out."

"You're the *substitute* teacher." She pivoted on one foot and stalked toward the bathroom without a backward glance.

Ayesha looked back at the closed classroom door. Great. She didn't have a key. She would have to knock and hope that one of the students would open it for her. Or maybe they wouldn't. Maybe they would just laugh from the window while they snapped pictures. She was just a substitute teacher, after all.

She leaned against the wall. *Is this what*

I'm supposed to be doing with my life?

When she had worked in insurance for a few years after graduating with her BSc, the only downside had been the boredom and a few unreasonable supervisors. But she'd had her own desk, she was assigned work that needed to be done on a computer, and mostly she was left alone to get on with it. The only time someone was rude to her was when her boss was having a bad day, and it was easy to avoid one person.

Now she was belittled by kids who weren't allowed to use the bathroom without permission, and left instructions by absent teachers who took delight in leaving work their students would hate. Or the same movie the class had watched so many times before.

Her cell phone rang with an unfamiliar number. She knew she shouldn't answer her phone during school, but what if it was an emergency?

"Assalamu Alaikum," a deep voice said. "Is this Sister Hafsa?"

"Who is this?" Ayesha said cautiously, though she had a pretty good idea.

"Khalid Mirza. From the mosque. The imam gave me your number." There was a burst of female laughter in the background and Khalid cleared his throat. "Sorry about that. I'm at work right now."

Where did he work, a beauty salon? Ayesha tried to picture Khalid surrounded by women in rollers waiting to get their hair blown out and hanging on his every word. "I'm at work too," Ayesha said.

There was a pause. "You have a job?" Khalid asked, surprised.

"I also dress myself, bathe myself, drive a car, and have opinions about things," Ayesha said.

"I didn't mean . . . I'm sorry to have assumed . . . When you picked up your cell phone, I just thought . . ." Khalid floundered.

Ayesha took pity on him. "I'm a high school teacher, and you're right. I shouldn't have picked up my phone during school hours. What can I do for you?"

"Are you free tonight?" he asked.

There was a long pause. "You have to give her a time!" someone hissed in the background. "Otherwise she's going to think you're weird."

Ayesha laughed out loud.

"Please excuse me," Khalid said. When he returned, his voice was muffled. "I had to go out in the hallway. My clients keep interrupting me. I wasn't trying to ask you out, before. That would be inappropriate."

166

"I understand," Ayesha said, matching his solemn voice, though she was smiling. "Now that you have explained your intentions so clearly, why don't you get to the actual reason for your phone call?"

There was an awkward pause before Khalid said, "The imam would like us to coordinate the social media campaign for the conference. Are you free to meet tonight at eight?"

"I don't think so," she said, stalling.

"We can meet earlier, if you wish. I am free at six. Or seven. Or even seven thirty."

This was getting strange. "Listen, I have to get back to class. We'll figure something out," she said, and before Khalid could reply, she ended the call.

Tanisha stood in front of her, hands on hips. "Was that your boyfriend?" she asked.

"No," Ayesha said.

"You're not supposed to pick up your phone during class," Tanisha said. Then she smiled. "Still, it's pretty badass of you to call your boyfriend when you should be watching *Mean Girls*."

"He's not my boyfriend!" Ayesha said.

"Whatevs." Tanisha shrugged. She sailed past Ayesha and rapped on the door, which immediately sprang open.

Ayesha crept into the class behind her,

back to Lindsay Lohan's high school jungle.

When she returned home that evening, the house was quiet. Her brother, Idris, sat at the dining room table fiddling with a camera.

"Where is everyone?" she said.

Idris jumped up and pointed the camera at her. "Do you have any last requests?"

Ayesha smiled. She hadn't seen him in such a playful mood in a long time. "A long bath and five million dollars, please," she said.

Saleha bustled into the room, holding a familiar pink shalwar kameez. She stopped at the sight of her daughter, and the camera. "Idris," she said sternly. "What are you doing?"

"Capturing every second," Idris said.

Saleha threw her son a warning glance, then smiled at her daughter. "Look what Hafsa lent you," she said, holding the suit up.

Ayesha swatted her mother's hand away. "I hate pink. Where's Nana?" she asked as she began climbing the stairs.

Idris's camera was still trained on his sister. "He went for a walk. He refused to have any part in this outmoded mating ritual."

168

Ayesha stopped dead. "What did you say?" she asked her brother.

"*Beta,* you don't have to wear pink," Saleha said, her hands clasped tightly in front of her. Her mother never called her by the Urdu endearment. "After our talk, I started to worry. And then when Nilofer called . . ." She trailed off in the face of her daughter's stony expression. "It will only take thirty minutes. Just meet the rishta, please. Nani already fried the samosas, and Masood and his mother are on the way."

Idris kept his camera fixed on Ayesha's face, capturing her swift transition from anger to a flash of vulnerable contemplation.

Hafsa was not the only one who could capture a man's attention.

Ayesha tried to shake off that shallow thought, but it lingered. She was twenty-seven years old, still young for so many things. Too young to die, too young not to start over. Still young enough to live with her family.

But she was too old for other things. Too old to never have held someone's hand. Too old to never have been kissed. Way too old to never have fallen in love or at least teetered on the brink of it.

Maybe she would find love, right here in

her own living room, while her mom and brother watched from the sidelines and wished her well. Maybe she would meet Masood and electricity would shoot through her fingertips, and her heart would start pounding when their eyes met for the first time. Why not?

Besides, she had told Khalid she was busy tonight.

"Okay," she said, to her mother's relief and Idris's delight. "Just this once."

When the doorbell rang, Ayesha was ready. Idris had tried to set up his camera on the dining room table — "So I can get a wide-angle shot" — but Nani made him put it away.

"Don't worry, I have another camera hidden in the room," Idris whispered to Ayesha. He danced away before she could demand he hand it over.

Saleha walked down the hallway, followed by the rishta, Masood, and his mother, Nilofer. Saleha made the introductions and they all looked awkwardly at one another.

Nilofer Aunty was a fashionable woman dressed in a shalwar kameez cut in the latest style, her dupatta shawl draped casually around her neck like an Hermès scarf. Her hair was pulled back in a neat bun, her makeup expertly applied. She took a seat on their old brown armchair and glanced around the tiny living room with appraising eyes. Her son was a stocky man with extremely broad shoulders, a barrel chest, and stubby legs. He was dressed in a green polo shirt and blue jeans with white socks.

Ayesha looked at Idris, who subtly motioned to the hanging spider plant in the corner of the room, the perfect hiding spot for the second video camera.

"This is an especially small house," Nilofer Aunty said, breaking the silence. "How do you all manage to live here together?" She asked the question mildly, like a scientist who had crash-landed in a strange new world.

"We all have our little spaces," Saleha said. "My parents are in the basement, and my children and I are upstairs."

"My house is easily twice the size of this, and there's only my husband and Masood. I never understood extended family living situations," she said. Then, as if remembering the purpose of her visit, she peered at Ayesha. "Your cousin Hafsa is prettier than you," she observed. "Younger too. Pity she rejected my Masood without even meeting him. I wanted to take a peek inside their house." Nilofer Aunty sounded so wistful

Ayesha nearly laughed out loud.

"I can give you a tour, if you like," Ayesha said. "They're offered every Tuesday afternoon. Admission is five dollars for adults."

Nilofer Aunty glared at her, but Masood cracked a smile.

"What did you study in school?" he asked. His voice was mild, his eyes fixed on her face like a moony calf.

"Life sciences, and then teaching."

Masood nodded slowly. "Teaching is a good fallback career."

Ayesha bristled at his knowing tone. "I wanted a job that challenged me, and I like working with kids."

They lapsed into silence again, and Saleha offered tea. Nilofer requested sparkling water — "Perrier, if you have it." Masood declined all offers of food and drink, explaining that he was on a strict diet regimen.

Ayesha looked at the clock. Only five minutes had passed. She had forgotten how uncomfortable it was to go on a blind date in front of her entire family.

"What about you, Masood?" she asked, casting about for a topic. "What line of work are you in?"

Masood and Nilofer Aunty looked at each other. "Consulting," he said quickly.

"What do you consult on?" Ayesha asked.

He hesitated. "Life."

"Do you mean you're a fortune teller, or a psychiatrist?" Idris asked. "And would you mind facing that way when you talk?" He motioned to the plant.

"I'm a life coach," Masood said. "For professional wrestlers mostly, but I work with all professional athletes."

Ayesha didn't look at her brother. "That must be an interesting job," she said. "Is there great demand for life coaches among professional wrestlers?"

"Professional wrestling is an elite sport that requires just as much mental stamina as basketball, soccer, or gymnastics," Masood said defensively. "People don't really get how tough it is to be a wrestler in today's competitive market. The Australians are really taking over. I blame the kangaroos."

Ayesha blinked. "The kangaroos?" she asked, as her mother entered the living room with a tray laden with water, tea, and cookies.

"Their national mascot is a kangaroo, so they really focus on jumping more than the rest of us. They're trying to trademark the move for Aussies only," Masood said bitterly. "I've seen a real uptick in business since the lawsuit."

Ayesha's eyes watered from biting her tongue. "I had no idea the world of wrestling was so fraught with international intrigue. You must need a PhD in conflict resolution to understand it all," she said, avoiding her brother's gaze.

"Actually, I think being an effective life coach is something you're born to do," Masood said. "Just like wrestling."

Saleha sat down abruptly on the couch. "You're a wrestler?" she asked. "Is that a real job?"

"My son could have gone pro and joined World Wrestling Entertainment, but he held back for the good of the community. His life-coaching skills were needed more than his Cross-Face Mississauga Eggplant move," Nilofer Aunty said, looking fondly at her son. She took a sip of her sparkling water and made a face. "I asked for Perrier, not no-name club soda." She stood up. "We have a few more girls to see today. We will be in touch if Masood thinks you will be a good fit for the position."

Masood smiled shyly at Ayesha. "Nice to meet you. Call me if you know anyone who needs my services." He passed her an embossed white card. "I'm trying to do some outreach in the Muslim community.

Being a pioneer is lonely."

Saleha accompanied the guests to the door while Ayesha and Idris remained in the living room, and the moment Masood and his mother left, they looked at each other and dissolved into giggles.

"Tell me that really happened. Tell me I'm not dreaming," Idris said, tears of laughter streaming down his face. "I'm going to get so many views when I post this on YouTube."

"You can't post it — promise you won't!" Ayesha was doubled over, holding her stomach.

"Fine, I'll wait until after your *nikah* to Masood." Still laughing, Idris picked a tiny device out from the hanging plant and strolled upstairs, leaving the plates and cups for Ayesha to clear up.

"That was interesting," Ayesha said when Saleha returned. "Maybe the next rishta will have a secret identity — stockbroker by day, rock star by night."

Saleha straightened the chairs.

"You have to admit it was funny," Ayesha said. "Idris caught the entire thing on camera, if you want an instant replay."

Saleha turned to face her daughter. "I thought this might be the solution, but I was wrong. Marriage is too important to leave to chance."

"What do you mean?"

"When I met your father, it was because I was at the wrong place at the wrong time. I don't want the same thing to happen to you."

" 'No sooner met but they looked; no sooner looked but they loved,' " Ayesha quoted softly.

Saleha was startled. "Why did you say that?" she said. "Who told you about that?"

"It's from *As You Like It,* Mom. Shake-speare."

Saleha turned away from her daughter. "No more rishtas," she said. "I would rather you stay single for the rest of your life than quote that fool poet and think the world is a comedy when it always turns out to be a tragedy." She walked upstairs, wiping her eyes.

Ayesha stared after her. What was that all about?

And what kind of *desi* mother didn't want her twenty-seven-year-old daughter to get married?

Ayesha checked the time on her cell phone: six twenty. Before she could change her mind, she texted Khalid.

My schedule just cleared up. I can meet

you tonight at the mosque after all. If you want.

Ayesha could pretend to be Hafsa for a little longer. She needed to get out of this crazy house.

Khalid replied immediately, almost as if he had been waiting by his phone. I'll be there in ten minutes.

CHAPTER FOURTEEN

Khalid sat in the mosque conference room facing the door, nervously waiting for Hafsa. His tasbih prayer beads clicked in his hands as he repeated, *"Subhanallah, Alhamdulilah, Allahu Akbar"* — Glory be to God, all praise to God, and God is great. The repetition of the familiar chant calmed him.

She entered, face drawn.

Brief and professional, Khalid reminded himself. *No random conversation, keep this business only.* "I googled Muslims in Action and you're right, there is very little online about our event. I can set up a website for our conference, and maybe you can do a write-up," he said.

"Have you ever had a rishta before?" she asked.

Khalid paused. "No," he said. "I've signed us up for a Facebook account. We can prepare a few posts in advance and ask prominent community members to help spread the word."

"I just had a rishta from a professional wrestler–slash–life coach."

"Oh, Masood," Khalid said.

"You know him?" she asked.

"Everybody knows Masood. He sponsors the youth basketball tournament every year. What do you think we should write for our first post?"

"It's not like I want an arranged marriage. It's just strange my Indian mother doesn't care if I stay single for the rest of my life. Don't you think that's strange?"

Khalid felt himself wavering. This beautiful girl actually wanted to talk to him, not laugh or scowl at his words. But if he looked up, her eyes would lock him in a tractor-beam trance. So he kept his gaze on the screen and his voice bland. "I think you should always listen to your mother. When the time is right, Ammi will find me a suitable wife. I really have no opinion on the matter. What color scheme best represents the conference? I was thinking yellow and purple."

She put her hand out. "Wait. You don't really believe that."

"We can do green and orange if you prefer," Khalid said. When Hafsa didn't respond, he looked up from the laptop screen. Her wide brown eyes were looking at him intently. She was wearing eyeliner, he noticed, which made her eyes look larger. He moved his gaze lower, to her soft, pink lips. Khalid swallowed.

"You don't honestly believe that your parents should pick out your spouse?" she asked.

Khalid forced himself to focus on the screen. *The conference,* he reminded himself severely. *Stick to the conference and stop staring at her like a girl-starved teenager.* "I suppose 'Hello, world' is too obvious for our first post," he said. "Your expert writer's eye would be of use here."

She stood up and started pacing the room.

"Obviously your parents should have some input on your partner," she said. "We're South Asian — you really do marry the whole family. But to let your parents choose for you, without any input of your own — I know you're traditional, but that's crazy. Even Hafsa wants to talk to one hundred guys before she picks one."

Khalid looked confused. "Hafsa? You mean you?" he said.

She didn't miss a beat. "Sometimes I refer to myself in the third person," she said. "And if you think purple and yellow or green and orange are good color combinations for a website, your dress sense no longer surprises me."

Khalid closed his eyes. This conversation was giving him a headache. He opened his eyes — it would be worse if she stopped talking.

"I've never been in a relationship before," Khalid said. He stopped, and the heat rose in his cheeks at this admission. He had been teased often for his lack of relationship status. He continued. "I've never had a girlfriend. How could I possibly know what I want in a wife? Ammi knows me better than anyone else, and she wants me to be happy. I trust her opinion and her choice."

Hafsa sat down abruptly. "I've never had a boyfriend either. That doesn't mean I want my family to pick out my husband like they're ordering something off Amazon."

Khalid kept his hands clasped tightly in front of him. "This is the way things are done, the best way to keep families united and avoid problems. Love comes after marriage, not before. Whatever you feel for someone before marriage is just attraction and chemistry. It's not real." He looked up at her. She looked irritated, thoughtful. *And beautiful,* Khalid thought, and swallowed hard.

"Your words sound rational, but it doesn't

seem like you completely believe them," she said slowly. "Does your mom ask you to dress like that?"

Khalid glanced down at his white robe, the tasbih prayer beads on his wrist. "This is who I am," he said. "I'm not hiding what's important to me."

"But don't you know how you look to everyone else?" she asked, sounding genuinely curious.

"You wear hijab," Khalid said. "That's an act of faith and bravery. All I'm doing is wearing a really long dress shirt. Besides, Ammi said the beard makes me look manly." He smiled, clearly taking her by surprise. She laughed, and his smile widened.

"Maybe you should write a poem about your rishta," he said.

"Are you mocking me?" she asked, face flushing.

"When something bothers me, I read the Quran and pray about it. You could try that too, but since you're a poet, you should write about it."

"I'm not a poet. I'm a substitute teacher."

"I heard you at Bella's," Khalid said, locking eyes with her again. "You're a poet." His pulse began to speed and he looked at her hands instead, her long, delicate fingers, smooth and copper-colored and . . .

"You could title it 'Rishti-culous,' " Khalid said, desperate to distract himself. "The poem, I mean."

" 'Rishta Rage,' " she said, smiling. " 'Runaway Rishta.' "

" 'Risht-ocracy,' " Khalid said.

" 'Hasta La Rishta,' " she said, laughing. "Have you seen the *Terminator* movies?"

Khalid froze. "No," he said, heart thudding painfully in his chest.

His sister had quoted Schwarzenegger too, right before she had disappeared from his life forever. The memory was still so painful, his hands clenched.

Zareena hugging him tightly at the airport, full of bravado and unshed tears, their mother shifting impatiently beside them.

"Did you even want to help with the conference?" he asked, his voice rough. "I'm not your friend, Hafsa. We need to focus."

Her face registered surprise and hurt before she wiped it clean of emotion. "White and black for the conference color scheme. We should put together an ironic video we can post on our website and YouTube. I'll take care of the posts." She spoke quickly, but he was not listening.

Khalid knew he had failed his sister. His guilt lurked below the dark shadow of his anger and rose to the surface whenever he thought of his grim-faced mother marching Zareena toward the security gates at Pearson International Airport. His sister, a light sheen of sweat on her face, had looked so meek. So hopeless.

He should have done something. He should have stopped them.

Instead, he had looked to his father for guidance and found none. Faheem couldn't bear to watch his daughter leave. He had kept his back to her the entire time.

Hafsa picked up her bag from the floor. "I should go. I think we're both having trouble staying focused right now."

She was almost at the car when Khalid caught up to her.

"I'm sorry," he said.

"You apologize an awful lot," she said. "You might want to get that checked out."

"I'm sor—" Khalid paused. A smile eased the grim line of his jaw. "I'll make an appointment with my doctor," he said instead. "Thank you for meeting with me, Hafsa."

Her answering smile faded. "Listen, Khalid. I don't know how much longer I can help with the conference. I'm very busy right now, with work." She didn't look at him.

"Aren't you afraid I'll ruin everything?" Khalid tried for a light tone, a return to the moment they had shared earlier in the conference room, but it was long gone.

"Men always expect women to pick up the pieces and then they swoop in and claim all the glory," she said, her voice flat. "If you ruin everything, you'll only prove me right."

The call for sunset prayer began, but Khalid didn't move. "I'll tell the imam you aren't feeling well."

"Don't make excuses for me."

Khalid watched her get into the car with a sick feeling in his stomach. "The mosque is going bankrupt!" he announced, surprising himself.

She stopped, door half-open. "That's impossible."

"The imam told me. That's why they want to host the conference. It will drum up donations and business. Otherwise they will have to sell the building. You don't want our mosque turned into condominiums, do you?"

She paused, biting her lip.

"Khalid, we're too different," she said quietly. "This isn't . . . real. Please, just let me go."

Ayesha drove straight to the Taj Mahal, but Hafsa wasn't home. "She's at the mosque," Samira Aunty said when she answered the door, cradling a cordless phone. Her aunt looked at her with disapproval. "Sulaiman told me you haven't been showing up at the mosque to help Hafsa like you promised."

Ayesha was tempted to tell her aunt the truth, but she swallowed her irritation. "I've been so busy with school," she said instead. "I'll try to do better." Back in her car, she texted Hafsa.

We need to talk. Where are you?

Hafsa replied almost immediately. Busy. Talk later.

Ayesha felt her face grow hot. Fine. I'll tell your parents who really attended those meetings.

There was a pause. Then: I'm at the mall. Usual spot.

The Scarborough Town Centre was the largest mall in the east end of the city, and one of the busiest. Ayesha parked close to the theaters and made her way through the food court to the bubble tea stall. She ordered a lychee mango drink and waited.

Hafsa was in front of the Laura Secord ice cream stall with a young man who was dressed in late-nineties fashion: baggy pants and wallet chain, Doc Martens, white tank top, and a single cigarette behind his ear.

His dark hair was buzzed, his skin a tanned taupe. As Ayesha watched, Hafsa leaned in close to the young man and whispered something. He nodded and took a seat at the food court. Ayesha got a good look at his face: baby round, light stubble, hooded eyes. There was something off-kilter about his carefully cultivated appearance. He looked like a little boy pretending to be a badass.

He was nothing like Khalid, she thought. Khalid, whose face transformed when he smiled, who had gentle brown eyes and broad shoulders hidden under his long robe, thick, curly hair beneath his prayer cap. Khalid was a surprise, Ayesha admitted to herself; funny and thoughtful and maybe even a tiny bit cute.

She shook her head. What was she thinking? Ayesha remembered her words to Clara only a few nights ago: *He's a fundamentalist.*

And Clara's response: *No, he's not. He's a good guy.*

Hafsa walked up to Ayesha, smiling but uncertain. "You've been avoiding me all week," she said.

Ayesha was still checking out Hafsa's friend. He had a lighter in his hand now and was flicking it on and off, moodily posing for the mall crowd. "What happened to one hundred rishtas and a wedding?"

Hafsa followed her gaze. "That's Haris. We're just friends."

"What do you and Haris talk about? Your twenty-two rishtas?"

Hafsa tossed her head. "Mostly he tells me how pretty I am, and I tell him about my business plans."

Ayesha closed her eyes. "Hafsa . . ." she began.

"Before you say anything, I want to thank you for covering for me. You're the best!" Hafsa leaned over the table to give her older cousin a half hug, but Ayesha was stiff.

"Marriage is a lot of responsibility," Ayesha began again.

Hafsa puffed out her cheeks, eyes scanning the food court. "As if you would know," she muttered.

Ayesha stopped, anger rising.

"You're acting like a child," she blurted. "Do you know how busy I am? I'm working all day, and then at night I go to these stupid meetings at the mosque for you! The least you can do is show up."

Hafsa's eyes filled with tears. "I know," she said. "I'm such a screwup."

Ayesha's anger immediately deflated, and she reached across to squeeze her cousin's hand. "Don't say that, Hafs."

Hafsa wiped her eyes. "I've had forty-five, you know."

"What are you talking about?"

"Proposals. Rishtas. All the guys were too poor, too ugly, too boring, or too old."

"You don't have to get married," Ayesha said. "Finish school. Start your business. You're only twenty, there's no rush."

"Yes, there is. I don't want to leave it too late and end up like you. You're almost thirty and nobody wants you." The note of pity in her cousin's voice was clear. "You think I'm silly and keep changing my mind about school, but I know what I want. I want to be rich and married. In the meantime, I want to have some fun with Haris."

Ayesha shook her head. "You're stalling. What have you been doing while I impersonated you at the mosque all week?"

"Dad was so happy when the imam told him I'd shown up. He offered to give me five thousand dollars for my business." Hafsa sniffed. "As if I can do anything with that."

Ayesha stared at her baby cousin, who loved flowers and makeup and thought that rishtas were knights coming to woo the princess. She didn't recognize the spoiled brat sitting in front of her.

As if sensing Ayesha's thoughts, Hafsa's

eyes flashed. "You always behave like the saintly star of the story. Well, you're not. Exciting things can happen to me too. You're not Jane Eyre. I'm going to find my Mr. Darcy, and all my problems will be solved!"

"I think you mean Elizabeth Bennet, not Jane Eyre," Ayesha said. "Mr. Darcy is the hero of *Pride and Prejudice.*"

For an instant, Hafsa's face wobbled. Then her eyes hardened. "You can tell my parents about the conference meetings if you want," she said. "They'll only blame you for not keeping a closer eye on me. And what kind of a saint will you be then?"

CHAPTER FIFTEEN

Khalid was having a hard time concentrating at work, and not only because Sheila was breathing down his neck about the WomenFirst Design account. His conversation last night with Hafsa kept playing over and over in his mind. They had been talking easily, enjoying themselves, and then he had messed it all up. What was wrong with him?

And what was wrong with orange and green or yellow and purple background colors? His mother owned plenty of shalwar kameez with similar color combinations.

When Clara dropped by during lunch, he was grateful for the distraction. Amir had gone out, and he was alone in the office.

"The word around the water cooler is you landed a very lucrative client. How did you manage that?"

Khalid looked sheepish. "I'm not entirely sure. I told them I hadn't designed a website since high school, but Lorraine and Vanessa said honesty was endearing in a man. I don't think Sheila is too happy about the situation."

He felt comfortable confiding in Clara. There was something about her that reminded him of his sister, Zareena. She listened to him, and her eyes never rested on his clothes or his beard with condescension. She accepted him as he was, and that gave him the courage to open up.

"I met your friend at the mosque," he said, careful to keep his voice nonchalant. "The poet from Bella's. We are working together on a community project."

Clara perked up at this, and he continued. "I annoyed her for some reason. I'm not sure what to do about it."

Clara pulled Amir's chair from his desk and sat down. "You like her," she said, stating a fact.

"I don't . . . I've never had a . . ." Khalid trailed off, but Clara's eyes were full of understanding.

"Yes," he said simply. "I like her."

Perhaps she would have some suggestions that might help his situation; Allah knew he could use it. Khalid waited patiently for her advice.

I like her. The words hung in the air between

them as Clara took in his finger-raked hair, the cookie crumbs on his desk. Poor Khalid. He really had no idea about what was going on. Not about the anger he had generated in Ayesha, or the trouble this account had caused at work.

Sheila had been so irate after the ladies at WomenFirst Design dismissed her, everyone was walking around on eggshells. She had fired an assistant yesterday for sniffling too loudly. Khalid wouldn't last two minutes if Sheila could figure out a way to fire him without Vanessa and Lorraine finding out.

And now this sudden, unexpected revelation about Ayesha. He clearly needed her help.

Clara had noticed the way her friend had looked at Khalid during her open mic performance — like she wanted to fry his beard with lightning bolts. No other man had ever roused that much emotion in Ayesha, ever.

"I told Sheila about your attempt to socialize with your coworkers, and she's really, really pleased," Clara lied. "Why don't you come over for dinner sometime next week, and we can talk job strategy? My partner, Rob, makes a yummy pad Thai."

Khalid appeared to consider the offer. "Will there be alcohol?"

"Only the finest nonalcoholic wine for you," Clara promised. *And my beautiful friend for dessert,* she thought. "I've been hearing rumors about you. Your saag paneer and kofta kebab have become the stuff of Christmas party legend."

"Cooking relaxes me," Khalid said.

"Women love a man who can cook," Clara said. "When Rob makes me an apology dinner, it's hard to stay mad at him."

She gave him a knowing look. Part of her mandate as HR manager was to make suggestions, plant ideas, and encourage her clients to add the water and sunshine necessary for them to blossom. Khalid was an intelligent man; she was sure he would put two and two together. And if he didn't — well, then he didn't deserve a chance with her friend.

She smiled her good-bye and left him to it.

Khalid furrowed his brows, thinking about Clara's cryptic advice. His forehead cleared. He would cook Hafsa a meal! What a brilliant solution. Before he could change his mind, he texted her.

Salams. I've enrolled in AA — Apologizers Anonymous — and I'm working through the steps. The next one is to make amends to people I've wronged.

His phone pinged with her response a few minutes later.

Ok, I'm intrigued. How do you make amends for this very serious and completely not imaginary problem?

Khalid typed quickly, before he lost his nerve.

Your forgiveness for a kofta?

There was a long pause, and Khalid stared at his phone, feeling nervous and exhilarated. A tiny voice urged him to back down, but for the first time in his life, he didn't pay it any attention.

His phone pinged with another message. 6 p.m. Meet me in the parking lot of your favorite lounge.

Ayesha parked her car and walked toward Khalid, who leaned against his rusting Honda and waited for her. He passed her a plastic container filled with rice and peas, kofta meatball curry, and a packet of homemade crispy *papad* lentil chips. The savory scent of cinnamon, cumin, cloves, coriander, and melted ghee enveloped her in a flavorful cloud when she lifted the lid. It smelled so good, she dug in right away, using the fork Khalid had packed. Teaching made her hungry.

"Your mom is a good cook," she said, chewing.

"I made it," he said absently. "Ammi is a terrible cook, actually."

Ayesha laughed softly and Khalid looked away. "I'm sorry about what happened at the mosque," he said to his shoes. "Something you said reminded me of my sister, and it's a painful subject."

"I didn't know you had a sister." Ayesha speared two peas on the tines of her plastic fork and popped them in her mouth.

"She doesn't live in Canada, and I haven't seen her in a long time," he said. "I shouldn't have snapped at you. Please don't give up on the conference because of what I said."

"I can't help you, Khalid," Ayesha said, her mouth full of kofta. "I've got a lot going on. Work, my family." But her will was weakening with every bite. "If you made me dinner again, I might change my mind."

"Ammi hates it when I cook," Khalid said. "My sister always loved my pasta."

"Tell me about her."

Khalid hesitated, as if judging if she truly wanted to know. "Her name is Zareena, and she's almost four years older than me. She lives in India."

Ayesha thought about this. She had assumed he was an only child. "Why India?"

"She married and moved there. Or rather, moved and then married."

Ayesha looked at him curiously. "That's a big decision, to reverse immigrate to a country your parents left behind. Does she like it there?"

This time he didn't hesitate. "I'm pretty sure she hates it." Khalid was silent for a beat. Then: "I've never told anyone that."

Ayesha picked at the rice, not sure what to say. "I have a little brother, Idris. He's seventeen, and sometimes it feels like we haven't had a proper conversation since he was seven and obsessed with Pokémon."

Khalid smiled briefly. "After she left, I didn't hear from her for a long time. I didn't handle her absence well. I went through a rebellious phase."

Ayesha nearly choked on a kofta. She tried to picture Khalid dressed like Haris, in low-slung jeans and gold chain, a cigarette behind his ear, white skullcap replaced by designer baseball hat. "What did you do, listen to Islamic spiritual music with the volume turned up? Take up the tabla drums and Sufi whirling?" she teased.

Khalid scuffed his foot against the loose gravel of the parking lot. "Something like that. Then Zareena started e-mailing me, and things got better. At least I knew she was okay. I put away my anger and started going to the mosque in my old neighborhood with my Abba. We went for Fajr and Isha prayer every day. He died last year."

Ayesha lowered her fork at his words; she wanted to reach out and squeeze his arm in sympathy. "I'm glad you had those moments with your dad before he passed. I lost my father too, when I was younger," she said, her voice quiet.

"The mosque was my refuge, if that makes any sense. I feel the same way about the Toronto Muslim Assembly. I have to help save it."

Ayesha replaced the lid on her half-eaten dinner and held it in front of her, glancing at Khalid's face in profile. He had long eyelashes and beautiful skin, big hands and thick fingers. She felt safe and comfortable beside him. *You are good and kind and wholly unexpected,* she thought with surprise.

"My Nani wants to teach me to cook," she said instead. "I'm scared I'll burn the house down. I think I embarrassed her a

198

few days ago. Some aunties came over and I told them I was too busy to learn how to fry frozen samosas."

"The first time I cooked an egg, I put it in the microwave and the yolk exploded. I wish I had someone like your Nani to teach me."

"Why don't you come over to my house for a lesson?" Ayesha asked.

They both froze at her words.

What have I done? Ayesha thought.

Khalid looked stunned. "Thank you for the offer," he said carefully.

"Is that a yes?" Ayesha asked, mirroring his cautious tone.

Khalid was silent for a moment, clearly thinking. "I'm free Monday night."

Monday her mother was working a double shift, and Idris had basketball practice and wouldn't be home until ten.

"Okay then," she said.

Ayesha could still taste the basmati rice on her lips, could still picture the look on Khalid's face as he talked about his father and his sister.

He's not so bad, she thought. How many guys cooked for someone they barely knew? Also, Nani would be thrilled to finally lure Ayesha into the kitchen.

She was rationalizing, and she knew it.

Her offer of a cooking lesson and Khalid's acceptance was spontaneous, and she regretted both. Khalid was a repressed mama's boy. Plus he thought her name was Hafsa. How could she explain any of this to her grandmother?

When she got home, Nana and Nani were sitting on the front lawn in plastic chairs. They greeted Ayesha as she got out of her car.

Nani gave Nana a meaningful look, and he stood up. "Jaanu, I was just about to take a walk before dinner. Will you accompany me to the park?" he said. Nani disappeared inside the house.

It was nearly seven, and the streets were filled with children. Basketball and cricket games were underway on driveways and streets, while other children skipped rope or formed whispering clusters on bicycles. Stately grandmothers in bright cotton saris kept a close eye on their young charges. The children knew they had time to play. Dinner wouldn't be served until eight, bedtime after ten. An ice-cream truck slowly cruised the street, a Pied Piper parting children from their allowance money.

When Ayesha had moved to Canada, the neighborhood park was the first place she'd felt safe. With baby Idris in a stroller and three-year-old Hafsa toddling beside Nana, she would race to the playground after school, ready to lay claim to the geo-dome in the center, a structure that stood nearly ten feet tall and resembled a metal lattice egg. When she climbed to the top, she would survey the park's inhabitants: schoolchildren playing tag, mothers pushing babies on the toddler swings. Her eyes had lingered on the fathers kicking soccer balls or throwing baseballs to their children. Nana let her stay there as long as she liked. He knew she would join them on the ground when she was ready.

Now they approached the playground and took a seat on a faded wooden park bench. "I spoke to the imam today after Zuhr prayer," Nana said. "Abdul Bari mentioned how pleased he is with Hafsa's help. It seems Hafsa has many creative ideas for the conference, and she has offered to recite one of her poems." Nana gave Ayesha a sidelong glance. "I am so happy to learn we have two poets in the family. Perhaps she was inspired by you, jaanu."

Ayesha turned her face away to mask her blush. Her grandfather continued.

"Shakespeare enjoyed a good farce. Separated twins, love triangles, and mistaken identity were his specialty. Yet it is through his tragedies that one learns the price of silence. 'False face must hide what the false heart doth know.' "

"Hafsa isn't Macbeth," Ayesha said.

"Macbeth did not start off evil. It was the choices he made that sent him down a dark path. Hafsa is not as silly as she appears, and you are not as strong. Your father placed a high value on loyalty as well, but he was an idealist who died for his beliefs." Nana stared at the play structure, cheerfully painted in primary colors and swarming with children. He turned to his eldest grandchild. "Beta, there is nothing worse than watching your loved ones suffer. Promise you will always choose laughter over tears. Promise you will choose to live in a comedy instead of a tragedy."

Ayesha ducked her head to hide her confusion. Nana spoke of Syed as if he were a freedom fighter. She wondered what romantic cause her father had sacrificed himself for, and if it had been worth leaving behind his heartbroken wife and children who barely remembered his face. Her mind raced with unanswered questions.

"Nana . . ." she started, but her voice trailed off. Her grandfather held himself so carefully, face lined with worry but filled with love. His brown eyes pleaded silently:

Don't ask me questions I can't bear to answer.
Ayesha looked away. "I promise."

CHAPTER SIXTEEN

Farzana pounced as soon as Khalid walked in the front door. "Where have you been?" she asked, wrapping a black hijab around her head. "I promised my friend Yasmeen I would visit today."

"Have a nice visit. I can make myself something for dinner," Khalid said.

Farzana fixed her son with a glare. "They are expecting you too, of course. You must drive me."

Khalid protested that he was hungry and tired, but his mother only sniffed. "If you keep eating so much, you'll get fat. Then it will be even harder to find a suitable wife. Hurry, I said we would be there for six thirty."

The rush hour traffic was brutal, a forty-minute slog north before Khalid parked in front of a two-story house with large windows overlooking a patterned-concrete driveway. Giant planters stood sentry on

204

either side of the granite walkway next to a manicured lawn.

Farzana looked impressed. "So pretty, no?" she said at the daffodils blooming on the front porch.

His mother's genial mood made Khalid nervous. "I'll wait in the car," he offered, but she insisted he join her.

"You're not a dog. Make sure you eat whatever they offer and then ask for more." She walked up to the double-door entrance.

Warning bells rang in Khalid's head. "Ammi, what is going on?"

"I told you, we're here to visit my old school friend. Also her youngest daughter, Ruhi. She's nineteen and quite lovely. Make sure you compliment her on the chai she brings for you."

Realization dawned: He was on his very first rishta visit. He was about to protest when he heard footsteps and giggling. The door was thrown open by Yasmeen Aunty, who greeted Farzana with rapturous air kisses.

Khalid hung back and felt eyes upon him. He looked down into the fierce gaze of a five-year-old boy.

"Ruhi Phuppo will NEVER marry you!" the boy said, and he kicked Khalid in the shin.

"Ow!" Khalid bent down to rub his leg. "What are you talking about?"

The little boy whacked him over the head with a stuffed orange tiger.

Yasmeen Aunty grabbed the little boy. "Adam, go to the kitchen for a special treat from your mother," she said, smiling at Khalid. "My oldest grandchild. He's very possessive of his phuppo aunt, my youngest daughter, Ruhi. She's so good with children. Do you like children, Khalid?"

"Um . . . I . . . Yes. I suppose," Khalid mumbled. Adam fixed him with an evil glare before trotting off in search of his treat.

On second thought, Khalid was pretty sure he didn't like kids.

"Maybe I should wait outside until you're done," he said to his mother.

The women started laughing. "You never told me he was *funny*!" Yasmeen Aunty said to Farzana. Then she turned to Khalid. "I haven't seen you in so long. Who knew you would turn into such a tall, handsome man? Please come inside. Ruhi will be right out."

She led them to a large living room stuffed with furniture — four couches crammed along the walls, a large coffee table, a credenza, a hutch, and a dining table. Khalid gingerly took a seat on a bright-green patterned couch.

A younger man who looked like Yasmeen's son, his wife, and Adam walked into the room and sat down. There was a moment of silence as the strangers looked at one another.

"How long have you lived in this house, Yasmeen?" Farzana asked brightly.

They chatted about the neighborhood, the proximity of the halal butcher, the astonishing number of halal restaurants that had sprung up in recent years ("No good — outside food is so bad for digestion," Farzana declared) and other topics unrelated to the real reason for their visit. Finally, after what felt like hours but was really only fifteen minutes, the main attraction entered the room.

Ruhi was slender and dressed in a mint-green shalwar kameez, her dupatta shawl pulled demurely over her head. She balanced a tray of tea and snacks, which she placed gracefully in front of Khalid before taking a seat beside her mother, eyes on the ground.

"You've gotten so tall since I saw you last, Ruhi. What are you studying in school?" Farzana asked her.

Ruhi's voice was so low, Khalid strained to hear it. "Early childhood education, Aunty."

"That will come in handy once you have children," Farzana said, smiling at her. "Do you read your prayers every day?"

"Yes, Aunty."

"And you live in an extended family, so you are used to listening to your elders."

"Yes, Aunty."

"How many dishes can you make?"

"Over twelve, Aunty. I'm also taking a course in Italian cooking."

Khalid wondered if his mother realized she was carrying the conversation by herself. Farzana looked over at Khalid. "My son loves pasta. Beta, do you have any questions for Ruhi?"

Khalid's neck prickled with discomfort. This whole setup felt wrong. He thought about his careful explanation to Hafsa about marriage, his confidence in his mother's method and in her selection of his wife. Was the process supposed to be this awkward? He had pictured his arranged marriage very differently, more sophisticated and mature, like a thoughtful business merger. This felt more like a backroom deal.

The rest of the family was staring at him — or in the case of Adam, shooting daggers at him — and he shook his head. Ruhi had yet to lift her eyes to look at him, and he shifted uneasily. Perhaps she shared Hafsa's disapproval for the arranged marriage process and wanted him gone.

The silence stretched as everyone tried to think of another topic of conversation.

"Maybe we should let the young people talk on their own," Yasmeen Aunty finally suggested. "They can sit at the dining table and get to know each other."

Farzana narrowed her eyes. "Khalid does not talk to women," she said. "It would not be proper."

Khalid flushed at his mother's words and their implication. Of course he spoke to women; he talked to Sheila, and Clara, and his clients at WomenFirst Design. He spoke to Hafsa — could not, in fact, stop thinking about their conversation. He wanted to correct his mother's ridiculous pronouncement, but Yasmeen Aunty hurried to respond.

"Of course, of course. Ruhi, help me make some more chai for Farzana Aunty."

Khalid wanted to disappear. He eyed the door and wondered how quickly he could orchestrate an escape. If Hafsa had been here instead of Ruhi, things would have been very different. She would have made jokes, laughed at his awkwardness, and asked inappropriate questions. He would have enjoyed every second.

He stood up in search of the washroom, which was in the hallway near the kitchen. Khalid's eyes looked wild in the vanity mirror, and he splashed cold water on his face. *This is what I wanted,* he reminded himself. *Love blossoms after marriage.*

When Khalid emerged, he was unsure whether to return to the living room or try to make a run for it. As he stood there considering his options, another conversation intruded on his thoughts. Yasmeen Aunty and Ruhi were talking in the kitchen, and Ruhi was not bothering to keep her voice down.

"Why aren't you saying anything?" Yasmeen Aunty asked in Urdu. "They will think you're mute!"

"I don't want to be here," Ruhi said, furious. "Farzana Aunty is a control freak, and her son is a boring mama's boy. Why are you making me do this?"

"Do you have any idea how rich they are? Farzana is always boasting about the condos she owns and their property in India. Be reasonable, Ruhi. If you marry him, you'll never have to work again. You can buy that BMW you always wanted."

Ruhi was silent. Then: "Fine. I'll talk to robot-boy."

Khalid walked quickly back to the living

room, heart thumping.

When Ruhi returned with another tray, she sat closer to Khalid. "Can I pour you some more tea?" she asked. "Milk and sugar?"

Khalid nodded and accepted the small china cup. She smiled shyly at him, then lowered her eyes and blushed becomingly. He gulped his tea and stood up. "Ammi, I have a meeting at the mosque tonight. We have to go."

Farzana paused midsentence, surprised. But Khalid was determined, and they left soon after.

"That's a good idea, to leave early," his mother said as they walked to the car. "We must maintain the upper hand."

Khalid kept his peace until they were in the car. "I don't want to marry that girl. She only talked to me because her mother forced her to."

Farzana patted her son's arm. "Beta, this is all just a game. I have no intention of letting you marry that minx. We are only testing the waters, that's all."

His mother's words made him uncomfortable. "This doesn't feel right, Ammi. How would you feel if someone spoke like that about Zareena?"

"With your sister, we had to take what we

could get," Farzana said. "I don't have to worry about that with you. Let me do my job."

Khalid remained silent on the drive back, his thoughts ricocheting around in his head. Maybe his mother was wrong. Maybe there were other ways to find a wife, methods that didn't involve awkward conversations and bribing possible brides with BMWs.

He thought about the cooking lesson with Hafsa's Nani, the one he had been planning to cancel. It might be nice to learn from an experienced cook after all.

Also, grandparents made great chaperones. He had a feeling that where Hafsa was concerned, he needed one. He didn't trust himself around her.

CHAPTER SEVENTEEN

Ayesha returned home from school on Monday with her stomach full of butterflies. She couldn't stop thinking about that night's cooking lesson. She had spent the entire day waiting for Khalid to cancel, so sure he would back out that she hadn't even bothered to ask Nani.

As the evening drew near, Ayesha's nervousness grew and she checked her phone for messages again and again. Finally she could put it off no longer.

Nani was alone in the kitchen drinking chai. "Remember you wanted to teach me how to cook?" Ayesha asked.

Her grandmother looked up briefly. She was reading an Urdu magazine with a picture of a police detective on the cover.

Ayesha shifted her weight, hands clasped behind her. "My friend . . ." she began, then stopped. Was Khalid her friend? A colleague? Her Muslim brother?

"This guy I know . . ." she started, and this time Nani closed her magazine and looked at her granddaughter.

"You're such a good cook," Ayesha began again. "I was telling him about your food, and he really wants to learn a few authentic recipes, so I thought maybe you could give him a lesson on how to make your delicious parathas."

Nani had a good poker face. "Is this the man you met the other night in the parking lot?" she asked. "The one from the mosque meetings?"

How did her Nani know about that? She was sure her grandmother didn't keep up with mosque happenings, and she had met Khalid far from prying Aunty-Brigade eyes.

Nani was waiting for an answer, her face expressionless.

"Yes," Ayesha said. "But how did you . . ." she trailed off as her grandmother shrugged.

"Imam Abdul Bari's receptionist mentioned the conference meetings when I saw her at Hakim bhai's grocery store last week. I assumed it was the same person who'd given you the plastic container of food. It makes sense to meet him somewhere far away from nosy aunties, and I know how fond you are of Bella's. But you didn't smell like cigarette smoke, as you usually do when you attend your poetry nights. So, the parking lot." Nani was perusing the magazine again and didn't notice Ayesha's astonishment. Her grandmother looked up and smiled slightly. "His garam masala blend was quite impressive. Is your young man a chef?" she asked.

"He's not my young man, and he's not a chef."

Nani nodded, turning a page of the magazine. "I can give him a lesson, so long as you promise to stay and learn something as well."

The doorbell rang, and a light sweat broke out on Ayesha's forehead.

"Can you give him a lesson right now?" she asked.

Nani put away her magazine, nonplussed. "Of course, rani," she said, pulling out bowls and ingredients from the cupboard.

"Right. Um," Ayesha floundered. "Can we just keep this between us? Mom will make a big deal, and Idris will take out his video camera. Also . . . he-thinks-I'm-Hafsa-I'll-explain-later." Ayesha's heart was pounding as she walked to the front door.

Khalid was dressed in a black robe, his hair wet from the shower. He thrust flowers, white carnations, into Ayesha's face. "For your Nani," he said, and then he stood looking stupidly at her, which made her feel a little better. He was nervous too.

She led him to the kitchen for introductions. Ayesha hadn't realized how tall Khalid was; he towered over Nani's diminutive form. Her grandmother looked up at him, coolly assessing.

"It must be nice to get out of the office and work with your hands," Nani said to Khalid. "Though making parathas is just as hard on your shoulders as sitting in front of a computer screen all day."

Khalid looked at Ayesha, who only shook her head. "You're right. I find cooking very relaxing," he said.

"Maybe you will cook for your wife one day," Nani said. "After you decide to settle down."

Khalid nodded, and Ayesha noticed that he didn't correct her grandmother. "Khalid's mother will find him a wife," she said to Nani.

"Then she should hurry up, before he finds a wife for himself," Nani answered.

Khalid hid his confusion by reaching for a notebook in his bag. He titled a blank page and watched Nani assemble ingredients: flour, water, oil, yogurt, salt, baking soda.

"Rani, give your friend an apron. I don't want him to get any flour on his clothes.

216

His mother will wonder what he has been doing."

Khalid gave Nani an appreciative glance and followed Ayesha to the pantry.

"Your grandmother is very perceptive," he whispered as she rummaged in the cupboard, digging under kitchen towels.

"She's happy to finally teach me a few things," she said, passing him an ancient blue apron. A current of electricity shot between them as their fingers touched. Khalid leaned in and Ayesha closed her eyes and inhaled his scent: soap and a hint of clean-smelling cologne.

"Thank you for inviting me," he said, his voice low and warm in her ear.

"Thank you for coming," she said, keeping her eyes on his hand, only inches from hers. He walked back out to the kitchen and Ayesha followed.

Khalid picked up his pen and made notes in his book as Nani placed two cups of flour in a large glass bowl, then sprinkled in salt and baking soda. She added yogurt, oil, and water, and started to mix with her hands. When Khalid asked how much of each ingredient she used, Nani shook her head.

"You need to use *andaza*," she said.

Ayesha smiled at her grandmother's use of the untranslatable concept of *andaza*.

"Nani, you can't just eyeball the ingredients," she said.

"Not everything needs to be measured. The most important step is to mix well and give the ingredients time to sit together," Nani said in Urdu. She kneaded as she talked, hands working until the dough became soft and pliable. She covered the bowl in plastic wrap and put it in the microwave.

"What now?" Khalid asked, pen poised.

"We let it rest and wait for it to rise," Nani said. She looked at Ayesha and then at Khalid. "I have to pray Asr. I'll be back," she said, and she left them alone at the kitchen table.

Khalid fiddled with his notebook. "I met a girl yesterday," he said. "My first rishta. Ammi ambushed me."

Ayesha sat up, a wisp of jealousy making her stomach clench. "Did you talk to her or stare at the floor?" she asked lightly.

"It wasn't just me. Everyone was staring at the floor. They had a really nice carpet."

Ayesha laughed, strangely relieved. "I told you, rishtas are the worst. So what do you think of your mother's taste? Do you still trust her?"

"Yes," Khalid said automatically. Then he added, "Though it was very awkward.

Especially when I overheard the girl's mother reprimanding her in the kitchen. I don't think she was happy to be there either."

Either. So he wasn't happy to be meeting other girls. Ayesha wanted to whoop. Instead she said, "If that's true, she's a fool. You're a catch, Khalid. A single, educated, pious Muslim man. All the mothers must be salivating at the thought of snatching you for their daughters."

"Not every mother," he said, looking at her.

Ayesha flushed but said playfully, "I'm the doomed spinster. When I finally have the time to look for a husband, I'll be thirty-five and all the good men will be taken. Maybe if I'm lucky, I'll find a second cousin in India who will marry me for my Canadian citizenship."

Khalid was doodling in his notebook. "Or you could look around right now," he said slowly, and Ayesha felt her hand tingling from where they had touched.

"Khalid . . ." she began, but Nani was back. She took the dough out of the microwave. It was softer, rising from the bowl. She made six portions and handed them each one small ball.

"There is a secret to the perfect paratha,"

Nani said in Urdu. With her thumb, she deftly made a well in the middle of her dough ball. Then she covered it with the sides of the dough, encasing the air pocket inside. "Leave a little space, right in the middle. The paratha needs it to grow and become soft. Without this space, it will be hard and lumpy, just another piece of bread."

Next they rolled out their portions. Ayesha's circle was deformed, but Khalid's came out perfectly round. She stuck out her tongue and he smiled.

Nani fried the paratha on a hot pan with oil. The bread rose against the heat, fluffing up like a dough balloon as Ayesha watched in delight.

"See what a little space can do?" Nani murmured.

Ayesha reached for the first one and split it with Khalid. It was warm and soft, chewy and delicious. She enjoyed every bite. "What do you think?" she asked him.

"Perfect," he said, eyes on her face. "I wouldn't change a thing."

Behind them, Nani hummed a few bars of a classic Bollywood tune and then called them back to roll out the rest of the dough.

When the parathas were done, Nani got out some canned mango pulp, and they all sat to eat at the kitchen table. She told them she hadn't known how to cook when she was first married. "We ate a lot of eggs," she said. "It was the only thing your Nana knew how to make."

"I didn't know Nana could cook," Ayesha said.

"He can't," Nani said. "When we were first married, I was in school studying to be a police officer. It was all those Hardy Boys and Agatha Christie mysteries he read to me. I wanted to be a detective, like Hercule Poirot or Miss Marple."

Ayesha burst out laughing at the thought of her grandmother, who didn't leave the house most days, investigating crimes and running after bad guys.

Nani lifted her chin, offended. "Don't laugh. I would have been very good at it too, except Allah decided I should be a mother first. A woman plays many roles in her life, and she must learn to accept them as they come. Men are not so flexible," she said, a half smile on her lips. "That's why it's important to find someone who complements you, rani. Someone to dream with you."

Ayesha walked Khalid to the door, and he took his time putting on his shoes. When he stood up, she noticed he had flour in his beard, and she reached out and absently brushed it away. His beard was soft, like spun cotton, and her hand lingered.

He clasped her wrist to stop her, and their eyes met — hers wide in sudden realization, his steady. Ayesha blushed bright red, embarrassed at violating their unspoken no-touch rule. He looked at her for a long moment, then gently, reluctantly, dropped her hand.

Her face still flaming, she stared at the tile floor, too embarrassed to say anything.

Khalid fiddled with the lock on the door. "Hafsa," he said in a low voice. "Have you ever wondered —"

His phone pinged and he frowned at it. When he looked up, the spell was broken. "Are you free tomorrow night?" he asked. "The imam wants us to check out the caterers for the conference."

They made plans to meet and Ayesha watched him turn and cross the street. She hadn't known he lived so close to her.

She shouldn't have touched him; she couldn't believe that she had. Yet her hands on his face felt natural and right. She could still feel the gentle pressure on her wrist from his warm hand, the heat in his eyes.

Whatever he was about to say, it could wait. A bit of space would help his words expand and grow soft. Ayesha could admit it now: Khalid wasn't like any other man she'd ever known.

Chapter Eighteen

Ayesha was late for work again. The reality of teaching was beginning to hit her now. She had been excited to start a new career when she had first graduated from teachers' college. That feeling had quickly been replaced — first, by the difficulty of securing a position, and then by the demands of substitute teaching. She had settled into a sort of routine and understood how exhausting it was just to teach, day in and day out. She was always "on," always responding to students, parents, other teachers. By the end of the day, she was so tired, she didn't have the energy to talk to her family. Her more seasoned teacher colleagues assured her that it would not always be like this. Give it five years, they said. Once you have your own class and have found your rhythm, teaching will be easier.

The thought of another five years made her even more tired.

Today Ayesha was substitute teaching two eleventh-grade English classes and one ninth-grade boys' gym class. The English students had an essay due tomorrow, and they were bent over laptops and papers, diligent and quiet. Gym class was something else altogether. The teacher had left convoluted, fussy instructions: The boys had seven minutes to change, three minutes to warm up, then fifteen minutes of basketball drills, followed by four rotations of games at ten minutes each. Ayesha's head spun trying to make it all out, and the end of the class found her standing on a chair in the middle of the gymnasium, keeping an eye on four simultaneous games of basketball and trying to make sure the boys didn't kill one another.

The principal, Mr. Evorem, poked his head into the main door. He drew back, perhaps at the pungent odor of teenage boy, and gave her a discreet thumbs-up. She jumped off the chair and smiled weakly.

"Come see me later," he called out to her.

"Miss, you're in trouble!" Nathan, one of the students, yelled as he threw a perfect three-pointer.

She dismissed the class and went in search of the principal.

Mr. Evorem was in his office, dusting

sports trophies.

"How are you enjoying our school, Miss Shamsi?" he asked. He continued before she answered. "Teaching is a challenging career, and the first few years can be quite tough. Stick with it, and it will reward you. I remember my first years in the classroom. There's nothing more satisfying than a happy, productive class." Ayesha recognized his wistful tone. She sounded like that too — when she talked about poetry.

"What subjects did you teach before you became a principal?" she asked.

"Math, science, gym. I still coach a few teams, but the admin work has to come first."

Ayesha knew he was being modest — Mr. Evorem organized half a dozen sports teams and tournaments, and he tried to attend every game played on school grounds.

"You're lucky to have a job that encourages your passion," she said.

"That's the thing about teaching. There are a lot of options. You just have to see where it takes you." He turned back to her, suddenly businesslike. "Miss Shamsi, I wanted to give you a heads-up. There might be an opening for a permanent teacher on our faculty in September."

Ayesha had waited for this moment for so

long, she didn't know how to react.

"Your students like you, and you work well with your fellow teachers. You've probably noticed that our student body is quite diverse. Our school board wants to see that diversity reflected in our new hires."

So they were looking for a token ethnic. Ayesha was familiar with the role; she had played it often enough. She heard Clara's scoffing voice in her head: *Who cares? It's a job, and you'll be good at it. Everyone needs an in, and if yours is hijab and brown skin, go for it!*

Ayesha knew she had potential. She could grow into a good teacher. Her thoughts traveled to Khalid and the way he spoke about his principles, about what he wanted. He was so sure of himself, so sure of the life he wanted to lead. She wanted to be that sure about something too.

She had told Khalid she wasn't looking for a husband, and she meant it. But as she stood at the precipice of a permanent teaching job, she wondered if this choice was really that inevitable or if it only felt that way.

And what had Khalid been about to say before he'd caught himself at the door last night?

Ayesha thought back to the way his eyes

had lingered on her face as they rolled out parathas, his uncertain reaction to that brief, forbidden caress. They were both so new at . . . whatever this was. Both inexperienced at relationships, at romance . . . and love? She mentally shook her head. This wasn't love. He didn't even know her real name. When they met at the caterer's tonight, she would have to pretend to be Hafsa again. The thought made her even more tired, and determined to move on with the rest of her life.

"Thank you," she said to Mr. Evorem, her voice firm. "I'm very interested in the position. It's all I have ever wanted."

The words were true, once. She just wasn't sure if they were anymore.

Khalid had slept well the previous night, which was surprising. Today was the twelfth anniversary of Zareena's banishment to India, an unmarked day of mourning on his calendar. Yet his memories of her today felt more like a dull ache, not the usual sharp pain of another year spent missing his sister.

Perhaps his optimism had something to do with Nani's cooking lesson yesterday. Hafsa's small house had been filled with shabby furniture, yet it had felt warm and inviting. He had been accepted and welcomed by her and Nani. The anniversary of his sister's banishment seemed less distressing as a result. He had wanted to say something to Hafsa last night about what he was feeling, but he'd lost his nerve. He rehearsed the words galloping around in his mind while he drove to the caterer the imam had chosen for the conference.

Have you ever wondered, Hafsa, what it would be like to spend your life with someone like me? Have you ever wondered, beautiful Hafsa, what it would be like to open your heart to something unexpected, someone wholly unanticipated? Because I am starting to wonder. Actually, I am having a hard time thinking of anything else.

Perhaps he would find the words today.

Khalid met Hafsa in the parking lot of Kamran's Superior Sweets at eight thirty that evening. As his eyes met hers, his courage failed him, and he politely asked after Nani instead. They walked into a restaurant with beige linoleum floors, greasy green wallpaper, and dingy white Formica tables. The place was famous for its extensive and well-priced catering selection. Kamran himself had presided over many mosque events, and his restaurant had catered more than half of the community weddings.

229

Khalid was surprised to see Tarek sitting at a table, a plate of samosas in front of him.

"I did not know you would be joining us, Brother Tarek," Khalid said, his hopes of having Hafsa to himself dashed.

"When the imam told me you were going to Kamran Khan's, I had to come too," Tarek said, smiling. "Best butter chicken in the city."

They settled around the table and Mr. Khan entered the dining room from the kitchen, wearing a black apron and a white T-shirt that strained against his potbelly.

"Who's getting married?" Kamran asked abruptly.

"The two of us, if Hafsa will have me," Tarek said, putting his arm casually on the back of Hafsa's chair.

Khalid stiffened.

"We're here to discuss catering for the conference at the Toronto Muslim Assembly. Imam Abdul Bari sent us," Hafsa said, moving her chair forward so Tarek's arm was dislodged.

Kamran opened an unstained page in his black notebook. "I can do both. Wedding and conference — I'll give you good price," he said.

Tarek leaned forward. "I'm still working on her, Brother. Give me a few weeks and we'll talk." He winked, and Kamran grinned, revealing teeth stained red with betel nut.

"I thought you were here to help," Hafsa said firmly to Tarek, but with a smile. "We need to focus."

"How can I focus when you're such a distraction?" Tarek asked. He turned to Khalid. "Don't you find it distracting to work with Hafsa?" His words were playful, but the look in his eyes was shrewd.

Khalid cleared his throat. "Sister Hafsa is very easy to work with," he said, avoiding eye contact with either of them.

Tarek laughed out loud. "I think Khalid just said he doesn't find you attractive. Which is good for me. Less competition."

Hafsa swatted Tarek's arm. "What's gotten into you?"

Tarek leaned in close. "Imam Abdul Bari isn't around to disapprove. I guess Brother Khalid will have to keep me in line. He's good at policing behavior."

Khalid clasped his hands tightly together. "Why don't we concentrate on the purpose of our visit," he said, indicating Kamran Khan, who was directing a waiter to set down plates of food and watching them with quiet amusement.

Tarek winked at Hafsa and offered her a

plate of sizzling chicken tikka. "Don't worry about upsetting Brother Khalid. We're old friends. Did you know he has an older sister?"

Hafsa shifted, clearly uncomfortable. Khalid felt her glance at him, but he kept his gaze on the lamb biryani. "How are the conference plans progressing with your team?" she asked instead. "Have you found any more female speakers?"

"I knew Zareena in high school, but I haven't seen her in at least twelve years," Tarek said. "Actually, I think it's been exactly twelve years." Tarek looked at Khalid, who remained silent. "When was the last time you saw your sister?" he asked, taking a bite of spinach pakora. The happy flirt of a few minutes ago was gone, replaced by a wolf in their midst.

"I am in regular communication with my sister," Khalid said. "Thank you for your concern. I will pass along your greetings, though I doubt if she remembers you. She has never mentioned your name before."

Tarek dropped the spinach pakora. "Too spicy," he whispered to Hafsa, who looked back and forth between the two men, confused. "Do you have friends that your parents don't know about, Hafsa? Or do you only ever talk to people who meet with your family's approval?" Tarek's tone was genial, but his eyes were hard.

"I think people's families are their own business," Hafsa said evenly. Khalid felt a flare of gratitude at her words. He took a bite of the biryani — it was quite good, though heavy on the ghee.

"Butter chicken is popular with the *goras*, the white people," Kamran offered helpfully. He spooned some onto their plates and then sat down, as if to watch what would happen next.

"I hate butter chicken," Khalid said to no one in particular.

"How's your mom?" Tarek asked him, leaning over Hafsa. "Your sister used to complain about her all the time."

"Butter chicken is bland and boring and completely predictable," Khalid said, ignoring Tarek.

"Do you know Khalid's mother, Hafsa? He calls her *Ammi*. Isn't that adorable?" Tarek turned to her. His smile was pointy.

"No," she said shortly. "Eat your food."

He glanced over at Khalid. "I haven't seen your Ammi in twelve years either."

"My mother is doing well, though she doesn't approve of your conference. She thinks it will encourage mixing between the young men and women." Khalid kept his voice even, but his heart was pounding. He didn't know why Tarek was bringing up Zareena and Ammi, but every instinct screamed at him to be careful.

"Ammi didn't approve of the company Zareena kept either," Tarek said. "She doesn't approve of anything she can't control. That must be why she is so happy to have you around. I bet you don't give her any trouble."

Khalid saw Hafsa look helplessly at Kamran Khan, who was sipping a cup of tea. He watched as Kamran shook his head at her, as if to say: *Girl, you don't know the things I've seen. What happens at the caterer's stays at the caterer's.*

"You seem to know a lot about my family," Khalid said. He felt rattled, but his tone was calm.

"You know what they say about gossip." Tarek leaned close. "Most of it is true, and whatever isn't is wishful thinking."

Hafsa smacked the table. "That. Is. Enough." She glared at Tarek, daring him to say another word, but the spirit that possessed him had vanished. He put his arm around her plastic chair, easy once more.

"Relax, Sister Hafsa," Tarek said, smiling his raffish Prince-Charming smile again. "I was just kidding."

Khalid sat silently for a moment. Then he grabbed his jacket and, after thanking Kamran, left the restaurant. Hafsa jumped up and followed him.

Tarek and Kamran were left alone at the table. The caterer began to stack the half-full dishes. He gave Tarek a conspiratorial wink. "It won't work, you know," he said in Urdu. "I have seen enough couples to know. You will never get that girl."

Tarek stared at Khalid through the restaurant window, a knowing, determined expression on his face. "I'm not worried about Hafsa," he responded to Kamran in perfect Urdu. "Women always come around to me, one way or another."

CHAPTER NINETEEN

Khalid was at his car when Ayesha called his name. He looked back at her, his face tight with anger.

"I don't need you to speak for me," he said.

Ayesha stopped short. "You were like two boys wrestling in the mud."

Khalid's fists curled. "I know most women are taken in by a pretty face, but I thought you were different. Tarek is trouble."

His accusations were unfair. As if Prince Charming could ever turn her head. She had been sticking up for him! "At least Tarek isn't afraid to make eye contact when he talks to me. Have you really not seen your sister in twelve years? Why on earth not?"

Khalid's expression hardened at her words. "You have no idea what is expected of me or how I feel about it. You can't be bothered to look beyond the surface."

Ayesha reeled back. "Me? What about you? You're so afraid, you run away whenever things get real. You're nothing but a coward!"

Khalid stepped closer, his eyes dark with anger. "At least I know what I want from my life. I know who I am. You can't make up your mind about anything."

His words struck harder than he could possibly realize. Ayesha thought of her mother, of Hafsa and Clara and even Khalid himself, and their utter certainty about everything. It was infuriating. She'd thought Khalid was different, but her first impression had been right after all: He was a judgmental conformist, content to bow mindlessly to tradition and the expectations of others.

Just like me. Her face flushed with anger, at him and at herself. "Your mother has you on a leash, and you're happy to be her puppet!" she said, hurling her words at him. "We don't live in India or Pakistan. You're allowed to choose your own wife and live your own life."

"For someone who claims to have no interest in finding a husband, you care an awful lot about who I marry," he threw back.

They glared at each other, furious and

helpless, their faces inches apart.

"Actually, you're wrong, Khalid," she said deliberately. "I don't care about you at all."

He jerked back, and the hurt on his face made her wince.

"I never expected you to," he said, more to himself than her. He unlocked his car and drove home.

When Ayesha returned home, her thoughts were churning. She was halfway up the stairs to her room when her mother called from the kitchen, taking her by surprise. It was a rare evening that found her mother home early.

"I heard back from Masood's mother," Saleha said. "He is interested in speaking further. I gave him your number."

Ayesha wanted to throw up her hands in fury. After a lifelong drought, suddenly it was raining men. She turned on her mother. "Masood the wrestler? You didn't like him. You told me finding a husband is too important to leave to the arranged marriage crapshoot."

"It turns out wrestling and life coaching pay well. His mother told me Masood is on his way to becoming a wealthy man."

Ayesha sat down at the kitchen table. "So now you want me to talk to him?"

Saleha took a seat beside her. "I want you to be safe, to keep your expectations reasonable."

Ayesha was silent, her thoughts lingering on Khalid again. "What about love?" she asked.

Saleha met her daughter's eye and then looked away. "I fell in love with your father, a long time ago. We were students at the university. He was so handsome and charming, so passionate about everything. All the girls had crushes on him, but he chose me," she said, and there was a trace of pride and wonder in her voice. "Your Nani didn't approve. His family wasn't rich, and he wanted to be a journalist. You got your literary skills from him."

Ayesha traced patterns on the tabletop, listening intently. Her mother never talked about her father, not in this kind of detail.

"Nana gave us his blessing. He knew it would break my heart to let Syed go. Your grandfather has always been a romantic. We married, we had you and then Idris, and we were so happy. When he died, I thought I would die too." A single tear traced a path down Saleha's cheek, and she smiled at her daughter. "Love is not enough. I thought it would be once, but after Syed died, I realized how much of myself was wrapped up in the idea of him. Perhaps Masood is not your ideal candidate, but he is a decent man. I don't think he would ask too much of you. You would be able to keep a part of you for yourself."

Ayesha paused, thinking about her job offer and the life she had vowed to lead. Her thoughts traveled back to Khalid, to his stricken face when she'd told him she didn't care. Maybe this was all for the best. Khalid was too conservative, too tied to his mother's commands. He could never make her happy.

The path was clear. It was time to start walking.

"I'll talk to Masood," she said to her mother.

The smell of onions and garam masala greeted Khalid as he parked his car in the driveway, and his stomach sank. His mother only cooked late at night when she was angry, and he didn't know if he had the energy to deal with that right now, on top of everything else.

"Assalamu Alaikum, Ammi," he called cautiously, but his stomach growled, betraying him. He hadn't eaten at Kamran's Superior Sweets. Khalid followed the smell of spices to the kitchen, where his mother stood sentry over four pots.

"Brother Tarek called," Farzana said. "He wanted to thank you for helping to pick out the food at the caterer's tonight." She gave the pot in front of her a violent stirring. "I have to learn what you are doing from strangers now. Who is this Tarek person?"

He leaned against the doorway. "Nobody."

"Why are you being so secretive? I'm your mother. I have a right to know what you are doing at all times."

Hafsa's words rang in his ears — *Your mother has you on a leash* — and Khalid flushed with shame and anger. "Tarek is from the conference committee. He was helping us pick out the caterer."

"Yes, Tarek mentioned that you and Hafsa were both there. Is this Brother Sulaiman Shamsi's daughter?" Farzana took two plates from the cupboard and ladled out a generous serving of rice, chicken, and naan.

"No, Hafsa's father died a long time ago. We all arrived in separate cars. She joined us after work."

Farzana's hand stilled over his plate. "Where does this Hafsa work?" she asked carefully.

"She's a high school teacher, I don't know where."

His mother's eyes were watchful as she

241

passed him the food. "I thought Hafsa's family lived in a big house nearby. The family is very rich."

Khalid swallowed the rice, which was too salty, and took a bite of chicken, which was dry and tasted sour from too much lemon. "I don't think their house is that large. They live across the street from us, in one of those old townhouses. You must be thinking of another family."

Farzana nodded, her lips thin. "Yes, of course, that must be it. Another family."

They ate their food in silence, both deep in thought.

As soon as Farzana was sure her son was upstairs in his bedroom with the door shut, she dialed Hafsa's house.

"This is Farzana," she said importantly into the receiver. "I must speak to Hafsa immediately. It is an urgent matter."

After a few minutes, a voice came on the line. "Who is this?"

Farzana resisted the urge to scold Hafsa for her rude lack of greeting. Instead, she coated her voice in honey and crooned, "Hafsa beti, this is Farzana Aunty. I came to see you a little while ago, do you remember?"

Hafsa's voice was wary. "Yes, I remember

you. I'll get my mom."

"No, wait!" Farzana said. "I'm calling to apologize." There was a pause, and Farzana continued. "Beti, when I met you, I was so overwhelmed by your beauty and refined behavior, I'm afraid I came off as quite rude. I was only thinking of my darling son, Khalid. He is such a sensitive boy. He could never handle being rejected by *you*."

Hafsa's voice softened, mollified. "That's okay, Aunty. I know how hard it can be for boys. I have received quite a few rishtas."

"I am not surprised at all. Though I know my Khalid is out of the running, whoever you decide to marry will be one lucky young man." Farzana was afraid she might be laying the compliments on a little thick, but Hafsa accepted the flattery easily.

"That's so kind of you, Farzana Aunty. Maybe I was too quick to reject your son. After all, I didn't even meet him."

Farzana's voice took on a sorrowful tone. "Oh my, this is embarrassing. It's just that my Khalid has moved on."

"What do you mean?"

"I would love to have a beautiful, modest young woman like you for my daughter-in-law. But I have one rule, Hafsa: A mother must never interfere in the lives of her children. If Khalid has taken a liking to your much older cousin Ayesha, who am I to object?"

"Ayesha? MY Ayesha?" Hafsa said loudly.

"Didn't your dear cousin tell you? Apparently they met while planning a conference at the mosque together."

"That's my conference!" Hafsa said. "She was covering for me, but I'm the real event planner!"

"I never meant to cause trouble," Farzana said sweetly. "I know how close the two of you are, and I'm sure Ayesha didn't purposely go behind your back and betray you. I only want what's best for my son."

On the other end of the line, Hafsa spluttered, and Farzana went in for the kill. "May I give you some advice? You must always guard against jealous family members who want what you have. If I were you, I would pretend to know nothing. Make your own plans behind the scenes, just as your cousin has done. I know my son better than anyone else, and I think he would be far happier with you than with someone as outspoken and opinionated as Ayesha."

Hafsa was silent, no doubt considering Farzana's words.

The older woman smiled thinly. These vain, silly girls. When Khalid had mentioned that "Hafsa" was a school teacher whose father had died years before, she had immediately realized that her innocent son was being duped. The real Hafsa might be rich and flighty, but she would be easier to control than Ayesha, an aging rishta-reject with strong opinions.

As for Khalid — he was a good boy, and he would do as he was told.

CHAPTER TWENTY

Salams, Ayesha. This is Masood. Save this number, it's my personal contact. I'm available any time, day or night. I look forward to getting to know you better.

Ayesha looked at her phone and sighed. It was lunchtime and she was sitting by herself in the staff room, a little-used corner of the school. She put her phone down and looked at the stale bagel she had packed that morning. In her rush to be on time for school, she hadn't even prepared it with cream cheese or peanut butter. She pushed the cold, empty bagel away and contemplated her meal options. She could make a takeout run, but there weren't any halal restaurants nearby, and the thought of greasy cafeteria food made her stomach turn. Her phone pinged again with another message from Masood:

I have met many young women, but I enjoyed meeting you the most. There's something special about you, Ayesha. I hope you felt our connection too.

She didn't need this right now.

Despite her resolution to move past Khalid, Ayesha couldn't stop thinking about their confrontation last night, couldn't stop replaying the words she had thrown at him: *You're a coward, a puppet, I don't care about you at all.* He had looked so resigned, as if her words were a confirmation of his own thoughts and not just her anger talking.

Ayesha wasn't sure what she felt for Khalid, but it was definitely not indifference.

She felt just as trapped by tradition and expectations as he did. It would be so easy to dismiss him, with his skullcap and long beard — to put him inside a box labeled "fundy" and ignore the things that didn't fit that role, like his kindness, his strength, his character, or the way he managed to look sexy in a white robe.

Ayesha flushed and took a long sip from her water bottle. Her phone pinged — Masood, again.

I'm confident that my unique life coaching services will enable you to find your Best

Self. When are you free for an initial consult? I'm teaching a preschool mixed martial arts class on Thursday, but otherwise I'm free.

Ayesha smiled and quickly texted him back:

I thought you wanted to talk to me, not take me on as a client.

He responded after a moment:

I'm sorry if I led you on. The truth is, I'm just not that into you. I hope we can be friends?

Ayesha laughed softly. Leave it to Masood to put things in perspective. Heartache and hastily uttered words were nothing in the face of farce. *I choose to live in a comedy.*

Only the very best of friends, she typed. She took a tiny bite of her bagel.

Clara called after school with an impromptu dinner invitation, and Ayesha accepted immediately. It would be good to see her friend and talk about something other than the mosque, Hafsa, and Khalid.

"Bring some nonalcoholic wine, the most

expensive you can find," Clara said.

At home, Ayesha threw on one of Idris's old hoodies and fished the cleanest-looking pair of yoga pants out of the pile in her closet. She had been too busy lately to do laundry. She wrapped a favorite black cotton hijab, the one she wore for quick errands, around her head and kissed Nani good-bye.

"Where are you going?" her grandmother asked. "Why are you wearing that?"

"Clara invited me over for a girls' night. I've been wearing teacher clothes all week and I want to be comfortable."

Ayesha arrived at the condo at seven thirty, and she already felt lighter. This was just what she needed — a night talking with her best friend. Rob was cooking in the kitchen with The Hurtin' Albertans turned way up while Clara tidied.

"Why are you dusting?" Ayesha asked, suddenly suspicious. "You never dust."

"My allergies are acting up," Clara said. She hugged Ayesha and they took a seat on the couch. Ayesha noticed the coffee table had been cleared of the usual magazines, plates, and mugs.

Clara was still dressed in her work clothes, a black skirt and white blouse. She hadn't taken off her makeup either.

"I think I'm underdressed," Ayesha said.

"No, you're fine!" Clara said in a high-pitched voice. "You look really, really . . . great. But you know, if you wanted to put on some makeup, just for fun, I bought a new lip gloss."

"You're acting weird."

"No, I'm not. Do you have a more colorful hijab you can throw on, maybe in the car?"

Ayesha gave her a strange look.

Clara stood up. "Let's open up that faux-wine you brought. Does it need to breathe?" She winked at Ayesha and ran to the kitchen to grab wineglasses.

"So, what's new?" Ayesha called out. "Your boss still a psycho?"

"You know, the usual. Nothing to report. Tell me about this conference you're helping organize."

Ayesha made a face. "I don't want to think about the mosque or my family tonight."

"Sure," Clara said, returning to the room, her eyes roaming around. "What's Hafsa up to?"

"Who cares? You keep telling me to focus on myself. My principal sort of offered me a permanent job in September."

"That's great," Clara said absently. "So, have you seen Khalid anywhere, like maybe at the mosque?"

"Clara, what's going on?"

"Nothing!" Clara said, her voice rising. "I just like to be kept in the loop. What's up with Hafsa?"

Ayesha sighed. Clara was distracted and spacey, like that time she'd smoked pot during frosh week. "I didn't want to bring this up because I know what you're going to say, but I saw Hafsa at the mall with this punk, Haris. I'm pretty sure he's her boyfriend. She's been hanging out with him while she sends me to conference planning meetings at the mosque in her place."

Clara started to laugh. "Your cousin wants to get married this summer and she has a boyfriend on the side? Maybe she's on to something. You should get a boy toy too."

Ayesha scowled. "My life is complicated enough. I told Hafsa she was being childish, and we got into a fight. She told me she wants to be married and rich, not poor and alone like me."

Clara sat down beside Ayesha. "Why do you put up with her?"

Ayesha shook her head. She couldn't explain it. The loyalty she felt for Hafsa was instinctive and unflinching and didn't make a lot of sense. It went back to her first few months in Canada, when Hafsa and her family had been her lifeboat in a new country.

Hafsa had been only three years old when Ayesha's family emigrated from India. During that time, playing with her baby cousin was the only ray of sunshine in her life. Even now, whenever she looked at her cousin, she saw the preschooler who had never left her alone, who had climbed into her lap and wiped away the tears Ayesha cried for her father and everything else she had left behind.

Clara wouldn't understand any of that, and so she changed the subject. "It gets worse. Everyone on the committee thinks I AM Hafsa!"

The doorbell rang, and Clara and Ayesha looked at each other.

"Did you invite someone else?" Ayesha asked, eyes narrowed.

Clara jumped up. "Don't-be-mad-I-invited-Khalid," she said in a rush.

"What?!" Ayesha said. She grabbed her bag. "I'm leaving."

Khalid, dressed in a neatly ironed white robe with jeans underneath, stood with a bouquet of tulips in his hands. His eyes widened at the sight of Ayesha.

"Hafsa?" he said. "What are you doing here?"

"Leaving." Ayesha brushed past him, catching the scent of soap and aftershave.

Clara ran after her, barefoot.

Ayesha jabbed the elevator button. "How could you invite him? What are you trying to do?"

Clara wrung her hands. "I know I should have told you. Please don't be angry. In my defense, I never said it was girls' night." Catching sight of Ayesha's stony expression, she backtracked. "It was wrong to trick you."

"I don't even like him. Why do you keep pushing us together?"

Clara's shoulders slumped, and she wrapped her arms around herself. "I don't know," she admitted. "You've seemed so unhappy lately . . . *I've* been so unhappy lately."

Ayesha's face softened, and she reached out to her friend.

"Rob and I . . . It's been so hard. Maybe I was looking for a distraction."

Ayesha gave her a disbelieving stare. "So you decided to set me up with the only Muslim guy you know?"

"He's not the only Muslim guy I know. There's Amir, and let's not forget the very sexy Mo from Bella's."

Ayesha smiled, and when the elevator arrived, she didn't step into it.

"Khalid is a good guy, and there's something about the two of you together that just feels right. Maybe you'll wind up as friends."

Ayesha looked away from Clara's earnest, open face. "I'm pretty sure he can't stand the sight of me right now."

"Rob made pad Thai," Clara said, wheedling. "He bought halal chicken. Khalid will probably leave before dessert, and then girls' night can begin again. Please."

Ayesha remembered the hurt look on Khalid's face the night before. Maybe there would be time between the faux-wine and pad Thai to apologize. She followed Clara back to the apartment.

Rob and Khalid were sitting on the couch. "Babe, Khalid said sugar dates are a superfood. I'm gonna put them in your morning smoothie," he said.

Khalid looked solemnly at Ayesha. "Assalamu Alaikum," he said. He held her gaze, looking a little shamefaced. She nodded at him.

Clara set the table while Rob brought out the food. Ayesha took a seat across from Khalid, who offered her the noodles first, before serving himself.

"You have a beautiful home," Khalid said

to Rob. "Did you move here directly after your wedding?"

Clara started coughing.

"We're not married," Rob said.

Khalid looked confused. "Clara informed me you have been together since university."

Rob nodded. "There's no need to make it official. It's not like either one of us is religious or anything. It's not a big deal. Right, babe?"

Clara forked pad Thai into her mouth and didn't say anything. Khalid's eyes rested on her.

"Marriage is not confined to a religious institution," he said. "It is a socially accepted symbol of commitment."

Rob laughed. "Clara said you were intense. Listen, man, we don't need it. Clara knows I'm in it for the long haul."

Ayesha took a bite of her noodles. "This is delicious, Rob," she said.

Khalid was not deterred. He speared a large piece of chicken and chewed thoughtfully. "Your presence in a relationship is not indicative of commitment but rather inertia. Standing before your friends and family and pledging your love and loyalty is an essential ingredient for a long-lasting union."

"Nah, man, we don't need it. Besides, I hate weddings."

Clara dropped her fork. "You never told me you hate weddings."

Rob looked at her, surprised. "Sure, I did."

"No. You didn't."

"Babe, I hate all that traditional stuff. Putting on a suit, buying shit from the registry. Everyone is so fake, and half the time the family is fighting like crazy and the couple are dead broke by the end of it. What's the point?" Rob took a big swallow of cola.

Clara jumped up, two red spots of color on her cheeks. "You have never — ever! — said you hated marriage," she said through gritted teeth.

"Whoa, babe. Settle down. I said I hate weddings. Not marriage."

"You need one before you can have the other!"

"Well, I think they're both pretty stupid," Rob said. "You're getting hysterical."

Clara looked as if she were about to explode. Khalid and Ayesha exchanged glances. "We should go," Ayesha said.

"Thank you for the meal. I have never eaten pad Thai with ketchup before," Khalid said.

Rob and Clara didn't notice as they slipped quietly out the door and walked silently, side by side, to the parking lot.

"That's two days now I've met you somewhere and left before finishing dinner," Khalid said. "Are you hungry?"

Ayesha knew he was trying to lighten the mood, but she felt annoyed. Why couldn't he just keep his opinions to himself and gossip about Rob and Clara afterward, like a normal person? "You shouldn't have brought up marriage," she told him. Her stomach rumbled, betraying her.

"There's a convenience store across the lot. I'll be right back." He strode off before Ayesha could say anything else.

She checked her phone. It was eight thirty, and the parking lot was deserted. She sat down on the curb by the condo entrance.

When Khalid returned, he was holding two iced slushies and a box of Twinkies. "Blue watermelon or red raspberry?" he asked her.

Ayesha reached for the raspberry slushie. "Clara and Rob have been together since freshman year," she said. "They met at a kegger during frosh week. Believe me, they don't need to get married. It's permanent."

Khalid unwrapped a Twinkie and took a large bite, sprinkling his beard with golden-yellow crumbs that he brushed away absently. "If it is permanent, they should have married years ago," he said.

"That's their business," Ayesha said.

"From the way Clara reacted, they are avoiding their business. The conversation is clearly overdue. This would never have happened if their parents were involved. Yet another example of the superiority of the arranged marriage process."

Ayesha rolled her eyes. "Not this again."

"They arranged the relationship themselves. There is no harm in letting their parents or their friends arrange the formality of a wedding." Khalid finished the Twinkie and leaned back on his elbows, staring up at the dark sky.

Ayesha looked at his face in profile. A few crumbs still clung to his beard, and she fought the urge to brush them away again. Instead she mirrored his position, leaning back and turning her face up to the dark night. She closed her eyes, feeling surprisingly at ease. "Tell me about your father," she said.

Khalid was quiet at first, then he spoke, his voice soft. "He died suddenly last year, a heart attack. Afterward, I dreamed about him every night for weeks. It was always the same dream. I was in the middle of a forest, somewhere in Algonquin Park. It was fall and the trees were red, yellow, and orange, so bright they looked like they were on fire. He always appeared out of thin air and sat beside me for a few minutes, dressed in his white robe. He never said anything. The imam told me it was my father's soul, visiting me in my sleep."

"I've never dreamed about my father," Ayesha said, wistful, her eyes open now. "He died so long ago, sometimes I can't even remember his face."

Khalid looked at her, and their eyes met.

"Why are you still single?" he asked. His question sounded like an accusation, and Ayesha looked away.

"Probably because I don't know how to cook," she said lightly. "Why do you want an arranged marriage?"

He hesitated. "I'm not sure I do anymore."

Ayesha smiled at him. "Got your eye on someone?"

Khalid was silent, and she took a sip of her slushie. "Do you believe men and women can be friends?" she asked.

"I do not think that men and women should be alone together or spend time with each other. That would be inappropriate."

"You're sitting here with me."

Khalid thought about this. "I probably shouldn't be."

"You can leave any time. Your car is right there."

"I wouldn't want to leave you alone in the dark."

"I'm an independent woman."

Khalid was silent again. "I don't want to leave," he said.

"You're very honest."

"I have been told it's one of my worst qualities." His smile was brief; his teeth shone in the semidarkness.

"I don't have anywhere I need to be right now either," Ayesha said.

They sipped their drinks and shared the box of Twinkies in silence. Sitting under the dim lamps, their bodies angled toward each other, they stared up at the stars together.

CHAPTER TWENTY-ONE

Ayesha mentally listed Khalid's pros and cons.

Con: He was a self-confessed fundy with no fashion sense and a controlling mother, and something was definitely up with his absentee sister.

Pro: He was an excellent cook, and when he wasn't trying too hard, he could be funny. Sometimes even on purpose.

Con: He wanted his mother to pick out his wife.

Pro: He said he wasn't so sure about that anymore.

Con: His beard was probably itchy.

Pro: His lips looked soft; she wondered what it would feel like to kiss him.

Ayesha leaned back against the headrest of her car and gripped the steering wheel. This was not the way things were supposed to happen. *Calm, clear, drama free.* Nothing about Khalid was any of those things. Even thinking about being with him made her heart race and her palms break out in a sweat.

She thought about how comfortable and excited she had felt sitting next to Khalid in the parking lot, the occasional hum of a train leaving the station nearby a buffer from the rest of the world. Their voices low and soft, faces illuminated by a lone street lamp. After they had eaten the last Twinkie and drunk the last of their slushies, they had walked to her car. Even then they'd lingered, not wanting to leave.

"When will I see you again?" he asked, leaning on her car window.

Ayesha smiled up at him. "At the next meeting. We have a conference to plan."

"And when the conference is over?"

"Then we'll see," she said. Their eyes locked and the air around them grew still.

"Inshallah," he said, straightening. God willing.

She felt light-headed even now, remembering the hungry way he had looked at her. She hadn't felt this loose-limbed and powerful since the last time she'd performed her poetry, onstage at Bella's. The night they had first met.

Ayesha parked her car in the driveway, a dreamy smile on her face as she walked up to her porch. Hafsa opened the front door.

"What are you doing here?" Ayesha asked. "Is everything okay?"

Her cousin enveloped her in a hug. "I have a surprise for you!" She led Ayesha into the living room, where the rest of her family was sitting. There was a festive air in the room, and boxes of sweets were being passed around. Sulaiman Mamu embraced Nana, and even her mother was smiling. Idris was videotaping everyone, while Nani sat in the back corner, her face inscrutable.

"What's going on?" Ayesha asked.

Hafsa's face glowed. "I'm so happy."

Samira Aunty came up to them. "Hafsa is engaged!" she said. "The first wedding in the family!"

Ayesha smiled so broadly, her face hurt. She was happy for everyone tonight. "Who's the lucky guy?" she asked.

"It is a good match," Samira Aunty said. "He is twenty-six years old, works in computers, and comes from a well-respected family. You don't know him — his name is Khalid Mirza."

Ayesha stopped breathing.

"Remember that crazy rishta with the two aunties who asked me all those questions?" Hafsa said. She had a smug, satisfied expression on her face. "Her son is Khalid. She called me a few days ago to apologize, and then she talked to Mom and Dad and they really hit it off. When they showed me his picture, I just knew he was the one!"

Ayesha sat down beside Nana. "I don't understand. You've never met him?"

"We'll meet at the engagement party on Sunday. The most important thing is, I'm getting married!"

Ayesha's mother sat down beside her, nibbling on a *chum chum,* a milky dessert dyed bright pink. She leaned over and whispered, "Khalid's family is extremely wealthy. They own land in India, and real estate all over Canada."

Ayesha's head spun. Khalid was rich? He always wore the same three robes, and the car he drove was even older and rustier than her own. She stood up and walked into the kitchen.

Nani followed her. She silently filled a glass with water and handed it to Ayesha. "What did Nana tell you the other day?" she asked her granddaughter.

Ayesha shook her head, eyes filling with tears. "He said a lot of things."

"What he said in the park: There is nothing worse than watching your loved ones suffer. Choose laughter over tears." Nani was grim-faced.

Ayesha tried to laugh, but it turned into a sob. "It's fine. I'm shocked, that's all. I just saw Khalid, and he said . . . and then to come home and find out that he belongs to Hafsa —" Her voice broke, and she buried her face in her hands, shoulders shaking silently.

Nani placed one warm hand on Ayesha's arm but otherwise made no move to comfort her. She waited until Ayesha had stopped shaking and passed her a slightly damp paper towel.

"Khalid does not belong to Hafsa. He does not belong to you either. He belongs to Allah, and Allah is the One who will determine your young man's fate, as well as yours." Nani looked determined, eyes unflinching. "Now you must do a very difficult thing. I know you can do it, because all your life you have done very difficult things. I want you to walk back into that room and congratulate Hafsa. Smile and hug her, as an older sister should."

"I can't," Ayesha whispered.

Nani placed her other hand on Ayesha's arm and gripped her, hard. "*Allah kassam,* I will find out what happened. I promise. Please, do as I say."

Ayesha wiped her eyes and smiled, lips trembling. She tried again, and her smile looked slightly more genuine. She walked back into the living room, ready to greet her family, mask firmly in place.

After Hafsa left the parking lot, Khalid stood staring after her car for a few moments, his heart light. He felt such an unfamiliar joy. He walked to where his car was parked, at the back of the lot, and pulled out the woven prayer rug that he kept in the trunk. Laying it flat on the grass beside the curb, he prayed two *rakats,* or units, of prayer. He felt the need to mark this moment. He needed to turn his face toward his Creator and give thanks for his life, and for the serendipitous series of events that had led him to Hafsa.

It was close to ten o'clock when Khalid pulled into the driveway of his house, and he cut the engine. He sat in the dark and relished the tiny ember of happiness in his chest.

Khalid had ignored the part of his life that others filled with relationships, biding his time until marriage to experience love, companionship, and the other perks of coupled life. In the meantime, work and the mosque helped to distract him from his single existence.

Now Khalid considered an alternate possibility. He pictured Hafsa once more. Sitting beside him in the parking lot, her dark eyes shining in the dim evening, the gentle and sometimes not-so-gentle way she teased him. The way her voice had softened the longer they talked, so he had to move even closer to her. Her black hijab had been coming loose on one side and he wondered what her hair looked like, whether it was long and flowing and softly scented like the rest of her. She smelled like jasmine and coconut. The urge to touch her had made him dizzy.

Khalid had never felt this way about anyone else. This tumbling, this lightening, this easing. Was this what it felt like to fall in love? It was so different than what he had expected. For the first time in his life, he could imagine what it must feel like to be drunk and completely unbalanced.

All the lights were on when he opened the front door and Farzana was waiting for him in the living room, along with Aliyah Aunty and a few other women he didn't recognize. His mother welcomed him, beaming, and he grinned back, pleased she looked so happy.

"Khalid, where have you been? I have glorious news!"

"I had dinner with a friend. Actually, I

have some news too."

Farzana waved his words away. "I found you the perfect wife. You're engaged to be married!"

Khalid was blinded by a flash of light. Aliyah Aunty grinned behind her cell phone. "Posted to Facebook," she said. "Congratulations, Farzana!"

"What?" he asked, staring stupidly, but his mother was surrounded by her friends, who crowded around with words of congratulations and suggestions for banquet halls and jewelers.

"*Mubarak.* I know you and Hafsa will be very happy," Aliyah Aunty said beside him.

Khalid's heart, which felt like it had stopped beating, began to thud in his chest. "What?" he repeated.

"Your Ammi and I went to see her a few weeks ago. Didn't you know? Maybe Farzana wanted to surprise you."

"I'm surprised," Khalid said. He felt behind him for the sofa and sat down.

"Their home is so beautiful. Farzana was a little concerned that Hafsa was too old for you, but I told her it would be a good match."

Khalid tried smiling. "I'm engaged to Hafsa," he said out loud, and the words sounded so sweet in his ears that he said it again. "I'm engaged to Hafsa!"

Farzana came up to them. "The engagement party will be Sunday," she told Khalid. "You will meet her for the first time then."

Khalid didn't tell his mother he had already met his future wife, or that he had come home tonight to tell her that he didn't want to be with anyone else. "Yes, Ammi," he said instead. His heart felt too big for his chest.

Farzana patted her son on the arm. "You are all I have left in this world, my most precious possession. I have chosen a bride who will make us both very happy." Farzana's eyes filled with tears and her lips trembled. Khalid embraced her, and Aliyah Aunty snapped another picture. "I promise you will be happy, *Allah kassam*," Farzana said. "As long as you listen to me. I know what is best for you."

CHAPTER TWENTY-TWO

Khalid should have been miserable at work, but instead he couldn't stop smiling. Even though Sheila had effectively demoted him from e-commerce manager to website developer, the sort of job performed by new graduates, he was too happy to feel the sting of humiliation. He had spent all week inputting data, and the only thing left was layout design. He was leaning toward brown and mustard yellow for the colors of the website, with a black background. Hafsa said black was classy.

The thought of Hafsa made him grin. His fiancée, Hafsa, thought black was classy. His fiancée, Hafsa, had excellent taste.

Clara spotted Khalid as he sat on the front steps of the Livetech building during the lunch hour and walked over. She asked him how work was going.

"Nothing has changed. I'm still designing a website for WomenFirst Design and Sheila still hates me," he said with a smile.

Clara sat down beside Khalid, tucking her knees under her. "Sheila hates everyone. She makes her assistant cry daily. Yesterday she fired three people in accounting because she was mad at her hairstylist. But she won't fire you. I'm not sure what you did, but your new lingerie clients love you."

"It is a mystery," Khalid said. "Let me ask you something. Do you think yellow and brown are ugly colors for a website?"

"Yes."

"What about orange and green?" Khalid said. "Purple and yellow?"

Clara winced. "Listen, I want to apologize for dinner last night. I'm so embarrassed."

"There is no need. How are you and Rob?"

"I don't know. I'm afraid Rob doesn't even know why I'm pissed." Clara's laughter was hollow. "Your arranged marriage idea is starting to sound really sensible. At least both parties know where they're headed."

"The Prophet Muhammad's wife Khadijah proposed to him," Khalid said. "She was fifteen years older, a rich widow, and they were happily married for decades. I think he liked her confidence." Khalid smiled again, eyes dreamy. Clara blinked at him.

"Have you talked to your friend today?"

Khalid asked her, and Clara shook her head. "Maybe you should call her," Khalid said. "Maybe she has news she is waiting to tell you."

Clara's cell phone pinged with another angry e-mail from Sheila and she rose, reluctantly, and took her leave.

Khalid's excitement made it hard for him to concentrate when he returned to his desk. He decided to write Zareena a quick e-mail:

Salams. I didn't want you to hear this from anyone else. I'm engaged! To that girl I was telling you about, Hafsa Shamsi! Ammi arranged the whole thing, without even knowing how I felt. You were right, Z, I do like her. A lot. The way things worked out, I know it was meant to be. I'm really happy. I'm even happier because Ammi arranged the entire thing!

Life is good. God is great. *Allahu Akbar!*

Khalid settled in to work, checking e-mails and fiddling with the website. Maybe lime green and electric orange? His cell phone beeped.

K,

Congrats! I didn't tell you before, but I heard Ammi was on the prowl for a docile little wifey for you. In fact, the aunties in my neighborhood asked for your picture to post on their rishta database. I gave them one from your third birthday party. You're naked and stuffing chocolate cake in your mouth. Iqram didn't think it was a good idea, but I thought the picture really captured your eyes.

Khalid's eye caught on the unfamiliar name — *Iqram?* That was the name of his sister's husband. Zareena never referred to him in her e-mails. He continued reading.

Also, I looked up Hafsa on Facebook. She doesn't really seem like your type, but what do I know? The last time I saw you, you were a sad, awkward fourteen-year-old boy who didn't talk to women. I'm sure you're completely different now.

— Z

P. S. Drivers who signal when they want to make a lane change.

P. P. S. You might not hear from me for

the next few days. I'm going on a trip. I promise I'll be in touch soon.

Khalid read the letter again, his eyes lingering on the name Iqram. Maybe this was a good sign. He looked around the office, noticing the quiet for the first time. Amir was sitting at his desk, staring intently at his monitor.

"I have some news for you," Khalid said, walking up behind Amir's desk. "Are you free Sunday?"

"Are we going to Bella's again? I knew you'd love it!"

"No, I'm inviting you to my . . ." Khalid's voice trailed off as he looked at Amir's computer. "What are you doing?" he asked, horrified.

There was a picture of a fully veiled Muslim woman looking coyly out from the screen. Beside her stood a woman in a translucent string bikini.

"I wanted to show you this amazing website. It's called unveiledhotties.com and all the women on it are Muslim. The whole site is full of women who wear hijab in real life, and if you click a button, you can see what they look like with their hijabs off. Some take off even more, if you're interested. But it's totally halal," Amir hurried to

274

assure Khalid. "If you like what you see, you can e-mail the administrator of the website and ask for the girl's hand in marriage."

Amir scrolled to a pretty woman wearing an innocent expression and a pink hijab. He clicked on it and all of a sudden the woman was looking lasciviously at the camera, one hand cupping a voluptuous naked breast. Khalid closed his eyes and turned away.

"This is completely inappropriate, especially at work. You could get fired for this!" Khalid said.

"It's not for me," Amir said, sounding wounded. "I get enough action. I was thinking about you. You know what Prophet Muhammad said: 'You're not truly a Muslim until you want for your brother what you want for yourself.' "

"I'm pretty sure the Prophet did not mean pornography!"

"It's not porn. It's a matrimonial service. I know how hung up you are on all that no-dating, marriage-only stuff."

The reminder of marriage put a smile back on Khalid's face. "Actually, that's what I wanted to tell you. I'm engaged! My mom picked out the perfect person for me. Remember Clara's friend from Bella's?"

"Mo said that chick was frigid."

Khalid gave Amir a warning look. "The engagement is Sunday. I'd like you to be there."

Amir closed the window on the website and looked at his friend. "Are you for real? I can't believe you did it — you actually got an arranged marriage. *Mubarak* and congrats! But I still think you should have a backup plan, in case things don't work out."

Usually this type of conversation would irritate Khalid, but nothing could dampen his good spirits today. In his own way, Amir was trying to be nice.

Khalid settled down to work on the WomenFirst webpage, but his thoughts continually drifted to Hafsa. He wondered what she was doing now. Maybe she was thinking about him and their life together too.

CHAPTER TWENTY-THREE

Nana sat at the kitchen table reading the newspaper while Nani loaded the dishwasher. It was nine in the morning and they were alone in the house. Ayesha and Idris were already gone for the day, and Saleha had not yet returned from her night shift at the hospital.

The only sound in the kitchen was the rustle of the newspaper. Nani, deep in thought, looked at her husband. "Nasir, I must go to the mosque," she said.

"The bus runs every fifteen minutes, Laik," Nana said. He peeked over the paper, eyes twinkling at his wife of more than fifty years.

"Hafsa's engagement was too quick," she said, ignoring her husband. He loved to tease her and it was no use encouraging him.

" 'Better three hours too soon than a minute too late,' " Nana quoted.

Nani paused in her cleanup. "Nasir, are you listening to me? Something is not right about this situation. I feel it in my knees. I was there when Farzana first saw Hafsa. She showed no interest in her at all."

Nana sipped his chai, his face unconcerned. "You didn't want Saleha to marry Syed because they'd known each other for too long. Now you don't want your granddaughter to marry this boy Khalid because she hasn't known him for long enough. If Hafsa is happy with her arrangement, who are we to interfere?"

Nani shook her head. She remembered Farzana's strange rishta visit, her deep antipathy to Ayesha. Farzana and her friend Aliyah had leveled a barrage of nosy questions at Hafsa and then left the house after only thirty minutes. Their rude dismissal of her granddaughters had left Nani in a foul temper for days afterward. She had no idea how such an engagement could possibly have come about — and so suddenly, with no word of warning to her or Nasir!

For the engagement to take place so soon after that strange cooking lesson was enough to raise her suspicions. Khalid and Ayesha had not stopped staring at each other while they rolled out their parathas; it was clear they were quietly falling in love. Had Farzana clued in and decided to do something about it?

She did not know Farzana well, as she was new to the neighborhood and to the mosque community. But from their brief interaction during the rishta visit, Laik had formed a clear picture of the woman's character. If Farzana suspected her only son was in danger of finding his own wife, she would consider it an attack on the very soul of her family traditions.

It was all so worrying. Yet Nasir continued to sit at the kitchen table and drink his chai and read his newspaper as if the fates of their grandchildren were not at stake.

"The seniors' social circle meets at the mosque in an hour. I must speak with Sister Joanne. Hurry up, jaan," Nani said to Nana. Sister Jo was on the executive board, and she volunteered at the mosque almost every day. If anyone knew what was going on, it would be her.

Nana stood and neatly folded his paper. "Laikunissa Begum," he said, calling his wife by her full name. "What are you up to?"

"I made a promise to Ayesha to get to the bottom of Hafsa's engagement, and I intend to keep it," Nani said in the determined tone her husband knew so well. He swallowed the dregs of his tea and went to change.

The seniors' social circle was a weekly meeting of all the older aunties and uncles in the neighborhood. Today the men were gathered in the cafeteria while a small group of women attended yoga class in the gym. Nani nodded at the women as she made her way through the group. Her friend Maryam signaled to her and made room on her purple yoga mat.

"Have you heard of yoga?" Maryam said. "It's the latest thing, Laik. So good for posture and breathing." Maryam was a cheerful woman from Sudan in her early sixties, the matriarch of a large family. She was usually busy babysitting her grandchildren; Nani had not seen her in months.

"I think I may have heard about this yoga," Nani said. "Is Sister Jo here today?"

"She's our teacher. She's running late, but this will give us a chance to catch up."

Nani settled next to her friend, and they chatted about their grandchildren. Maryam was halfway through a long-winded anecdote about her youngest grandson when Sister Jo walked into the gymnasium, unbuckling a bicycle helmet and apologizing profusely. She was a long-faced white woman in her late fifties, dressed today in a tailored white hijab tied close to her face, a white turtleneck with long sleeves, its hem brushing her knees, and black yoga pants. After a quick greeting, the class began.

Nani followed along as best she could, moving stiffly from child pose to warrior stance. "I hear Sister Farzana is on the mosque executive board now," she whispered to Maryam when they stretched into cat pose.

Maryam wrinkled her nose. "I don't like that woman. So bossy and old-fashioned. She told me I should wear a black abaya and slippers when I come to the mosque. What is wrong with track pants and Nike shoes?"

Nani nodded in sympathy. "I hear she has only one son."

Maryam clucked. "Yes, poor thing. That's the problem. She doesn't have anything else to occupy her time. No job, her husband died last year, and her daughter lives somewhere else."

"What is her son like?"

Maryam shrugged. "Rasool sees him at prayers." Rasool was Maryam's husband. "Khalid is quiet but close to the imam. I think he is helping with that conference."

They were in boat pose now, and Maryam leaned close to Nani. "Farzana was boasting to me only last week that her son would marry a girl of her choosing." She giggled. "When I tried to introduce my children to suitable spouses, they laughed in my face. They are all married now. Children must be allowed to lead their own lives, Laik."

After the class, Nani approached Joanne, who was rolling up her yoga mat.

"Sister Laik, I know that look on your face," Sister Jo said, smiling. "What are you up to?"

"You sound like Nasir," Nani grumbled. "What do you think of Farzana?"

Sister Jo's smile dimmed slightly. "I don't really know her. She invited me to her house for an impromptu party. I think she is trying to make friends and find her place."

Nani kept her tone casual. "Was there any particular reason for the party?"

Sister Jo looked uncomfortable and reached down to pick up her bicycle helmet, fiddling with the chin strap. "I don't like to gossip, Laik, but it was very strange. I thought it was just a dinner party, and I brought chickpea salad. When I arrived, all the women were dressed up in fancy outfits and putting henna on their hands. Around ten, her son, Khalid, came home." She paused, uncertain how to continue. "I found out the party was actually Khalid's engagement celebration."

Nani nodded, thinking. "Was Khalid happy?"

Sister Jo shifted her weight to her other leg. "He seemed shocked by the news. I don't think he knew about it at all. I must admit, his reaction concerned me. When my daughter asked us to help her look for a husband two years ago, I made sure she was comfortable with every introduction we arranged. After all, she was the one getting married, not me." Sister Jo lowered her eyes, thinking. "Every family is different, of course."

Nani remained silent at this diplomatic answer. "Did Khalid know who he was engaged to?"

Sister Jo shook her head. "Not at first, but Aliyah told him. I was so relieved to see him smiling. It makes me so happy to see the young people in our community settling down. I hope they will bring their children to the mosque one day."

"*Inshallah*. Love is a powerful force," Nani said.

Sister Jo reached down for her bag, and when she straightened up, her troubled expression was replaced with a smile. "Hafsa is your son Sulaiman's daughter! Now your questions make sense. Brother Khalid is a kind and respectful young man." She hesitated, choosing her words. "I would only be concerned about Sister Farzana. Some of the other women at the mosque are uncomfortable with her conservative beliefs." Jo fixed the bike helmet to her head and smiled wryly. "At the party, Farzana held a *halaqa* study circle just before dinner. She talked about the importance of modesty. She made sure to mention that a pious Muslim woman should never ride a bicycle, as it draws too much attention to her legs." Sister Jo sighed, her amusement replaced by worry. "Such rigid thinking has no place in our community, Laik."

On the car ride home Nana asked, "How is your investigation progressing? Have you found a suspect yet?"

Nani shifted irritably. "Make fun if you like. Ayesha is heartbroken, and I fear Hafsa has made a mistake."

"Jaan, sometimes it is better to let things work out on their own."

Nani's eyes softened as she looked at his lined, well-loved face. "Of course, Nasir," she answered. "You are so right."

Nana smiled. He knew that it was not in his wife's nature to let matters rest, not until she was satisfied. "Laik, why did you not join the RCMP? They always get their man."

Because this time I am after a woman. Laik closed her eyes and organized her thoughts.

After lunch, Nani told Nana she was going for a walk, and she left before he could offer to accompany her. She brought the cane she kept to nudge objects off the top shelf in the kitchen and set off in the direction of the park.

She slowed in front of a large house with a double-car garage and looked around; the coast was clear. Leaning heavily on her cane, she dragged her foot painfully, her face screwed up in feigned agony. She shuffled to the front of the house and rang the doorbell.

A few moments passed before the door opened. A woman in her early fifties, wearing an ugly orange cotton shalwar kameez, opened the door. She had a bright-purple scarf wrapped around her head, which clashed painfully with her clothes.

"Assalamu Alaikum, Farzana," Nani said, making her voice sound old and querulous. "I am Hafsa's Nani. Samira told us the good news about the engagement yesterday and I decided to visit you. I'm afraid the walk was too much for me." She tried her best to look weak and helpless, and Farzana, after a moment's hesitation, led Nani

285

into the family room and offered her water or tea.

Nani requested tea because it would take longer to prepare. She was instantly on her feet and poking around when Farzana retreated to the kitchen to boil water.

The room looked as if it had been decorated by a toddler obsessed with primary colors — bright-blue curtains, a vibrant green carpet, and a yellow blanket on the brown leather couch. There were no pictures on the walls, and the TV looked as if it was not used much; a stack of newspapers was piled in front of it.

Farzana returned with a small cup of tea, and Nani noted the absence of the usual cookies or snacks. She clearly wanted to give her no reason to dawdle.

"You have a lovely house," Nani said, trying to sound breathless. She took a sip of the tea — it was weak and lukewarm. "Delicious chai," she lied.

Farzana smiled at Nani, but her eyes weren't friendly. "I'm surprised Samira didn't accompany you. We need to finalize the guest list for the engagement party."

Nani ignored her. "This is quite a large house for only you and your son. I heard your daughter lives in India. Does she visit often? I hope she will join us for the engagement on Sunday."

Farzana flinched at the mention of her daughter. "Zareena is quite busy. I doubt she will be able to make it back for the ceremony. A girl belongs to her husband's family after she marries. I'm sure you agree."

Nani watched Farzana over the rim of her cup. Underneath her words and bluster, Farzana was clearly afraid. She masked it with anger, but the fear was just below the surface, and Nani pitied her for it.

"Every family has its own problems," Nani said mildly. "I'm sure the issues with your daughter will resolve with time."

Farzana gripped the arm of her chair and attempted to smile again. "There is no problem. Why would you say that?"

"Hafsa is very young," Nani said, ignoring the question. "She has been sheltered from many things. I hope Khalid will make her happy."

Farzana shook her head. "Your grand-daughter comes from a good family, and girls should be married young, otherwise they become stubborn and set in their ways."

Nani put her cup down. "You remind me of my sister-in-law. She has eight children who live all over the world, but she is very lonely. None of her children visit much. She was too controlling when they were younger and didn't let them make their own decisions when they grew."

Farzana bristled. "Khalid is a good boy. He will do as I say."

Nani leaned forward. "But will he forgive you?"

Farzana froze. "What do you mean?"

"You know that Ayesha and Hafsa are two different people. Your son trusts you to do the right thing. How will he feel when he discovers that you purposely arranged his marriage to the wrong Hafsa?" Nani had no proof that Farzana knew about the identity mix-up and nothing but her intuition guiding her. She only hoped that she was wrong.

"Ayesha is too old for him. She is not suitable!" Farzana stood up, eyes bright with anger. "She is fatherless, and she does not know how to speak to her elders. My son deserves better."

Nani felt a deep well of sadness open inside her. So it was true: This blustering, angry woman had arranged the marriage of her only son to a woman he didn't know, instead of allowing him to follow his heart.

She put a hand on the armchair and made a big show of slowly standing up, her arms shaking for added emphasis. Farzana sighed

288

and leaned over to help; Nani grabbed her hand in a viselike grip. "Ayesha is the best person I know," she said to Farzana, her voice cold and resolute. "Khalid would be lucky to marry her."

A look of alarm crossed Farzana's face. "What will you do?" she asked.

Nani stood up straight, all trace of the frail old woman gone now, and Farzana shrunk under her gaze.

"Aunty, will you tell my Khalid? Will you tell Ayesha?" Farzana asked again.

"No," Nani said. She walked to the door and slipped on her shoes. "I did not come here to threaten or blackmail, only to warn you. Your plan will not work. Please do the right thing. Break off Khalid's engagement to the wrong Hafsa. Let your son go, before you lose him forever."

Nani walked back to her house, shaken. She was reasonably certain Farzana would not listen to her advice, but she wanted to give her a chance anyway. Everyone was capable of change, though she doubted Farzana would take the opportunity.

Nana was right — she must let events run their course. Things would work out on their own. *Inshallah.*

CHAPTER TWENTY-FOUR

Ayesha was grateful for the superhero movie the ninth-grade math teacher had left for her class. She was distracted, and could not stop running through the events of last night: Hafsa's happiness, the giddy smiles on her aunt's and uncle's faces . . .

Her own crushing pain.

Nani would know what to do. Her grandparents had never let her down before. Her grandmother would make her inquiries and find out what was really going on. Perhaps there had been a mistake. Perhaps Hafsa's fiancé wasn't Khalid after all. He would still be single and everything could go back to normal.

Whatever her "normal" turned out to be.

Nani waited for Ayesha after school in the basement suite she shared with Nana. It was small and poorly lit, with thin beige carpet and faux-oak-paneled walls. There was a small bedroom behind a larger living room area, and a tiny bathroom with a standing shower. Despite the dim lighting and cramped dimensions, the space felt warm and inviting, the furniture outdated but comfortable. The walls of the living room were lined with Ikea bookshelves bought second-hand and filled with Nana's new collection, carefully built up since his move to the country seventeen years ago.

When her granddaughter appeared at the bottom of the stairs, Nani motioned for her to take a seat on the large floral-cushioned rattan sofa. Ayesha was pale, with shadows under her eyes. Nana sat on his usual armchair, reading a biography of Shakespeare.

"Did you find out anything? Did you talk to anyone, to his mother or Khalid or —" Ayesha's voice broke, and Nani looked at Nana, who quietly left the room.

Nani stroked Ayesha's hair, just as she used to do when Ayesha was a child missing her father. "I spoke to some people about Farzana, and then I spoke to Farzana herself."

"Was it all a misunderstanding? Has there been some mistake?" Ayesha looked at her grandmother with eyes filled with hope, and Nani's heart contracted.

She shook her head. "No, jaanu, there was no mistake. Khalid is engaged to our Hafsa."

Ayesha took a shaky breath. "Was he using me?"

"I don't know," Nani said. She wiped the tears leaking from Ayesha's eyes. "You have always been so capable and strong, even as a child. This is painful news and there is no clear solution. For my part, I think you should follow your heart."

"What does that mean?" Ayesha's voice was a whisper.

Nani looked down at her hands. "It is difficult to know what to do, and I cannot help you decide," she said, hating herself. "I am sorry."

Nana tiptoed into the living room after Ayesha left. He settled down with his book, glancing surreptitiously at his wife. "I hope you know what you are doing, Laik," he said.

Nani was lost in thought. "This morning you said I didn't want Saleha to marry Syed because they'd known each other for too long. That's not the reason why."

Nana said nothing, only turned a page of his book.

"It wasn't because he wanted to be a journalist, or because he was poor," Nani continued.

"It was so long ago. What is meant to be has already happened," Nana said.

"I knew they weren't right for each other from the beginning. Saleha loved him too much. Syed loved her as well, but not as she loved him."

"What does that have to do with Ayesha? She was crying when she left. I saw her tears."

Nani stood, her shoulders set back. "Nasir, you were right. We must let the young people sort things out on their own. If I say anything about what I have learned, I will be stepping between Sulaiman and Saleha, between Ayesha and Hafsa, and no good can come of that. Also, Ayesha needs to be sure of her feelings for Khalid, and this will help her decide. I know Khalid has already made his decision about her. I saw it on his face clearly, when they cooked together. Farzana's wishes are already irrelevant. Nothing will change his mind now."

" 'Love sought is good, but given unsought better,' " Nana quoted. "What if you are wrong?"

Nani didn't answer. She was confident, but she also knew that nothing was certain. Right now, all she had was faith.

■ ■ ■ ■

FOLLOW your heart. Ayesha expected that sort of romantic drivel from Nana, not her sensible Nani. She wiped her eyes, but the tears kept falling.

She had spent so long fighting against what she felt for Khalid. Now that it was too late, she could finally admit it: She liked Khalid. A lot. She'd thought he liked her too . . . but clearly not enough to defy his mother.

Follow your heart.

Ayesha looked out the upstairs living room window at the neighborhood children playing basketball and skipping rope, blissfully unaware of the drama unfolding a few houses away. She grabbed her purse and car keys.

Five minutes later, she rang the doorbell of the Taj Mahal. Hafsa answered with a big smile.

"I was just thinking about you! Come help me pick out my engagement dress. I have it narrowed down to a long red shalwar kameez with gold embroidery and mirror work, or a white *lengha* skirt with lace and beadwork on the tunic. I'm getting a dress for you too — in pink!" Hafsa's cheeks were

294

rosy, her eyes shining with the excitement of a big purchase.

Ayesha didn't move, and Hafsa's face filled with concern. "What's wrong?"

"Why are you marrying Khalid?" Ayesha asked.

Hafsa's eyes darted away from her cousin's face and back. "I . . . He sent me a rishta and I accepted. Why, what did you hear?" Her cheeks flushed an even deeper red.

"You don't even know him. Why are you doing this? What about Haris?" Ayesha stepped into the house, one foot in front of the other. Blood was thumping in her veins so loudly she could hardly hear her cousin's answer.

Hafsa lifted her hand as if waving away her cousin's objections. "Happiness in marriage is a matter of chance. The less you know about the person, the better. What really matters is family and money."

"You can't believe that," Ayesha said.

Hafsa tossed her head. "Khalid will do whatever his mom tells him, and Farzana Aunty and I understand each other. We both get something out of this arrangement. As for Haris, I'll get rid of him after the wedding."

Ayesha stared at her cousin. "That's disgusting."

Hafsa's lip trembled. "This is hard for me too. Everything comes so easy for you, Ashi Apa. You've always done well at school, you have your poems, and you have Clara. Everyone looks up to you. Meanwhile, I'm just spoiled, silly Hafsa, who can't decide what she wants to study at community college. The family screwup. Sometimes I think my dad likes you better than me."

Ayesha knew Hafsa was being manipulative, but still she wavered. "That's not true."

A single tear streaked down her cousin's smooth porcelain cheek. "I just want to make my parents happy. Dad is thrilled with the engagement, and Mom is so happy to see me settled. They've both done so much for me. I owe them this. You understand — you owe them too."

Ayesha was silent. *You owe them too.* If it hadn't been for Sulaiman Mamu, she wouldn't be here right now. She would be in India, along with her mother, Idris, Nana, and Nani. She owed her uncle for the very life she led. He had rescued her family, had gifted them with the house they lived in, had taken Ayesha into his confidence and told her his worries for Hafsa. She had promised him she would keep an eye on her young cousin.

It was meant to be Hafsa all along, she realized with a jolt. Hafsa was supposed to be at all those planning meetings. Hafsa was supposed to meet Khalid and fall for him. Not her. Ayesha had been the placeholder, the understudy who had passed herself off as someone else because she was tired of being the boring, reliable saint.

It was time to gracefully exit the stage and let the real star shine.

"Are you sure this is what you want?" she asked carefully. "Are you sure Khalid is the one?"

Hafsa looked at her. "I've never been more sure of anything in my life."

"I'm going to kick her skinny ass. That bitch!" Clara stared at her friend in shock.

Ayesha's face was puffy from crying. She had driven directly to Clara's house after her confrontation with Hafsa.

Ayesha shook her head. Khalid was wrong for her. They didn't want the same things. A shared love of Twinkies and parathas was no basis for a long-lasting relationship.

The words were starting to sound convincing. Maybe if she said them out loud, she would actually believe them. "It would never work between us," she said.

"That doesn't mean you should give him to your cousin without a fight!" Clara grabbed Ayesha's phone and waved it in her face. "Text him. Call him. Ask what's going on."

"And should I tell him that it's Hafsa or Ayesha on the line?" She covered her face with her hands, voice muffled. "I can't believe I've been so stupid." Tears leaked down the sides of her face, pooling beneath her palms.

Clara gently lifted her friend's hands and looked at her seriously. "Don't call my best friend stupid. She's the smartest girl I know," she said. "Text him. This is Khalid we're talking about. He'll understand."

Ayesha wiped her eyes and sat up. "No, he won't. He hates anything deceitful. He won't even wear a regular shirt because he doesn't want to hide his identity. There were so many times I could have told him who I really was. Maybe I knew he wanted someone like Hafsa all along, not me." She shook her head. "Besides, my uncle has given me so much. I can give him this one small thing."

Clara threw up her hands in frustration. "What is wrong with you? Hafsa only wants him for his money. What about what Khalid wants? He likes you. I saw you two sitting outside my house last night."

Ayesha wiped her face. "He told me he

298

wanted an arranged marriage, and his mother has made her choice. Farzana probably showed Khalid a picture of Hafsa and he forgot all about me. It's done. I'll get over him."

"You're making a mistake," Clara said. "When I met Rob, I wasn't looking for anything either. I was only eighteen! But I knew, after only a few days, that this was it. When I saw you with Khalid, it was the same thing. You just fit. I'm not sure why, but it works."

Ayesha turned her head away and bit down on her lip. She had cried during the entire drive to Clara's house, and now her head felt swollen, her ears full of cotton.

Clara sensed her advantage and pressed. "Just text him. You'll always regret it if you don't."

That night as Ayesha lay in bed surrounded by sodden tissues, her purple notebook flung to the floor, she took out her cell phone and sent Khalid a single question:

Are you happy?

Khalid responded an instant later:

I am getting exactly what I wanted. I have never been happier.

CHAPTER TWENTY-FIVE

Ayesha had already set up two dozen folding chairs in the Taj Mahal for the engagement ceremony. Now she held two colorful silk saris in her arms, with instructions from Samira Aunty to "hang them on the wall like streamers, jaanu," before the guests arrived to witness the engagement of (the real) Hafsa and Khalid.

Ayesha was dressed in a hot-pink shalwar kameez covered in gold embroidery, her ornate dupatta shawl a leaden weight on her shoulder. The outfit was uncomfortable and itchy, but Hafsa had insisted that her sisters and cousin dress the same. Hafsa had settled on the white *lengha* dress, which was decorated with so much lace and beadwork that it weighed close to ten pounds. It had also cost $2,000, and had the label of a famous designer.

Sulaiman Mamu walked past Ayesha, his stomach straining against a too-tight white sherwani, a traditional shalwar kameez that resembled a long suit jacket. He was adjusting a stiff brown felt prayer hat on his head.

"Have the caterers arrived yet?" he asked Samira Aunty, who was taking out plates and cutlery from the hutch. "They're late. I told you to order from Kamran Khan."

Her uncle wandered back into the living room and gave Ayesha a wan smile. "I hope this makes Hafsa happy," he remarked, looking vaguely at the golden balloon arc and paper lanterns.

"I'm sure it will be fine," Ayesha assured him.

Her uncle wiped his forehead with a handkerchief. "Thank you for helping set up. Everyone has been so busy with shopping and buying things. The expenses . . ." He trailed off, looking worried.

Ayesha reassured him that everything was under control and that Hafsa was ecstatic. Her cousin was a bubbly ball of energy, delighting in every detail and crowing about all the money her engagement had cost, according to her mother and Idris.

In contrast, Ayesha had spent the days following Hafsa's engagement alternately crying and writing bad poetry until, disgusted with her swollen-eyed self, she had arrived at the house early this morning to run errands and generally be helpful.

It was nobody's fault that Khalid had chosen the real Hafsa instead of the real Ayesha. He had been upfront about his plans to marry the woman his mother chose, just as she had been honest about her disinterest in marriage. This overblown reaction was simple . . . disappointment. Misplaced, ill-advised disappointment. Khalid said he was happy. And once Khalid officially became engaged to Hafsa, Ayesha could continue with her plan to teach high school, write poetry, and die alone.

What about the way he looked at you? What about the pull between you? What about that night you looked up at the stars together, outside Clara's condo?

Ayesha pushed these unhelpful thoughts away. Hafsa was the princess, and princesses always got their happily-ever-afters. Ayesha was the one left wearing the itchy, uncomfortable dress and running last-minute errands, watching as everyone around her got exactly what they wanted.

Except I am *getting what I wanted,* she thought as she unraveled six yards of silk sari and held it up against the wall. *I wanted nothing. And in a few short hours, all my dreams will come true.*

Ayesha lifted the sari up to the corner of

the wall behind the dining table, as high as she could reach. She was looking around for a stool when an arm reached above her to grasp one end of the sari.

Ayesha looked up into Khalid's face. She dropped the sari.

"What are you doing here?"

He was dressed in a dark blue robe and white kufi, a red cotton scarf hanging from his neck. He looked so handsome with his curly black hair and soft brown eyes framed by thick lashes, a serious expression on his face. She looked away, biting her lip.

All Hafsa's. He belongs to her now.

"I didn't think your family would make you decorate by yourself, not today." He looked at her pink shalwar, his eyes traveling up to her face. "You are so beautiful."

Ayesha started, her eyes wide. "What?"

Khalid dropped his half of the sari and stepped closer. Ayesha could feel the heat from his body, smell the subtle cologne. She closed her eyes and inhaled deeply.

"I got you an engagement gift." He pressed a clumsily wrapped package into her numb hands, and his fingers deliberately brushed against her palm.

Ayesha ripped open the wrapping and her hands caressed a notebook bound in supple blue leather. It was the sort of notebook she'd always pictured carrying, perfect for writing poetry but too expensive and impractical. The sort of notebook nobody else had ever thought to buy for her.

When she looked up, his expression was full of want.

"Open the book," he commanded softly, moving closer until his scarf brushed against her arm.

She lifted the front cover, reading the inscription in Khalid's precise handwriting:

When I think of you, I see my future.

"It's for your poetry," he explained with a smile. "I like to imagine you writing in a notebook I gave you." He looked at her intently. "I hope that's not too corny."

Ayesha didn't know where to look. *He doesn't know,* she thought wildly. *He still thinks I'm Hafsa.* Joy wrestled with rising panic. Joy that he still wanted her, plain Ayesha, and not beautiful Hafsa. Panic at his disappointment when he learned the truth. She wouldn't be able to stand watching the affection and longing drain from his eyes when his real fiancée walked into the room dressed in white.

She looked around, hoping for Idris or Nana or even Hafsa to wander by and save her, but they were all alone.

"I never believed in love before marriage. At least, I didn't until I met you," Khalid continued. "I am so happy Ammi picked you to be my wife. I will try very hard to be a good husband." His breath was warm and sweet on her cheek, and his thumb rubbed the silky material of her sleeve slowly, back and forth.

Ayesha felt a rising nausea in her stomach. She scrambled back, and his eyes, heavy-lidded, widened slightly in confusion.

She had to tell him, right now.

"Khalid, I'm not . . . My name isn't . . . This is all a big misunderstanding . . ." she began.

Farzana strode over to them. "What are you doing here?" she asked her son. She looked at Ayesha, and her face shifted, from fear to determination. "Why are you standing here talking to Hafsa's cousin?" she said.

Khalid recoiled as if slapped. "This is Hafsa. My fiancée."

Farzana shook her head. "This is Ayesha. Hafsa's much older, unmarried cousin. Hafsa is much prettier than her, with lighter-colored skin too."

Khalid's eyes snapped back to Ayesha and they stared at each other for a long moment before he dropped his gaze. Ayesha said nothing, her helplessness making her fists open and close. She heard the clock tick slowly, but her eyes were riveted to his face. *Please don't hate me.* The words remained locked in her throat.

She watched him struggle to maintain his composure, jaw clenching. She took a step toward him, but he moved back, his body rigid with the effort of keeping silent. When he looked up again, his eyes were blank.

"Ayesha," he said. It was a cold, impartial statement.

She didn't say anything, and he allowed himself to be led out of the house, where the rest of his family waited for the engagement ceremony to begin.

"Tala al badru alayna . . ." The voice of Yusuf Islam, aka former 1970s folk singer Cat Stevens, drifted into the house. As the drums began to beat over the speakers, Khalid and his mother walked inside, followed by Aliyah Aunty and a half-dozen distant relatives rounded up to inflate their numbers. Khalid's family held large platters piled with food, Indian sweets, and gift bags filled with clothes and jewelry for the bride.

Khalid followed his mother into the living room where Hafsa sat, her face covered by a sheer white dupatta shawl. He took his place beside her, his face carved from granite.

Ayesha missed the grand entrance. She was in the bathroom, the taps turned on full blast, sobbing.

Samira Aunty dragged Ayesha to the family room for pictures after the brief engagement ceremony.

"I have to help in the kitchen," Ayesha said. "The uncles expect tea."

But her aunt insisted Ayesha stand beside a beaming Hafsa and stone-faced Khalid.

"I'm so happy, Ashi Apa," Hafsa said, hugging her cousin tight. "This picture will look great for my business, Happily Ever After Event Planning."

Ayesha looked over at Khalid, who was staring straight ahead.

"Have you talked to your . . . fiancé yet?" she whispered to Hafsa.

Her cousin looked dismissively at Khalid. "I think he's shy. Come look at the gold jewelry his mom bought me!" She dragged Ayesha to a large tray holding three gold jewelry sets. "I don't really like the design, but I can sell them and buy new ones. And look at all the shalwar kameez!" She pointed to five large platters heaped with clothing. "Last year's fashion, but I can sell them on eBay and buy better ones. I'm the luckiest girl in the world!"

Ayesha looked over at Khalid again. He stared at his hands as the guests piled their plates with biryani, butter chicken, and aloo gobi.

A hand wrapped around her waist and squeezed. Samira Aunty's face was flushed with excitement. "One down, three daughters to go. It is such a relief to have Hafsa settled. You can't imagine the strain. Khalid is such a handsome man, don't you think?"

Ayesha glanced over at Khalid, but he was gone. Had he run away?

"Mom has a crush on him," eleven-year-old Hira said. "She keeps talking about his regal nose."

The girls giggled, and Ayesha used the opportunity to slip away. She had to find Khalid; she had to explain herself. She had to wipe that blank look from his face.

He was not in the kitchen, or the foyer. She didn't find him in the living room, dining room, servery, or family room. She checked inside the walk-in hall closet, just in case, but he wasn't there either. A quick peek outside confirmed his car was still parked in the driveway.

"Looking for someone in particular, Ayesha?" Farzana said.

Khalid's mother was dressed in a peacock-blue shalwar kameez with a black abaya on top like an overcoat. She was wearing a matching blue hijab, her face bare of makeup.

"Assalamu Alaikum, Aunty," Ayesha said politely. "Would you like tea? I'm making some right now."

Farzana drew closer to Ayesha, an unkind smile hovering at the edge of her mouth. "I know you went to the caterer's with my Khalid."

"How about coffee?" Ayesha asked, backing away.

"I should be thanking you, actually. So should Hafsa."

Ayesha's heart started to pound. What was Farzana talking about? "You know how cranky the uncles get without their chai," Ayesha said, but Farzana grabbed her arm and pulled her close.

"You're a schoolteacher, but you know nothing about people," she said.

Ayesha tried to twist out of Farzana's grip, but the older woman held her fast.

"When Khalid spoke about the teacher who was helping him plan the conference, I knew it was time for him to get married. Before he was duped by a pathetic spinster pretending to be more than she was." Farzana's sharp eyes traveled over Ayesha's tight pink suit.

Ayesha was confused. "You knew he thought I was Hafsa?"

"Don't be ridiculous," Farzana said. "I had no idea about your duplicity. Besides, the rishta to your cousin had already been sent. When your cousin spoke with me on the phone, I realized she would be the perfect daughter-in-law."

"What about Khalid? Do you think she will be the perfect wife for him?" Ayesha asked, her mind working furiously.

"He doesn't know what he wants," Farzana said. "That's why he has me, to protect him from people who wish to take advantage of his innocence." She paused, staring at Ayesha. "I think I will take that tea after all. Extra-hot, two sugars, served in a china cup."

Khalid was in the garage. It was the only quiet place in the house, and he needed to think.

I'm engaged to a stranger. Not the Hafsa I thought I knew, but a child more excited by new toys than by the person in front of her. Hafs-*Ayesha* was probably laughing at him right now. Awkward, gullible Khalid, too dumb to know when he was being played.

311

He angrily wiped his eyes.

He thought about the casual banter between Hafs-*Ayesha* and Tarek at the caterer's. Tarek probably knew all about this farce too; he was probably laughing at him the entire time. He closed his eyes and saw Hafs-*Ayesha* sitting beside him in Clara's condo parking lot. He pictured her onstage at Bella's, reciting her poem — that stupid poem! Then he saw her smile, dark eyes laughing up at him, and he shivered.

Zareena had been a liar too. She had lied about where she was going and who she was with. She had asked Khalid to lie for her again and again. Every time she lied, Khalid felt used, and he promised himself he would stop covering for her. Then every time, he would give in and make new excuses for his sister, the one who knew him best in the world. The only one who had ever had his back.

Until the day Zareena's lies came crashing down.

He'd lost his only sister because of her lies, and because of his cover-up.

He wasn't going to fall for another person's lies, not again. Ayesha couldn't be trusted. Ayesha could go to hell.

Khalid smelled something burning.

■ ■ ■ ■

Ayesha needed to leave. Now.

Farzana had known Ayesha was pretending to be Hafsa. She'd known her son thought he was getting engaged to the wrong girl. Ayesha saw through her denials. What kind of mother did that to her own son?

There was no way to fix this. Not here, not now.

She walked straight out of the house without bothering to put her shoes on. She got as far as the sidewalk when Hira caught up with her.

"Where are you going?" her little cousin asked.

Ayesha didn't answer, only walking faster.

"You're not wearing any shoes."

Ayesha started to sprint, but Hira kept up easily.

"Go . . . back . . . home," Ayesha panted.

"I'm bored," Hira said. The little brat hadn't even worked up a sweat. "Is this what happens when you get old, Ashi Apa?"

"What?" Ayesha gasped.

"You forget things like shoes, you stop breathing so good when you run, and then you die?"

313

Ayesha stopped running and took deep, cleansing breaths, hands on her knees.

"Your toe is bleeding. Probably from the glass back there," Hira said.

Ayesha straightened up and kept walking toward her house, Hira beside her. At the door, Hira took out a blue leather-bound notebook.

"You forgot this at our house," she said. "I saw Khalid bhai give it to you." She looked at her cousin curiously. "He seemed really happy to see you at first, and then he got mad. What did you say to him?"

Ayesha took the notebook from her cousin. "Nothing," she said. "I didn't say a thing."

Hira shrugged and turned to go. "I'll tell everyone you were feeling sad," she said. "On account of your bleeding feet."

Ayesha walked into the empty house in a daze, her feet stinging. She collapsed on the kitchen table, opened the notebook, and started to write.

Things I should have said to you but only know how to write:

    1. I'm not who I never said I was.
    2. Not that I ever wanted to be.
    3. And yet that night, the stars twinkling,

Twinkies in your beard,
4. You smiled and leaned close.
5. Sometimes these things happen.
6. I hope you will be happy with her.
7. The way you never could be with me.
8. I'm not wifely material because
9. I'm who I said I never was.
10. And I'm not sure, yet, who that "was" could possibly turn out to be.

Nana stood by the side door entrance to the garage, holding a half-finished cigarette. "Please do not tell my granddaughter," he said when he spotted Khalid. "She does not approve of my habit. Of course, her disapproval makes me want to smoke more."

"I don't know your granddaughter," Khalid said.

"Well then, let's speak no more of this. Let us speak instead of a more interesting topic. Why is the fiancé hiding in the garage during his engagement?"

"I'm not hiding."

"You remind me of my granddaughter. Lovely girl," Nana said, lighting another cigarette. "Except when she's nagging me about smoking."

Khalid waved his hand in front of his face to dissipate the smoke. "I should get back," he said.

Nana said nothing, and Khalid didn't move. Then Nana said softly, " 'We are such stuff as dreams are made on, and our little life is rounded with a sleep.' "

The words were familiar. "I've seen you before," Khalid said. "You're always at the mosque."

"I am old and have nothing else to do," Nana said. "What is your excuse?"

Khalid smiled. Nana continued. "I think you are avoiding my initial question, which makes me even more eager to hear your answer. Tell me: Are you happy?"

"Happiness comes after the wedding," Khalid said, looking away.

"You speak of love," Nana said. "Love blossoms after the wedding, in the arrangements typical to our people. Happiness is a seed that takes root in your soul. Tell me, on this day of all days, are you capable of happiness?"

Khalid reached over and snagged a cigarette from Nana's pack. He lit it expertly and took a deep drag. "I thought I was. Now I don't know."

Nana nodded slowly. "The question remains: Is it you or the person to whom you have pledged your life who presents the problem?"

Khalid threw the cigarette down and

ground it under his foot. "I don't know that either."

Nana clapped him on the shoulder. "Then you know your quest. May Allah guide your journey."

CHAPTER TWENTY-SIX

Over breakfast Monday morning, Farzana asked Khalid about the conference.

"Perhaps it will be best if you tell the imam you can no longer help," she said, putting another greasy, overcooked aloo paratha — potato-stuffed flatbread — onto his plate. "We have a wedding to plan."

Khalid swallowed the paratha with difficulty. He doubted his mother had bothered to put an air pocket inside. It tasted like plywood and sat unhappily in his stomach.

"Ammi, about the wedding," Khalid started.

"It will be the event of the year, don't worry about that," Farzana said. "We'll have to limit the nikah guest list to six hundred people. Maybe we should hold it in an outdoor tent. Or at the Hollywood Princess convention center. You can walk down their crystal staircase and pose beside the marble fountain."

"Ammi, I was thinking," Khalid began again.

"As for the *walima* reception, I don't see how we can get away with less than one thousand guests. Your father knew so many people, and Sulaiman will have to invite his business contacts. We must finalize the date."

"I don't want to marry Hafsa," Khalid blurted.

Farzana waved at him dismissively. "Of course you do. I think a simple floral arrangement is so classy for centerpieces, no? With a colorful spotlight on each table in green, red, and yellow."

"I don't even know her," he said, and his voice was mutinous.

"Khalid, what is going on? You told me you would be happy with whomever I chose. Did something happen to change your mind?" Farzana looked sharply at her son. "Hafsa Shamsi will be the perfect daughter-in-law. She is a pious, well-behaved girl from a prominent family. What more do you want?"

Khalid pictured Ayesha's face yesterday. She looked tired. Maybe she'd been wondering how to tell him the truth. Or maybe she'd been laughing at how easy he was to fool. His jaw clenched.

"There is no such thing as love before marriage," Farzana continued.

"Khadijah was attracted to Prophet Muhammad, peace be upon him, before she married him," Khalid said.

"I'm sure her father arranged it all beforehand," Farzana said.

"She was a widow fifteen years his senior, and she proposed to him."

Farzana stared at her son. "Do you want to humiliate our family after we gave our word to Hafsa? How can you do this to me, after everything I've been through, after everything your sister put me through? She never listened either." Her voice cracked.

Khalid couldn't stand to see his mother cry, and he was still so angry with Ayesha. Either way, he didn't see how he could win. "Ammi, I'm sorry. Of course, you're right. I will marry Hafsa."

Farzana's face cleared. "She will make me so happy, Khalid. You'll see. Your children will take care of me in my old age. If your sister had only listened as you do, she would still be with us."

"I want her to come to the wedding."

Farzana started tidying up the kitchen, her back to Khalid. "Invite who to the wedding?"

"Zareena. I want to send her an invitation

320

and a plane ticket."

Farzana picked up a cloth and started scrubbing the stovetop. "Don't be ridiculous, Khalid. What would people say? She doesn't belong here anymore."

"She's not dead, Ammi," Khalid said. "You sent her to India."

Farzana rinsed the cloth and wrung it in the sink. "As far as I'm concerned, I have no daughter."

Khalid finished his breakfast quietly, but he was unable to silence the doubts sprouting like mushrooms on an old tree stump. It would be so easy to go along with what his mother declared. It would be so easy to get out of her way and let her plan the wedding of the year, filled with Sulaiman's business acquaintances and his parents' friends.

But did that mean he had to sacrifice himself in the process? Wasn't he entitled to his own opinions about who he invited to his own wedding, or even who he married at his own wedding? Khalid felt an uneasy melancholy settle over his stomach, full now with the unhappy parathas. He remembered the flatbread he had made with Ayesha and Nani — light, crispy, soft. He remembered her tentative hand on his face, the soft expression in her eyes so different from the one that Hafsa — the real Hafsa — had worn during their engagement.

What should he do? Ammi had promised his hand in marriage; he was getting exactly what he said he wanted. Except now he didn't want it anymore.

On the bus, Khalid checked his inbox, but there were no messages, and Zareena had said she was going on a trip. He wrote a quick e-mail to her anyway.

Salams. My engagement was yesterday. Hafsa turned out to be someone else entirely. I had her confused with her cousin, Ayesha Shamsi. But Ammi is very happy and I know I will be too, eventually. Keep July free for the wedding. You're invited and you're coming. No arguments.

Write me back soon. I really need to hear from you.

— K

He pressed Send and looked out the window at the traffic speeding by, everyone in a hurry to get somewhere. His mother was right; the engagement was done. He had given his word that he would marry Hafsa, and it would be wrong to go back on a promise. Besides, Hafsa was the perfect wife for him. Young, attractive, religious, from a good family. What more could he want?

Khalid settled down in his seat and willed the bus to drive more slowly. It was only taking him to work, and from work back home, on and on, with no end in sight.

When Khalid arrived at Livetech, Amir had just come out of the bathroom with a towel and toothbrush. When he smiled at Khalid, there was a little bit of toothpaste foam on the side of his mouth.

"K-Man!" he said, raising his hand for a high-five. "You look worse than me, and I was drinking and clubbing all night. I hope I've been a bad influence on you." He eyed Khalid's rumpled white robe and bloodshot eyes. "Let me guess — late-night study circle? Pre-dawn prayer jam?"

Khalid ignored Amir and sat down at his desk. He rubbed his eyes and waited for his laptop to start. "I'm fine," he said. "Just some issues at home."

"What are you talking about? You live with your mom and she does everything for you."

Khalid looked down at his hands. Was this how Amir saw him, as a weak-willed man tied to his mother's every whim? He glanced at his phone. Zareena hadn't e-mailed or texted. His stomach churned ominously.

"Do you have anything to eat?" he asked Amir.

Amir reached into his desk drawer and held out a granola bar to Khalid. When Khalid reached for it, Amir pulled it back slightly. "Not until you tell me what's going on. Have you decided to break bad and join the dark side? Why do you keep looking at your phone? Are you expecting a special lady to call? Or maybe ladies? You dawg!"

Khalid snatched the granola bar from Amir and unwrapped it.

"You didn't come to my engagement," he said, his mouth full of chewy oats and chocolate chips.

Amir settled down in his chair. "I was a little tied up, bro. There was this girl and she was into handcuffs."

Khalid put out his hand to stop Amir. "Something happened at the engagement. Hafsa Shamsi isn't who I thought she was. The girl from Bella's is someone else. Her name is Ayesha."

"Wait, so who are you engaged to?"

"I told you, Ayesha's younger cousin Hafsa."

"Is she hot?" Amir turned to his laptop and opened his Facebook account, fingers flying. After a moment, he gave a low whistle. "She's smoking. Maybe I should give this arranged marriage thing a chance. So what's the problem?"

Khalid shook his head. "No problem. Ammi's happy, and this is what I said I wanted."

Amir started typing again. "Ayesha doesn't even have a profile. Only serial killers aren't on social media. You dodged a bullet, bro."

Khalid slumped in his seat. "I didn't even talk to Hafsa at our engagement. How can I marry someone I don't know?"

"Who cares. She's hot!"

"Whenever I talk to Ayesha, she makes me laugh, and she gives me a hard time, and . . ." Khalid trailed off. "And now I'm engaged to her cousin."

Amir started laughing. "K-Man! You gots girl troubles! I never thought I'd see the day. Maybe you should take a look at that matrimonial service I showed you the other day. Or better yet, come out with us tonight."

"How is that going to help me? All you do is drink and pick up women, and I'm already engaged."

"We need a designated driver. Also, you have no experience with women. But me and my boys, we could counsel the UN on the ladies, you know what I'm saying?"

Khalid looked at his phone again. Zareena still hadn't responded, and he didn't have anyone else he could ask for advice. "Okay," he said. "I guess."

"Wise Men's Council, baby!" Amir said. "We'll sort you out pronto." He paused. "So, does Hafsa have a younger sister?"

CHAPTER TWENTY-SEVEN

As a show of support, Ayesha agreed to accompany Hafsa to the next mosque planning meeting. Maybe she would have a chance to explain herself to Khalid, or at least to apologize.

Khalid was the only person in the seminar room when they arrived, and he stood up when they walked in. "Assalamu Alaikum," he said, looking at Ayesha in surprise. "What are you doing here?"

Hafsa stepped forward, commanding his attention. "Hi, sweetie. Remember me?"

"Of course, *meri dil,*" he said, using the Urdu word for heart. "I'm happy to see you. There is a lot of work that needs to be done for the conference and we can use the extra help."

"I'm sure Ayesha tried her best, but she has zero event-planning experience. I'm the interesting one in the family," Hafsa said, giggling. "But at least she's reliable. You know what they say: Those who can't, teach."

Ayesha flinched and contemplated the door. She had accompanied her cousin as a goodwill gesture. Now she wondered why she had even bothered. This was not going to end well, she knew it. She wanted to leave right now, except Hafsa had driven them both here.

Hafsa took a seat beside Khalid and leaned forward. "I thought we could use this time to get to know each other. What do you do for fun?"

Ayesha selected a seat on the other side of the conference room, far away from the happy couple. She couldn't bear to watch Hafsa fawn. All thoughts of apologizing to Khalid vanished. She wanted to disappear.

Khalid frowned at Hafsa. "I'm not sure what you mean. I enjoy reading the Quran and attending daily prayers at the mosque. I also spend a lot of time helping the imam."

Hafsa wrinkled her nose. "No, I mean for *fun,*" she insisted. "Like, do you watch movies? TV shows?"

Ayesha glanced over. Khalid was leaning away from Hafsa. The look on his face was so funny that Ayesha smiled. Khalid looked over and frowned at her. "What are you doing here?" he asked again.

"Hafsa wanted me to come. We're family now, so I thought . . ." She trailed off. Khalid was staring at her. He had called her beautiful yesterday, and he'd given her a present — an engagement gift, she supposed. She thought about the poem she had written on the first page. "Thank you for the notebook," she said.

Khalid's eyes were still on her, as if searching for an answer to a question. "Why didn't you —" he said, but Ayesha cut him off.

"I'm sorry. You have no idea how sorry I am."

Hafsa glanced from Ayesha to Khalid and back. She tried to recapture Khalid's attention. "I bet you're more of a sports guy. I can tell you work out."

"I play basketball," he offered, looking at his fiancée. Hafsa brightened, until he added, ". . . At the mosque on Friday nights."

Ayesha laughed. "Hafsa loves coming to the mosque," she teased.

Hafsa shifted uncomfortably. "I mean, sure, the mosque is really great and all . . . but don't you think it's a little dank?"

"There's a chandelier," Khalid offered. "Besides, you come to the mosque to pray."

"I can pray at home, where it doesn't smell like dirty feet," Hafsa replied.

Ayesha's phone buzzed with an incoming text from Masood:

Salam. I haven't heard from you. I hope you weren't offended when I wrote that I'm not into you. At all. Not even a little bit. I still think you're a great person, despite all your negative energy. Have you ever considered wrestling? With your repressed frustration, you'd be a natural. I could be your coach. We just need to find a signature move.

Hafsa said brightly, "But with all the wedding stuff, the shopping and parties, there won't be time for all this." She waved her hand around the room.

Khalid looked pained, and Ayesha felt sorry for him. "The shopping is for you, Hafsa," she said. "Khalid just has to show up on the wedding day." *Wedding day.* She blinked rapidly.

"Are you also employed, like your cousin?" Khalid asked Hafsa, making an attempt at conversation.

"Dad promised he would give me some money to launch my company, Happily Ever After Event Planning, just as soon as we get married." Hafsa nodded dismissively toward Ayesha. "She has to work. When her dad died, he left them with nothing. It's a big mystery in our family. My mom said he was involved in something illegal. Maybe he was a gangster!" Hafsa giggled.

"You are speaking of her deceased father, Hafsa," Khalid said gently. "There is nothing amusing about that." He turned to Ayesha. She couldn't tell what he was thinking. "How old were you when he died?"

"I was ten. We left India soon after and moved to Toronto. I lost my father and my country at the same time."

"Yeah, but who would want to stay in *India*?" Hafsa said. "There are cows and amputated beggars everywhere, and people poop in the middle of the street. Why are you talking about things that happened so long ago?"

Ayesha and Khalid had no reply to this ignorant image, both shocked into silence. Hafsa had already moved on, her gaze fixed on the door.

Tarek had just entered the room, dressed in a tight-fitting white shirt. Its top two buttons were undone, showing off a smooth, sculpted chest. With his gray pants and hair carefully gelled into mussed-up peaks, Tarek was a fashion model straight off the runway.

"Who is *that*?" Hafsa said, her eyes fixed on Tarek's face. When he caught Hafsa's eye, he gave her a slow, lazy smile.

Ayesha and Khalid exchanged a glance, and then looked away. After what had happened at Kamran's Superior Sweets, Tarek had morphed from Prince Charming to Big Bad Wolf in Ayesha's eyes, and right now he was eyeing Hafsa hungrily. From the concerned expression on Khalid's face, he was having similar thoughts.

Ayesha's phone pinged again — another text message from Masood.

How about "Punch of the Seven Veils" for your signature move? Just think about it. The FIRST Muslim hijab-wearing wrestler. You could be famous!

Ayesha turned her phone to silent. Imam Abdul Bari had followed behind Tarek, and he lit up when he spotted Ayesha. "I knew you would return, Sister Hafsa," he said.

She shifted uncomfortably. "Actually, my name is Ayesha. This is my cousin Hafsa. I was just filling in for her. She's the real event planner, and also Khalid's new fiancée."

Hafsa was still staring at Tarek, the thrill on her face obvious when he selected the seat beside her.

"Congratulations on your engagement,"

332

Tarek purred to Hafsa. "I bet you weren't on the market for very long."

Hafsa preened. "Is that shirt from the Armani Spring collection?"

Tarek leaned close. "Observant and beautiful," he said softly. "This conference is sure to be a success."

"Let's get started," Ayesha said sharply. "Since you missed the last few meetings, Hafsa, we'll have to get you up to speed."

Hafsa laughed. "My cousin is always so focused on the goal. I prefer to enjoy the journey."

"I've always admired the way Ayesha gets straight to the heart of the matter," Khalid cut in. "Brother Tarek, what is on the agenda for today?"

Tarek called the meeting to order and updated everyone on the progress so far, his eyes lingering on Hafsa as he talked. Khalid didn't notice. He stared at the table, or took notes in a blue leather notebook that was familiar to Ayesha.

He bought us matching notebooks, she realized with a lurch.

Tarek asked about the website, and Khalid filled him in. "Sister Ayesha suggested black and white as the color theme, and I have come up with a beta of the website. The attendees will be able to pay for tickets online as well. What is the banking information?"

"I'll get that to you," Tarek said. "So we have agenda and speakers confirmed. Sister Hafs . . . I mean, *Ayesha* will open the conference with a poem. We are on track for a successful event. Now we just need to figure out the marketing tag line and mission statement to tell the speakers, so their speeches can align."

"And decorations," Hafsa said. "I think we should go with something classy. How about a 1920s theme? Like that movie with Leonardo DiCaprio, *The Good Greatsby.*"

Everyone paused. "You mean *The Great Gatsby,*" Ayesha said. "I'm not sure that's the right theme for an Islamic event."

Hafsa shook her head. "Ashi Apa, you should leave the event planning to the experts. Trust me, it's perfect. You know how there was Prohibition in the 1920s? And we're like a Muslim conference and don't drink alcohol? Plus, those flapper dresses are loose, like abayas, and all the men can wear three-piece suits, and we can maybe play some jazz music to get everyone in the mood."

"We're planning a conference, not a costume party, Hafsa," Ayesha said. "What's next, give everyone a Tommy gun in their swag bag, and open a speakeasy in the gym?" Ayesha and Khalid shared a smile.

Hafsa caught the glance between them and stood up, furious. "You know what? I don't need this. This conference sounds super boring. I'm leaving!" She flounced out of the room.

Ayesha sighed, but Tarek stood up. "I'll go talk to her," he said, just as the door was flung open and Farzana entered.

"Imam Abdul Bari, I have arrived!" she announced.

The imam's smile tightened. "Welcome, Sister Farzana," Abdul Bari said. "We weren't expecting you, but please join us."

"You cannot stop me from attending this meeting!" Farzana said, hands on hips. "I am a member of the executive board. Everything that happens in this building is *under my domain*!" She took a seat at the head of the table and Khalid sunk low in his chair.

Tarek, still standing, looked as if he had seen a ghost. His breathing was shallow as he lowered himself into his seat.

The imam cleared his throat, smile stapled to his face. "You are always welcome, Sister Farzana. I value input from all community members."

Ayesha was impressed with Abdul Bari's people-management skills. She knew he was a veteran of seven mosques and was likely familiar with people like Farzana: They were both the sources and disseminators of all community gossip. Except Farzana was even worse than an idle gossip, Ayesha realized. She was an active troublemaker, so consumed with the need to control those around her that she would even lie to her own son. Ayesha struggled to remain calm. It would be no use making a scene, not here.

"We were just about to decide on a marketing tag line for the conference. Two suggestions previously raised were 'Muslims in the Twenty-First Century,' or 'Beyond the Sands of Time: Examining Faith in the Modern World,' " Imam Abdul Bari said to the group.

Farzana looked disgusted. "This is what you have been wasting your time on, Khalid? Themes and silly discussions? How are you going to make any *money* for this mosque?"

The imam, no doubt spotting a chance to get rid of Farzana, said, "I'm afraid this is all dull work, Sister. I'm sure your talents are better employed elsewhere."

"No, no — the problem is that your choices are terrible and you are wasting too much time in pointless debate. The theme will be "Islam: The Only Pure Choice." I'll order a banner and flyers tomorrow. As for the tag line, let's keep it simple: "Follow Islam, Stay Pure." The colors will be white and green, like the Pakistani flag."

"Sister Farzana, you can't just bulldoze our meeting," Ayesha said, her resolve to be quiet rupturing with an almost audible crack.

"You don't think Islam is the only pure choice?" Farzana asked. "What kind of a Muslim are you?"

"You're twisting my words," Ayesha said, her face turning red.

"Perhaps it is your heart that is twisted. Everyone knows you were impersonating your cousin Hafsa for several weeks. Jealousy is so ugly in a woman."

Ayesha was shocked but didn't back down. "Insults are not going to work, Farzana Aunty. You have two options: Stay and contribute to the discussion in a respectful manner, or leave."

The two women glared at each other. Farzana turned to the imam. "Abdul Bari, I am appalled at the shameful behavior of your committee members. The executive board will be hearing about this. Let's go, Khalid. The caterer is waiting for us." She stalked out of the room. After a moment of embarrassed silence, Khalid followed.

The imam stood up slowly, a pained expression on his face. "As much as I enjoyed your reprimand, Sister Ayesha, Farzana is a force of nature. Perhaps in the future we should all moderate our tone when dealing with her."

"She's a bully!" Ayesha said. Her heart was pounding.

"I am afraid she will make good on her threat to speak to the executive board. I had to fight very hard to get them to agree to the conference in the first place. They only went along with the idea due to our financial problems. I will attempt to calm her down," Abdul Bari said, and he walked swiftly out of the room, leaving Tarek and Ayesha alone.

Tarek glanced at Ayesha, then away. He seemed quieter since Farzana had arrived, his usual swagger gone. Maybe he disapproved of her words too.

"Come on," Tarek said to Ayesha, grabbing his car keys. "I'll drive you home."

"I can't stand that woman," Ayesha said a few minutes later, taking a seat in Tarek's Lexus SUV. "I can't believe she's related to Khalid. He's so different from his mother."

"You mean he's not dogmatic and stubborn about his beliefs?"

Ayesha stopped, considering. "Well, I think I understand the beard and robes a bit better now. Imagine having Farzana for a mother. What would that do to a person?"

Tarek's shoulders hunched, and he gripped the steering wheel tightly.

"It's hard to imagine," he agreed, his voice thin. Tarek took a deep, steadying breath, and smiled slyly at Ayesha. "You like him."

"He's engaged to my cousin."

"I mean you *really* like him."

Ayesha flushed. "No, I don't."

Tarek looked at her. "You can do better."

"I know a Muslim woman's love life is an open book, but can we please move on to the next chapter?"

Tarek laughed. "You're funny. I like that." His smile faded, and his face grew serious. "Actually, I'm glad this happened. I wanted to talk to you about something serious. How long have you known Khalid?"

"Not long. He's new to the neighborhood. Why?"

"Did you do a background check on the family before Hafsa's engagement?"

Ayesha raised her eyebrows. "I'm sure the usual inquiries were made. What's going on?"

Tarek shifted in his seat, his eyebrows angling down so that he resembled a regretful puppy. "I really don't like to gossip, but when it comes to marriage, you have to tell the truth. I know Khalid Mirza's family. We both used to live in the west end of the city."

Ayesha nodded her head. She had a bad feeling about this.

"You probably remember the way I behaved at the caterer's." Tarek looked embarrassed. "I'm sorry about that. I was upset because Khalid has everyone fooled. You see, I knew his sister."

"Khalid told me about her. She lives in India. Zareena, right?"

Tarek sighed at her name. "There was a big scandal, years ago. Zareena got into some kind of trouble, and her family freaked out. They shipped her to some relatives in India and forced her into an arranged marriage."

Ayesha's hand was at her mouth. She had heard stories of girls being forced into marriages against their will, of course. It happened around the world, across different religions and cultures, and the practice disgusted her. The thought of Khalid going along with such a despicable plan made her ill.

"Are you sure?" she asked. Then she remembered the conversation she'd had with Khalid about his sister:

Does she enjoy living in India?

No. I'm pretty sure she hates it.

Tarek's mouth was set in a grim line. "Hafsa seems like a sweet kid. I just want to make sure she knows what kind of family she's marrying into." He reached over and squeezed Ayesha's arm. "I know you'll do the right thing."

Ayesha's stomach twisted at his words. Was he telling the truth? Tarek was too smooth, too polished to be entirely trusted. But then, what did he have to gain by lying about Khalid's family? If what he said was true, then her cousin was about to make a terrible mistake. Sulaiman Mamu and Samira Aunty had agreed to the engagement because they thought Khalid came from a good family. How would they react once they found out Khalid's parents had forced Zareena into an unwanted marriage? Maybe all his solicitousness, his gentleness, was nothing but an act. Maybe he actually fit the stereotype of the domineering, terrifying man who forced his will upon the vulnerable women in his life.

She recalled Khalid's face, his gentle eyes, the inscription he wrote inside the notebook he had bought for her back when he thought she would become his wife. Was this the man her cousin was engaged to marry, or was he really some other, darker figure?

What had Hafsa gotten herself into?

CHAPTER TWENTY-EIGHT

Farzana did all the talking at the caterer's, speaking over Kamran Khan himself.

"I want butter chicken, vegetable *tawa,* palak paneer, veal korma, and meat biryani. Fresh, now — none of that old mutton you people like to sneak in. We'll have Amritsar fish pakoras and *channa chaat* for appetizers."

"Madam, fish is one dollar extra," Mr. Khan said, but Farzana waved her hand.

"Don't forget how many people are coming to this wedding. Good advertising for you. You should be doing it for free, actually. Now for dessert, I want mango kulfi and *ras malai.*"

"Kulfi is two dollars extra, madam," Mr. Khan said, but he kept his gaze on his notebook as he spoke, and Farzana ignored him. She continued talking about tasting menus while Khalid wondered what he was doing there.

He watched his mother berate, order, and boss around Kamran. She criticized his managerial style, questioned the freshness of his chicken, and ridiculed his knowledge of basmati rice. Mr. Khan, usually a gruff and taciturn man, accepted it all so meekly.

"Ammi, don't talk to him like that," Khalid said, interrupting her lecture on the right brand of paneer. "He knows what he's doing, otherwise why would we be here?"

Farzana and Mr. Khan turned to look at him.

"Khalid, *chup,*" she said, shushing him. She turned back to the caterer. "My son doesn't know what he's talking about."

Khalid felt the first tendrils of anger warming his feet. "I do know what I'm talking about," he said evenly. "So does Mr. Khan, and the imam, and Ayesha, and —"

"Ayesha, Ayesha, Ayesha!" Farzana said. "Two weeks back I never heard of this girl, and now all I hear is her name! Khalid, I forbid you to speak to her again! In fact, we will never speak of her at all!"

"That might be difficult, since I'm marrying her cousin," Khalid said. The anger was licking at his shins now, traveling up his legs and warming his fingertips. "You were out of line at the conference meeting, Ammi."

"Ayesha disrespected me, and now you?

Your father would be so ashamed."

"I thought you said you were never going to speak her name again," Khalid said.

Mr. Khan leaned back, clearly enjoying the exchange. "Would madam like some chai?" he asked genially. They both ignored him.

"Ammi, you are the one who is being disrespectful. The way you behaved at the conference meeting was wrong. You tried to take over everything, you didn't listen to anyone, and you picked a fight with Ayesha for no reason! You drag me here, and you don't even ask what I want to eat at my own wedding reception!" Khalid's face was flushed.

"What do you want, then, Khalid?" Farzana shouted. "I do everything for you, and this is the thanks I get. Tell him, then, if you know everything. Tell Mr. Khan what it is you want!"

"I don't know what I want!" Khalid yelled. "But I do know one thing — I don't want butter chicken! It's too sweet, and everyone serves it all the time. It's boring!"

Farzana nodded at the caterer. "You heard my son. No butter chicken on the menu."

Kamran Khan carefully made a notation in his black notebook. "Would sahib like chicken tikka instead?" he asked Khalid.

Farzana sniffed loudly and made a big production of wiping her eyes.

Khalid nodded, deflated and too tired to argue.

Avoiding eye contact, they continued with the order.

Khalid met up with Amir, Ethan, and Mo at Bella's after dropping his mother home.

"Damn, Khalid, how did a guy like you score a girl like *that*?" Ethan asked. He stared at the Facebook picture of Hafsa on Amir's phone. Khalid reached over the table and put his hand over the screen.

"Please do not ogle my fiancée," he said calmly.

"Well, then tell your fiancée to put on one of those face-mask niqab things. Sister is *fiiiiine*!" Ethan high-fived Amir, and Khalid wondered what he was doing there.

"I think I should go," he said.

"Wait, wait. Cool it, brother," Amir said. "Ethan is just having some fun with you. This is what yo' boys do, all right? Now before the Wise Men's Council begins, we need to have our opening ceremony."

Mo, Amir, and Ethan quickly downed shots. "Okay. The Wise Men's Council will now decide whether the hottie with the body —"

Khalid moved to walk away.

"— I mean, the good Muslim girl," Amir said hastily, "is the one for K-Man here, or whether he should dump her and go after her cousin Ayesha."

"Wasn't that the poet chick from last time?" Ethan asked. "Dude, you need to expand your social circle."

Khalid only frowned. He wouldn't be here if Zareena would just e-mail him back, or text, or even call.

Mo slapped the table. "I got it. You should marry the hottie and fool around with the cousin on the side." He high-fived Ethan and Amir.

"That is disgusting. I'm going to the mosque," Khalid said, but Amir grabbed his arm.

"Joke-shhh," he slurred. " 'Member? We're jush joking with you."

"You're drunk," Khalid said. "You only had one shot."

"Had five more outside," Amir said proudly.

Khalid passed him his club soda. "Drink this, please. I don't want you to pass out before you get home."

"What home?" Ethan laughed, but Amir dutifully drank the club soda.

"So what should Khalid do?" Amir asked

after a few seconds of chugging to clear his head.

"I don't get it. Why are you marrying the hottie if you like her cousin?" Ethan asked. "Why are you getting married at all? You're not forty, and she's not pregnant." He paused. "Is she pregnant?"

Mo and Amir fell against one another, laughing.

"No, she is not with child," Khalid said tightly. "She's a virgin, and so am I."

There was a stunned silence among the men.

"You're not supposed to say that *out loud,*" Mo said. "There are women present."

"You must be going out of your mind," Ethan said. "I lost it when I was fourteen."

"I was twelve," Mo bragged.

"I was nine!" Amir said.

"And you're all such wonderful models of manhood," Khalid said.

"K-Man, sarcasm don't look good on you," Amir said. "Okay, maybe I was sixteen. How do you deal?"

Khalid shrugged. He regretted being so forthcoming. "It can be uncomfortable at times. However, I want to wait until I am married."

"Then go with the hottie," Ethan advised. "You want your first to be worth the wait."

"You mean my only. I have no intention of sleeping with anyone other than my wife."

"Don't you mean *wives*," Mo said. "You can have four, you know." He nudged Khalid, waggling his eyebrows suggestively.

"One is sufficient for me. Amir, you brought me here to make fun of me, didn't you?" Khalid looked around at the men and sighed. "I should have known better."

This time Amir didn't stop him when he walked away.

Andy the Bouncer nodded at Khalid at the door. "You with those idiots?"

Khalid shook his head. "Definitely not."

"Look at that A-meer guy. It's a new girl every night. Like he doesn't have his own place or something. He's pathetic."

Khalid looked back at Amir, who was flirting with a brunette in a halter top. She was laughing and he was leaning close. Khalid noticed the stubble on his friend's face, recognized the familiar emerald-green shirt and black pants.

Andy looked disgusted, and Khalid gripped his keys. He contemplated returning to the table, but when he looked back, Amir was gone.

On the way to the car, Khalid checked his phone again. Still no word from Zareena.

Chapter Twenty-Nine

The waiting room was full when Ayesha brought Nana in for his six-month checkup with Dr. Adams, the cardiologist. Nana had a heart condition — a very minor one, he assured Ayesha — that had to be monitored regularly.

"Remember, you promised to tell Dr. Adams about your smoking," she said.

"I do not wish to alarm him. It is only the occasional cigarette." Nana looked at his granddaughter to see if she bought his story.

She didn't. "You promised to quit."

"A man my age has few joys left in life," Nana began, but Ayesha stopped him.

"If you don't tell Dr. Adams, I will."

"He always sides with you. Actually, jaanu, I would like to switch doctors. It is my right as a patient."

The chore of taking Nana to the doctor had fallen to Ayesha after he had declared several years ago that he no longer believed in Western medicine.

"Your blood pressure medication is the only thing that is keeping you alive, you idiot," Nani had said when she found out.

"It is Allah who is keeping me alive," he argued. That hadn't worked either, and now his days of solitary doctor visits were a thing of the past.

Ayesha's phone pinged with an incoming text message. It was Masood again:

I'm about to trademark "Punch of the Seven Veils." If you don't want it, one of my preschool mixed martial arts students is showing a lot of promise. Actually, she reminds me of you. If not wrestling, how about joining a Fight Club? I hear they're really relaxing.

Ayesha smiled and put her phone away. Though she had never responded to his notes, Masood's texts were a comforting absurdity.

Nana leaned back in his chair. "Beti, tell me the truth. Are you angry with Nani?"

"I don't know what you're talking about."

"There are no secrets between married people. I know that Nani conducted an investigation on your behalf and that it was unsuccessful. Are you very hurt?"

Ayesha bit her bottom lip. "I'm happy for Hafsa and Khalid. Even if the only reason they are getting married is to please their parents."

Nana bowed his head, his face somber. He seemed to be thinking something over.

" 'The robbed that smiles steals something from the thief,' " he offered instead.

Ayesha remained silent. Sometimes, even Shakespeare could offer no comfort. Right now, she was also worried about Tarek's warning. She had been turning it over and over in her head all day, trying to figure out the right course of action. Perhaps Nana could provide some guidance.

"What would you do if you heard something very bad about Khalid and his family?" she asked.

Her grandfather picked up a magazine from the shelf. "Is this 'something' from a reliable source?"

Ayesha thought about Tarek. He was unpredictable and moody, but he seemed familiar with Khalid's family. Besides, only a monster would make up such a terrible story. It had to be true. She nodded and filled her grandfather in on the details. His face grew serious and he bowed his head.

"This is a dreadful accusation indeed," Nana said. "If it is true, Hafsa cannot marry into such a family."

A sadness filled Ayesha. If the story was true, Farzana was even worse than she had thought. It also meant Khalid was hiding the forced marriage and banishment of his sister. The idea horrified her.

Dr. Adams emerged from his office and smiled at Nana, who rose. "Leave this matter with me only. I will attempt to ascertain the veracity of this story," her grandfather said.

Except Ayesha couldn't leave it with Nana. She had promised Sulaiman Mamu she would keep an eye on Hafsa. She called Clara from the waiting room and related Tarek's accusations.

When she finished, Clara was silent, thinking. "I find this hard to believe. I can't imagine Khalid would keep quiet about something so underhanded," she said, and Ayesha felt relieved. Clara continued. "Still, you never know what happens in people's families. I think you should tell Hafsa. We don't know if it's true, and there's no point telling her parents yet. But she has a right to hear these rumors and decide what she wants to do."

Clara was right. Khalid had looked so sad when he'd spoken about his sister. Or maybe that was his shame coming through.

It wasn't like she really knew him. Did she?

"What would Nana do?" Clara asked.

Ayesha smiled. They played this game often, whenever they were confronted with an ethical quandary. What would Nana do? "He'd say, 'Family first.' Then he would remind me that Sulaiman Mamu rushed to Hyderabad after my father died and saved us all."

"What would Samira Aunty do?"

"Don't be so melodramatic, Ayesha. The wedding show must go on!" Ayesha mocked, and Clara laughed at her impersonation.

"Right. What would Hafsa do?"

"I don't know anymore," Ayesha said slowly.

"Remember when she was twelve years old, and you told her Veer Patel was only talking to her because he wanted a nude picture?"

Ayesha laughed. "Who knew twelve-year-olds were such creeps?"

"She didn't believe you, and she screamed at you in front of her friends. Don't be so sure Hafsa's going to appreciate your warning, or listen to your words," Clara said.

"The moment Tarek told me about Khalid's family, it became my responsibility."

Clara was silent, and Ayesha wondered if she disapproved. "I'm thinking of breaking

353

up with Rob," she said instead.

"It's not because of what Khalid said over dinner, is it?"

"Rob's not ready to move forward, and I don't know how much longer I can wait. Ten years with him, and it's all come to nothing."

"Clara, it wasn't nothing. You mean the world to Rob. If it's not meant to be, you will be the world to someone else. You need a nosy aunty to send him a rishta. A professional matchmaker to put him on the spot."

Clara cleared her throat, and Ayesha heard the rustle of tissue.

"I'm sorry to bother you with my stupid problems right now," Ayesha said.

Clara laughed, her voice shaky. "You should talk to Hafsa. It might not do any good, but I know it will bother you if you don't."

Nana emerged from the doctor's office, smiling. "I am very healthy and will live to be one hundred and five, according to Dr. Adams," he said to Ayesha.

She drove them home in silence, thinking about her cousin. She had a pretty good idea where she was right now, and her news would not wait.

"Tell Nani I'll be back. I have to do something first," she said.

■ ■ ■ ■

Hafsa was sitting in the food court of the mall, a container of fries in front of her, three little paper cups filled with assorted seasonings arranged neatly in a row on the table. She was methodically covering a fry with cajun powder when Ayesha settled into the seat opposite.

"Someone's sitting there," Hafsa said without looking up. "Don't you have a conference to plan, Miss Perfect?"

Ayesha ignored her. Every time she talked to Hafsa lately, she was drawn into her rabbit hole of drama. She could feel it happening again, and she fought against the current, toward the shores of reason.

"I have something to tell you about Khalid and his family. I'm not sure if it's true, but I think you need to hear this anyway and decide for yourself. Khalid has an older sister, Zareena. A few years ago her family forced her to marry someone in India."

Hafsa continued to eat her fries, not making eye contact. "So?"

"This is bad, Hafs. Just think of the family you are marrying into."

Hafsa shook her head. "Let me get this straight. You heard some gossip about Khalid and, based on these unfounded rumors, you think I should dump him?"

"It's a trustworthy source. I'm only trying to look out for you."

"If Khalid is as terrible as you say, I'll divorce him. That way I get to keep his money *and* the money Dad promised for the wedding."

Ayesha reeled back. "That's horrible."

Hafsa's eyes flashed. "Even more horrible than making a move on your cousin's rishta?" she snapped. "I know all about your little romance with Khalid. His mother told me everything."

"Is that why you said yes to him? To get back at me?"

Hafsa shrugged. "Not everything is about you."

Ayesha stared at her, wondering how Hafsa could sit there calmly eating junk food while her words ripped out her heart.

"I'm done making excuses for you, Hafsa. You're an adult. You'll just have to live with the consequences of your actions, like everyone else."

CHAPTER THIRTY

"Sister Farzana! What are you doing here?" It was Monday morning, and Tarek was loitering inside the Toronto Muslim Assembly, waiting for the weekly executive board meeting to finish. For extra emphasis, he turned on the full force of his megawatt smile.

Farzana sniffed dismissively. "If you are here to talk me out of complaining about Ayesha's behavior, you are too late. The executive board is considering their options." She looked Tarek up and down, taking in his fashionably distressed jeans, ankle boots, and black leather motorcycle jacket.

"Are you even capable of growing a beard?" she asked.

Tarek's smile didn't falter. "I have been attempting a beard for years. Your son is my new role model. You have done such a good job raising him."

357

Farzana relaxed, slightly. "What do you want?"

Tarek eyed her. He had never sought Farzana out before, not in all these years. She had become a bogeyman in his mind, the manufacturer of his greatest disappointment. But after her performance at the conference meeting, he had finally been able to see her for who she truly was: a pathetic caricature, a puffed-up phony who needed to be knocked off her self-righteous pedestal.

And he happened to have motive, opportunity, and a great big baseball bat ready to take a swing at her perfectly choreographed life.

"I was very moved by your efficient choice of decor and theme at our last meeting." Tarek placed a hand on his heart.

Farzana's scowl dropped, replaced with something that might one day grow up to be a smile. Or at least a not-frown. "Young people must listen to their elders, who have experience and know better."

"I couldn't agree more. I have so much respect for my parents. They moved to Canada from Pakistan, leaving everything they knew and loved behind. As children, we have to acknowledge that sacrifice with absolute obedience."

Farzana relaxed some more, the not-frown tightening into an upturned grimace. Tarek recognized his moment, gleeful. "Actually, I was hoping to run into you today. I have some disturbing information about Imam Abdul Bari, and I need to tell someone I can trust."

Farzana pounced. "You can trust me. I only have the mosque's best interests in mind." They walked to the conference room for privacy, and Farzana looked eagerly at Tarek.

"Sister Farzana, I'm sure you have heard that the Toronto Muslim Assembly is nearly bankrupt. However, I recently discovered the reason for these troubling financial problems."

Tarek drew out the moment as long as possible, closing his eyes for added emphasis, as if the words were too painful to be spoken out loud.

"Imam Abdul Bari is stealing from the mosque," Tarek announced, his voice mournful. "He requested all the funds collected from the conference be deposited into his bank account. I don't know what to do," he added.

"We must catch him in the act and then expose him to the congregation as a crook," Farzana said. "I never liked the imam. He smiles too much."

"What a great idea," Tarek said. "In the meantime, I'll deposit the money into another bank account, for safekeeping."

He watched Farzana take the bait as expected: She was always so quick to think badly of others. Tarek flexed his fingers and imagined himself gripping a baseball bat of truth. He pictured himself taking a swing and shattering Farzana's biggest secret, straight into the wide-open sunshine.

Tarek returned to the mosque a few days later at sunset. He made sure to wait by the entrance of the prayer hall for Khalid and rearranged his expression into one of delighted surprise when he spotted the taller man.

"Assalamu Alaikum, Khalid," he said, shaking his hand. "I'm so happy I bumped into you." Tarek suggested they grab coffee and discuss the conference details. With less than a week to go, there was still a lot to do. After the prayer, they made their way across the street to a Tim Hortons coffee shop.

"How long have you been running these conferences?" Khalid asked Tarek after they'd ordered their drinks and donuts.

"This will be my fifth year. I recognized a real need in the Muslim community to discuss ideas with other stakeholders," Tarek said. "That's why we started the summer conference, to attract the youth. I only hope we can help with the Toronto Muslim Assembly's financial problems."

Khalid looked bleak. "Over five hundred people preregistered, but I don't know if it's enough. We need a miracle to save the mosque."

"Please make sure all the registration proceeds are deposited to the Muslims in Action bank account."

Khalid looked confused. "The imam said the registration money should be deposited into the mosque account, so we could pay our debts immediately."

Tarek shook his head. "I'm afraid for tax purposes, the money must first go into my organization's account. Otherwise it won't be a charitable tax write-off. I cleared all this with your mother, and since she's on the executive board, I'm sure it will be fine with the imam as well."

Khalid frowned. "I need to double-check with Abdul Bari," he said.

Tarek examined Khalid. He was so tightly wound that all he needed was a little push. "Congratulations on your engagement," he said casually. "Hafsa is a special girl."

Khalid nodded, still frowning. "I think the

imam is in his office. I should talk with him about the money right now."

Tarek ignored him. "I'm thinking of getting married soon too. Do you know if Sister Ayesha is single?"

Khalid froze. "Why do you want to know?" he asked, keeping his voice even.

"I need a wife who is practical and capable. Ayesha had the best ideas for the conference during our meetings. Besides, she has a really lovely smile. I'm thinking of approaching her father."

"Her father is dead," Khalid blurted.

"Her mother, then."

"I don't think she's on good terms with her mother either." Khalid gulped the hot coffee, exclaiming as he scalded his tongue.

Tarek eyed Khalid like a falcon going in for the kill. "I hope I haven't offended you. I really admire her character, and I thought I would ask your opinion. I noticed you have become close. Is she in a relationship?"

Khalid took a large, vicious bite of his donut. "As far as I know, Ayesha is single and available for anyone who's interested in her."

"Anyone except you," Tarek said softly. "Isn't that right?"

"I don't know what you're talking about."

"An engagement is not the same thing as

362

a nikah, Khalid. You're not married to Hafsa. Yet."

"Hafsa makes my mother happy. Love blossoms after the wedding," Khalid said automatically.

Tarek regarded Khalid for a long moment. "You know that's not true. I think it's time you stopped lying to yourself."

Khalid toyed with his empty coffee cup. He didn't meet Tarek's eyes.

"I loved someone very deeply, a long time ago," Tarek said. "Things didn't work out, but I never forgot her. You never forget your first love. As a Muslim, can you really stand in front of Allah and pledge to love only Hafsa when your heart belongs to someone else?"

Khalid looked up; he must have caught something in Tarek's expression, because he said softly, "I don't know what to do. I can't stop thinking about her."

"I think you do know. You're just scared," Tarek said, trying to keep a satisfied smile from playing at the corners of his mouth. Really, if he had known Khalid and Farzana were so easy to manipulate, he would have exorcised his anger years ago. He continued, "If I were you, I wouldn't delay even for a single moment. A girl like Ayesha — well, she won't stay single for very long."

CHAPTER THIRTY-ONE

Khalid felt reinvigorated. He knew now what he had to do, and he went over the list in his mind: (1) Ayesha, (2) Zareena, (3) Amir. Heart, family, friend.

He took a small detour on his way to work. When he arrived at his office at eight, Amir was lying on the sofa, one arm thrown over his face, fast asleep.

Khalid didn't know how he had missed the signs: Amir's backpack was under his desk, stuffed with clothes; a bag of toiletries, which he had mistaken for a large pencil case, sat on a shelf; there was a towel on the back of his rolling chair; and he kept a toothbrush in his drawer.

Amir had been sleeping at work for weeks. Andy the Bouncer had helped him to connect the dots: His friend was homeless.

Khalid nudged Amir awake. "Here," he said, passing him a plastic hotel key card.

"What's this?" Amir asked, sitting up.

"Room 522. I paid for two weeks. It's close to work and the subway. Just until you get back on your feet."

Amir looked at the plastic card, the usual smirking smile gone. "I don't need your pity. I'm fine, okay?" He held the key card with the tips of his fingers.

Khalid shifted, feeling awkward. This conversation had gone a little differently in his head. He tried a joke to lighten the mood. "How could someone like me pity you? You get all the ladies, and I can't even decide on one."

Amir smiled, but his eyes were wary. He examined the card: *Sleep-time Inn.* "Too cheap to spring for a Marriott?" He placed the room key on Khalid's desk.

"I have a wedding to pay for," Khalid said weakly.

Amir sat up, rubbing his eyes. "Look at the two of us. We're pathetic, bro. I don't know who's sadder — you're still a virgin, and I got no place to stay." He paused, thinking, and his face brightened. "Actually, I think it's you. Definitely more sad."

Khalid looked at his feet. "I think you have a drinking problem, Amir. I looked it up and there is an AA meeting nearby. I think you should go."

"Nah, man. Not really my scene. I just hit

a rough patch. I'll be all right."

Khalid sighed and closed his eyes. ". . . I could go with you, if you want."

Some of the old fire lit up Amir's eyes. "K-Man at an AA meeting? This I gotta see!" He slapped him on the back and headed off to the bathroom with his toothbrush.

Time for item number 2: Zareena. His sister had warned him she would be busy for a few days, but it was strange that she hadn't responded to his last pleading e-mail. He found her cell number in his contacts and dialed.

The phone rang twice before it connected and a singsongy voice chirped, "The number you are calling has been disconnected." It repeated the message in Hindi, Telugu, and Marathi while Khalid stared. Zareena would have told him if she had changed phone numbers. His fingers shaking, he quickly typed an e-mail:

Salams. Haven't heard from you in a while. Are you okay? I'm starting to worry. Please respond.

He pressed Send and tried to concentrate on the website for WomenFirst Design. Despite his earlier discomfort and irritation with the project, everything was going well. He had Sheila, of all people, to thank for this. She had wanted to humiliate him by taking him off e-commerce and network security work to focus on the lingerie website exclusively. Which meant that for the past few weeks, his sole job had been to brush up on his website design skills. The end result was a huge update from their existing platform. He hoped Vanessa and Lorraine would be pleased when he presented it to them next week.

Tomorrow was also the first day of the conference. Khalid had taken the day off to help with setup and to coordinate the Singles Mixer in the evening. He wasn't exactly sure what a Muslim Singles Mixer was — maybe all the parents mingled, with their children's pictures and marriage résumés in hand? Regardless, he would be present at the mosque for the entire day. And so would Ayesha.

Khalid felt a current of excitement rush through him at the thought. He hoped he would be able to steal a moment to speak with her, now that he finally had something to say. If all went well, he would soon be standing before Allah and pledging his love and loyalty to the right woman.

Amir returned from the bathroom. He

picked up the room key from Khalid's desk and slipped it into his pocket. "What time is this meeting? I have a hot date with a Pilates instructor after work."

The nearest AA meeting was held in the basement of the Holy Ghost Baptist Church, a five-minute walk from Livetech. Amir was in a good mood as they walked, smiling and joking as he chatted with Khalid, but he stopped abruptly at the entrance.

"Listen, maybe you should go on without me," he said.

Khalid took note of the semiwild look in Amir's eyes, the grimace masquerading as a smile. "Amir, I'm not an alcoholic."

"The first step is admitting you have a problem."

Khalid paused, unsure what to do. Then he grabbed Amir's arm and pulled, hard. Amir planted his feet firmly on the ground, but after a second he went limp and allowed himself to be led, like a child, to the basement of the church. The meeting was already in session, a small group of about fifteen people who took no notice of the new members. The participants were sitting on metal folding chairs or standing at the back of the room while a young woman talked at the front.

"It wasn't until I ran out of money to buy diapers for my three-month-old son that I knew I had hit bottom," the woman said. She was a petite white woman, dressed in a pastel sweater set straight out of 1995, with matching slacks. A string of pearls hung from her neck, and she reached for them often as she spoke. "My husband and I weren't really talking. He didn't know how to tell me I had a problem, but I knew. I just didn't know what to do about it." There was sympathetic nodding from the crowd.

The moderator squeezed the woman's shoulder and read from a book, going over the twelve steps. The group broke for coffee and cookies, and the participants milled around; a few exchanged smiles with Khalid. Amir kept his eyes on the ground, arms tightly folded. He looked terrified.

An older woman with long graying hair approached Khalid. "Welcome, friend. My name is Joyce. First time?" Khalid nodded.

"I am here with my friend," he said, pointing to Amir, who had his back to Khalid and refused to make eye contact.

"Taking the first step is incredibly brave," she said to Khalid. "I know your religious tradition forbids alcohol, so good for you."

Amir glanced over at Khalid, who looked confused. His usual smirk began to creep back onto his face and he put an arm around his friend. "I kept telling him the same thing. He isn't going to get better without help."

Joyce patted Khalid on the arm. "Do you drink because you're angry at the United States and their foreign policy?"

"I am sorry, Joyce, you have made an error. I am not an alcoholic."

"Alcoholism is a disease that convinces you that you do not have it," Joyce said, smiling. "Your friend was right to convince you to come. We're going to be sharing more stories soon, and I hope you'll feel comfortable speaking to the group."

Looking far more cheerful and at ease, Amir filled a Styrofoam cup with strong coffee, grabbed a jelly cookie, and took a seat on one of the chairs arranged in a circle.

The moderator, a preppy-looking white man with blocky glasses and a careful comb-over, began with the nondenominational prayer and welcome. "AA is a fellowship of men and women who share their experience, strength, and hope with one another. Welcome new and returning friends. We recognize that alcoholism is a disease, and we ask for a higher power to help us deal with our addiction. Would anyone else like to share their struggle to-day?"

Amir lifted his hand. "My friend Khalid would," he said.

A dozen eyes looked at Khalid, taking in his white robe, skullcap, and unruly beard.

"I'm not an alcoholic," Khalid said.

"She's called Cleopatra — the Queen of Denial!" an older black man said from across the circle, and everyone laughed.

Khalid sighed. If this was the role he had to play to help his friend, he would do it. He sat up straight. "My faith is strong, and it has carried me through many dark times. I love Allah, and when I pray I feel at peace. But for the past little while, some things have bothered me. My mother wants me to be the perfect, dutiful son, but I am afraid I have lived by her rules at the expense of my own desires. I thought I knew what I wanted from life. I thought I knew exactly how my life should be lived, but I was wrong."

The group was silent, thoughtful, and Khalid continued.

"Then I met a girl, and I started to wonder — maybe there was another way."

"Khalid, can you be more specific?" the moderator asked.

"My mother is very controlling," Khalid said, and as the words left his mouth, he re-

371

alized they were true, even if he had never acknowledged them before. "I used to think she knew what was best for me, but lately . . . Well, I had to reconsider everything when she forced me into an engagement with a stranger."

"How awful," Joyce said. "That's barbaric!"

Khalid shook his head. "It's not awful. It's what I thought I wanted, but after I met Ayesha, I realized there were many paths to love and happiness, and they didn't all involve arranged marriage. When I came to that realization, it made me wonder what else my mother was wrong about. Like my sister."

The moderator looked puzzled. "When did you start to drink?"

"Throughout," Amir interrupted, catching Khalid's eye. "He's been drunk pretty much every day for the last year. That's why he's so broke. His roommates kicked him out when he used his rent money for booze for the fourth time. He can't go home to his dad, not after the last time he messed up. His friends are no help either, and he has a lot of pride. Maybe too much."

Khalid nodded, holding Amir's eye. "I'm only sorry I didn't realize it earlier, so I could help . . . myself."

Amir half-shrugged. "This is a good first step. Maybe now you won't feel so lost and alone."

"Wherever you go, there you are," Joyce said, patting Khalid on the knee.

Khalid wasn't sure what she meant, but he appreciated the support. The meeting wrapped up soon afterward, and Amir and Khalid walked out together.

"That felt really good," Khalid said. "Let me know if you want me to come with you again."

Amir laughed and then stopped in front of the crosswalk to face Khalid. "I came to Canada from Afghanistan when I was fourteen," he said. "When I close my eyes at night, I can still hear the bombs. My mother and my sisters are still there. We buried them a week before we left." Amir's arms were crossed tightly once more, and he shifted his weight from foot to foot. "Sometimes I just want to drown out the bombs, you know?"

Khalid nodded, even though he didn't know, not really. "My mosque is hosting a youth conference this weekend," he said instead. "No alcohol, but there will be a Singles Mixer. Why don't you come?"

Amir grinned at his friend. "You can't turn it off, can you?"

■ ■ ■ ■

Khalid waited until he returned home to call Zareena's landline, the number she'd told him to call only in case of emergency. His bedroom door was locked, and his nervousness grew the longer the phone rang.

Finally, after the twentieth ring, someone picked up. "Haaaallow?" a man's voice called into the receiver. Was this Iqram, Zareena's husband? He sounded angry.

"Assalamu Alaikum. This is Khalid Mirza, Zareena's brother. I'm calling from Canada. Can I please speak to my sister?"

There was a moment of silence as the message floated across the ocean. Then the man started to laugh, a choking, wheezing sound that chilled Khalid.

"Gone!" the man barked. He reverted to Urdu and said, "If you're her brother, where have you been all these years? She's never spoken about you, not once."

"What do you mean she's gone?" Khalid asked, his heart pounding. He'd known something was wrong. "Where did she go?"

"Ungrateful girl, lazy and selfish. You know she burned my breakfast every morning? On purpose too. You can have her back."

"But, but . . . she's not here," Khalid said. "Please, sir. Where is my sister?"

The man cackled, his voice nasty and insinuating. "Are you really her brother? Maybe you're her boyfriend, the one she's always texting and e-mailing. I tell you, she's gone. Long gone! Forget her!" The man slammed the receiver down, and Khalid frantically called back, but it was no use. The phone rang and rang, forty times, a hundred times, but no one picked up.

CHAPTER THIRTY-TWO

When Ayesha entered the mosque at nine on Friday morning, she was surprised to see Farzana, not Tarek, ordering around the crew of volunteers who were setting up for the conference. Everyone was petrified of her booming voice, and they jumped to attention as she strode around, criticizing everything they did.

"Where is Tarek?" she asked.

Farzana didn't look at her. "I am not his keeper. Brother Tarek informed me he was finishing up a delicate matter that required his attention. He requested I step in to ensure things progressed smoothly."

You didn't even want this conference to happen, Ayesha thought. *What's going on?*

Khalid stood on the stage, untangling power cords for the microphone and projector. He looked distracted but waved when he saw her. She frowned and walked away.

By noon, the gym was set up with enough

tables and chairs to accommodate more than five hundred conference attendees. The registration table by the front doors was staffed by three frightened-looking members of the youth committee, and conference signs had been posted everywhere, zealously taped to concrete walls by Aliyah Aunty's teenage children. Other volunteers had set up tables and assembled copies of the conference program.

Ayesha was inside the large outdoor tent that would host the Singles Mixer that night. Khalid found her counting out cutlery for dinner.

"Assalamu Alaikum," he greeted her. "Can I help you with that?"

He looked tired, as if he had not slept well last night. She wondered if he was worried about something. Ayesha returned his salams, her tone wary. Clara had cautioned against jumping to conclusions, but she wasn't sure what to think of Khalid, not after Tarek's disclosure.

"I'm fine," she said, and she turned away. "I'm sure your mother needs your help inside."

Khalid spoke from behind her. "If you have some time later tonight, I would like to speak to you regarding a personal matter."

"We have nothing more to say to each other," Ayesha said, dumping a pile of forks on a table with a clatter.

Khalid walked around the table to face her. "What if I bring you some kofta and paratha, will you talk to me then?"

Ayesha looked up. He had a half smile on his face. A curl had come loose from his white cap, and his hands were folded in front of him, as if in prayer. He met her gaze and then leaned forward. "Please," he said softly. "Ayesha, I can't stand this. I miss you."

Hafsa came bounding up to them, and Ayesha jumped away, her heart thumping. "What are you doing here?" she asked, her voice breathy.

"I'm here to help, obviously." Hafsa looked from Khalid to Ayesha, clearly annoyed. She turned to Khalid. "Why don't you show me where the decorations are, sweetness?" she cooed. "I'll probably need some help with that heavy banner your mother ordered. You're so strong — would you mind?"

Khalid gave Ayesha one last lingering look before following Hafsa inside the mosque.

The imam trotted up to Ayesha, his face wreathed in smiles. "Thank you for all your hard work, Sister Ayesha. Your website and posts have accomplished their goal. The conference is a success!"

Ayesha smiled, caught up with the imam's enthusiasm. "I'm so happy things worked out. Where is Brother Tarek? I thought he would be here directing the setup."

Imam Abdul Bari cleared his throat. "He did not show up this morning. He left a voice message saying that he would be present this afternoon, that he had put Sister Farzana in charge while he attended to some personal business."

"When will Sheikh Rafeek arrive?" Ayesha asked.

A look of panic crossed the imam's face.

"Let me guess. Tarek promised to take care of that." Ayesha sighed. "I'll pick him up from the airport. Don't worry, Sister Farzana has everything under control here."

The imam smiled. "She is a force to be reckoned with."

"Like a Category 4 hurricane," Ayesha agreed.

"Make sure you are back in time for your poetry recitation!" the imam called out to her, but Ayesha didn't hear him as she hurried to the parking lot.

"Ayesha!" a voice called out, and she spotted Masood. She wasn't in the mood for another ridiculous conversation and ducked behind her car, but it was too late. He was already striding toward her.

"You never texted me back." Masood was wearing a short-sleeved black button-down shirt and khakis, his hair slicked back. On his shirt was the logo for his company, Better Life Wholistic.

Ayesha stood up and pasted a smile on her face, resigned to a few minutes of catch-up chat. "I was busy with work. Nice to see you again, Masood," she said.

"I'm here for the conference. I can usually sign a few clients at these events. Where are you going?"

Ayesha explained about the guest speaker, her hand hovering above the car door handle. "I'm in a rush. We'll talk again soon —"

But Masood ignored her and opened the passenger-side door. "I love Sheikh Rafeek," he said, getting in and fastening his seat belt. "His lecture on the power of positive thinking made me step up my life-coaching business."

Ayesha was about to protest when the rear door opened and a familiar figure dived into the backseat, her head down. "Drive, drive, drive!" Hafsa whispered loudly. "Before that crazy woman makes me do anything else!"

Ayesha didn't have time to argue with

these two idiots. She just got in the car and turned on the radio.

"Ooooh, I love this song!" Hafsa said. "Turn up the volume!"

Ayesha's grip on the steering wheel tightened as Masood blasted the music. She turned onto the main street and drove toward Highway 401 as Masood and Hafsa sang along to Usher's "DJ Got Us Fallin' in Love."

Tarek sidled up to Farzana, who was barking at two terrified teenagers.

"Where have you been?" she asked, her voice contemptuous.

Tarek motioned for her to follow him to a quiet corner of the mosque. "I knew you would have things under control here. I was gathering evidence for that issue we discussed." He took out a flash drive and passed it to Farzana.

"This will prove the imam is a thief and a liar?" she asked.

Tarek nodded. "Make sure you play it in front of as many witnesses as possible. There's no telling what Abdul Bari will do once the truth is revealed. Open the file titled 'Just Desserts' and press Play."

Farzana tucked the flash drive into her pocket. "I'm glad you're not completely useless," she said. "I'll make sure this little bomb goes off in front of the entire congregation. The imam must be brought to justice."

Hafsa and Masood were both singing along with Usher — at the top of their lungs and off-key. Ayesha reached out and snapped the music off, and there was a sudden silence.

"You know, I can do the Usher dance," Masood offered. "I know all the moves. It's important for wrestlers to be light on their feet."

"You're a wrestler?" Hafsa asked, sticking her head between the two front seats to appraise Masood.

"I know the moves to Beyoncé's 'Single Ladies' too," Masood said.

Ayesha tried not to picture Masood in a unitard. "Let me introduce you: Hafsa, this is Masood."

"Now I'm a life coach for wrestlers. You wouldn't believe the problems we face in our industry. And do we get the same respect? No, it's all about hockey players and soccer jocks."

Hafsa nodded. "People don't understand how difficult it can be to forge your own path and take risks. We can't all hide in our classrooms."

Ayesha cut her eyes at her cousin in the rearview mirror. "Or depend on Daddy's money," she said.

"I'm sensing some tension in the car," Masood said. "Let's try a breathing exercise. Everyone close your eyes."

Ayesha's knuckles were white on the steering wheel. "Hafsa doesn't need a life coach. She needs a psychiatrist."

"I consider myself a doctor of the heart," Masood said. "How about a motivational mantra?"

"Don't bother," Hafsa snapped back. "Ayesha knows what's best for her, and for everyone else too. Also, she's always right."

"I'm only trying to look out for you, but you keep pushing me away," Ayesha said.

"You're not my mother. Stop telling me what to do," Hafsa said.

"Sounds like there are some real issues here," Masood said. "Why don't you book an appointment? Introductory sessions are free."

"Shut up, Masood," Hafsa and Ayesha chorused.

"All right, I'll do one right now, on the house." Masood rubbed his hands together, then he put a finger to his forehead, closing his eyes.

"I thought he said he was a life coach, not a psychic," Hafsa whispered.

"He's a lunatic. One of your rishta cast-offs. Please thank your mother for me," Ayesha said.

"Ladies, this petty bickering conceals a deeper issue. Tell me, Ayesha — have you suffered a significant loss in your life?" Masood asked.

"No," Ayesha said. "Mind your own business."

"Her father died when she was a kid, in India," Hafsa said.

Ayesha frowned at her cousin. "I don't want to talk about this, especially not with *you*. You told Khalid it would be funny if my dead father turned out to be a gangster!"

Masood turned to Hafsa. "I can't help unless I know what happened."

"I heard my dad talking about it once with my mom," Hafsa said in a halting voice. "Something about a 'facade.' I don't know what that means."

Masood looked pensive. "This early loss has led Ayesha to be particularly protective of the people she loves. Hafsa, meanwhile, is chafing under the restrictions and expectations placed on her. Tell me, Hafsa, have you made any significant decisions lately?"

It was Hafsa's turn to squirm. "I'm getting married soon, and Ayesha keeps interfering because she's jealous."

Masood steepled his fingers together. "You are engaging upon the more adult path of matrimony, which frightens your cousin, who is afraid she will lose you, or that you will get hurt. My diagnosis, as an accredited life coach, is to confront your feelings head-on. Do some light meditation, followed by power wrestling three times a week."

There was silence in the car. Ayesha didn't know whether she should laugh or pull over and smack Masood.

"You're a genius," Hafsa broke in, her voice awed. "Ayesha, I'm sorry for what I said about your dad, but I have no intention of being killed by a facade or whatever." Her voice softened. "I know you don't agree with my decisions and actions, but I'm an adult."

Ayesha felt a lightening at these words, as if an unacknowledged weight had been lifted from her shoulders. Masood was a goof, but maybe he was on to something. She hated fighting with Hafsa, and this sort-of apology was probably the closest her cousin would get to admitting fault. It was enough, for now. There was a way forward from here.

They arrived at the airport. Ayesha parked in the carpool lane and leaned back to squeeze her cousin's shoulder. "I told you I was done telling you what to do. Just be smart, and be careful."

Hafsa car-hugged her. "I promise."

Ayesha glanced over at Masood. His beatific smile had turned smug. "Don't go all fan-boy on me now, but I think that's Sheikh Rafeek." She nodded in the direction of a short man wearing horn-rimmed glasses, dressed in a gray three-piece suit.

Masood squealed. "Sheikh Rafeek! Over here! Can you sign my business card?"

Moments later, distinguished guest speaker in tow, they headed back to the mosque.

The number of conference attendees had swelled significantly since they'd left, and Ayesha had a hard time finding a parking spot. She dropped the sheikh, Hafsa, and Masood at the front entrance and drove around to the overflow parking lot.

Tarek was talking to Farzana near the back doors. She disappeared inside the building, but Tarek spotted Ayesha and waved.

"I was hoping to catch up with you. I'm so impressed with the way you all worked together to make our conference a success," he said as she walked up to the mosque.

Ayesha gave him a hard look. "Where were you?"

Tarek shrugged. "Did you tell Hafsa about Khalid and his sister?"

Ayesha shook her head. "It doesn't matter. The wedding is still on."

"I was afraid of that." He paused. "There's more to the story, but I need to know I can trust you. I'm breaking someone's confidence if I tell you the rest." He put his arm around her shoulder and guided her to the other side of the entranceway, where it was quiet. The look on his face was serious. He took a deep, shuddering breath.

Alarmed, Ayesha peered at him. "Tarek, what's going on?"

He wiped his face. "It's been so long. I thought I was over her."

Ayesha's eyes widened at his implication.

"Zareena wasn't just someone I knew. She was my . . . We met in junior year. We were together for two years before . . ." He covered his face with his hands and fought to regain his composure. "I told you her family forced her into marriage, but I didn't tell you why. It was my fault." Tarek's fists clenched and his eyes were wet. "You know how conservative their family is. When Khalid told his parents about us, about the baby, they flipped out."

Ayesha gasped. Khalid had told his mother that Zareena had a boyfriend? That Zareena had been *pregnant*? She knew he was judgmental, but he must have realized how badly his mother would react to this news. Or was Khalid really that naive, that stupid?

Tarek's fists were clenched, and he spoke now in a low, urgent voice.

"I didn't know she was pregnant, not until afterward. Her parents were so angry when they found out. They beat her —" His voice cracked. "She lost the baby. Our baby. They nearly killed her, and when they sent her away, I didn't even have a chance to say good-bye." Tarek's eyes were red-rimmed. "You have to save your cousin," he said.

Ayesha knew with certainty that he was telling the truth. She reached a shaky hand out to steady herself on the rough concrete wall of the mosque. And now Hafsa was engaged to marry into this dangerous, unstable family.

A volunteer peeked his head outside the door. "Sister Ayesha, I've been looking everywhere for you," the volunteer said. "You're up next. It's time to recite your poem."

388

Khalid watched Ayesha walk onto the stage, her face pale as she stood in front of almost six hundred people. He watched as her graceful hands straightened her purple hijab and adjusted her blue tunic shirt, her expression calm and resolute. *She is so beautiful,* he thought. She was the most beautiful woman he had ever seen, and after this performance, he would tell her how he felt. How he had felt about her from the first moment he saw her.

Khalid was in love with Ayesha, and every second spent without her was wasted.

Ayesha performed a minute adjustment to her microphone, her eyes roving through the crowd. Khalid moved to the center of the room, and she seemed to freeze at the sight of him. He was too far away to catch the expression in her eyes.

"Assalamu Alaikum," she said, her voice tinny in the microphone. "I had another poem prepared for you today, but I changed my mind. In the face of darkness, sometimes the only response is Shakespeare."

The crowd murmured, looking around in confusion. Ayesha took a deep breath and leaned forward. In a different voice, one strong and clear and powerful, her limbs loose and languid, she recited:

Tomorrow, and tomorrow, and tomorrow,
Creeps in this petty pace from day to day,
To the last syllable of recorded time;
And all our yesterdays have lighted fools
The way to dusty death. Out, out, brief
    candle!
Life's but a walking shadow, a poor
    player,
That struts and frets his hour upon the
    stage,
And then is heard no more. It is a tale
Told by an idiot, full of sound and fury,
Signifying nothing.

There was silence after she finished, and Ayesha kept her head lowered. When she looked up, there were tears on her face, and she stared across the room at Khalid in abject misery.

Then she walked off the stage without another word.

Khalid followed her to the parking lot. Ayesha stood by her car, fumbling with her keys. They slipped from her hands, and he bent down to pick them up. She looked at him again, and Khalid was lost.

A man less in love, less filled with purpose, might have hesitated at this point. But Khalid could sooner stop Niagara Falls from flowing than stop the words bubbling from his lips.

"I've tried so hard to control my feelings for you, to banish them from my heart, but my struggles have been in vain. I must be allowed to speak freely. Ayesha, I'm in love with you."

Ayesha's back was to the car, and her hand gripped the door handle tightly.

Emboldened by her silence, Khalid continued. "I know this might come as a shock to you. I don't believe in love before marriage. I know I have questioned your religious convictions in the past, but you can work on your faith. I'm a good catch for someone of your age and social standing. My family is rich and I have a good job. You can quit teaching and focus on writing your little poems. I will approach your mother to decide on a wedding date as soon as possible." Khalid smiled at Ayesha, his speech complete.

Ayesha straightened up and put a hand out to stop him from saying anything further. "It is customary to wait for the girl's response before you start planning the wedding."

Khalid froze. "What do you mean?" he asked.

"My answer to your proposal is . . . no."

"I don't understand," Khalid said.

"I mean no. No, I will not marry you. No, there is no possible chance that I could ever love you, or want you for my husband."

Khalid took a step backward. "You like me. I know you do."

"If you like me, or love me as you claim, why would you ask me to marry you in the most insulting way possible? You question my faith, insult my family, my job, you belittle my poetry and then tell me that you love me against your will, against your very beliefs."

"I am trying to be honest," he said. "Should I hide my struggles?"

Ayesha's face flushed with rage. "Even if I could overlook all of that, I could never marry you because *you're still engaged to my cousin*! Or are you so shallow and selfish you've already forgotten her?"

Khalid jerked back as if slapped. Ayesha continued, relentless.

"In fact, you can say good-bye to that arrangement as well. Do you think I would allow my cousin to marry into a family who beat their only daughter half to death and then forced her into an arranged marriage in India?"

"Who told you that?" he asked.

"I know what you did to Zareena. You're a monster, and the worst type of Muslim, a coward and a hypocrite. I wouldn't marry you if you put a gun to my head!"

She snatched her car keys from his numb fingers and drove out of his life.

CHAPTER THIRTY-FOUR

Khalid couldn't move. He was afraid his legs wouldn't support his weight and he stood still, a mannequin rooted to the spot.

Ayesha thought he was a monster.

He was still engaged to Hafsa.

And what about Zareena? He didn't even know if his only sister was safe or not. Ayesha was right: He was shallow and selfish.

Shame washed over Khalid in great, heaving waves, and he wanted to bury his face in his hands, but he still couldn't move.

He was such a fool.

What had Ayesha heard about Zareena?

And what was he thinking, asking another girl to marry him when he was still engaged to her cousin? Or before he heard back from his sister?

Stupid, stupid, stupid.

Nothing could possibly make this moment worse. Nothing.

"K-Man! Where's the party at?" Amir asked, Ethan and Mo ambling beside him.

Ayesha was shaking so hard she had to pull over to the side of the road. She buried her face in the steering wheel.

A tap on her window made her look up from her sodden arms, but there was no one there. She wiped her eyes and drove to her neighborhood park. She didn't want to go home, and she didn't trust herself to call Clara. She couldn't talk to Nana, or Hafsa, or her mother. They would just pat her on the shoulder while she sobbed.

She didn't want their pity. Ayesha didn't want to explain or cry, because she was furious. She hadn't been this angry in a long time. Probably not since she'd first moved to Canada, when her anger had been a dark ball that sat where her heart should be, and she so desperately missed her father.

The park was nearly deserted, only a few teenagers talking quietly by the swings, a mom and toddler by the slides. She sat down on a bench near the geo-dome.

She'd thought Khalid was different from other men, but her first impression had been correct after all. Ayesha recalled the judgmental way he had spoken about her at Bella's. He looked down on every Muslim who didn't live up to his narrow views of piety and goodness.

At least with Tarek, you expected it; he was a player, and there was always a game. Even Masood was predictable, with his ridiculous self-importance. But Khalid was the worst. He was a hypocrite, so convinced of his moral superiority that he almost had her fooled.

But what about the way he encouraged you to perform poetry at the conference? a nagging voice whispered in her mind. *What about the way he speaks of Zareena? He isn't a woman-hater. He is a person, complicated and confused. Just like you.* But she pushed those thoughts away. She would not be taken in again.

He said he loved her.

He had called her poems "little."

He said he loved her.

He had insulted her family, thrown his wealth and privilege in her face.

But he said he loved her.

Ayesha stood up from the bench, hands curled into fists. She started running, away from the park, toward the track beside the baseball diamond. Blood pounded in her ears as her feet smacked against the soft brown gravel of the field. She was wearing black heels, but her rage urged her on.

No man had ever told her he loved her before.

Ayesha hated him for that, probably most of all.

All of this would have been different if her father had still been alive. Her mother wouldn't be at work all the time or have such a negative view on marriage. They might still be living in India. Right now, that sounded like a good alternative to her life here.

If she was still in India, she never would have met Khalid. She would have been at peace.

Amir sat beside Khalid on the parking lot curb. He had sent Ethan and Mo away to mingle with the other singles. He had never seen his friend like this.

"She hates me," Khalid said.

"I'm sure she only dislikes you, like, a lot," Amir said, patting him on the shoulder. "Why did you ask her to marry you?"

"I love her. I thought she'd say yes. I'm such an idiot."

"Maybe you should have broken things off with her cousin before you made a move."

Khalid looked up at Amir. "You're not very good at this."

Amir's eyes rested on two figures, a man and a woman, standing just outside the tent. Their heads were together and the man was speaking urgently.

"Isn't that hottie hijabi your fiancée?" Amir asked, nodding in the couple's direction. Khalid recognized Hafsa, talking to Tarek.

"You mean my soon-to-be-*ex*-fiancée." Khalid got to his feet.

"I'll be here to help her pick up the pieces. Though it looks like I might have to get past that guy first. You know he's putting the moves on your girl, right?" Amir said as Tarek gave Hafsa a hug, taking her by surprise. After a moment's hesitation, she hugged him back.

"I'm not judging the behavior or actions of anyone else ever again," Khalid declared.

Amir's eyes were still on Hafsa and Tarek. "You better keep an eye on that guy, Khalid. He's a shady scuzzball."

Khalid shook his head. "No more judgments. No more assumptions."

"Trust me on this one. Takes one to know one." Amir stood beside Khalid and punched him lightly on the shoulder. "I know it hurts now, and it will probably hurt tomorrow, but eventually, like maybe after a few years, you'll get over it."

"You're really terrible at this," Khalid said, but he punched Amir back. He started walking toward Hafsa.

Breaking up with Hafsa was quick. Khalid found the words flowed from him easily, as if he had been rehearsing them for weeks.

"I have spent a lot of time thinking about our relationship. I've prayed about it too, and I now realize we are not compatible. I can't make you happy. Please forgive me for any pain I've caused you."

Hafsa was shocked. *"You're* breaking up with *me?"* she asked. She put a hand on her hip. "Do you know how many people told me to dump you? Haris, Ayesha, Tarek. *I'm* dumping *you,* and don't you dare try to say anything different!"

Khalid bowed his head. "I would never speak publicly about our private business."

"I could have had any guy," Hafsa said. "I *settled* for you. You will never do better than me. Never!" Her eyes were flashing, her voice raised.

"I never set out to cause you pain."

"If you think you can get with my cousin now, forget it. She hates your crazy beard, your stupid clothes, your obsession with the *mosque.* Enjoy being alone for the rest of your life!" Hafsa stalked off.

Khalid looked over and caught the eye of Amir, who gave him a thumbs-up. He waited for some emotion to hit him. Hafsa was his mother's choice; he should be upset that his perfect arranged marriage had disintegrated. But the only thing he felt was an overwhelming sense of relief.

Feeling lighter than a man with a broken heart had any right to be, Khalid wandered into the outdoor tent, where the Singles Mixer was in full swing. He might as well make sure the rest of the conference attendees were having a good time.

Khalid had been surprised to learn that a Singles Mixer did not involve parents. Instead the young people chatted together on their own. As he approached the tent, he noted all the seats at the tables were filled. The moderator, a young woman dressed in a colorful abaya robe and hijab, stood at the front, directing young men and women through a round of speed-introductions. The inside of the tent was draped in gauzy red fabric, and gently glowing paper lanterns hung from the ceiling. The room was perfumed with the smell of freshly mowed lawn, and it buzzed with energy and lively conversation.

He wondered how his life would have unfolded if he had been a participant at the

Singles Mixer and met Ayesha for the first time today. Maybe they would be talking and smiling at each other, like the couple in front of him.

"There are many paths to love," Imam Abdul Bari said, surveying the scene before him with a satisfied smile. "The executive board had reservations about this event. I told them, if we do not make space for love in our mosque, the young people will look elsewhere." He patted Khalid on the shoulder. "Though the more traditional route works as well, of course."

"Hafsa and I are no longer engaged," Khalid said.

"Oh, thank God," Imam Abdul Bari said. "I did not want to say anything earlier, but I have never seen a couple more ill-matched."

Khalid cracked a smile. "If anyone asks, she dumped me."

"Now you are free to pursue Ayesha," the imam continued happily. "A more compatible scenario. September is a good month for weddings, and I happen to have an opening in my schedule. I would very much like to perform the ceremony."

Khalid looked at the young couple in front of him again. The girl, wearing a bright-green patterned hijab, was writing something down on a piece of paper. She passed it to her partner, a serious-looking young man with glasses and a goatee. He carefully pocketed the note and returned her smile.

"No more rushing into things," Khalid said out loud.

The imam peered at him. "What do you mean?"

"I was so afraid of losing Ayesha I didn't think things through. It's not enough to find someone you love. You have to be ready for that love, and ready to make changes to welcome it into your life."

A few young women and men at the tables in front nudged their friends. One serious-looking man with a neatly trimmed beard looked up.

"That's the problem these days. The guys all want perfect Bollywood divas," one of the young women, a petite girl in a black-and-white striped hijab, offered to Khalid and the imam.

"And the girls have all these high expectations of us," a young man with square black glasses added. "Like, how much money are you making? How big is your house? What car do you drive?"

"The aunties are the worst," the girl continued. "We get ranked on skin color, height, weight, our parents' social circle . . .

If we haven't settled down by thirty, we're failures."

"Or there's something wrong with us," another man, chubby and wearing a wrinkled cotton shirt, chimed in. "I'm thirty-five and single. I was in school and in debt for years. I didn't want to burden another person with all of that."

"Allah placed love in your hearts and created you as two separate individuals," the imam said. "The Islamic view of marriage is not the same as secular romantic love." He paused, thinking. "I have been married for more than twenty-five years, and my wife and I are vastly different people. I think the reason we are still married and happy, most of the time, is because we have learned to forgive each other for not being the Ideal. We accept each other's limitations."

The young singles stared at the imam, unimpressed by his prosaic description of married life. Everyone except Khalid, who gripped the imam's arm hard. "Where is my mother?" he asked.

The imam patted him on the shoulder. "I try never to know the answer to that question."

Khalid walked swiftly toward the gym.

Farzana was in the gym with her friends

when Khalid approached and asked her if he could have a word in private. They walked outside to the main entrance, where they stood flanked by four large mirrored doors and an imposing stone staircase no one ever used. Khalid and Farzana were alone.

All of the adrenaline from his encounter with Hafsa was still coursing through him, and the imam's words echoed in his mind. He needed to confront his mother, now.

"The imam is stealing money from the mosque," Farzana said, interrupting his thoughts. "I have notified the mosque president. I knew Abdul Bari was a crook."

"Ammi, why don't you want Zareena to attend my wedding?" Khalid asked.

"I was going to notify the police, but there is no reason to air our dirty laundry in public. We will have him banished from the property. I will hire the next imam, someone young and pliable."

Khalid looked at his mother in exasperation. "The imam is not a thief. Ammi, why did you send Zareena away?"

"People must pay for their mistakes. It is best if these matters are dealt with quickly and quietly."

Khalid wasn't sure if his mother was talking about the imam or his sister. He pressed the issue. "Why didn't you call her after Abba died? Why haven't you talked to her since you sent her away?"

"Khalid, you need to focus. The imam is a thief! Make a citizen's arrest."

Khalid felt a rising frustration with his mother. Ayesha's accusations about his sister were painful and had stirred up so many unhappy memories. He wanted to shake his mother out of her rigid thinking. "I send Zareena money every month," he said abruptly. "We have been in touch for over ten years."

Farzana started. "Foolish boy. She's using you."

"She was seventeen and she made a mistake," Khalid said.

Farzana drew herself up. "She was an embarrassment, and it was my job to correct her behavior. She's lucky I was so gentle."

Khalid felt disgust at his mother's words. Had she always been like this, self-righteous and cruel? Was it possible that he had simply never noticed? "She's your only daughter and you treated her like a criminal. Zareena deserved better."

"If you won't confront the imam, I will. I don't know what's gotten into you lately, Khalid. I hope this isn't Hafsa's influence."

Khalid was angry now, and he couldn't stop the words from slipping from his mouth. "Hafsa and I are no longer engaged."

Farzana continued as if he hadn't spoken. "It is a good thing your fiancée is so young and well behaved. She will listen to me when I advise her."

"Ammi, did you hear me? We're not getting married anymore."

"Yes, you are."

"No," Khalid said. "We're not."

Farzana looked at her son for the first time since they had walked out together. He recognized the stricken expression on her face, and his voice softened. He took her hand.

"I want you to be part of my life, Ammi, but it's time I made my own decisions and learned to live with the consequences. Whatever they turn out to be."

Farzana snatched her hand away. "You will leave me too. Just like your father and your sister before him."

Khalid wanted to reassure his mother that he would never abandon her. A part of him wished he could take back his words. He didn't want to hurt her. But he also felt a sense of lightness and relief. For the first time in his life, he had told his mother what he actually thought about something, and it felt fantastic.

"Yo, K-Man!" Amir stood at the bottom of the staircase. "Your ex-hottie just got in a car with Mr. Shady. I told you to watch out for him. She gave me this." He held out a Post-it note. "I didn't read it," he lied.

Khalid turned to his mother. "Ammi, who told you the imam was stealing the conference funds?"

Farzana wiped her eyes. "Tarek. He's a good boy. He wanted to warn me."

Khalid ran down the stairs. He snatched the note from Amir's outstretched hands and read it quickly. His mother joined him, and her eyes widened as she read over his shoulder.

"The reason I know the imam could not possibly have stolen the conference money is because I set up the website myself," Khalid said. "All registrants paid directly into the Muslims in Action account, the same account controlled by Brother Tarek. He told me he cleared it with you."

"He told me the imam was a crook and that he would keep the money safe for the mosque."

Farzana and Khalid looked at each other, panic clear on their faces. Khalid did a quick calculation: tens of thousands of dollars in desperately needed donations, gone.

CHAPTER THIRTY-FIVE

A small crowd had gathered in the parking lot. Hafsa's parents stood apart, frantically dialing their daughter's cell phone over and over.

"Hafsa would never get into a car with a strange man. Something must have upset her," Samira Aunty said.

Something like a semipublic breakup? Khalid and Amir exchanged glances, thinking of the Post-it note in Khalid's pocket.

I'm going to have some fun with a real man — he's hot, rich, and totally into me. Tell everyone I'll be in touch after our nikah. And don't forget — I dumped YOU!

Khalid assumed she was joking about the nikah. Hafsa wanted a big, showy wedding. He felt the first flicker of guilt. "I'm sure she's fine," he said out loud, but no one paid him any attention. He wished Ayesha were here. Even if she yelled at him, he would feel better.

The imam plucked at Khalid's sleeve. "I hate to think the worst of a fellow Muslim, but it is better to have all the facts," he said. "How much money was deposited into the Muslims in Action account?"

"A lot. Enough to buy us a few months of breathing room."

The imam closed his eyes. *"Subhanallah."*

"I'm sure Brother Tarek took Hafsa to run an errand. Or perhaps out for coffee. He wouldn't steal from a mosque, and even if he was that reprehensible, I'm sure Sister Hafsa would convince him otherwise," Khalid said, trying to sound reassuring.

Abdul Bari looked pale. " 'The pens have been lifted, and the pages have dried,' " he quoted.

After Hafsa's parents made a call to the police, the crowd dissipated and Khalid drove his mother home.

Farzana was uncharacteristically silent, but she perked up as he pulled into their driveway. "Now that Hafsa has run away with Tarek, we can cancel the wedding. I never liked her anyway. The mistake we made was trying to find a girl here instead of in India. I have another girl in mind for you. Her name is Zulfat and she lives in

410

Hyderabad. She's seventeen, and if we start the sponsorship now, she can immigrate to Canada soon."

Khalid stared at his mother. She couldn't be serious.

Farzana crossed her arms. "What if I telephone Zareena and invite her to visit?"

Khalid took the key out of the ignition. He thought about his sister, who hadn't returned any of his texts or e-mails. He had buried his worry for her, just as he had buried his feelings of loss and guilt. No more.

If he had been looking for a sign that he had made the right decision, his mother's attempt to arrange his marriage to another stranger, and cajole his obedience by promising to telephone Zareena, was better than a burning bush. For better or for worse, he had taken the first few steps toward a new life.

"Zareena is no longer part of your life," he said softly. "You have no daughter. Remember?"

Khalid paced his room, his thoughts jumbled. It wasn't just that Hafsa had run away with Tarek. It wasn't just that Ayesha had stomped on his heart. Or that his only sister had vanished. Something else was bothering him. Khalid couldn't stop replaying Ayesha's words: *Gun to my head . . . Coward and hypocrite . . . You beat your sister almost to death . . .*

He paused, rewinding. That last allegation, at least, he could answer. Khalid reached for his blue leather notebook, the twin of the one he had bought for Ayesha back when he'd thought his life would unfold exactly as planned.

He began to write.

The townhouse was quiet when he walked over, but the lights were on. A young man opened the door and looked Khalid up and down.

"I heard Hafsa dumped you and ran off with some pretty boy," the young man said.

Khalid remembered him now: Ayesha's brother, Idris. "Is your sister here?"

Idris yelled for Ayesha before letting him into the living room. He perched on the arm of a saggy sofa.

"Is that beard for real?" Idris said. "I forgot to ask at the engagement."

"Yes."

"Solid."

There was a moment of silence. Then: "I hear you're rich."

"My mother has money, not me."

412

"That's probably why Hafsa dumped you. I'm going to be rich one day. I'm killer at writing code. Maybe you could come work for me." He reached into his pocket and handed Khalid a business card.

Khalid took it and nodded gravely. "I'd like that."

Satisfied, Idris wandered away. Khalid stood up and walked around the small living room. There was a framed picture of the Kaaba on the wall, along with a print of the Prophet's Mosque in Medina. On a small side table, a large white marble model of the Taj Mahal was prominently displayed. His eyes lingered on the model, and he thought about the legendary love Emperor Shah Jahan had for his wife Mumtaz Mahal. After he was deposed by his sons, Shah Jahan had spent his last days staring through the window of his jail cell at his wife's tomb. It came to represent his deep grief and love.

Ayesha slowly walked down the stairs, watching him stare at the Taj.

"It belongs to my Nani. A wedding gift, I think," she said to his back.

"I'm sorry," he said. She didn't smile.

"Why did you come?" Her voice was flinty.

He moved toward her, reaching first for the letter, but pulling out Hafsa's Post-it note instead.

Ayesha read quickly, shaking her head in disgust. "Did she break things off with you?"

Khalid shifted his weight. "That is what the note claims," he said. "I didn't want to show this to her parents at the mosque. They were already frantic. I thought I'd ask if you had any idea where she might have gone. Does she like to frequent a particular park, or . . ." He trailed off. Ayesha was laughing softly.

"Shouldn't you know this stuff? After all, you were engaged to be married. You should be able to read her like an open book."

The mocking tone in her voice made Khalid wince. She was so angry with him. She had every right to be.

"I knew her better yesterday than the day before," he said. "However, a few weeks' acquaintance is not enough to sustain a working knowledge of another person."

"But it's enough time to decide to marry them?" Ayesha asked, fixing him with her dark eyes.

Khalid looked away. He didn't know why he was so shy to admit the truth now: She was right. He wasn't ready to get married, not to Hafsa. He should never have played along with the engagement, not after he'd discovered the identity mix-up.

"That's what I thought," Ayesha said.

414

"Since you're not together anymore, I don't think this is any of your concern. I'll tell Sulaiman Mamu about the note. They might have some ideas. We'll handle it from here."

"How are they?" Khalid asked.

"Samira Aunty has taken to her bed. Sulaiman Mamu is trying to stay calm. When I left, he was calling around to hospitals."

Khalid stood to go. "I'm so sorry, Ayesha —" he began.

"I'll let you know if we hear anything," she said. She didn't look at him. "It's been a long day."

She walked him to the door. He wanted to reach out and take her hand, to reassure her that everything would work out, but there were too many lies between them already. He said salam and closed the door behind him.

Before he could stop himself, he slipped the letter underneath the doorjamb. Now it was in Allah's hands.

Ayesha heard the rustle of paper from the kitchen. She picked up the thick white envelope, weighing its heft. Curiosity wrestled with anger and won. She read the letter upstairs in her room.

415

Dear Ayesha,

Thank you for accepting this letter. You have made your intentions clear, and this is not a request to reconsider. I respect you too much to assume you do not know your own mind.

However, honor compels me to answer the other charges leveled against me. I have always found it challenging to express my thoughts in person, and I was in some distress during our exchange this afternoon. In truth, I find it difficult to speak coherently in your presence.

Sometimes it is also hard to breathe.

Ayesha's heart beat fast as she read the line over again before moving on.

Firstly, you accused me of insulting your family and your faithfulness. I apologize for offending you. You are right — I have a tendency toward judgment and have decided from this point forward to suspend all assumptions.

As for the second charge: I do not wish to hide my initial impression of you. When we first met, you were performing in a bar . . . sorry, lounge. The second time we met, you were impersonating your cousin and misrepresenting yourself to an imam. I can add, however, that upon getting to know you I have come to realize you are a loyal, intelligent, outspoken person who has made great sacrifices for the people you love and the principles you live by. That is the definition of faith in my mind.

Next, my reference to your "little poems." I haven't known you for very long, but in all that time, you have never displayed any pride in your art. When you were asked to perform at the conference, you were reluctant. Yet when you recited your work at Bella's, you were extraordinary. You are upset with me for belittling your work, yet you seem to have little regard for it yourself.

Finally, my opinions regarding arranged marriage: I must address these along with the most serious of your accusations — the alleged beating, nearly to death, of my sister, Zareena.

Zareena is almost four years older than me. I have heard that an age difference of this amount usually results in children who are raised independently. Certainly, my sister and I are very different people. She is an extrovert, popular, and adventurous. In contrast I am an introvert, preferring my own company to that of most others. Yet we got along quite well, until she started high school. At that point our paths drifted as she began to hang out with friends who preferred to party rather than to attend class. She became more and more extreme in her behavior, and though I covered for her as much as possible, our parents knew something was not right.

I am not telling you this to condone what came next.

In her junior year, when she was seventeen years old, something happened to Zareena that threw my parents over the edge. I'm not entirely sure what. I suspect she was arrested, or caught in a compromising situation. Regardless, the fallout was terrible. They took her out of school, and within two weeks had sent her to Hyderabad, India, where she was married to a distant cousin.

She was sent to Hyderabad against her will, and married against her will. For this, there is no excuse. But she was never beaten, of that I am certain.

To be honest, I'm not sure if this distinction makes any difference. I am certain her banishment led to my father's early death. My sister's absence haunts me still, and though I am in regular contact with her through text and e-mail, I have not seen her in twelve years. Fear of hurting my mother's feelings has kept me from visiting her in India.

I failed Zareena by keeping silent when I should have defended her. I'm not sure I will ever forgive myself for being such a coward.

My opinions regarding arranged marriage hardened against the backdrop of this experience. I wanted my family involved in my choice of spouse. My mother insisted that she would select my wife, and after I witnessed the way the situation with Zareena blew our family apart, I agreed. This was why I went along with my engagement to your cousin Hafsa even though I knew my heart was claimed by you.

I realize I was wrong. I ended things with Hafsa before she ran off, and I informed my mother that I will find my own wife, and make my own decisions, from this point forward.

Yours always,
Khalid Ahmed Mirza

Ayesha didn't know what to make of the letter. At first she read it with a rising anger.

How dare Khalid think this flimsy piece of paper could excuse everything?

But she read the letter again, and her heart twisted once more on, "Sometimes it is also hard to breathe."

Don't be fooled by flattery, she told herself severely. *He's still a judgmental jerk.*

She felt another pang when she reread what he had written about his sister: "I'm not sure I will ever forgive myself for being such a coward."

"My heart was claimed by you." Ayesha read that line over, shaking her head.

Jerk.

Reformed jerk?

Still a jerk.

She folded the letter carefully and stuck it inside her desk drawer, underneath a pile of receipts. Then she pulled it out again and read it once more.

"Yours always."

She threw up her hands and put the letter in her bag. For safekeeping.

Chapter Thirty-Six

It was Monday, and Hafsa had been missing for more than two days.

Ayesha was in no mood to teach, so she stayed home to help Nana prepare for his gardening competition the next week. When disaster struck, the world kept turning. Nana had ten large bags of bright-red mulch to spread around his carefully pruned plants, and they worked in silence, letting the weak spring light slowly warm them.

"Are you worried about Hafsa?" Ayesha asked.

Nana gently placed a handful of mulch around his herb garden. "I am sure she is in a spa somewhere, or perhaps shopping," he said.

Ayesha hesitated, wondering whether to tell Nana about the note Khalid had shown her yesterday, but her grandfather beat her to it.

"Your Nani told me that last night was

not the first time Khalid had entered our home." He looked at Ayesha, but she said nothing. "He is an admirable young man, but like Hafsa, he needs to grow up."

"What do you mean?"

"Every person experiences a moment of reckoning, jaanu. Khalid stands on the threshold of his destiny. It is evident he dumped Hafsa. A young woman as proud as your cousin would crow about her actions, not run away. Perhaps Khalid realized his heart belonged elsewhere," Nana said, giving Ayesha a significant look. "If that is the case, I am afraid he miscalculated."

Ayesha's heart started beating faster. "Why do you think that?"

"He will feel honor-bound to Hafsa, now. If his actions led to her hasty exodus, he will feel responsible for the fallout."

"It's not Khalid's fault Hafsa ran away from home."

Ayesha was not sure why she was sticking up for Khalid. His proposal, coming so soon after Tarek's revelation, had only angered her. And his letter last night had left her confused. Even though all evidence pointed to Tarek as the villain, Ayesha could not forget the stricken look on Tarek's face when he had told her about Zareena and their lost baby. She didn't know what to think.

Nana picked up a trowel and carefully dug out a weed, lifting it from the ground by its roots. "If I do not weed my garden, my beloved flowers will die, asphyxiated by vicious forces whose only goal is colonization. If you choose to plant the flowers, you make a choice to be responsible over other living things. Khalid is not a man who takes his responsibilities lightly."

Ayesha's heart sank as she recognized the truth of her grandfather's words. If Khalid had dumped Hafsa (likely), throwing her into an irrational tizzy (very likely), and causing her to run off with the unsuitable and possibly criminal Tarek (ditto), then Khalid would feel duty-bound to help in some way. And she had banished him last night.

Which left her exactly where she had been at the start of this whole sorry debacle: stuck. Ayesha laid her trowel down on the ground. The mulch was spread over most of the flower beds. Nana's garden was ready for the expert panel of judges.

Ayesha looked around her, trying to find a pattern in his planting of hibiscus, zucchini, violets, lavender, clover, and rocket. "I can't figure out your theme this year."

Nana stood up, grimacing as he stretched. "I titled it 'Double Service.' Every flower is both pleasing to the eye and edible. I wished to explore the theme of usefulness versus appearance. Flowers are so often mistaken as superfluous, yet their purpose is intricate and clever. They attract pollinators, ensuring their survival, and in turn they are consumed for their nutritional value. Never underestimate a flower."

Ayesha laughed. Hafsa would get a kick out of her grandfather's garden. She was like a flower herself: beautiful, ornamental, shrewd. Her smile faded. Ayesha hadn't returned to the Taj Mahal since the night her cousin ran away, but now her purpose was clear. She had to tell them about Hafsa's note.

Samira Aunty, self-appointed mourner-in-chief, had set up residence in the family room. She was surrounded by half-empty cups of tea and wads of used-up tissues, and had spent the past two days receiving a parade of nosy aunties eager to gawk at the mighty Shamsi family brought so low. Thankfully, the only other people at home when Ayesha entered the house were Sulaiman Mamu, Nani, and her younger cousins. She didn't think she could stand making small talk with the Aunty Brigade. She quickly relayed her information about the Post-it note.

"Why hasn't she called? How long does it take to get a quick nikah done somewhere? There are plenty of mosques in the city," Samira Aunty said to Ayesha.

Sulaiman Mamu looked bleak, his face lined and haggard from lack of sleep. Ayesha was filled with guilt. He had asked her to keep an eye on Hafsa, and look what had happened.

"I'm sorry, Mamu," she said. "This is all my fault."

Sulaiman Mamu shook his head. "The only people at fault are currently not answering their cell phones," he said. "Hafsa has been thoughtless and cruel. This note proves it. As for Tarek, I do not know him, but he cannot possibly be a good man. What does he want with Hafsa?"

This question had troubled Ayesha as well. Hafsa's motivation, she understood. Even as a child she'd been impulsive and had lashed out at others when thwarted.

But what was in it for Tarek? Maybe he was just as thoughtless as her cousin.

Except Ayesha didn't think so.

Tarek was a dishonest scoundrel, but he wasn't dumb. Muslims in Action was a well-recognized brand, known for its famous speakers and for running conferences around the country.

So what was his motivation? If he routinely ran off with conference funds and pretty young girls, he would have lost credibility a long time ago. Ayesha was willing to make a sizable bet that this was the first time Tarek had done something so brazen.

Again: Why?

If he was looking to blackmail Sulaiman Mamu, why hadn't they heard anything from him yet?

Even Hafsa's most epic sulks never lasted this long. Ayesha couldn't help thinking that maybe Hafsa was being held against her will somewhere, bound and gagged, crying for help, begging for mercy.

Ayesha shook her head, dismissing the unhelpful thought.

"How could she do this to me?" Samira Aunty asked Ayesha. "We had so much fun picking out her wedding *lengha.* It cost five thousand dollars and is being shipped from Pakistan direct! When I think of all the gold jewelry she picked out for the wedding just sitting in the bank deposit box . . ." Her face crumpled.

Her aunt was a silly woman, but Ayesha remembered that when she had first moved

426

to Toronto, Samira Aunty had been so kind to her. She had bought her a new bed to squeeze in beside Hafsa's princess canopy, and lavender sheets and new red pajamas to make her feel welcome.

"I've been hearing such terrible things about Tarek," Samira Aunty said when she'd calmed down. "Every visitor who arrives has a fresh story of his indecent behavior."

"When I called the Muslims in Action office, they said he wasn't answering his phone. I asked about the money, and they didn't know about that either," Ayesha said. "It sounds like he had been keeping them in the dark about our entire conference. They thought I was calling about another conference, the one being held in July."

"We talked to the police this morning," her cousin Maliha said. "Witnesses said she got into Tarek's car willingly. They can't get involved unless there's an actual crime."

Samira sniffed loudly. "My beautiful daughter is lost to me! What will people think?"

Ayesha could imagine what people would think. Hafsa would be branded unmarriageable. Her hasty actions would be a dark cloud over her family for years, affecting their social standing as well as the marital prospects of her younger sisters and even

427

Ayesha herself. A small voice in her mind mocked: *Khalid will never want you now. You're tainted by association.*

She hated this, hated the double standard for men and women. But unlike Hafsa, Ayesha had never tried to shape the world in her image. She had always seen the world and the people who inhabited it exactly as they were: flawed, imperfect, eager to think the worst of others while excusing their own misdeeds.

Ayesha recalled the mercurial Tarek, his wolf's smile at the caterer's, his smooth dealings with her and Hafsa. Then she thought about Khalid, who couldn't edit his doubts or conceal his thought process, even when he was asking her to marry him. She felt foolish, and the knowledge settled into her heart like a stone: Tarek was a beautiful liar and Khalid was awkwardly honest. Where did that leave her?

She checked her phone for the hundredth time that day and sent another text: *Hafsa. We're worried sick. Call or text. I'm begging you.*

It wasn't until after she pressed Send that she had a brainwave. If her cousin wouldn't answer any of her messages, maybe there was someone else who would know something: Hafsa's mall-rat "friend," Haris.

She gave her aunt a quick hug and promised to call her later that night, perhaps with good news.

Haris was in the food court eating chili-cheese fries. The moment Ayesha spotted him, she wanted to hug him for being so predictable. She plopped down in the seat across from him and gave him her most severe teacher look.

"Where's Hafsa?"

Haris leaned back in his seat, a smear of liquid cheddar at the corner of his mouth. "Who?"

Ayesha grabbed the chili fries and dumped them into a garbage can.

"Hey!" Haris said, his eyes widening in surprise. "What the hell!"

She slammed her hand down, hard. People at nearby tables glanced over uneasily, and Haris looked ready to bolt.

"Where. Is. Hafsa," Ayesha asked. She was enjoying the tough girl act. If the mall food court was his preferred hangout, he wouldn't want to chance being thrown out by security. Ayesha, on the other hand, had no such qualms. She hated malls.

"Relax, aiiight?" Haris said, motioning for her to calm down. "I don't know where she is. I haven't seen her in a few days."

Ayesha reached out to grab him, but he leaned away, waving his hands in the air. She noticed how young he was. His facial hair hadn't even really come in yet, and his efforts at shaving were clumsy.

"It's the truth, I swear."

"She ran off with someone else," Ayesha said. "Tarek Khan. Do you know him?"

Harris looked around as if bored, his bravado back. "We weren't going steady, you know? She could do whatever. We were only hanging out."

"Did she say anything to you about where she wanted to go or what she wanted to do?"

Haris shrugged. "She complained about her family a lot. Kept talking about her big business plans, how her dad wouldn't give her enough money. She was a whiny little bitch. I was going to dump her ass anyway."

Ayesha's hand flew of its own accord, and she slapped him, hard, across the face. They both looked stunned.

"What'd you do that for?" he asked, holding his cheek. "I told you what you wanted."

Ayesha spied the security guard heading toward them, and stood. "You're disgusting," she said. She turned and ran for the exit.

CHAPTER THIRTY-SEVEN

Khalid called in sick on Monday. He e-mailed Amir to reschedule the meeting with WomenFirst Design. If anything counted as a genuine family emergency, it was the current chaos that was his life.

He lay in bed staring at the ceiling. How had he arrived here? The plan was for him to marry the pious, modest woman his mother picked out. Not to fall in love with someone like Ayesha, agree to marry someone like Hafsa, and then help a scoundrel like Tarek bankrupt the mosque, all in the span of a few weeks.

Allah was testing him, and he was failing.

Khalid flipped onto his side and checked the time on his cell phone. It was nine in the morning and he hadn't heard Ammi in the kitchen. She had been so secretive since the conference, distracted and silent, leaving the house for hours at a time with no explanation. One more thing to add to his growing list of worries.

The doorbell finally roused him out of bed, and he padded downstairs in bare feet and pajamas, his hair and beard standing in tufts around his head like a lion's mane.

A young woman dressed in a black cotton shalwar kameez stood on the landing, a red suitcase by her side. Her face was round, eyes the same color and shape as his own. A dupatta shawl loosely covered her hair. One hand clutched the bag, the other cradled her large, very pregnant belly.

Khalid's face drained of blood and he clutched the door, knees buckling.

"Zareena?" he asked, his voice hoarse.

His sister threw down her bag and launched herself into his arms.

Zareena refused to come inside the house, so Khalid picked up her suitcase and carry-on bag — she had come straight from the airport — and they walked to the park, which was empty this early in the morning.

Khalid could not stop staring at his sister. When she had lived with them, she'd hated to wear shalwar kameez or any traditional clothing, preferring hip huggers, platform heels, and belly tops. The minute she was out of Farzana's criticizing glare, she would put on bright-red lipstick, tease her hair, and coat her eyes in black liner and sooty eyeshadow. The Zareena that Khalid remembered looked like an indie rock star. The Zareena sitting beside him looked like an Indian housewife. She saw him staring and grinned mischievously, and Khalid caught a glimpse of his long-lost sister behind her tired, jet-lagged face.

"You look like you're about to go on religious pilgrimage," Zareena said, nodding at the gray robe Khalid had thrown on before they left the house. "Have you heard of beard clippers?"

"I've been trying to e-mail and text. I even called, but some man said you were gone. I was so worried."

Zareena laughed, and Khalid realized how much he had missed the sound. "My father-in-law. He's so dramatic. Iqram and I lived with him, and when we told him we were moving to Canada, he didn't take it well. Did he complain I burned his breakfast every day?" Zareena laughed again. "He's sweet, really. He's going to be lonely without us."

Khalid's gaze was now fixed on her swollen belly. "How far along are you?" he asked.

Zareena's hands tightened around her stomach. "Almost seven months. We gave up, and then it happened. She's the reason

I'm here. I've been thinking about coming back for years, but when I found out I was pregnant, that I was having a girl, I knew it was time."

Khalid didn't know how to ask the next question. "You and your husband . . ." he began.

"Iqram and I are still together," Zareena said firmly. "I'm going to sponsor him just as soon as I get settled."

Khalid was silent. "I don't understand," he said.

Zareena stood up. "I came back to face her," she said. "I came here straight from the airport. Twelve years without a call or letter. I wanted her to see I'm still alive and doing well." Zareena's shoulders drooped. "When you opened the door, I lost my nerve."

Khalid didn't know what to say. "You must be tired," he said awkwardly.

Zareena smiled at him again. "You have no idea. Could I trouble you for a ride?" She was crashing with an old high school friend, Lauren, and refused Khalid's offer to stay at the house. He drove her to the small east-end bungalow and took her bags inside. Then he stood on the porch, fidgeting.

"Can I see you tomorrow?" he asked.

"I'll even let you take me out for dinner." Zareena hugged him, holding him close. Khalid hugged her back carefully — he didn't want to hurt his soon-to-be niece.

"I was so afraid something had happened to you. I didn't know what to do," he said, his voice trembling.

"You're the reason I could come back. All that money you sent . . . I saved every cent."

Khalid called in sick the next day too, and accompanied his sister to Ikea. Zareena joked she was a cheap date as they stood in line at the cafeteria, Khalid holding her tray while she picked out dinner: a small carton of 2% milk, almond Daim cake, and vegetarian meatballs. Khalid's stomach felt queasy, and he settled for a cup of coffee, black with three sugars.

They moved into a table in the back corner. Zareena's eyes rested on a toddler evading the grasp of his mother.

"We could have gone somewhere else to eat," Khalid said.

"I like the food here. Also, I need to buy some furniture," Zareena said. "A bed, crib, some sheets, a dresser."

"We're not just here for the food?"

Zareena smiled. "I found an apartment close by. I need to show that I have a place to live, and a job, before I can sponsor Iqram." She hesitated. "The landlord wants someone to cosign the lease. Lauren said she'd do it, but if you're willing . . ."

Khalid nodded. "Of course. I'm not sure where you'll be able to find any work, in your condition."

Zareena shrugged. "Even if it's tutoring or babysitting, I'll do anything for my family."

Khalid smiled at his sister. "You're so different."

"You're not the same skinny little boy either." Zareena took a careful bite of the Daim cake and closed her eyes. "So good," she said. "I'm sorry I didn't reply to your e-mails. I meant to, but packing up everything to move here took so much time. How's your fiancée?"

Khalid's smile faltered. "We didn't work out."

"Probably a good thing. You seemed more into that other girl, Ayesha."

Khalid's smile completely disappeared. "That didn't work out either."

"And here you are, taking your homeless, knocked-up big sister to Ikea. I don't know who has it worse."

Khalid looked at his sister — newly immigrated, financially insecure, emotionally vulnerable. Yet her face was glowing, and the teasing smile blossomed repeatedly on her face. "I think you're amazing," he said.

Zareena squeezed his arm. "Right back at you. Now let's go check out some cheap double beds."

She was careful with her money. She picked out a simple crib and dresser and a plain double bed; a queen might not fit in the rental basement apartment. A small sofa and armchair completed her purchase, and she refused Khalid's offer to pay. On the drive home, she leaned her head against the window and fiddled with the radio.

"I'm moving into my new place tomorrow," Zareena said. "Maybe you can come over. Bless it with your beard or something."

Khalid parked the car in Lauren's driveway. "Do you need more money? For groceries or something."

Zareena shook her head. "You already gave me some, remember? Every month for years."

"It was nothing," he said. "I should have done more. Zareena —"

But she was already opening the door and stepping out. "Let's talk tomorrow," she said. "My feet are killing me, and this conversation can wait one more night."

He watched her waddle to the front door.

The light turned on and Lauren let his sister in out of the cold.

CHAPTER THIRTY-EIGHT

When Khalid arrived at work on Wednesday, the office was empty. Amir was not sleeping on the couch, and his friend's desk was devoid of toiletries. Khalid settled into his chair and checked his e-mail. The presentation meeting with WomenFirst Design was scheduled for today. Maybe Sheila would be so pleased with his work that she'd let him go home early. He'd promised Zareena he would assemble the Ikea furniture.

He entered his username and password, and a screen popped up: ACCESS DENIED. PLEASE SEE NETWORK SECURITY ADMINISTRATION.

What was going on?

The phone rang, Sheila's assistant on the line. "I'm calling to remind you about your meeting with Ms. Watts. You're already five minutes late."

Mystified, Khalid hurried up to Sheila's office. She was waiting with a smirk on her

439

face, Clara beside her looking stricken.

"Late again, Khalid," Sheila said.

"I seem to be locked out of my workstation," he said. "I apologize. I did not know about this meeting in advance."

"You always have an excuse, don't you?" Sheila walked around to the other side of the desk and perched in front of Khalid. "There is no excuse for your behavior this time."

Khalid was confused. "I'm sorry?"

"Khalid Mirza, you have been found in violation of the employee code of conduct. Effective immediately, you are no longer an employee of Livetech Solutions. Please hand in your badge and security clearance, and clear out your personal effects immediately," Sheila said.

Shocked, Khalid gaped at Sheila. "What did I do?" he asked.

Sheila looked at Clara, who was sitting up very straight and trying not to cry. "We found pornography on your personal workstation. Does the website Unveiled Hotties mean anything to you?" she asked, not meeting his eyes.

Khalid's momentary confusion cleared. That stupid matrimonial service Amir had found! "It's not mine."

"It is a subscription service, and it was ac-

440

cessed several times last week," Sheila said. "What you do in your personal time is your own business, but to spend company time trolling the internet for exploited brides is truly disgusting."

Clara handed Khalid a form detailing the terms of his termination. "I'm sorry, Khalid, but there really are no other options in these situations." Her voice was shaky.

Khalid's face reddened in anger. "I would never use such a service. This is all a grave misunderstanding."

Sheila's mouth curled in disdain, but Clara motioned for her to keep quiet. "Please just sign the form, Khalid. You'll get some severance."

Khalid bowed his head, as if in prayer. The only sound in the office was the steady tick of an ornate desk clock. He thought about the five years he had worked at Livetech, happy ones until Sheila showed up and launched her campaign against him. The only reason he'd wanted to keep this job was to send money to Zareena. But his sister was here now, and eager for independence. He picked up the pen and signed.

Khalid returned to his office trailed by two security guards.

"What's going on, bro?" Amir asked. His hair was still wet from his morning shower.

Khalid didn't pause, emptying drawers into his backpack. "I've been fired. They found porn on my computer. A website called Unveiled Hotties. Perhaps you've heard of it?"

Amir reared back as if slapped. "No, no, no," he whispered under his breath. He leaned over Khalid's desk, punching in a code to override the lockout window, and clicked on an icon at the bottom of the screen.

The website, filled with nude or half-clothed women draped in some form of hijab or traditional clothing, popped up. Amir looked at Khalid with a stricken expression. "I logged on one night and paid for a subscription. It was a joke, a gag engagement gift," he said. "I must have forgotten to cancel it."

"You were probably drunk," Khalid said. The images scrolled past at a leisurely pace. "You were so bummed about your girl problems, I thought this might help."

Khalid gently placed his hand on Amir's shoulder. "I don't find mistreating young women the least bit helpful," he said.

He finished throwing his possessions into his bag, then removed his security badge. "I was supposed to present my website to WomenFirst Design today. I feel bad I am letting them down."

Amir looked puzzled. "What are you talking about, bro? They came here yesterday. Sheila showed them everything you've done so far and they seemed really happy."

Khalid closed his eyes. This wasn't about pornography on his workstation. It was about the very lucrative WomenFirst Design account. Sheila wanted to take all the credit and leave him with nothing but a lousy severance.

Amir looked guilty and unhappy. "This is all my fault," he said. "If they fire you, they'll have to fire me too. I'll tell the Shark I paid for the subscription."

Khalid shook his head. "There's no point. I was on my way out anyway. Sheila made sure of that."

Amir straightened, staring down at the computer. He clicked on a picture. "Is that Hafsa?"

The picture featured a young woman in a pink floral hijab and long gown. She was smiling brightly into the camera, looking young and vulnerable. *Our Latest Unveiled Hottie!* the banner ad screamed underneath. *Local Girl Bares All! $19.99 for a Sneak Preview!*

Khalid stared at the familiar face, horrified. "It can't be. How did those pictures even get there?" But he recognized that dress. She had been wearing it the last time he had seen her, at the mosque conference. Somehow, Tarek was involved in all of this.

"It looks like there's some kind of auction for the pictures," Amir said, clicking on the link. He looked up at Khalid. "I wonder if she even knows."

Khalid lifted his bulging backpack and nodded at the security guards, who were watching his every move. "Take care of yourself."

Amir hugged Khalid. "I'm going to make this up to you, K-Man," he said. "I'll find a way to make this right with Sheila."

But Khalid's thoughts were not on Livetech anymore.

He had more pressing concerns: how to help his pregnant sister, Zareena, and how to save Hafsa from public humiliation.

Khalid paced the living room of his sister's basement apartment, fingers raking his hair. Zareena's Ikea furniture lay in unassembled piles on the floor. He couldn't concentrate on anything, couldn't stop thinking about what had happened at Livetech.

The worst part, worse even than the contempt on Sheila's face, was the disappointment on Clara's. He had expected

Sheila to jump to conclusions, but Clara wouldn't even meet his eye or give him the chance to explain. In the end, she couldn't reconcile the Khalid she had invited into her home with the person he looked like: the women-hating, backward-thinking Muslim man.

That thought hurt most of all.

Zareena sat on the newly assembled Poäng armchair and watched him with amusement.

"You're going to wear a hole in my carpet, and I want to get my security deposit back," she joked, but he ignored her. She took another sip of chai and looked around her new home.

His sister had a peaceful expression on her face, and Khalid paused in his pacing, struck once again by how much she had changed. The old Zareena had worn her discontent like a dark cloak. The old Zareena would have been unhappy with everything in this room.

"Well, if you're not going to tell me what's wrong, let me at least make you dinner." She disappeared into the kitchen and returned fifteen minutes later with an overcooked egg that had somehow cooled to freezing, paired with dry toast. One thing at least was the same: She was a terrible cook.

"Iqram used to do most of the cooking back home. His chicken *karahi* is amazing," she said wistfully.

Khalid stopped pacing but remained standing, taking a small bite of toast. He mulled over Zareena's use of "back home." If India was "back home," what was she doing here?

"Home is wherever my family is," Zareena said, reading Khalid's mind. "You'll know what I mean when you get married."

"But you were forced into marriage," Khalid said. "Ammi didn't give you a choice."

Zareena became very still. "Your memory is very clear. Do you know the whole story?"

Khalid shook his head, feeling a familiar frustration.

"There was someone else, before Iqram. I was obsessed with him," Zareena said, sighing. "The way you are at that age." She glanced at Khalid. "The way most people are at that age," she amended. "We were only seventeen years old, and we were crazy about each other. I used to sneak out almost every night to see him. I was so happy," she said, closing her eyes. She looked at her brother, who shifted uncomfortably. "Then I found out I was pregnant."

It was Khalid's turn to be still.

"I didn't tell him. I didn't want to be a

mom at seventeen. So I made arrangements at a clinic, and I had an abortion." Zareena was silent now, cradling her stomach. "I don't regret it," she said softly. "I went on a school day during lunch and was back for gym class. Nobody knew except Lauren."

"Who was he?" Khalid asked.

Zareena didn't answer. She looked like she was in a trance, thinking of events long ago. "I thought I was okay. I didn't want anyone to know or suspect, and I didn't take care of myself. I collapsed after school by my locker. There was so much blood." Zareena was speaking into her lap now, wiping her eyes. "That's how Ammi and Abba found out. The doctor told them I had nearly died from the hemorrhaging."

"I didn't know," Khalid said, leaning forward to grip his sister's hands.

"If there's one thing our family is good at, it's keeping secrets," Zareena said, smiling. "When I got to Hyderabad, the nikah was done before I knew what was happening. Afterward, when they left me alone with Iqram, it was terrible. He had no idea what was going on. His mother had arranged the whole thing. He was pretty surprised to be stuck with me." She laughed. "By that point, I wasn't crying anymore. I was angry."

"A nikah is not valid without the bride's

consent," Khalid said.

"He never gave up on me," Zareena said, a note of wonder creeping into her voice. "He was so gentle, even when I was throwing things at his head and swearing at him in English, French, and Urdu."

Khalid shook his head. "I don't understand," he said.

"He made me donuts," she said simply. "All the things I was craving: poutine, pizza, spaghetti, cheeseburgers. He showed me the Charminar temple and the Taj Mahal. He waited for me. He never left, not once. I fell in love with the person I saw reflected in his eyes."

"Are you sure it wasn't . . . Stockholm syndrome?" Khalid asked carefully.

Zareena's laughter was buoyant, contagious. "Let me show you something." She rummaged through her suitcase and extracted a photo album. She passed it to Khalid, and he looked through Zareena's life in Hyderabad with her husband. In one picture, they posed in front of a squat, whitewashed house with adobe tile; in another, they stood beside a small blue hatchback car; another featured the couple in front of a street vendor.

Iqram was a skinny man with warm, sepia-toned skin, gangly legs and arms, short black hair, and intelligent eyes. He didn't smile in any of the pictures but stood stiffly, a stance that emphasized his angular features and square jaw. He stared directly at the camera, or more often at his wife. Zareena was smiling in each one.

"I didn't expect it to happen," Zareena said, looking at the pictures with Khalid. "It's not the same as what I felt for . . . him."

"You never mentioned Iqram in any of your letters. You kept including the things you missed about Canada. You never wanted any of this!" Khalid said. He took a deep breath and said the words he had wanted to say since Zareena had shown up on his porch. Since the day she had left. "I'm sorry this happened to you. I should have spoken up. I should have said something. I knew what Ammi and Abba were planning, but I was a coward." His voice broke.

Zareena gently took the photo album away from Khalid. "Do you remember what I was like, before?" she asked him. "I was skipping every class, getting drunk on weekends, partying with my friends. I wasn't doing well and I wasn't happy. I'm not sure where I'd be right now if I'd kept heading in that direction."

Khalid shook his head. "That's no excuse."

"Sending me to India was awful. What Ammi did was wrong, and I will never forgive her. But I also came back partly to show her that I turned out okay." Zareena started laughing again. "You know what I just realized? I'm the one who found love after marriage, and you're the one who fell in love first."

"I told you, all of that is over."

Zareena poked Khalid. "I don't care what you say. You're not a coward. You never have been."

Khalid felt lighter at his sister's words. He put his plate in the sink and stood in the middle of the living room, consumed by a restless energy that made his feet itch. He had to do something. He had to act.

"Why don't you call Ayesha?" Zareena suggested. "Send her roses. People love to forgive. It makes them feel so magnanimous."

"I'm not sure that will work."

"Do you know why Iqram and I are still together? Those first few months he let me know he was all in. He wanted me, no matter the past. If you run away in the face of a little conflict, you're not ready to settle down."

Khalid considered his sister's words. He didn't have an answer for her. So instead he asked, "Who was the guy? Do I know him?"

Zareena shook her head. "You're changing the subject. Are you ready for marriage or not?"

"Did you go to school with him?"

"Yes. Now answer my question."

Khalid sat, mulling this over. "He never contacted you again? Not even after the abortion?"

Zareena was silent. "He came to the airport. I saw him in the crowd, but it was too late."

Khalid thought this over. "I think about Ayesha all the time. I can see us together so clearly."

"I haven't thought about my ex in years," Zareena said. "I wonder where Tarek is right now, and whether he still thinks about me. I hope he's moved on, the way I have."

Khalid froze, and then the blood began pounding through his veins. "What did you say?" he asked, already reaching for his cell phone.

He knew what he had to do now.

He called Amir.

"K-Man!" Amir yelled.

"I can hear you just fine, Amir. Keep your voice down."

"Oh, sorry. Let me get out of here."

Khalid waited, and the thumping bass and music faded.

"I have some good news for you," Amir said before Khalid could say a word. "You're going to get your job back."

Khalid paused. "What are you talking about?"

"Don't get mad. You know that hot HR chick?"

"She has a name. Clara. Use it."

"Yeah, yeah. Well, I sort of used our surveillance equipment to bug her office a few weeks ago."

"Amir!"

"It's cool. I told her, she hit me, we're fine. It's not like she ever stripped in the room or anything. But she did have a lot of very interesting convos with Sheila."

Khalid paused, then he said, "I can't think about that now. What do you know about tracking a website? I think Tarek might be running Unveiled Hotties, but I need proof. If we find him, we might find Hafsa too."

"I'll do what I can," Amir said. "Hey, I think I found a place to stay, but I need a roommate. You interested?"

Khalid promised to think about it, and hung up. Next, he texted Idris:

Salams, Mr. Killer Code. How would you like to help find your cousin?

Idris responded immediately: I'm in.

Khalid made one final call, to Imam Abdul Bari. The imam answered after three rings, and his voice sounded hollow.

"What I feared most has come to pass. I informed the executive committee of the actions of Brother Tarek, and the missing money. They were quite angry."

"What happened?" Khalid asked, his heart sinking.

"There will be an emergency general body meeting on Saturday morning to inform the community of our dire financial situation." The imam paused. "The mosque will be sold to cover our debts. I have been in touch with Muslims in Action and they are in complete disarray, their reputation in tatters with the disappearance of Brother Tarek. I have also been informed that my services as imam will not be needed following the meeting."

Khalid was aghast. "They can't do that!"

"I'm afraid they already have," the imam said. "May Allah forgive us all."

CHAPTER THIRTY-NINE

Ayesha returned to the Taj Mahal after school to sit with Samira Aunty. She didn't know what else to do. Her uncle had been gone all day, driving to the different mosques in the city looking for anyone who might know something. When he returned that evening, he looked pale and ten years older. He walked straight to his office and shut the door firmly behind him. Ayesha followed and knocked tentatively. When he didn't answer, she entered.

Sulaiman Mamu had his head in his hands, his shoulders shaking with silent sobs. Ayesha hurried to his side.

"It will be all right," she said. "Hafsa is fine."

Sulaiman Mamu looked up at his niece with haunted eyes. "How can she be all right when she's with that man?" he asked. "I've been making inquiries. Everyone I talk to has nothing good to say about Tarek. He

454

has run up debts. He hasn't paid his vendors what they are owed. There are rumors about other young women."

"Has he gotten in touch with you?"

Sulaiman Mamu looked bleak. "For hush money? He seduced the wrong girl."

"What do you mean?"

"Ayesha beti, there is no more money." Sulaiman Mamu's eyes were red and bloodshot. "My business has not been doing well. I put off selling the house until after the wedding. Now I'm only sorry I didn't set aside money to pay off rascals who set out to ruin my daughter."

"Hafsa is not ruined," Ayesha said.

"Her reputation is in tatters and the vultures are circling."

"Let them circle!" Ayesha said loudly. She lowered her voice. "There must be something we can do."

Sulaiman Mamu slumped in his chair. "I have called everyone I know. The police refuse to take this seriously, and perhaps they are right. There is no criminal activity here. Hafsa has only turned her backs on us and everything we hold dear. She has shredded our hearts, that is all."

Ayesha felt helpless. "Tell me what to do. How can I help?"

Sulaiman Mamu shook his head. "All we

can do now is pray."

There would be plans to make and more people to call tomorrow. Tonight, Ayesha set her alarm for three o'clock. She remembered from Sunday school that the early morning hours were a particularly good time to ask Allah for a favor.

When her alarm went off, Ayesha made *wudu* and headed downstairs to the family room, the warmest room in the house.

She arranged her prayer mat in the darkened space and began to pray. The familiar rhythm calmed her racing mind. When she finished, she sat cross-legged on the prayer mat, her hands upturned in supplication. *Please, God. Please.*

The sound of a key in the lock broke her concentration, and she looked up to see her mother home after a double shift at the hospital. Saleha took off her rubber-soled hospital shoes and came to sit on the couch near her kneeling daughter, sighing a little as she sank into the worn cushions.

"Did you know Mamu was having money trouble?" Ayesha asked.

Saleha stretched her arms up. "I had my suspicions, but he is a proud man. He will bounce back."

Ayesha felt a prickle of irritation. "You

haven't gone to see him since Hafsa took off."

Saleha looked at her daughter, who was full of indignation. "I call every day, several times," she said mildly. "This is a waiting game."

Ayesha folded up her prayer mat, her movements jerky, not looking at her mother. Saleha watched silently.

"I know this must be hard for you," Saleha began.

"You have no idea what this is like!" Ayesha shouted. "You have no idea what it's like to wait for someone you love to come home, not knowing if they're safe or all right or —" She bit off the rest of the sentence, catching sight of her mother's bemused face.

"I do know what it's like," Saleha said quietly. "I remember very well. Your father was missing for more than a week before they found his body, but I knew on the first night that he was dead. I felt it, here." Saleha pointed to her stomach. "When you love someone the way I loved him, you just know."

Ayesha looked down at her lap. She had never heard her mother say she'd loved Syed. Most of the time, Saleha sounded bitter and angry when she spoke of her husband, if she spoke of him at all. Ayesha remembered Nana's words so long ago: *Your mother's anger conceals a very great love.*

"How did he die?" Ayesha asked. She expected to be rebuffed as usual. She expected Saleha to walk away, as she had so many times before. But her mother didn't move.

"Syed was a journalist. He covered local politics and he was ambitious; he wanted to cover the big stories. Sometimes he traveled to other cities, mostly Mumbai. This was before cell phones and the internet, so when he was gone, I had no way to get in touch with him. He wanted to be on the scene, to write about the way regular people's lives were affected by poverty and crime. He thought of himself as a crusader for justice." Saleha smiled faintly. "I worried about him every time he left the house."

Ayesha watched her mother, afraid to speak, afraid to break the spell.

"In December 1992, the Babri mosque was destroyed by Hindu extremists in Ayodhya, Uttar Pradesh. It was built in the sixteenth century, and a mob ripped it apart in a few hours."

Ayesha had heard about this, a long time ago.

"It made everyone so angry," Saleha said,

her voice low. "The Muslims, the Hindus. The entire country was so tense. I was afraid to go outside with you and Idris. You were just children. Then Syed told me he was leaving us in Hyderabad. He was going to Mumbai to cover the story." Saleha wiped the tears streaming down her cheeks. "We fought. I was so angry at him for even thinking about leaving us alone, but he said he had to go."

Ayesha remembered this, she realized. She had been nine years old, and her parents were arguing in the other room as she ate breakfast. Her parents never fought, or not so she could hear. Her mother was hysterical, her father's deep voice placating. She remembered running up to her father after he strode out of the bedroom. He bent down to hug her, and she inhaled the scent of him — cardamom mixed with sweat and the sandalwood powder he used for deodorant. He held on tightly for a few moments before releasing her. "Be a good girl. Take care of your mother and brother," he had told her.

"The *fassaad* —" Saleha began.

Ayesha jerked at the word. Hafsa said Sulaiman Mamu had used the word "facade" in connection to her father's death.

"The *fassaad* — the riots — they started

almost immediately. The worst were in Mumbai," Saleha continued. "All that rage and hate and fear exploded. Shops were destroyed, houses, entire neighborhoods burned to the ground. So many people died . . . two thousand people murdered in four weeks."

Ayesha's hands began to shake. She did not want to hear any more, but Saleha couldn't stop now, her words flowing from a newly unsealed faucet.

"The first few days, he filed his story without any trouble. He called me when he got there, and he sounded so excited. I knew he was doing what he loved, chasing a big story. The third day, he didn't file his story. His editor called me, asking if he had been in touch. That's when I knew."

Ayesha put her hand to her mouth.

"Your father was killed during one of the riots. He went to the wrong neighborhood and got caught up in the fighting. He was beaten to death."

A sob escaped Ayesha, and Saleha got off the couch and crouched beside her daughter, cradling her.

"I couldn't tell you before," Saleha said. "I didn't have the words. After they found his body, I had to go into hiding. He was the journalist who had reported on the riots, and even dead, he was a threat. I took you and Idris and left everything. We moved from house to house for weeks until Sulaiman could bribe the right official in India, and then we came to Canada as refugees. Nana and Nani came too. They couldn't bear to stay behind, not after everything."

Saleha hugged Ayesha again. "You were so brave. You've always been so brave." She smiled through her tears, then straightened, wiping her eyes. "I know Hafsa is all right. I know it in my heart, in my *jigar,*" she said, using the Urdu word for liver. "If there was anything I could have done to change what happened to your father, I would have done it. I would have crawled on my knees, swallowed my pride, handcuffed him to the door. I would have done anything."

Ayesha nodded. Sometimes prayers floated up to heaven. Sometimes they hung around here on earth and waited for you.

She would help get her cousin back. And when Hafsa had returned, safe and unharmed, Ayesha would focus on her own life, and begin to chase her own dreams.

CHAPTER FORTY

Hafsa had been missing for a week when Ayesha accompanied Sulaiman Mamu to the police station to make an official Missing Persons report. A young female police officer, Constable Lukie, carefully noted down the details of the disappearance and accepted the small picture of Hafsa.

"In situations like this, most of the time the person shows up. Maybe she was angry and wanted to punish you. Was there some sort of argument? Was she being forced into something?" the young officer asked, keeping her voice carefully neutral. Ayesha noticed her cool appraisal of them, the quick glance at her hijab.

"Hafsa was not being forced into an arranged marriage, if that's what you think," Ayesha said, but Sulaiman Mamu motioned for her to calm down.

"Please. Find my daughter," he said quietly. Sulaiman Mamu's face was gaunt and gray; there were deep lines etched under his eyes. He looked older than Nana.

Constable Lukie softened. "We'll do everything we can," she promised.

Samira Aunty still required around-the-clock attention from her family and help to deal with the steady stream of visitors. The Aunty Brigade were in daily attendance, eager to share increasingly scandalous rumors about Tarek: He was a master in the art of seduction; he was a gambler who owed money to the Punjabi mafia; he was wanted in Saudi Arabia for public indecency; he was the prodigal son of a Pakistani billionaire; he owned a dot-com that specialized in ethnic pornography. With every outlandish story, Hafsa's actions appeared more and more foolish, her reputation sinking deeper into the mud.

When Nana returned from Friday Jumah prayers at the mosque, he looked despondent. "There is a general body meeting tomorrow. The mosque is bankrupt, and Tarek has absconded with the funds. Sulaiman is too proud to go. Will you accompany me, jaanu?"

She didn't want to go. She would go. " 'Live like you're in a comedy, not a tragedy,' right?" Ayesha said.

Nana smiled, relieved. "This is simply the

plot twist at the end of act four."

On Saturday, eight days after Hafsa's disappearance, Ayesha dressed quickly for the general body meeting, pulling on a black abaya and a simple white hijab. She felt a knot of anxiety in the pit of her stomach.

Nana was waiting for her downstairs, dressed in a crisp white shalwar kameez and brown karakul prayer cap.

"I dreamed of Hafsa last night," Nana said.

"Was she okay?"

"It was her wedding day, and she was complaining about the caterers." Nana smiled at Ayesha, squeezing her hand. "The groom was not Tarek."

Ayesha shook her head. "She's been living with him for more than a week. If the groom isn't Tarek, who will it be?"

Nana looked straight ahead. "I only wish her safe return home." He paused. "After that, I will hire some very strong men to teach Tarek a painful lesson."

Ayesha laughed as they settled into the car. "I thought you were a pacifist."

"Naturally," Nana said. "Which is why I will simply watch."

The parking lot at the mosque was full. A podium and screen were set up onstage, and the crowd was on edge, shifting and muttering. Nana and Ayesha found two seats together in the middle of the room.

An elderly woman sat beside them. She was holding tasbih prayer beads. "I heard the bank will take the building and turn it into a shopping mall. This is all the imam's fault."

Ayesha glanced around, searching for friendly faces. She spotted Khalid standing near the front, his hands clasped in front of him, his expression unreadable.

Imam Abdul Bari walked onto the stage, followed by Sister Farzana and a wiry, bearded man wearing large aviator glasses. A tense muttering ran through the crowd. The imam stood up to start the meeting with a prayer, but Sister Farzana grasped the microphone. "Assalamu Alaikum, brothers and sisters," she began, her perky voice contrasting with the mood of the room. "We are here to discuss the financial catastrophe caused by the imam."

More muttering from the crowd. A man in the back yelled, "Where did our donations go?"

The wiry man stood up and introduced himself as Aziz, the president of the executive board.

"We have prepared a slide show detailing

our options. We are beseeching the community's immediate financial aid to meet our creditors' demands," Aziz said.

"How can we trust you?" another man shouted from the back. "Crooks!"

A scuffle broke out, and Aziz motioned to two security guards, who quelled the dispute.

"All hecklers will be removed from the premises," Aziz said, his forehead shining with nervous sweat.

"This isn't good," Ayesha said. The room felt as if it were closing in. Nana put his arm protectively around the back of her chair. "Nothing will happen," he assured her. "We are among our own people."

Aziz fiddled with a remote control that turned on the LCD projector, and Farzana seized the opportunity to grab the microphone again.

"I can no longer stand idly by as our mosque is dismantled. The executive board is trying to cover up a terrible scandal," she announced. The crowd leaned forward, hanging off her every word. Farzana glared out at the audience, her eyes settling on a figure seated in the front dressed in black, hood pulled up.

"Imam Abdul Bari is the one who is guilty! He stole from the mosque! I move for his immediate removal and a suspension of the executive board," she said loudly.

Ayesha gasped. "She's lying! It was Tarek. She knows it was Tarek!"

The crowd began to jeer. A few of the people at the back of the hall got to their feet. Nana squeezed Ayesha's shoulder and eyed the nearest exit.

Aziz was looking at Farzana, aghast, and Imam Abdul Bari had his head in his hands. Farzana took a flash drive from her pocket and plugged it into the laptop. "I have proof!" she said as she clicked on a video file. It began to play just as Khalid reached the stage.

"Ammi, what are you doing?" Khalid asked. The microphone caught his words, echoing them around the room.

She shrugged him off. "I know what is best," she said. "Tarek has been in touch. He has all the financial records. He was set up. The imam is guilty."

Khalid reached for the microphone, but his hand froze. Tarek's face beamed at the crowd from the screen.

"Assalamu Alaikum. This video is not about Imam Abdul Bari," a smiling Tarek boomed, the sound on high. "It is about identifying your true enemies. The person you should all fear is the one standing

467

before you: Sister Farzana."

Farzana gaped at the video, stunned. She reached for the remote, jabbing at the Off button so hard it flew across the stage.

Video-Tarek was grim-faced, his voice persuasive. "Farzana pretends to be a pious Muslim, but she is hiding a terrible secret. Twelve years ago, when she found out her only daughter, Zareena, had had an abortion, she did something unthinkable. She forced her into an arranged marriage with a stranger in India, and then she flew back to Canada, leaving her daughter all alone. She was only seventeen years old." A picture of Zareena appeared on the screen, her skin splotchy with traces of acne, a carefree smile on her face. The audience gasped, and Farzana shrunk back.

The video continued.

"This past year she arranged the marriage of her son, Khalid, an awkward fanatic with no friends, to Hafsa, the daughter of Brother Sulaiman. She did this even though she knew Khalid was in love with someone else. She was willing to doom Hafsa to an unhappy marriage just so she could remain in control of her son's life." A picture of Hafsa popped up on the screen, smiling innocently at the camera.

A murmur of shock spread through the

crowd. A few silently vowed to come to the mosque more often. Who knew it was better than reality TV?

Farzana, alone at the podium, stood frozen. She felt around for support and sat down. Khalid's face was devoid of color as he watched the video with the rest of the crowd.

Tarek's voice continued, hard and unflinching. "In fact, this whole setup was her idea. She wanted to accuse the imam of something so she could convince you all to fire him and construct her own puppet regime. I know, because I helped her. I supplied her with evidence of the imam's thieving. But here's the truth: There is no evidence. I made it all up when I became concerned with her selfish desire for power. Take a look around the room, brothers and sisters, and ask yourselves one question: Who shamelessly took advantage of an *Islamic conference* to further their own agenda? Who accused an innocent imam with no real evidence? Who is manipulating you and wasting your time?"

More muttering from the crowd, and nods of agreement. The woman beside Ayesha clicked her tasbih beads. "That man is right. I never liked Farzana," she said.

A picture of Farzana flashed on the screen

with the word *MENACE* underneath. "Take a good look, brothers and sisters. You cannot trust this woman. She is not worthy of your respect. As a symbol of my sincere intentions, I have already returned the money from the conference. I only took it to keep it safe from *her.*"

The video ended, and there was a moment of silence. Sister Farzana stood up, swaying slightly. Her lips moved as if she was about to say something. She sat back down, and her face sagged.

The crowd was on its feet now, people pushing to the front as the microphone fell from Farzana's hands. She caught Ayesha's eye. *Unhappy,* Ayesha thought. Farzana stood alone and abandoned.

The imam picked up the microphone and fixed it to his robe. Then he began to recite a chapter from the Quran, his voice echoing over the loud yells and sounds of people arguing in the gym. Slowly the crowd calmed down as Imam Abdul Bari's recitation flowed through the congregation.

The figure dressed in the black hoodie detached itself from the crowd and slunk into the hallway, tailed by Khalid in his white robe. Ayesha squeezed Nana's hand and followed right behind them. The man in the black hoodie looked familiar.

470

In the empty hallway, Khalid's voice bellowed out, "TAREK, STOP!"

Tarek turned around, smirking.

Khalid walked swiftly up to Tarek and punched him in the face. Tarek fell to the ground.

"So typical of you extremists," he sneered, rubbing his jaw. "You always resort to violence."

Khalid stood over him, massaging his split fist. "Why did you do it?" he asked.

Tarek slowly sat up as Ayesha bounded over to them.

"Where's Hafsa?" she demanded.

Khalid raised his fist again. "Tell me why!"

Tarek shrugged. "You don't recognize me, do you? We only saw each other once, at the airport twelve years ago. Your mother took Zareena away from me. I tried to put it all behind me, even after Lauren told me about the abortion, but I couldn't. When I met you and your mother again, I realized she was still a monster. I had to do something."

Khalid slowly sank down to his haunches, looking dazed. "I don't understand."

"I wanted to humiliate your *Ammi* in public. To unmask her as a hypocrite and fraud in front of everyone. She sent away her own daughter to India because she was afraid of losing face in front of those people.

471

Now no one will ever talk to her again."

"What about Hafsa?" Ayesha asked.

Tarek shrugged again. "She was Khalid's fiancée, Farzana's carefully hand-picked selection. I thought it would kill her if she knew her precious arranged bride was with me. I'm done with her now. I dropped her off at home."

Ayesha made a move toward him, but Tarek scrambled away. "I'm a hero," he said over his shoulder. "Farzana is a bully. Someone had to teach her a lesson. Don't behave like you're any better than me. When I told you Khalid and his family almost killed Zareena, you believed me." He started laughing, and the ugly sound bounced off the concrete walls. "Of course you did. He even looks like a villain. You swallowed every word because in your heart, you don't trust him, and you never will."

Khalid and Ayesha stared at each other. "It's not true," she said, her voice small.

There was a wail from the gym. With an apologetic look at Ayesha, Khalid ran off to find his mother. When Ayesha looked back, Tarek was gone.

CHAPTER FORTY-ONE

Ammi said nothing on the ride home, her silence more disturbing than the running commentary Khalid had expected.

"Ammi," Khalid said.

"I don't want to talk about it." She turned away from him, her face to the window.

"All of this happened because we don't talk about anything," Khalid said, keeping his voice gentle. "Please, Ammi."

But she refused to say another word. He unlocked the front door and she walked inside the house, her eyes staring resolutely ahead. He followed her inside; he had never seen his mother like this. She was always talking, complaining, ranting, bending others to her will. Never silent.

"Why did you accuse the imam when you knew Tarek took the money?" Khalid asked. He stood in the hallway, watching as she climbed the stairs.

Still Farzana said nothing.

Khalid followed her to her room. His mother reached for something at the back of her closet, standing on tiptoe to remove a heavy silver picture frame from the top shelf before she took a seat on the bed. Khalid recognized himself and his sister in the picture.

Zareena was nine years old in the photo, a laughing, happy girl, her hair in two long braids, dressed in a bright-pink frock that appeared hand-stitched. Khalid was five years old, solemn and frowning at the camera, holding a red toy car tightly in his hand.

"I was afraid of the shame, afraid of what others would think," she said quietly. "I don't know how else to be. Now I am ruined."

Khalid took a deep breath. He wanted to ask her if Video-Tarek was telling the truth. Had she really arranged his marriage to Hafsa, knowing that he wanted to marry Ayesha? But when he opened his mouth, he said, "I'm moving out."

Farzana nodded, her face frozen and expressionless. "Nani Laik was right: I have lost everything."

It was Hafsa's turn to cry on the family room couch. "He told me he loved me!"

she sobbed. "We were getting married. I was organizing the wedding and you were all invited."

"Hafsa, why didn't you call us?" Samira Aunty asked, stroking her daughter's hair.

Hafsa sat up, lower lip trembling. A week in hiding with her lover had left her unchanged. "I wanted it to be a surprise," she said. "Tarek thought it would be such good fun. No one has ever done a surprise wedding before. It might have become a thing. We were going to film it, like a commercial for my business!" She burst into tears again and her sisters crowded around, comforting her and offering tissues.

Ayesha left the family commiserating with Hafsa and headed to the front door. She took a seat on the marble porch steps. Idris found her there a few minutes later and they sat in silence, breathing in the fresh air of spring.

"I can't believe Tarek got away with everything," Ayesha said.

"He'll get what's coming to him," Idris said.

"You mean in the afterlife?"

Idris shrugged. "I just wanted to make sure Hafs was all right. Tell Mom I'll be back late."

"Where are you going?"

Idris shrugged again. "Some things can't wait for the afterlife."

Khalid was sipping his double-double when Amir and Idris slouched into the Tim Hortons. He waved them over. Amir sidled into the plastic booth and gave Khalid a side-hug. "I got the info on Mr. Shady. He tried to use a proxy address, but when I contacted the web hosting company and explained he didn't have the models' permission to post those pictures, they told me what I wanted to know. They don't want any trouble with the law."

Idris slouched low in his seat. "I've been digging through his business. Tarek was pulling in some serious cash with his ethnic porn. He launched Unveiled Hotties a few years ago, and it's popular. The Hafsa pics are still up, but only the ones where she's clothed. He wants a bidding war for the other ones." Idris's tone was flat, but his eyes flashed with anger.

"Have you come up with the interface and nag screen?" Khalid asked, and Idris nodded.

They went over the plan once more as they finished their coffee and donuts.

Amir pulled Khalid aside at the door. "Clara wants to talk to you about your job,"

476

he said. "She's got some ideas about how to use the video footage."

Khalid was surprised. "Clara wants to help?"

"It was her idea. When I told her what really happened, she felt awful. The Shark is cold, man. She's got to be put down."

Khalid shook his head. "I just want to move forward and forget about Livetech."

"If you don't stop Sheila, she'll do the same thing to the next socially awkward religious nut who tries to get a job there," Amir said.

Khalid smiled. "Who are you calling socially awkward?"

Amir returned Khalid's smile, then gave his friend a long, considering look, one that took in his wrinkled white robe, crumpled track pants, and full beard. "No offense, Khalid, but if you walk into Livetech dressed like that, they'll probably call CSIS."

"What do you suggest?"

Amir clapped Khalid on the shoulder. "Brother, you don't know how long I've wanted to say this: You need a makeover. Right after Operation Vengeance."

Chapter Forty-Two

Tarek sat in his apartment, wearing gray boxer shorts and a ratty white T-shirt, enjoying the silence. Hafsa was finally gone, but the pictures he'd taken of her had generated a lot of interest on his website. Life was good.

His new idea, inspired by Hafsa, was a stroke of genius: Get local Muslim women to take their clothes off for money in front of the camera. Or at least, women posing as local Muslims. A sort of *Girls Gone Wild,* except with frolicking, veiled women. It would add to his current product line of exotic girls from around the world. He would be rich!

Tarek had never thought he would make his mark peddling porn, but the Islamic conference scene was turning out to be a complicated front. He should just stick to porn, which was a comfortable, discreet way to make money. He made a mental note to send Hafsa a gift basket for her contribution to his empire.

His phone pinged. It was an e-mail notification, sent to his private account.

To: eyecandyz@unveiledhotties.com
From: brotha-undercova@elude.com
Subject: lawyers

The damage that this leak has done to my personal and professional reputation is irreparable. My wife is already threatening divorce and my business partners have expressed their reservations. If I go down, you will too.

Especially now that I know your name.

> Yours sincerely,
> Thomas L.

What the hell is going on? Tarek opened his website and input his administrator password. When he pressed Enter, a message popped up:

You no longer have access to this website. Your website has been infected with a virus made especially for you by Vengeance Productions. Welcome to the new world order, SUCKA!

Tarek tried the password again, but the same message popped up. This had to be some twisted joke. His cell phone pinged with another e-mail:

To: eyecandyz@unveiledhotties.com
From: johnnybhai@denote.com
Subject: you're dead

According to the e-mail I received earlier today, you own unveiledhotties.com.

I'm usually a peaceful man, but when my entire contacts list receives the sort of e-mail your company sent out, it makes me very, very angry. What I do on my own time is my own business and I don't appreciate being played for a fool. I'll be visiting your place of business this afternoon to air my grievances in a more thorough manner.

Sincerely,
Javed

Tarek scrolled to the bottom, where he read the e-mail that Thomas and Javed, along with everyone else on their contacts lists, had received that morning:

To: All subscribers of
   unveiledhotties.com
From: Owner and CEO
   <eyecandyz@unveiledhotties.com>
Subject: Road to Damascus

You have been a valued customer of my specialized services for the past several years. As a purveyor of Muslim adult entertainment, my commitment to expanding audiences and tastes is unparalleled. I have provided pictures and videos of exotic women in various poses and positions, all engaged in the seductive arts.

However, despite the fact that my website has made me a wealthy man, from a spiritual and moral viewpoint, I am bankrupt. I have recently seen the light and learned the error of my ways. In order to make a full and complete repentance, I have decided to give up all haram activities and confess my sins. And since my sins include yours, I am forwarding this e-mail to everyone on your contacts list.

All of your contacts will receive this e-mail, along with a complete list of the services I have provided for you over the years. For a full record of all transac-

481

tions, please click <u>here</u>.

I sincerely hope and pray that this will help you on the road to your personal redemption.

Sincerely yours,
Tarek Khan,
CEO, unveiledhotties.com
101 Star Team Blvd., Ste. #300 / Buzz: 333
Toronto, ON
416-555-2055

Tarek sat rooted to the spot, at the center of a spiraling tornado of panic and fear. His doorbell buzzed and his cell phone started ringing and pinging simultaneously with incoming messages. *I'm a dead man.*

Chapter Forty-Three

Hafsa hadn't left the house since she'd returned almost one week ago, and Samira Aunty was worried. She called Ayesha on Thursday evening, her voice like honey.

"Beti, why haven't you visited? Hafsa misses you so much. Maybe when you come to see her, you can talk to her about what happened. I think she might be suffering from *post-traumatic stress*," her aunt said confidentially.

Ayesha doubted this, but she agreed to a Bollywood night and a return to some kind of normalcy.

"Maybe you can ask her what happened with Tarek. Maybe they are actually married and just having a little tiff," Samira Aunty continued.

Oh God, anything but that, Ayesha thought. A quickie marriage might assuage the gossip wildfire burning in the community, but Ayesha knew it would be better in the long

483

run if Hafsa was not married to a lying, manipulative ass.

She kept this thought to herself, just as she had the confrontation with Tarek at the mosque. Mostly because she couldn't believe that a decade-old revenge plot was the reason behind their current situation. She also couldn't forget the look on Farzana's face as the mosque crowd jeered. Khalid's mother might be a wannabe-despot, but her schemes brought her no joy, and Ayesha pitied her.

Her thoughts on Khalid were not so easily sorted. As satisfying as it had been to watch Khalid punch Tarek, her mind kept drifting to the way his face had crumpled when Tarek revealed his true motivations. She wondered if Khalid felt as confused as she did. Or maybe he was too busy trying to deal with the buried ghosts of his past, suddenly thrust into the harsh glare of his community's consciousness.

Or perhaps he was wondering if Tarek's last taunting words to her were true: *When I told you Khalid and his family almost killed Zareena, you believed me . . . He even looks like a villain . . . In your heart, you don't trust him, and you never will.*

Ayesha shook her head. On that point, at least, Tarek was wrong. She knew Khalid

484

could never be a villain. If anything, he was her hero.

Hafsa was waiting for Ayesha with chicken wings, two pizzas, and the 1960 classic Bollywood blockbuster *Mughal-e-Azam,* the doomed Mughal-era love story of dancer Anarkali and her lover, Prince Saleem, fully remastered in color.

"I like the black-and-white version better," Ayesha said as she reached for honey-garlic wings.

"You can see the clothes better in color," Hafsa said. She was dressed in pink flannel pajamas, bunny slippers on her feet. She looked like a five-foot-three-inch toddler, but Ayesha didn't comment. The room was littered with Amazon purchases; Sulaiman Mamu clearly hadn't told his daughter about their financial difficulties.

"How are you doing?" Ayesha asked, taking a sip of cola. "Your mom is worried about you. She said you haven't left the house or talked to anyone."

Hafsa shrugged. "Everyone's still mad at me."

Ayesha picked halal pepperoni off her pizza. "Have you apologized?"

"I didn't do anything wrong. I'm an adult!"

"You didn't behave like an adult. You disappeared without a trace. We were worried you were dead or being held for ransom."

"My cell phone died. It's not my fault."

Ayesha gave her cousin a skeptical look. "Come on, Hafsa. You were mad, and you ran away and made everyone crazy with worry. You're not a little kid anymore. You put us through hell, and for what?"

Hafsa looked down at her hands. "He said he loved me," she said.

"Tarek wanted to hurt Khalid and Farzana, and he used you and the mosque to do it."

"Nobody gets it!" Hafsa's face was streaked with tears. "He lied to me. He used me."

"Why didn't you call?"

"I was too embarrassed," she said in a small voice. "I thought running away would be such good fun. You all think I'm stupid."

"Not stupid. Selfish and careless, maybe." Ayesha eyed her cousin, exasperated. "Did Khalid break up with you?"

Hafsa nodded.

"And you were angry and ran off with the first pretty boy who looked at you." Ayesha shook her head. "You're better than this, Hafs. I know you are. You don't need to be married to matter, you don't need a man's attention to be loved, and you don't need to run away to teach us a lesson. We love you, but you treat us like dirt." Ayesha held her gaze. "You treat me like dirt."

Hafsa dropped her eyes, quiet. A look of shame passed across her face as the truth of her actions finally seemed to hit home. When she looked back at Ayesha, her eyes were filled with remorse. "I'm sorry. I'll do better," she said.

"Promise?"

"I swear," she said, looking around her room. "I swear on the color pink, I'll be better."

She reached for the remote and turned on the movie. "Madhubala is totally hot," Hafsa said, referring to the female star of *Mughal-e-Azam.* She was finished with the subject of Tarek, for now. "I don't get why she went for Dilip Kumar. He looks so old in this movie. He's no Shah Rukh Khan."

"Shah Rukh wasn't even born when this movie was released," Ayesha said, settling down beside Hafsa.

Hafsa wasn't listening. "The first wedding I plan will have a *Mughal-e-Azam* theme. Anarkali dresses and feathered caps and mirrors everywhere. The entrance song will be 'Pyar Kya To Darna Kya,' " she said, referencing the hit song from the movie.

The title meant "Why fear if you are in love?"

Ayesha smiled at her cousin, who was watching the opening credits of the movie closely. "I can't wait to see it, Hafs," she said. "I know it will be beautiful."

CHAPTER FORTY-FOUR

"Are you sure about this?" Khalid was nervous, looking at himself in the bathroom mirror.

"Bro. Trust me." Amir flicked a piece of fluff from Khalid's shoulder. "Say *bismillah* and go."

"I feel ridiculous." Khalid tugged on his tie, and Amir slapped his hand away.

"You look great. And remember: You're still you, no matter how you dress."

Khalid emerged from the bathroom in the lobby of Livetech and walked to the reception desk, his heart pounding.

He smiled at the receptionist, a grouchy gargoyle named Sandra who hadn't looked twice at Khalid in the five years he'd worked there. Today, she straightened up when she saw him approach, reaching up to adjust her hair.

"Hello, I'm here to see Sheila Watts," he said, smiling widely.

Sandra flushed and licked her lips. "Sure thing. What's your name, honey?"

No one had ever called Khalid "honey" before.

"David McGyver," he said.

"You can go right up. It's the third floor, second door on the right. Ms. Watts is expecting you." Her eyes followed him to the elevator, and he waved at her as the doors closed.

Stick to the plan. Amir had been very insistent. Clara had made the appointment, Amir had equipped Khalid with the audio recording and image upgrade so he looked the part of a client, but the rest was up to him. He resisted the urge to pull off his tie. How did people dress like this every day? He felt so restricted.

Sheila stood up and held out her hand to shake when Khalid entered the office.

"David, so nice to meet you," she said, smiling.

He hesitated for only a fraction of a second, then firmly grasped her hand and shook. Sheila didn't recognize him until she looked into his eyes, and then she froze. Her expression tightened as she took in the familiar-looking stranger.

Khalid was dressed in a crisp white shirt with jet-black cufflinks, a skinny paisley tie with matching pocket square, and a brand-new navy blue suit, slim cut to emphasize his tall frame. His hair had been closely cropped, and his beard, untouched since he had started growing it in tenth grade, was neatly trimmed.

"Khalid?" Sheila said, not believing her eyes.

Khalid sat down and looked genially at his former boss. "Hello, Sheila." He figured he had the upper hand for another few minutes, until the shock of seeing him wore off. After that, she would remember that she had fired him ten days ago and call security.

He took a deep, calming breath and smiled at her, channeling his inner shark, or at least, dolphin. "This is a courtesy visit. I have such happy memories of Livetech. Did you know I worked here as an intern in university? John, the director before you, hired me as soon as I graduated. I would hate to sour my fond memories with anything as ugly as a lawsuit."

Sheila leaned back, trying to regain control of the situation. "Pornography was found on your workstation, a clear violation of the employee code of conduct. You were terminated as a result. Any lawsuit would be dismissed immediately."

"Yet when Amir confessed he was the one who paid for the subscription and showed you the network log and receipts, you did nothing."

"You have no proof of that," Sheila said quickly.

"Admit it, Sheila. You don't like me because I'm Muslim."

Sheila pasted a wounded look on her face. "I find that highly insulting. Amir still works here."

"Amir is a light-skinned Persian man who does not identify as Muslim. My appearance makes you uncomfortable."

"Employee dress code —" Sheila started, but Khalid interrupted her by pulling out a printed copy of Livetech's code of conduct. He took his time riffling through the pages before reading aloud:

" 'Livetech recognizes the rights of all employees to express their religious beliefs through dress and behavior. Livetech encourages all such religious freedoms and supports a diverse and respectful work environment.' "

Sheila blanched. "Well, in your case . . ." she said, stumbling over her words.

"I'm a peaceful man," Khalid said. He realized he was enjoying himself. "But when the NCCM — a Muslim advocacy group, perhaps you have heard of them? — approached me looking for a test case on workplace Islamophobia, I considered it my duty to speak up."

Sheila straightened. "You can't prove anything."

Khalid leaned forward and placed his iPhone on the table. He pressed Play and Sheila's voice was clear: "I can't stand men like Khalid. They come to our country and expect us to change everything for them. He's probably got some sixteen-year-old virgin waiting for him in the desert."

Khalid pressed pause. "There's video too," he said.

For a moment, Sheila said nothing. "What do you want?" she asked.

"I'm a reasonable man. I know you probably don't hate an entire religious group, not all 1.8 billion of us. I know this all boils down to money. You presented the website I made to WomenFirst Design and took all the credit. I'm going to call them today and explain the situation. And when they offer me a job, Livetech will not sue me for non-competition. Because if they do, I'll come straight back here to your office. With my lawyer."

"Khalid, be reasonable. It's a twelve-million-dollar account!"

Khalid stood up, looking down at Sheila. From this vantage point, she looked so small. "Then consider this a very expensive lesson on the dangers of workplace discrimination. The choice is yours."

Sheila didn't look at him as he left her office. Outside, he texted Amir:

It's done. Thanks for the audio file and the makeover.

Clara emerged from the side entrance where she had been waiting and stood beside Khalid.

"How did it go?" she asked.

"She crumpled like a used tissue."

"Gross." Clara eyed the suit. "Somehow, the makeover just isn't . . . you."

Khalid loosened his tie and ran a hand through his neatly combed hair, messing it up. "What about now?"

"I miss the white dress."

"I think I held on to the robe for too long. Just like I held on to some other things. But I'm learning to let go and 'edit,' as Amir would say."

They smiled at each other.

"Thank you," Khalid said. "For everything. Please let me know if I can return the favor."

Clara was thoughtful. "Actually, I've been thinking about what you said before. About your Prophet Muhammad and his wife Khadijah."

Chapter Forty-Five

LOVE COMES FROM BELOW

The words fall from above, dust in an old
　house
Coating everything, blurring lines,
　softening forms, covering up
Love rises, a well filled for the first time,
Drop by drop
Transparent and clean, giver of hope and
　life
I see you now.
I see myself.
I see us.
I'm ready
For something new.

Ayesha sat back, frowning at the words. She was sitting on a bench near the baseball diamond outside Brookridge High, enjoying a moment of quiet after school. The poem was rough, but it felt like a distilled truth.

She flipped through the pages of her blue notebook, reading over the half-dozen poems she had written in the past two weeks, since Hafsa's return. One way or another, they all said the same thing: She was ready for change, ready for something different.

In reality, not much had changed since the general body meeting. Though Tarek had returned the money as promised, the mosque's financial future remained uncertain, and her family was still tainted. Samira Aunty's story (Hafsa had been kidnapped by a con man and held for ransom) didn't hold much water with the Aunty Brigade, who were busy feeding off the entrails of the biggest scandal to rock their community in years. But her aunt was an old hand at the rumor mill; she knew things would settle down, eventually.

Hafsa was quieter now, her old playful fire subdued. Ayesha suspected she was suffering from a slightly bruised ego but would make a full recovery in time. Besides, the sun was shining, and June had arrived. Everything was sane and hopeful in June, even irreversible life decisions.

Ayesha looked up and spotted Mr. Evorem on the baseball diamond, watching the junior boys' team practice. She squared her shoulders, put the notebook away, and walked over to him.

"How are your classes?" he asked her, his eyes on the boys. He winced as the outfielder missed the catch. "Any plans for the summer?"

Ayesha chatted for a few minutes before growing silent. When she didn't leave, Mr. Evorem turned to look at her. "Was there something else, Miss Shamsi?" he asked politely.

Ayesha shifted. She had practiced her speech in the staff bathroom, but now she didn't know how to begin.

His eyes were kind, the laugh lines that bracketed his mouth deeply etched, his crow's feet a permanent notation from too many seasons watching school teams go to bat, or run after a black-and-white ball, or throw the perfect spiral. Mr. Evorem belonged here. She didn't.

"I won't be returning next year," she said.

Mr. Evorem took a moment to absorb the news. A good poker face was essential for a high school principal. "I thought you wanted to be a teacher."

Ayesha shrugged helplessly, unsure how to turn her churning thoughts into words. "I did too. There was so much pressure to take the road more traveled. I didn't want to disappoint my family. But now I think I'm ready to chase a dream."

Mr. Evorem looked back at the field, smiling at the firm *thwack* as the bat made contact with the ball, watching it sail past second base. "I admire your bravery. Where will you go? Dreamers need to eat too."

"I was thinking overseas. See the world, write."

Mr. Evorem nodded. "Just remember to pack light. Dreams tend to shatter if you're carrying other people's hopes around with you." He shook Ayesha's hand and wished her good luck. "A good teacher grows, they're not born. If you ever change your mind, let me know. I think you have potential."

Ayesha promised to keep in touch and left him staring after his team.

Hafsa's red Mercedes SLK was in the driveway when Ayesha returned from school. All Ayesha wanted to do was change into her yoga pants, crawl into bed, and try not to think about the perfectly good job she had thrown away because of something a man she had decided never to talk to again had written in a letter she couldn't forget.

Hafsa was waiting for her on the porch steps, and she had that look on her face, the one that said she wouldn't be easy to dismiss. Still, Ayesha tried.

"Hafs, I have a splitting headache," she said.

"So take an Advil. I need to talk to you."

Ayesha had been secretly enjoying the new, quieter, less needy Hafsa. The one who didn't whine or complain when Ayesha wanted time to write, and think.

And also quit her job.

Maybe there were advantages to constantly getting sucked into Hafsa's vortex of trouble.

Her cousin followed her into the house as she dropped her purse by the door and kicked off her shoes. Hafsa plopped down on the couch. "Make me a tea too," she said. "Where is everyone?"

Ayesha looked around, noticing the stillness. She busied herself with the chai and soon carried out two steaming mugs.

"Not even a cookie?" Hafsa pouted. "Though I shouldn't. I have to watch my weight."

"Why bother?" Ayesha said, sighing. "It's not like you're getting married."

"Actually," Hafsa said, smiling. "I am."

Ayesha froze, her tea halfway to her mouth. "What?"

"I'm getting married!" Hafsa said. "It's

someone you know."

"I think you've exhausted the list of men we have in common," Ayesha said.

"Remember Masood?" Hafsa asked.

"What?" Life-coach-wrestler Masood?

"Don't be mad. We sort of bonded on that car ride to the airport, before I ran off with Tarek. He texted me when I came back and it sort of fell into place."

"This can't be happening," Ayesha said. "I thought you were swearing off men for a while."

"Masood said you'd say that. He thinks you're closed-minded," Hafsa said. "You really need to open yourself up to the possibility of loss and gain. The world of wrestling is full of psychological complexity. Masood said if people understood it better, they would have a better understanding of *themselves.*"

"This is a joke, right?"

Hafsa shook her head. "He said he loves me, and he doesn't care about Tarek or the pictures. We're going into business together. We're going to be rich!"

"What pictures?"

Hafsa waved her hand. "The banquet hall is already booked from the other wedding. There's no sense losing the deposit for the caterers too. Dad actually smiled when I

501

told him, especially because Masood said he'd pay for everything. We only have a month to plan, but I can do it."

Ayesha put the chai down. "Hafsa. What pictures?"

Hafsa shifted uncomfortably. "They were supposed to be just for Tarek. We were going to get married, remember?"

Ayesha closed her eyes, trying to breathe. "Where are the pictures now?"

Hafsa shifted her gaze around the room. "He told me he was posting them on his website, unveiledhotties.com. He was going to auction them — me — off. Bastard."

"Oh my God," Ayesha said. "Why didn't you say anything?"

"It was humiliating."

Ayesha started to pace. "What are we going to do? We have to tell the police."

Hafsa was shaking her head. "The website's gone," she said. "I checked it yesterday. There's some letter he wrote about having a change of heart. All the pics of those other women are down too."

"How? What happened?"

"Who cares? I'm getting married!"

Ayesha didn't know what to say. "Congratulations?"

"Thank you," Hafsa said demurely. "It's at the end of July, so you have lots of time to buy a few dresses and get your eyebrows waxed. They're, like, out of control." She stood up. "I have to go. I need to talk to Nadya, my assistant. This wedding is going to be epic!"

Hafsa let herself out. Once she'd closed the door behind her, Idris peeked down from the railing.

"She always has to be first in everything."

"She's marrying Masood," Ayesha said. "Masood! He was texting me only two weeks ago, offering to coach me in wrestling. What happened?"

"Maybe they bonded over their broken hearts," Idris said. "Though Runaway Bride doesn't exactly have a good track record."

Ayesha picked up her tea, now cold, and took a sip. "Did you know about the pictures on Tarek's website? Hafsa said he had a change of heart." She punched in the URL on her phone and clicked on the "Open Letter to My Subscribers," reading quickly.

"This doesn't even sound like Tarek," Ayesha said. "Actually, this sounds a bit like . . ." She looked at her brother, who had a half-guilty/half-coy expression on his face. "Idris," she said sternly. "Tell me what happened, *right now.*"

CHAPTER FORTY-SIX

When Khalid contacted WomenFirst Design after his confrontation with Sheila, Vanessa and Lorraine tut-tutted through his story.

"I knew there was something wrong when that cow told us you quit. How soon can you start?"

He explained about his sister and the impending birth. Vanessa and Lorraine congratulated him. "Work from home for a while. We need you."

Khalid was feeling happier than he had in weeks. He drove from the apartment he now shared with the sober-so-far Amir to his sister's basement unit.

"I can't get over your new look," Zareena said when she opened the door. "Like a secret service agent. All you need is an earpiece and Ray Bans." Khalid followed her down the hall into the main room. Zareena had decorated. There were pretty purple drapes on the window, photographs in frames on the coffee table, and a vase with flowers on a shelf. "Don't worry, I didn't cook," she added.

They split a frozen pizza and bagged salad while Khalid told Zareena about Livetech, and Tarek's website.

"I'd like to think Tarek wasn't always this horrible," Zareena said. "At one point, he had excellent taste in women."

Khalid hesitated. He wasn't going to mention the confrontation he'd had with Tarek outside the mosque, but his sister deserved to know the full story. "He told me he did it all for you. He said he loved you, that Ammi pulled you two apart. He was trying to get his revenge or something."

Zareena smiled, her hand on her stomach. "He can blame the past if he likes, but we never fit, not like you and Ayesha."

"Ayesha hates me."

Zareena laughed, a teasing sound. "If you told me she was indifferent, or she had moved on, I'd tell you to give up. I don't think this is the end of the story for you. You should pray about it and wait for a sign. Isn't that your thing?"

Khalid took a bite of his pizza. It was overcooked and tasted like particleboard. Next time he visited, he would pick up groceries and cook a few meals for his sister.

His niece deserved the very best.

His phone rang and he made a face — it was his mother. "Assalamu Alaikum, Ammi," he said.

His mother called several times a day. She still couldn't believe he wasn't starving and falling apart on his own.

"Khalid, you must come home immediately," Farzana said. "We must plan your wedding."

Khalid smiled. His mother was a lot easier to deal with now that he no longer lived with her. "No, thank you. I'm good."

"I have just learned that Hafsa is getting married! On what was supposed to be your wedding day. It's an outrage, not to mention totally tactless."

Khalid was surprised. He hadn't expected Hafsa to mourn their engagement, but two weeks seemed a little fast. "I'm happy she found someone," he said.

"She had the cheek to send you an invitation but not me. I was going to be her mother-in-law!"

Zareena looked at him curiously. *Everything okay?* she mouthed.

"Hafsa invited me to her wedding?" Khalid said, shocked. His mind focused: *Ayesha will be there.*

"Everyone is going, if only to see if the

tramp actually makes it to the nikah this time or runs away with the caterer," said Farzana.

"Ammi, I have to go. I'll visit soon." Khalid hung up.

Zareena smiled at him. "I think you just got your sign."

CHAPTER FORTY-SEVEN

Ayesha wasn't sure what to expect when she walked into the Hollywood Princess banquet hall on the last Saturday in July. Hafsa, Samira Aunty, and Nadya, the assistant/new BFF, had been running around with self-important expressions on their faces for weeks, tightlipped about everything: color scheme, centerpieces, decor . . . All was shrouded in a cloud of secrecy. Hafsa was going to get her surprise wedding after all.

Most South Asian weddings were multiday occasions, with the mehndi henna party, nikah wedding ceremony, and *walima* reception all as separate events, but Hafsa wanted to keep things simple with a one-day extravaganza. From discreet hints dropped by Samira Aunty, Ayesha knew that the decorations alone had cost over six figures, the entire tab covered by Masood.

Which probably explained the smile on Sulaiman Mamu's face as he greeted Ayesha and the rest of the family in the banquet hall parking lot.

All amusing familial observations vanished when Ayesha walked up to the main entrance with her grandparents, Idris, and her mother. The Hollywood Princess banquet hall had been completely transformed into a Mughal-era palace.

Ayesha walked around, marveling at the intricate details. Hafsa had commissioned a scaffold to extend across the entranceway of the banquet hall, bearing a plasterboard replica of a palace entrance, complete with mosaic tiles arranged in Islamic geometric patterns and two thin pillars that framed a small dome and marble arch. Thick Persian rugs covered the floors, and chandeliers twinkled red and green. The pillars inside the banquet hall were decorated with more multicolored mosaic tiles, and tabla and sitar players, seated on a gold-fringed rug in the foyer, strummed classical Indian music. Ayesha spotted Hafsa by the grand hall, wearing a headset and a pink-and-cream *lengha* dress, her makeup dramatic.

"You should be hiding in the bridal room," Ayesha said.

Hafsa placed a hand on the microphone of her headset, her smile radiant. "I wanted to make sure everything was running

509

smoothly. What do you think?"

"I'm speechless."

"It's from the movie *Mughal-e-Azam,* remember? I couldn't get it out of my head after we watched it. I think it will be great for business." She gestured toward a table set up at the entrance, where Nadya sat surrounded by flyers and business cards. A large pink sign proclaimed HAPPILY EVER AFTER EVENT PLANNING. Beside it, another table advertised Masood's Better Life Wholistic wrestling life-coach services.

"This way we can claim the wedding on our taxes," Hafsa said. "It was Masood's idea."

A female server in a white-and-red Anarkali dress, with an embroidered prayer cap set at a rakish angle, walked past with a tray of mango lassi.

"Is that the dress Madhubala was wearing in the movie?" Ayesha asked.

Hafsa nodded. "All the male servers are in white sherwanis with turbans and fake swords."

Ayesha shook her head. "I can't believe you did all this in one month. I'm so proud of you."

Hafsa looked down. "I had a lot of time to think. Ayesha, I'm sorry for the way I treated you. I was competitive and jealous. I hope you can forgive me."

Ayesha hugged her cousin, holding her close. "Just tell me you're happy."

"Masood is solid," Hafsa said. "I know we'll do well together."

Ayesha nodded, relieved and impressed that Hafsa was capable of making decisions devoid of drama and lies.

Hafsa fiddled with the heavy gold-and-crystal embroidery on her tunic. "I was jealous because I knew Khalid liked you, not me."

Ayesha didn't know where to look. "Nothing happened."

Hafsa burst out laughing. "I know that! Duh. But in his heart, he was in love with you all along. He was marrying me for his crazy mother. You can't blame me for being angry about that."

Ayesha gripped her cousin's hand. "I don't blame you for anything."

Hafsa shook her head impatiently. "I know you don't." She took a deep breath. "If you're still interested, I think you should go for it. Khalid is a good guy. He might even be good enough for you."

Hafsa wiped her eyes, smearing some of her mascara. She looked ruefully at her henna-covered finger. "There goes my makeup. I should fix it before the video rolls. Masood will be here any minute on his white horse. There isn't an elephant to be had for love or money in Toronto." She turned toward the bridal room, then turned back. "Don't be mad, but I invited Khalid to the wedding." She smiled mischievously. "Just promise me one thing: If you're going to make a scene, do it after the cake cutting. You wouldn't believe how much I paid for the Taj Mahal cake."

Khalid was wearing the navy blue suit, paisley tie, and pocket square again, hair slicked back and beard trimmed close to his face.

As he walked into the hall, the groups of young women gathered by the entrance paused in their chatter to stare at him, but he didn't notice. His hands were clammy on the wedding present Zareena had picked out, some sort of crystal bowl and gift card. His eyes scanned the crowd, looking for Ayesha.

There were over eight hundred people admiring the decorations while they waited in line for appetizers. He paced the hall, looking closely at all the young women who might be Ayesha but weren't. A few smiled back at the handsome, intense stranger in the navy blue suit.

He made his way to the head table where Hafsa, dressed as a Mughal princess in an empire-waist cream-and-pink *lengha,* sat on a rented throne made of inlaid tile, mirror, and gold paint. An oversize pearl *maang tika* adorned her forehead, and her hands were covered with henna and diamonds. Painted red lips curved in a smile at Khalid's approach. He shook hands with Masood, who was dressed in a cream-and-gold suit that looked like it had been removed from a museum, before turning to the bride.

"*Mubarak,* Hafsa," Khalid said, offering his congratulations.

She looked at his outfit with approval. "I don't know if I should be irritated you never dressed like that when we were together, or happy for Ayesha," she said. "No drama until after the cake, okay?"

The irony of the Queen of Drama asking him to cool it was not lost on him. "I promise."

"I got you both in the same room. What you do next is up to you."

Dinner was a sit-down affair. The servers, in their *Mughal-e-Azam* finery, paraded to the center of the hall with steel dome–covered dishes of mutton biryani, *haleem,* and Mughlai chicken. They uncovered the platters in a flourish and Hafsa clapped. The rest of the servers began dishing out the food while the guests, reveling in their luck, dug into the meal. Khalid chatted with the people seated at his table, his eyes continually scanning the room for Ayesha, but she was nowhere to be found.

Musicians entertained the crowd with Urdu poetry after dinner, ghazals on love and loss that made the older aunties cry. Then the Hyderabadi comic poets took over, and soon the Urdu-speaking guests were rollicking with laughter and translating mother-in-law jokes to their non-Urdu-speaking table partners.

Khalid wandered outside the main hall to the tea and coffee station. He spotted Nana in a starched black sherwani with silver buttons, standing beside Nani, resplendent in a light green sari. The older woman smiled at Khalid and motioned him closer.

"I know who you are looking for," she said quietly, in English. "You've been looking for her all your life. When you find her, I hope you will remember my words: Always dream together, raja. Always leave space in your life to grow and soften."

Khalid inclined his head before turning to greet Nana. "Assalamu Alaikum," he said politely. "Are you enjoying the Urdu poetry?"

"I'm more of a Shakespeare man," Nana said. "My favorite are the comedies. Weddings are such a cheerful way to end a story, don't you think? So full of hope and promise. And love."

Khalid nodded in agreement. He handed a cup of tea to Nana.

" 'Let me not to the marriage of true minds admit impediments,' " Nana quoted, his voice a deep rumble. " 'Love is not love which alters when it alteration finds, or bends with the remover to remove: O, no! It is an ever-fixed mark that looks on tempests and is never shaken.' " He twinkled at Khalid. "I believe they are cutting the cake. A Taj Mahal, commissioned at great expense by the bride. Completely tacky, of course." Nana nodded at Khalid. "Perhaps you will be good enough to inform my granddaughter, Ayesha. She enjoys wedding cake."

Khalid turned around slowly.

Ayesha was dressed in a white sari flecked with silver. Her white hijab was tied away from her face, a sparkly crystal *maang tika* on her forehead. Her bangles were silver and diamond, and flashed cold fire at her wrists. Khalid's breath caught at the sight of her, and her eyes widened in shock at his altered appearance.

The strains of the song "Pyar Kya To

Darna Kya" floated out of the main hall as Khalid walked to her. "I've been looking for you everywhere," he said.

"Hafsa said no drama before cake," she said, her voice warm and low. "Did someone take you shopping?"

"My friend Amir. Do you like it?"

Ayesha didn't answer, but her eyes lingered on his broad shoulders, neatly combed hair, and trimmed beard.

They drifted down the hallway together, drawing curious looks from cranky toddlers and the parents stuck entertaining them. They left the hall, and stood outside in the humid night.

"Idris told me what you did to Tarek's website," Ayesha said. "I wanted to thank you, on behalf of my family. It would have destroyed my aunt and uncle if those pictures of Hafsa had remained online." Ayesha didn't look at him. "What Tarek said that day . . . He was wrong. I trust you. It took me a while, but I know who you really are."

Khalid forced himself to focus on the conversation, despite his racing heart. The urge to gather her in his arms was overpowering.

"Tarek hurt my sister too," he said. "He had to be stopped. I'm happy to spare your family any pain, but I confess I wasn't thinking about them. I thought only of you."

Ayesha turned to face him. "Your mother doesn't like me, and I don't want to come between you and your family when you've already lost so much. I know how it feels to lose someone important." She looked at her hands, covered in henna for the wedding, and traced the design of a vine from index finger to wrist. Khalid watched, mesmerized, wanting to press his mouth to her delicate palms.

"When my father died, my mother fell apart," Ayesha said. "She cried for weeks, and when we moved to Canada, she didn't get out of bed for a long time. If that was love, I wanted no part. Love takes your heart and leaves you with nothing. It makes you forget your children, your family. It steals your very self. So I closed off my heart, telling myself I was better without it. Nothing could be worth such pain. That's why I fought so hard when I realized I was falling for you." Ayesha looked up, and they stared at each other.

"We're so different, Khalid. You accused me once of not knowing what I wanted in life, and you were right. I was lost for so long, but you helped me see myself. I know what I want now: I want to travel the world. I want to paint pictures with my words. But most of all, I want you."

Khalid gathered his courage. The time to speak was now.

"I asked you a question, at the wrong time and the wrong place and in the worst possible way. I was devastated when you refused me, but you were right. My mother taught me there was only one way to be a good Muslim, that any other way was misguided. You showed me that faith was a wide road. I was harsh; you taught me compassion. I was judgmental; you taught me to be brave and open. Please, tell me we still have a chance. I need you in my life, Ayesha. My heart is yours to take." He closed his eyes and prayed.

When he opened them, she was smiling at him.

"Yes," she said. "Yes, I have changed my mind. I will marry you, Khalid."

He wanted to be very, very sure. "Yes?" he repeated.

She leaned closer, until there was barely any space between them. "Yes."

CHAPTER FORTY-EIGHT

Ayesha was trying to distract Clara and failing miserably.

"Anything new at work?" she asked her friend.

"Sheila's trying to find out who gave Khalid the security footage. She suspects me and Amir, of course." Clara bit her lip. "I'll have to look for a new job and a new apartment soon."

"The only thing you'll have to search for is honeymoon destinations."

Clara started to pace. "What's taking him so long? Rob is going to think this is stupid. I'm such an idiot!"

Ayesha smiled at her friend. She had been doing a lot of smiling lately. Her family had been surprised (except for Nana, Nani, Hafsa, and Idris, of course) but happy to hear her good news. Her future mother-in-law was less happy, but Khalid had assured her that Farzana would calm down. Eventually. In the meantime, Zareena's warm welcome made up for the frosty reception from Khalid's mother.

She only had two conditions for Khalid. First, their wedding would be held next summer. Ayesha figured this would give them enough time to get to know each other better and be absolutely sure about the marriage. Second, the wedding would be small; one Mughal palace in the family was more than enough.

Clara stopped pacing. "I'm not even *desi*. What was I thinking?"

"Arranged marriages are not only practiced by South Asians. They're common all over the world. Think of it as a facilitated introduction," Ayesha soothed.

"I don't need to be introduced to my own boyfriend!" Clara said. She sank to the ground, moaning, her head in her hands. "What made me think it was a good idea to send Rob a rishta in the first place?"

Khalid was back in his white robe and track pants. His hair was neatly trimmed under the skullcap, but he had decided to let his beard grow out again. Ayesha had told him she liked it.

He sat on the couch and gazed at Clara's boyfriend. Rob looked back, uneasy.

"What did you want to talk to me about, bro?" Rob asked, taking a swig from his Budweiser.

Khalid took a sip of his club soda. "I am here to present you with a proposal of marriage, on behalf of Clara Taylor," he said.

Rob's expression changed from wary to bewildered. "Huh?"

"As her representative, I am here to make an offer of marriage," Khalid repeated. "After careful consideration of the many years she has spent in your company, Clara has decided you will make an excellent husband and father to her future children. If this proposal is acceptable to you, we can commence with formal negotiations."

Rob put the beer down on the coffee table. "Are you nuts?"

Khalid, who had been warned that Rob would likely respond with these exact words, continued with his speech. "If her marriage proposal is not acceptable to you, she will withdraw her name from the lease on the apartment, as well as other aspects of your life together."

Rob leaned back on the sofa. "Hold on a sec. She said that?"

Khalid nodded his head. "As her representative, I can tell you that Clara loves you dearly, and she is eager to move the relationship to the next level."

Rob picked up his beer and took another sip, thinking. "Why didn't she just ask me herself?"

"Why didn't you ask her?" Khalid countered. "I believe she was also inspired by Prophet Muhammad, peace be upon him. His wife Khadijah was an older, very clever businesswoman who proposed to him."

"This for real?"

"Marriage is no laughing matter. If you require further time to consider your rishta, you can contact me with your answer." Khalid held out a business card with *Khalid Mirza, Website Consultant* embossed on the front, along with his e-mail and phone number.

Rob stared at it, then at Khalid, eyes lingering on his thick beard. He shook his head slowly. "Clara's crazy, but I can't imagine my life without her, and I guess this is what she wants." He sat up, and in a formal voice said, "I accept Clara Taylor's offer of marriage."

Khalid smiled. "An excellent decision. Let's discuss dowry."

Ayesha read the text message and whooped loudly.

"What does it say?" Clara asked, looking

up from her prone position on the floor.

"Mubarak," Ayesha said, congratulating her friend. "You're engaged. Khalid said Rob agreed to a dowry too."

Clara sat up, dazed. "I don't need a dowry."

"He offered to pay for a honeymoon in Hawaii."

Clara beamed. "Did I tell you how much I like Khalid?"

Ayesha thought about the Taj Mahal, and Shah Jahan's love for his wife Mumtaz Mahal. Then she thought about her father, who had sacrificed his family for his ideals, and Khalid, her future husband, who had rediscovered his ideals when he fell in love.

"Nana would quote Shakespeare or maybe Rumi," Clara said. " 'All's well that ends well.' "

Ayesha shook her head. Sometimes there were no words, only sunshine on your heart. *Alhamdulilah.*

ACKNOWLEDGMENTS

Bismillah.

Bringing a book into the world is the work of many hands, and I have a list of people to thank.

Thank you to my wonderful agent, Ann Collette, for joining the Muslim open call, for picking me out of the slush pile and for believing in my Muslim romantic comedy.

Many thanks to the team at HarperCollins Canada and especially my editor, Jennifer Lambert. You are always right, and so gracious when I am wrong. Thank you for sending me the world's greatest e-mail.

Huge thanks to my amazing U.S. editor, Cindy Hwang, as well as the fantastic team at Berkley for bringing *Ayesha at Last* to the United States! I am forever grateful for your support and encouragement, and so proud to be part of the Berkley fam!

Every writer needs a village, and my village would not be complete without my

#SistersOfThePen:

Sajidah, my writing soul sister: You called me every day to check in (and make sure I was on task). You read my drafts and mentored me through every step. I am in awe of your talent and so thankful to have you in my life.

Ausma, meeting you was written in the stars. You read my first draft overnight and wrote me the kind of critique letter every writer dreams about. Your talent is matched only by your generous heart.

Rukhsana, for wise counsel, blunt honesty, and your beautiful books. Khalid jumped, fully formed, into my imagination during a shared meal with you years ago. Thank you.

My first readers: Tricia, Aminah, Nina. This book is better because of your input.

I am grateful to my parents, Mohammed and Azmat. I won the genetic lottery when I was born to the kindest, strongest, and best people I know. Thanks also to my mother-in-law, Fouzia, for the hint about leaving space for the perfect paratha, and for your compassion. For my brother, Atif: Your impish sense of humor is surpassed only by your bravery. To the rest of my large, wonderful Indian family: I love you all. Thank you for putting up with me.

To my sons, Mustafa and Ibrahim, whose

disinterest in my writing career has always kept me grounded: You are my favorite people in the world.

Thank you to the Toronto Muslim community. I grew up attending study circles, conferences, lectures, picnics, fund-raising dinners, and sleepovers at mosques around the city. Through them, I found myself.

Many thanks to Mary Vallis, Amber Shortt, Kate Robertson. Writing my column "Samosas and Maple Syrup" for the *Toronto Star* helped me realize I was a writer.

And finally, to my husband, Imtiaz: You are the sunshine on my heart. Thank you for dreaming with me.

SHAKESPEARE IN
AYESHA AT LAST

PAGE 43
Oh, she doth teach the torches to burn bright! . . . Beauty too rich for use, for earth too dear. So shows a snowy dove trooping with crows. As yonder lady o'er her fellows shows.
— *Romeo and Juliet,* Act 1, Scene 5

PAGE 49
Self-love . . . is not so vile a sin as self-neglecting.
— *Henry V,* Act 2, Scene 4

PAGE 76
We know what we are, but know not what we may be.
— *Hamlet,* Act 4, Scene 5

PAGES 78, 176
No sooner met but they looked, no sooner looked but they loved, no sooner loved but

they sighed, no sooner sighed but they asked one another the reason, no sooner knew the reason but they sought the remedy; and in these degrees have they made a pair of stairs to marriage.

— *As You Like It,* Act 5, Scene 2

PAGE 113

The rose looks fair, but fairer we it deem, / For that sweet odor, which doth in it live.

— Sonnet 54

PAGE 202

False face must hide what the false heart doth know.

— *Macbeth,* Act 1, Scene 7

PAGE 277

Better three hours too soon than a minute too late.

— *The Merry Wives of Windsor,* Act 2, Scene 2

PAGE 293

Love sought is good, but given unsought better.

— *Twelfth Night,* Act 3, Scene 1

PAGE 316

We are such stuff as dreams are made

on, and our little life is rounded with a sleep.

—— *The Tempest,* Act 4, Scene 1

PAGE 351

The robbed that smiles steals something from the thief.

—— *Othello,* Act 1, Scene 3

PAGE 390

Tomorrow, and tomorrow, and tomorrow,
Creeps in this petty pace from day to day,
To the last syllable of recorded time;
And all our yesterdays have lighted fools
The way to dusty death. Out, out, brief
    candle!
Life's but a walking shadow, a poor
    player,
That struts and frets his hour upon the
    stage,
And then is heard no more. It is a tale
Told by an idiot, full of sound and fury,
Signifying nothing.

—— *Macbeth,* Act 5, Scene 5

PAGE 515

Let me not to the marriage of true minds / Admit impediments. Love is not love / Which alters when it alteration finds, / Or bends with the remover to remove: / O,

531

no! It is an ever-fixed mark / That looks on tempests and is never shaken.
— Sonnet 116

PAGE 523
All's well that ends well.
— A play of the same name

NANI'S DELICIOUS
HOMEMADE CHAI

Chai means "tea" in Hindi/Urdu. Yes, that means every time someone orders "chai tea" at Starbucks, they are really ordering "tea tea"! While tea remains the most popular drink in the world next to water, chai is often made with a spice mix in addition to tea leaves, which adds a vibrant, aromatic flavor. It is also often cooked for a long time to strengthen the potency and deepen the taste of the brew.

Ingredients
3 cups milk
2 cups water
3/4 tsp cardamom seeds, ground up
1 stick of cinnamon
3–4 cloves (optional)
4 teabags of orange pekoe tea or 5 tsp of
   loose-leaf black tea

Bring the milk, water, spices, and tea to a

boil in a medium pot. Make sure it doesn't boil over! Lower heat and let simmer on the stove for 20–25 minutes, longer if you want a stronger tasting chai. Skim milk skin off the top, or use a sieve to pour chai into small mugs. Sweeten with sugar or honey to your taste. This recipe yields three cups. Enjoy!

(with thanks to Sameena Ali)

ABOUT THE AUTHOR

Uzma Jalaluddin is a teacher and also writes a funny parenting column named 'Samosas and Maple Syrup' for the Toronto Star, Canada's largest daily newspaper. Her debut novel is *Ayesha at Last*.

The employees of Thorndike Press hope you have enjoyed this Large Print book. All our Thorndike, Wheeler, and Kennebec Large Print titles are designed for easy reading, and all our books are made to last. Other Thorndike Press Large Print books are available at your library, through selected bookstores, or directly from us.

For information about titles, please call:
(800) 223-1244

or visit our website at:
gale.com/thorndike

To share your comments, please write:
Publisher
Thorndike Press
10 Water St., Suite 310
Waterville, ME 04901